IN GENEVA,

a Howard Hughes-style oil tycoon makes a proposal to Arab representatives that shocks even them.

IN PARIS,

the beautiful daughter of an American presidential candidate must choose between saving her father or satisfying her lover.

IN MEXICO,

a mansion full of corpses yields a nightmare legacy of the Nazi past that has refused to die.

IN WASHINGTON, D.C.,

the White House is the goal of a man who may be just one more murder from getting there. . . .

THE
PHANTOM
CONSPIRACY

THE
PHANTOM
CONSPIRACY

— By —

Michael Barak

A SIGNET BOOK
NEW AMERICAN LIBRARY
TIMES MIRROR

Publisher's Note

This novel is a work of fiction. Names, characters, places, and incidents are either the product of the author's imagination or, if real, are used fictitiously.

NAL BOOKS ARE AVAILABLE AT QUANTITY DISCOUNTS WHEN USED TO PROMOTE PRODUCTS OR SERVICES. FOR INFORMATION PLEASE WRITE TO PREMIUM MARKETING DIVISION, THE NEW AMERICAN LIBRARY, INC., 1633 BROADWAY, NEW YORK, NEW YORK 10019.

SIGNET TRADEMARK REG. U.S. PAT. OFF. AND FOREIGN COUNTRIES
REGISTERED TRADEMARK—MARCA REGISTRADA
HECHO EN CHICAGO, U.S.A.

SIGNET, SIGNET CLASSICS, MENTOR, PLUME, MERIDIAN AND NAL BOOKS are published by The New American Library, Inc., 1633 Broadway, New York, New York 10019

First Signet Printing, September, 1981

1 2 3 4 5 6 7 8 9

PRINTED IN THE UNITED STATES OF AMERICA

For Jo, with love

CONTENTS

Prologue:

August 15:

THREAT

"... Therefore I accept with gratitude, humility and pride, our party's nomination for the presidency of the United States."

The last words of the candidate were drowned in the loud cheer of thousands of delegates, rising to their feet. Clusters of multicolored balloons hovered in the air; young campaign volunteers jumped, shouted and waved their red-white-and-blue hats; hundreds of cardboard signs emerged all over, displaying the convention verdict: "Jefferson for President." The deafening roar of the electrified crowd seemed to shake the very foundations of the Miami Convention Center.

The nominee paused and patiently waited for the cheers to subside. His smile disappeared from his rugged features. Deep furrows emerged in the large clear forehead. The bushy white-and-black eyebrows joined over the piercing blue eyes. Jefferson tossed back his mass of graying hair as he thrust his chin forward. "I call upon you, members and supporters of our party, and all my fellow Americans, to join forces in a tremendous effort to save America." A grim note slipped into his voice. "Our nation is in danger. Not in danger of war and destruction by our traditional foes. But in danger of strangulation by the hands of a new, ruthless enemy, who is relentlessly driving us down on our knees. And my duty is to warn you that if we don't resolve to take our fate in our hands, this beloved country of ours is doomed."

A hush descended upon the huge assembly and the television cameras focused in on a close-up of James Jefferson's face. "I am going to name that enemy, now, and I am going to tell you what I believe we should do."

Five thousand miles away, in a plush office in Geneva, a man leaned toward his television set, intently watching the tough, sunburned face of Jefferson that filled the screen.

1

Owing to the time difference, it was past midnight in Switzerland and the local television stations had signed off their broadcasts for the day. But the office of Sheikh Ali Shazli, chairman of the Organization of Petroleum Exporting Countries (OPEC), was equipped with a special Omega television set, capable of monitoring broadcasts directly from communication-satellite transmissions.

"The enemy"—Jefferson drew a deep breath—"is the international organization which controls most of the world's oil. During the last ten years this organization has increased oil prices by four hundred percent, simultaneously cutting down production by twenty-five percent. Our economy cannot cope either with the soaring price of energy or with its shortage. America faces the worst economic crisis since the crash of nineteen twenty-nine. Plants and factories are being closed all over the nation. Unemployment has reached unprecedented figures. The average American citizen cannot properly heat his home in the bitter months of winter or cool it in the summer; he cannot afford to drive the car of his choice. He is even denied the freedom to travel around this vast land of ours, the cost often being beyond his means. Inflation is rising at a most alarming pace. And what is the purpose of all that?" He paused and looked straight into the cameras facing the podium. "The purpose, my fellow Americans, is not to bring more equality to the world, to take from the rich nations in order to help the poor. We would have gladly accepted any sacrifice for such a noble endeavor."

He paused again. Shazli's well-manicured hand drew a black, gold-tipped Sobranie cigarette from a hand-carved ivory box on his desk, and lit it with his Cartier lighter.

"No," Jefferson was saying. "The blackmail to which this nation is being subjected is aimed to fill the coffers of a handful of arrogant and greedy sheikhs, to allow them to acquire control over the world's wealth and economy, and to make them the financial rulers of our planet."

The unlisted phone on Shazli's desk buzzed discreetly, but the OPEC chairman ignored it. He was closely watching Jefferson's face on the screen. Sparks of anger seemed to explode in the steel-blue eyes. "Our nation has been yielding to this degrading humiliation for too long. A President of the United States said, a few years ago, that OPEC holds an ax over our heads, and we stretch our necks. Well, we shall not stretch them anymore. We shall place before the oil blackmailers the clear-cut choice: either they will lower their prices and resume full production—or we shall go there ourselves and take the oil we need."

For a split second the stunned audience held its breath. Then a somewhat hesitant applause started at the center of the hall, gradually spreading. It lacked, however, the intensity and the enthusiasm of the former ovation.

The phone buzzed again, and this time Shazli picked it up. "Are you listening to the speech, Ali?" The voice on the other end of the line was deep, controlled, and carried an unmistakable American accent.

The Arab recognized it ot once. "Of course, Bill. Well, what do you think?"

"You know exactly what I think," the voice said angrily. "I warned you, months ago. The bastard said it at last, in so many words."

Sheikh Shazli pressed the volume button on the remote-control panel and the candidate's voice subsided. "Yes, he said it. And he sounds like he means it."

"Of course he means it. Now, do you still think that we shouldn't interfere? Or maybe 'tough J.J.' has made you change your mind?"

The chairman of OPEC drew on his cigarette. "I think you are right," he conceded. "That man should be stopped." On the silent screen of the television Jefferson and his running mate were holding hands, smiling broadly and waving to the crowd.

"Now you are talking sense," the American said. "Should I come and see you, in Geneva?"

Shazli blew a spiral of bluish smoke and closed his eyes in thought. A summer storm was brewing outside and heavy drops of rain splattered on the large windowpanes behind him.

"No," he said finally. "This would draw too much attention. I am due in Caracas next week, for the South American conference. I can make a short stop in New York, between planes."

"Fine. Let's meet then in my New York office." The man called Bill attempted a joke. "It's air-conditioned, you know, energy crisis or not."

Shazli laughed nervously. "I'd rather not come to your office. Not now. Why . . . why don't you send a car to pick me up at the airport and join me later? We could talk in the car, for as long as we wish. You have enough gasoline for such a purpose, don't you?"

3

Bill chuckled, but his voice remained tense. "That's fine with me. We'll work out the details with your staff. I am glad that finally we see the situation eye to eye. Jefferson should be stopped."

"I agree," Shazli muttered, and with a swift, violent gesture killed his cigarette in the big ashtray on his desk. "He should never become President. Never."

Shortly after 10 P.M. Washington time, Vice-President Wheeler briskly stepped out of the East Room entrance of the White House. The lawn and the immaculate facade of the building were bathed in dazzling light as teams of technicians busily tested microphones and cameras. All the major television networks, radio stations and national newspapers had sent their reporters to the White House as soon as word had come that Vice-President Wheeler, his party's candidate for the presidency, had been summoned to the Oval Office.

Wheeler looked crisp, confident and in the best of moods. His blond-gray hair, parted in the fashion made famous by the late John F. Kennedy, made him look younger, almost boyish. That impression was accentuated by a slim body, alert blue eyes and an easy smile revealing two rows of perfect teeth. He did not look surprised at the sight of the crowd that expected him. An old hand at politics, he knew the media were eager to get his reaction to Jefferson's bombshell at the convention, and he was ready to give it to them. As a matter of fact, his urgent summons by the President had been prearranged between them, in a hurried telephone conversation barely minutes after the speech. They had agreed that the announcement of a nonscheduled meeting between the President and Wheeler would add dramatic impact to the Vice-President's first public appearance after the Jefferson speech. Moreover, it would enhance the President's endorsement of Wheeler's position.

Lawrence Wheeler stopped in front of the battery of microphones and smiled. "My, what a reception," he said pleasantly, blinking in the glare of the floodlights.

"Mr. Vice-President!" Rachel Burke, the blond, curvaceous CBS reporter, knew how to use her advantages, as she boldly advanced toward him, microphone outstretched. "Would you comment on Senator Jefferson's speech, sir?"

Wheeler nodded and a grave look came into his eyes. "I certainly will, Miss Burke." He paused to recollect his well-rehearsed statement. "Senator Jefferson has just pledged that

4

if he is elected President, he will declare war on the oil-producing states. This statement should cause grave concern to all Americans. We still bear in our flesh scars of the Vietnam War. We don't want any more bloodshed. We don't want our finest young men to die in foreign lands, fighting useless battles. We don't want to subjugate other nations and to trample their legitimate rights. Senator Jefferson advocates a return to gunboat policy and to the most cynical practices of colonialism. I am convinced that no sane American would support a bloody adventure that might easily trigger a new World War."

"Mr. President!" George Bernstein of WNEW called, and was rewarded with an outburst of laughter from his colleagues. Wheeler smiled at him. "May I quote you on that, Mr. Bernstein?" The reporter joined the laughter, then quickly corrected himself. "Mr. *Vice*-President, did you discuss Senator Jefferson's speech with the President?"

"Yes, we did discuss it."

"What was the President's reaction?"

"I believe that the President will make his stand clear at his forthcoming press conference," Wheeler replied. "Yet I can already tell you that his reaction was as indignant as mine." He smiled. "Maybe a little more strongly worded, but then, he wasn't speaking to the press."

"Will you quote the exact words of the President?" Mike Shean of NBC intervened.

"No, I certainly will not," Wheeler said. "Why don't you guys use your imagination? You are so good at it, sometimes." Another wave of laughter greeted his words, and he knew that he had conveyed the message: The President was angry, very angry with Jefferson's speech.

Wheeler calmly surveyed his audience. "Yes, Mr. Scarlatti."

The dark, mousy reporter of *The Washington Post* was an old friend and confidant; he was bound to ask a sympathetic question.

"What do you intend to do about the energy crisis if you are elected, Mr. Vice-President?"

"I intend to overcome it by an overall plan, which in no case implies launching a war against any friendly nation," Wheeler answered. "And let me tell you that the oil-producing nations are, and have always been, our friends. As far as my plan is concerned, a team of the finest experts in this country is working very closely with me on the details of my program, which will be disclosed shortly. I can already reveal its main points. If I am elected, my first initiative will be to tour the capitals of the oil-producing states. I shall carry out firm and exhaustive talks with their leaders. At the conclusion of the tour I shall invite those statesmen to an international conference in Washington, to work out together a new system of oil exploitation that will ensure a steady supply of energy for the future." He stopped at that point, knowing that it was a good lead for tomorrow's headlines: "Wheeler pledges to go on personal mission to oil capitals, and to call world energy conference."

He intended to keep it there, when the loud baritone of Burt Hardy from the *Los Angeles Times* boomed over the babble of voices: "Mr. Vice-President, are you aware that Senator Jefferson's speech reflects the feelings of a great many Americans?"

Lines of scorn appeared at the edges of Wheeler's mouth and he answered curtly: "No, Mr. Hardy, I am certainly not aware of that. Thank you and good night to all of you."

He strode purposefully to his car. He knew that his performance had been good, almost flawless. And yet, Hardy's question gnawed at him and caused him a vague feeling of discomfort.

Except for a few illuminated shop windows, the rue des Délices was dark and deserted. The gray OPEC building was equally plunged in darkness. A single light was visible at the top floor, but the regulars of rue des Délices had grown accustomed to the unconventional working hours of Sheikh Ali Shazli. He was alone in his office now, going through a voluminous file of current paperwork and sipping frequently from a tiny cup of thick, sugary tea. A big copper teapot full of the hot liquid was simmering on an electric plate beside the large mahogany desk. The addiction to tea seemed to be a rare indication of the Bedouin origins of the cultivated, urbane Arab. A tall, swarthy man of forty-five, Shazli had graduated from Trinity College and spoke English with an Oxford accent. He was always impeccably dressed in expensive suits, made to measure by the best Savile Row tailors in London. His colleagues used to joke that when occasionally he donned his traditional Arab clothes—the long loose *galabia* and the *kaffiyeh* headdress—he looked like a Swiss amateur rehearsing for the part of Lawrence of Arabia. Only a closer look at the thin, intelligent face could discern the

6

subtle traits of a Saudi prince: the liquid black eyes, the sharp, slightly curved nose with its delicate nostrils, the over-full lips.

Shazli seemed to be more at home in the glass-and-con-crete pyramids of the West than in the mosques and *suqs* of his homeland. And yet, only seventy years ago his grandfa-ther had had his newborn twin daughters buried alive in the sand dunes of the Najd desert, refusing to bear the ignominy of becoming "Abu'l Banat"—a girls' father; the Bedouin sheikh had watched the burial of the screaming infants, mur-muring prayers to Allah the merciful for a male child who would restore his honor. That child had been Ali Shazli's fa-ther.

Only fifty years ago Shazli's mother, then a teenager in the wastelands of the Hijāz, had been cruelly circumcised by the women of her tribe in a traditional ceremony intended to dis-connect pleasure from sex and to assure that intercourse should be a mere duty of the wife to her husband. The eldest women of the tribe had cut the edge of her clitoris, thus kill-ing her sexual sensations and denying her, forever, the feeling of orgasm. A few months later, on the eve of her marriage, the thirteen-year-old girl was deflowered not by the penis, but by a violent thrust of her fiancé's thumb, in front of all the family women, who held her arms and parted her legs. When blood oozed between the legs of the sobbing girl, the eldest women's faces broke into toothless grins: The child was a vir-gin all right and everyone saw it. Therefore the family honor was safe.

There had been some changes since on the shores of the Red Sea. They didn't bury girls alive anymore, and only in the remote regions did they circumcise women and publicly pierce a bride's maidenhead. But they still used to apply the strict laws of the Koran in the marketplace in Jiddah; the court executioner would cut thieves' arms and legs and be-head assassins with his curved scimitar, the same that ap-peared on the green flag of Arabia under the inscription, "There is no God but Allah and Muhammad is His Prophet."

Ali Shazli never forgot where he came from. Although moving with remarkable ease in the spheres of Western business and politics, in private he strictly observed the basic commandments of his religion. A devout Muslim, he would kneel five times a day on a small threadbare carpet he had brought all the way from Jiddah, and prostrate his body in the direction of Mecca, eyes closed, his lips murmuring holy

7

verses. He wouldn't touch alcohol and wouldn't eat pork. In the first drawer of his desk he always kept two editions of the Koran, in Arabic and in English. He would quote extensively from those holy scriptures while negotiating, yet many of his European business associates were convinced that this was one more trick of the cunning Arab.

Cunning he was indeed, a real desert fox, smoothly planning his moves, cleverly disguising his intentions. He had risen quickly to the position of oil minister in the Saudi Arabian government; barely two years later he had been elected chairman by his peers at the OPEC council. Many predicted for him a brilliant future, in his country and in world politics as well. And when openly branding OPEC as the enemy, James Jefferson had to realize that in the person of its chairman he had found a formidable enemy.

Yet that enemy had kept a surprisingly low profile in the twenty-four hours that had elapsed since Jefferson's speech. Shazli had doggedly refused to issue any statement to the press or to comment on the threat voiced by the American candidate. "We do not mix in the internal affairs of other nations," was all he would say for publication. He had rejected the demand of several OPEC leaders for an emergency meeting of the council. "Our next regular meeting is scheduled for the end of the week," he had pointed out, "and as far as I am concerned, no new item should be added to the agenda."

His meek reaction was not caused by cowardice or confusion. On the contrary: Jefferson had challenged him to a deadly duel, and he was going to strike back. But with his own weapons, at his own convenience, and far, very far from the public eye.

In the stillness of the night he heard the soft purr of a slowing motorcar. He swiveled his chair and looked down from the window. A silver-gray Mercedes had drawn to a halt by the sidewalk. Five people got out. One of them unlocked the front door of the OPEC building and remained outside. The other four quickly moved in; a few seconds later he heard the whir of the elevator. He lit a cigarette and leaned back, savoring the pungent smoke while awaiting his late-night guests.

The leather-padded door swung noiselessly on its hinges. The first to enter, as always, was Ahmed Abd-el-Krim, the oil minister of Algeria. He was a heavyset, thick-waisted man, and his curly hair, flat nose and protruding lower lip attested to his Berber origins. His short arms and legs and his clumsy

8

movements made him look like a peasant. Even the best-tailored suit that draped his overweight frame looked borrowed. But he didn't seem to care much for his appearance. He exuded an air of confidence and power, and his tiny bead eyes had a cold, mean look. During the Algerian war for independence, twenty years ago, he had been one of the most feared field commanders of the FLN underground. When France finally retreated from Algeria, he was charged with hunting down the former collaborationists with the French regime. While other FLN commanders instigated a long series of trials against the traitors, not a single trial had been held in Abd-el-Krim's region. There were rumors, never investigated, of tortures, mass executions, hamlets burned to the ground with their entire populations. When questioned about those stories by foreign reporters, government spokesmen would shrug them off as "gross exaggerations." As Shazli got up from his chair to shake Abd-el-Krim's callused hand, and looked briefly into the small cruel eyes, he wondered once again if the reports were exaggerated.

Abd-el-Krim was followed by Adnan Baghdadi, the Iraqi permanent representative at the OPEC council. He held only the rank of ambassador, which was a junior position compared to the ministerial status of most of his colleagues. All of them knew that his appointment to the council was a kind of semi-exile from the turbulent political arena in his country. Formerly the right hand of President Ahmed Hassan al-Bakr, he had been very close to the helm of power; but his pro-Soviet views, which had propelled him to the top, had also caused his downfall. When Iraq had decided to adopt a more balanced foreign policy, and al-Bakr had resigned, Baghdadi had been exiled to Geneva. Yet the mere fact that he was not hanged with the other thirty-six purported traitors to the Baathist revolution proved that his intelligence and diplomatic skill were held in high esteem by the new regime. At sixty-two he was a disillusioned man on the verge of old age, and his sallow face, topped with a few wisps of snow-white hair, bore a permanent expression of bitterness.

Sheikh Munir Badran, the oil minister of Kuwait, was certainly the most exuberant of the small group. A greasy smile was painted over his oval, cherubic face and his darting brown eyes seemed to shine with the knowledge of secret pleasures. A pleasure-seeker he was indeed, and Geneva's conservative diplomatic community was shocked again and again by the wild rumors about Badran's scandalous behavior. There had been an affair with a little Swiss boy, a report about regular orgies with teenaged nymphets in the lavish villa of the Sheikh, the present of a Patek Philippe watch to a male ballet dancer from the Opéra de Paris, screenings of hard-core pornographic movies, and even the unexplained drowning of a young Swedish model in Lake Geneva, not far from Badran's private beach. But the sleazy, round little minister managed to sail unperturbedly through all those storms. Being a cousin and close friend of the emir of Kuwait, his position at home was secure; as far as the local authorities were concerned, he knew exactly how, when and whom to bribe. The Swiss police hushed the scandals, the government officials looked the other way, and nosy press correspondents often got free tickets to Kuwait, where they enjoyed sumptuous treatment in Badran's summer palace.

The lively little man happily threw both his arms around Shazli's neck and pressed his wet lips on his cheeks. Shazli had no choice but to submit, barely concealing his disgust. He hated those traditional effusions of Arab brotherhood and embraced his peers and superiors only in public, when the mere handshake might be considered as aloofness or even lese majesty.

The last man to enter did not try to embrace Shazli. He was the youngest of the group—just thirty-five—and could have been a very handsome man if not for something ascetic in his sunken cheeks and the chilling, fanatical expression of his strangely opaque eyes. The resemblance he bore to Muammar al Qadhafi, the dictator of Libya, was striking; it was further enhanced by his having copied to perfection Qadhafi's mannerisms. Karim Nusserat was a member of the same nomad tribe as the unpredictable colonel, and shared his religious fanaticism as well as his hatred of the West. Yet behind the disturbing eyes of the Libyan deputy foreign minister lay an incisive mind, which grasped complex situations and knew how to accept—if not to formulate—logical and inevitable conclusions.

When his guests were seated, Shazli obligingly poured them tiny cups of steaming tea and returned to his chair. Over the rim of his cup he surveyed the four well-dressed people who were his closest advisers and formed, at his side, the unofficial leadership of OPEC. In recent years quite a few non-Arab countries had joined the organization, which the press had labeled "the most exclusive club in the world." The newcomers, and particularly the South Americans, steadily supported

Shazli's policy. Yet he was reluctant to admit any non-Arab into his inner circle, where the real decisions were made. For a short while after the revolution in Iran, he had invited the representative of the Ayatollah Khomeini to their secret meetings, but after a few weeks he had stopped doing so. Khomeini's regime was too unstable, a new internal strife was brewing and the risks of a leak were considerable.

None of the four members of his private council had questioned his decision to ban the Iranians. At least not openly. Baghdadi, the Iraqi ambassador, was a broken man and regularly adopted a passive attitude. Sheikh Badran was a fool, too busy planning his next ejaculation to argue with Shazli, whom he sincerely admired. The chairman was aware, though, that the two others, Libya's Nusserat and Algeria's Abd-el-Krim, secretly coveted his position. Nusserat was not a dangerous contender; the council of OPEC would never elect the fanatical envoy of Qadhafi as chairman. But Abd-el-Krim was different. He was ambitious, intelligent and radical. He had already emerged as the leader of the extremist wing in the OPEC council. Lately, the moderate Arab states had become the object of a growing criticism by the radicals, who pressed for a tougher attitude toward the West. Shazli had subtly yielded to the pressure without appearing to do so, and had emerged from the storms, feathers unruffled. Tonight, however, he felt for the first time that his personal position was at stake. Until now he had been the only man who knew how to talk to the Americans and maneuver them into painful concessions. But if Jefferson won, and an open conflict erupted between America and OPEC, the moderates would be washed out and he would be the first to go, his gifts becoming obsolete. If he wanted to maintain his position at the head of OPEC, he had to keep America submissive and docile. He had to prove that he was the only person capable of assuring the steady flow of dollars from the West. It was either him—or Jefferson. That's why he had to crush the presidential candidate.

"*Markhaban*—welcome," he softly said in Arabic. He went suavely through the inevitable procedure of small talk, inquiring about the health of his guests, the well-being of their families, the latest news from their capitals. Then he moved to the subject of the meeting. "You certainly heard or read Jefferson's speech. It is very disturbing. I presume that you have been in contact with your governments during the day.

Our organization and our countries have been openly threatened. We must define, tonight, our course of action."

An ironic smile flourished on Abd-el-Krim's lips. *Rubbish,* the Algerian's smile seemed to say, *you don't need our advice, and you have already chosen your course of action. You need us as a rubber stamp to approve your own decision and to cover you if your plan fails.*

Shazli held Abd-el-Krim's eyes for a second. *Yes, that is true,* his eyes spoke back, *but then you would never dare to say it aloud.*

"I want him dead," Nusserat suddenly spat in a voice heavy with hatred. "We must kill him like a dog. He shouldn't live to be elected."

Sheikh Badran's lips twitched nervously, panic flashed in his eyes and he threw an alarmed glance around him, as if looking for help.

Shazli looked earnestly at the young Libyan. "You suggest that we arrange his killing," he said slowly, and his voice was very respectful. "Do you have an idea how we should do that?"

Nusserat was briefly taken aback. He had expected a flat rejection and was not prepared to offer a practical proposal. It was Baghdadi, unexpectedly, who gave him the necessary respite to shape his thoughts.

"Let's not panic," he soothingly said. "Who would vote for him? The Americans are afraid of war. He has no chance to be elected."

"Are you ready to take the risk?" Shazli asked him, eyelids half closed. "We all believe his chances are slim, but what if the contrary happens? Karim has a suggestion, let's hear him." He turned back to Nusserat.

The Libyan shifted on his chair. "We should speak with Arafat. No, no . . ." He raised his hand when he saw the expressions on the faces around him. "I don't mean that the PLO should do that. I don't mean that an Arab should do that. It is stupid; it is too dangerous. But Arafat's people have contacts with other groups—the Japanese Red Army, the Irish, the German Baader-Mein . . . Meinhof Gang." He had difficulty pronouncing the last name.

Abd-el-Krim looked at Nusserat condescendingly. He took a sip from his cup but quickly put it down, finding the tea too sweet for his taste. "When Ali asked you if you have a suggestion, he meant a suggestion for an operation that in no way could be connected with us, do you understand? In no

12

way," he repeated, looking around him. He turned to the Libyan again and explained, as if to a small child: "If anybody succeeds in linking Jefferson's death to us, it will be even a greater disaster than if he is elected. He will become a martyr, a saint. His insane idea will become a moral commandment. Every American will be in the streets screaming for revenge and urging the government to send the Marines to the Middle East."

Shazli was listening attentively, his head bowed in deference. "What would you suggest, Ahmed?" he asked, and his voice conveyed the great importance he attached to the Algerian's opinion.

"He is a son of death," Abd-el-Krim muttered through clenched teeth, using the old Arab expression for a man who has to die. "We have to explore every possible way, to see if his death could be arranged. But not by us. By somebody else. If we don't get absolute guarantees that we'll be kept out of the affair, we should look for a different solution."

"What kind of solution?" Badran asked. The little Kuwaiti was scared by the ugly turn that the conversation was taking.

"A way must be found to discredit Jefferson in the eyes of the American public," Abd-el-Krim said forcefully. "What kind of man is he? He has no wife. What did she die of? He has money. Where did he get it? He is a politician, and politicians are filthy and dishonest men. He is a nonbeliever; he must be sinning in private or have sinned in the past. Somebody should find it and show it, and if it does not exist—invent it!" Beads of sweat popped out on his forehead as he talked.

The chairman nodded. Abd-el-Krim was an intelligent man. He had said exactly what Shazli had hoped he would.

"Bill Murphy called me last night," Shazli said in the same soft voice, busying himself with another cup of tea. "He said he wanted to talk to me about the removal of Jefferson."

"Don't trust him," Nusserat hissed angrily. "It must be a trap. I know those Americans, trying all kinds of dirty tricks to fool us. Don't talk to him, I tell you!"

The Iraqi ambassador, Baghdadi, patiently waited for the Libyan's outburst to fade away, and with an imperceptible nod attracted the chairman's attention. "Are you sure that Bill Murphy is our ally in that matter?"

"Yes," Shazli firmly said. "It's been months—since the primaries, as a matter of fact—that he has been pestering me about Jefferson. He hates the man, fears him and wants him out, at all costs."

"Why?" Baghdadi asked in the same candid voice. "Why go to such extremes?"

"The reasons are quite evident, I believe." Shazli lit another of his cigarettes and Abd-el-Krim wrinkled his nose. "As president of American Oil, his policy has been total cooperation with us. Everything he possesses, and every penny of his oil companies, is invested in our holdings. His operating credits come from our funds. If OPEC is forced to withdraw from the United States, American Oil will be bankrupt in twenty-four hours."

"Murphy wouldn't kill for that," Baghdadi reflected.

"Not only for that. But there are two more reasons. Murphy sincerely believes in long-term cooperation between his country and OPEC. He is convinced that Wheeler will seek an arrangement with us. He fears that Jefferson is a danger for America, and might start World War Three."

Baghdadi raised his eyebrows skeptically and an ironic smile flourished on his lips. "So the man is a patriot and a peace lover." He smirked. "How nice." He didn't seem to value Murphy's idealism. "Now, what is the other reason?"

"The other and most important reason," Shazli said with the shadow of a smile, "is sheer ambition. Murphy craves power. He has wanted money and he has got it. Now he wants power. I have received a very reliable report that Wheeler has promised to make him Energy Secretary. And a man like Murphy would sell his own mother for a cabinet appointment."

Baghdadi nodded. "That makes sense. I would not count on his patriotism. That is nonsense. But we all know that he is a greedy man. He is motivated by lust for money and power. Therefore, we are the key, and Jefferson is the obstacle." He paused and crossed his legs. "Yes, I believe that we can count on him."

"Should I talk to him then?" Shazli asked and let his gaze wander around the room. "I mean, ask him what solution he has to offer to the problem we are facing." Baghdadi and Badran nodded their approval. Nusserat seemed lost in thought, absently biting his lower lip, while Abd-el-Krim looked at Shazli, his head slightly cocked to one side, as if he were trying to figure out his real game.

"I have to go to Caracas next week," Shazli said and his face lit up with a sudden idea. "I can stop on the way in

14

New York and meet Murphy, very discreetly of course, to hear what he has in mind."

"Good idea," Baghdadi said and got up. "Do that. But be careful. And don't let him talk you into an assassination. We are still paying the price for that madman Sirhan Sirhan."

"Sirhan was a freedom fighter!" Nusserat jumped to his feet, his face flushed. "How dare you!"

But for once, Baghdadi didn't listen to him. He dismissed the cocky Libyan with a deprecatory gesture of his hand and walked out, followed by Sheikh Badran. Nusserat hesitated a moment, then followed them, mumbling to himself.

The last to leave was Ahmed Abd-el-Krim. On the threshold he suddenly turned to Shazli with a sly smile. "I think that you had it all set. You had fixed the appointment with Bill Murphy beforehand, hadn't you?"

Shazli bowed ceremoniously and his hand gracefully fluttered over his chest, mouth and forehead, in the traditional Arab greeting. *"Salaam Alaykum,* go in peace, my brother," he said pleasantly.

The black limousine smoothly sailed through the sparse midday traffic. Behind the drawn curtains of its rear section, Bill Murphy opened a built-in small refrigerator and took out a jug of orange juice and two chilled glasses. He filled the glasses and handed one to Shazli.

"Thank you," the OPEC chairman said, pulling the curtain and throwing an absent look at the sun-drenched Van Wyck Expressway. "You don't have to drink that because of me, Bill. You can have liquor; I don't mind."

"It's too early for booze," Murphy smiled. He had a cold, tight smile, devoid of any warmth. He was approaching sixty, a big muscular man with a bald head, protruding jaw, and coal-black eyes surrounded by a web of tiny wrinkles. An air of confidence emanated from his bulky figure, and yet he treated the much younger Shazli with respect and even deference. He took a folded sheet of paper from his pocket and passed it to the OPEC chairman. "I thought you would be interested in this. The latest Harris poll."

Shazli unfolded the crisp paper and perused it attentively. His face clouded. "When did you get that? I didn't see it in the papers."

"It will be released only tomorrow. I got it from a friend who works for Harris. There is also a Gallup poll coming which will confirm this one, give or take half a percent."

Shazli nodded.

"Well, what do you think, Ali?"

"I don't like it," Shazli said. "Three percent increase in a week? I assumed that Jefferson's rating would drop for a couple of weeks at least after the speech."

"What worries me is California and New York." Murphy leaned over and pointed at two figures in the report. "Jefferson gained here one-point-eight percent and here one-point-three percent. And these are supposed to be the liberal strongholds of America."

Shazli shook his head. "But they suffered the worst oil shortage in the country. I warned you then not to go too hard on them, remember? But you wouldn't listen." He fell silent for a moment and looked at the document again. "On the other hand, there is no change in Wheeler's popularity. He still has a considerable lead."

"But the gap has narrowed by three percent. We are now forty against twenty-three, with thirty-seven percent undecided and two more months to go."

"I know," Shazli sighed. "I still cannot believe it. I cannot believe that America might elect such a reactionary for President."

"Oh, they might do it all right," Murphy muttered, and a concerned look sneaked into the charcoal eyes. "First, he is not so much of a reactionary. On issues other than energy his record is very liberal. Second, as far as oil is concerned, many people in this country feel that they have been bullied around too much by you guys." He shot a quick glance at Shazli. "They crave a strong leadership. Five years ago a political scientist in Harvard wrote an article about the pendulum swing in public opinion, from one extreme to the other. He predicted that after the anti-Vietnam movement reached its peak, there would be a conservative upsurge. That's the pendulum, all right."

Shazli took a silk kerchief from his breast pocket and wiped his lips. He looked at his watch. "I have to be back at the airport in thirty-five minutes, Bill."

"Right." The president of American Oil leaned back in his seat. "Right," he repeated. "It's time to talk business."

Shazli soundlessly motioned toward the massive back of the driver, sitting woodenly beyond the glass partition.

"That's okay," Murphy assured him. "The glass is completely soundproof. He can't hear a word, unless I press this button." He pointed at a small panel on his right. "Well?"

Shazli looked at him searchingly. "Do you have any practical suggestion or just a general idea?"

"It might be a practical suggestion," Murphy said very slowly, very carefully. "I know somebody who is able to get in touch with a person or several persons who can do the job. It's completely foolproof. Nobody would trace it to us in a million years."

"So you do have an assassination in mind," Shazli said, without looking at him.

Murphy drew a deep breath. "He must be removed."

"You must be aware of the fact"—Shazli's tone was formal—"that my government and my organization will never condone murder, in any form."

"Oh, shit." Murphy was very tense and his features were drawn. "Don't give me that lawyer's talk, Ali. This is a question of life and death for all of us. I tell you—those guys can remove Jefferson. We shall not know who they are and they will not know who we are. Nobody will discover the connection, never!"

"Nonsense," Shazli snapped with an abruptness that was completely out of character. "Don't buy that from anybody, Bill, and don't sell it to me. These perfect operations, with mysterious killers whom nobody knows, who change their disguises and their papers five times a day—that's cheap Hollywood stuff. There is no such a thing as a completely foolproof conspiracy. I shall know about it, my closest friends will know about it, you will, the go-between will, one or two other men, maybe the killer himself . . ."

"The killer will be removed immediately after the hit."

"Sure, sure," Shazli said mockingly. "But the man who would remove him might go to prison. And he will have a story to tell."

"He'll be well paid." Murphy said it with a sullen expression.

"And what if something misfires?" Shazli said heatedly. "And if Jefferson doesn't die? Or the killer is not 'removed,' as you say? Or he goes to prison for life and a clever prosecutor offers him to trade a name or two for his freedom? And what will you do when the best investigators and the ablest reporters in this country start nosing around? They're still digging in Kennedy's murder, after all these years. And what if something leaks from the OPEC council? How do you know there are no CIA agents or Israelis or I don't know what in Riyadh, or Baghdad, or Tripoli?" He took his gold cigarette case out of his inner pocket and nervously lit a black Sobranie. "And there is another angle to this affair, Bill," he pointed out, checking his temper. "Let's assume, just for the sake of argument, that everything works according to plan. You, me, OPEC, my government, your go-between—all of us will be bound to each other for life. Tomorrow you might become Energy Secretary . . ."

"Oh, you've heard about that," Murphy muttered, surprised.

"Yes, I have." He ignored the annoyed expression on Murphy's face. "As I was saying, tomorrow you might become Energy Secretary and you might have to disagree or even clash with me. But you won't dare, because I know your secret. And I won't dare because you know my secret. And you might lose your position, and I might lose mine. And then one day, in five, ten, fifteen years, somebody will talk, or make a confession on his deathbed, or write a book—they all do now—and sell us down the river for a nice bundle. No, Bill. I've thought it over, believe me. And if that is what you have to offer, I must say no." He leaned back in his seat and closed his eyes.

"So you're letting me down," Murphy said angrily. "You are not ready to prevent that sonofabitch from becoming President."

Shazli opened his eyes and looked at Murphy in mild surprise. "Come on, Bill, you are more clever than that. You know I want Jefferson out. But there must be another way."

"What way?"

Shazli stubbed out his cigarette and immediately lit another. "You don't have to murder a man physically to kill his political chances. If you manage to smear him, tarnish his public image, create the impression that he is unreliable, or a crook, a homosexual, a drug addict, whatever, you can have him out of the race in no time. What was the name of McGovern's mate, the guy who withdrew when they blew the story about his psychiatric treatment?"

"Eagleton," Murphy grunted.

"Eagleton, right. And how long did Teddy Kennedy lie low after Chappaquiddick? Twelve years? And Muskie's breakdown, remember?" He angrily removed a speck of tobacco from the tip of his tongue. "Do I have to give you more examples? Why don't you put your best men to work and check Jefferson thoroughly? You have good connections in the CIA and the FBI. You told me you were CIA once. Okay, then

18

pry in Jefferson's past, probe his private life, his business, his army record. Find out all about him since he used to piss in his pants. I am sure you'll discover something. And that's legitimate, and one hundred percent legal. That's not murder!"

"And if I don't find a thing? If the man is kosher?"

"Nobody is. But if Jefferson is so . . . kosher"—Shazli smiled at the Jewish word—"then invent something. Start a rumor, trump up a charge on him, throw the insinuations to the public on the eve of Election Day, don't give him time to clear himself. And if anything is needed to build or support the allegations against him—I'll help you. You'll need secret funds from a foreign source—I'll get them for you. You'll need men—I'll get you good men. That's the way we should operate, Bill."

Murphy shrunk in his corner for a long moment. "It won't work, Ali," he said stubbornly. "Jefferson is a well-known public figure; nobody has ever found a thing against him."

"Maybe they haven't tried hard enough," Shazli shot back. "Anyway, that's the only plan we in OPEC will go along with," he added with finality.

Murphy retreated into a hostile silence. His lips were angrily compressed, and he ran his left thumb back and forth along the jutting line of his jaw.

Shazli looked at his watch and became his old suave self again. "Before we part, I must ask you for something, Bill," he said in a friendly tone, subtly veiling the threat he was to convey. "If you have already started making your plans to 'remove' Jefferson—I beg you to drop them. I am afraid that you are not free to do it anymore. Not after this conversation. You are very close to us, you are associated with us, and people know it. One day somebody might learn that we met a week after Jefferson's speech and so many weeks before . . . before an attempt was made on his life. We'll get involved, just because of that. We can't afford it. We have cooperated with you for years, to the benefit of both sides. We want to develop this relationship in the future. If you had any plans, please, call them off."

"Is that a threat?" Murphy asked aggressively, his hand freezing in midair.

"Of course not." Shazli looked hurt. "You know me better. I am just asking for a token of your friendship."

They rode in silence all the way back to Kennedy Airport.

Two weeks later, the unlisted phone rang in Shazli's office. He picked up the receiver.

"It's me," Bill Murphy said. He sounded taut and reserved. "I think I have found something. I got a plan and a timetable worked out."

"That's real good news, Bill," Shazli said warmly, and took a sip of his fragrant tea. "I'd love to hear about it."

Chapter One:

October 18:

TREASURE

The girl leaned over the table, pushing aside her bell-shaped cognac glass. "You want to come with me to Lothar Club?" She smiled mischievously and her pearly teeth glowed in the half darkness. "It is *privat,* but the *Direktor,* he is *mein Freund.* There is a *Schwimmbad*—pool—with lights and music. Girls must take off all clothes"—she made quick undressing motions with her hands—"and men stay only with shorts. You want, *ja*?"

Clint Craig frowned and took a long sip of his drink, watching her warily over the rim of his glass. She had seemed to him so demure, so hesitant, when he had picked her up in the lobby of the Frankfurt Intercontinental Hotel; and now, barely one drink and two dances later, she made such a wanton offer! A tiny warning bell started ringing in the back of his mind. Could she be . . . ? No, it didn't make sense. She was pretty, neat, well-dressed and had rather reluctantly agreed to have a drink in the Prolog bar after a couple of minutes of idle talk in front of the gift-shop window. He had even felt a twinge of male pride for having broken her initial resistance.

And yet . . . She looked at him engagingly, waiting for his answer. He smiled brightly. "I don't feel like it right now, Marianne." She had said that was her name. "I'll tell you what. Let's have dinner first, and then we shall decide where to go. Okay?" As she seemed doubtful, he reached over the table and rubbed her cheek with his fingers.

Her reaction was amazing. She moved back sharply and a hard look came into her eyes. "Don't touch my face and my hair," she said in a low voice. "Only one man can touch my face and my hair. My boyfriend. You and me, we can do everything *zusammen,* very good things." Her red lips curved into a suggestive smile. "But without touch face."

He cursed inwardly. So she was a whore all right. A wave of anger swept him, anger directed at himself for being so stupid. "And you want money, of course," he snapped. It was not a question; it was a statement.

She nodded matter-of-factly. "I need money."

He sighed, gulped the rest of his drink and put his glass on the table. "I am sorry," he said, trying to be polite. "I shall not pay any money. I'll go now." He beckoned to the waiter, a blond boy in bow tie, who was busy mixing a drink behind the bar.

She eyed him with hostility. "So you go," she said. "But I want another drink!"

"All right," he said angrily, and tersely spoke to the waiter who bent over him. "Bring the lady another drink and let me have the check." He lit a cigarillo, snapped the lid of the oblong box, and replaced it in the inner breast pocket of his blazer.

She was watching him sullenly. "And if I want another drink later, when you are not here?" she asked in a loud voice. Gone were the gentleness and the shyness, and there was something utterly vulgar in the way she spoke now, striving to divest him of a small bill, at least. A silver-haired man, sitting alone by a nearby table, slowly turned around and stared at him.

"If you want another drink, find somebody else to buy it," he flared.

"I made big mistake," she said aggressively, ignoring the curious looks that converged on their table from all over. "I knew you were not a man who pay me. You think you can get girls for nothing, because you are attractive."

He didn't answer. The waiter was beside him, placing a second glass of cognac in front of the girl, beaming his flashlight on the check. Clint reached in his pocket, peeled two twenty-mark bills from the wad of German money and, without waiting for the change, strode out of the bar and into the brightly lit lobby. He was furious with himself.

Only when he stood outside, in the cool, invigorating air of the Frankfurt night, did his anger slowly subside. He should not have been rude to the girl; she was only trying to make a living. But for him, the scene at the bar had been the culmination of a rough day. Just one of those days when nothing seems to come out right. The Pan Am night flight from New York had been overcrowded with publishers and agents coming to the Book Fair, blabbing loudly about the deals they were about to close; he could not get a single minute of sleep. At the airport, another disappointment was in store. All the good hotels in town were full, the clerk at the Welcome desk apologized. He had to settle for a third-rate *pension* room on the outskirts of Frankfurt. But the most frustrating experience had been the visit, this afternoon, to the fair—the *Buch Messe*. He had walked for hours among the thousands of international stands in *Halle Fünf*—Hall Five—and had scanned the stands for the familiar dust jacket; but his last novel was to be seen only on the racks of his Swedish and Dutch publishers. The Americans, the French, the British, the Italians, had not even put it on display. He visited his publishers, feeling deeply humiliated to stand in line before their stands only to be gratified with a perfunctory handshake and a few routine formulas. He asked how his novel was doing and got the same answer over and over again: "We can't tell yet. . . . At this point the sales are rather moderate. . . . No, it's doubtful if any further publicity would help; you see, there were very few quotable reviews. . . . No, I wouldn't say that the book didn't succeed; it still might catch on. Unfortunately, the book clubs turned it down. . . . If we had only got a movie deal . . ." And then the publisher's eye would suddenly peer over his shoulder at an important customer, and he would get the message, shake the outstretched hand and move over.

He had left the fairgrounds with a bitter taste in his mouth. There was no use pretending: another of his novels had failed. In the cab on his way back to town, he was already trying to think up an excuse, to justify his failure in his own eyes. Everything had been different once. Had he only persevered . . . Hell, what difference did it make? He was on the decline, and his humiliating tour at the fair was an experience which he now wanted to efface from his memory. Maybe that was why he had approached the lonely girl who stood by the gift shop—an unconscious attempt to restore some of his badly shaken confidence. But his bad luck had stuck to him till the very end, and he had picked a hooker.

He sighed wearily and walked down the Gutleutstrasse. He knew himself pretty well. He would have a bad night, but tomorrow morning his natural optimism would prevail. And for tomorrow morning he had a breakfast appointment with Peter Bohlen. Clint had something that might—that should—interest his American publisher. Still, he had to play it very cool, very cautious. The project was based on Peter's idea, but then Peter himself was unpredictable; if he didn't feel like it now, he might dismiss it right away. And Peter was his last chance.

He looked at his watch. Only nine-thirty. What if he dropped in the Frankfurter Hof for a last drink? It could take his mind off things, and he might meet a friend or two.

He strode past the arched facade of the hotel court that gave the Kaiserplatz its touch of class, turned the corner and walked in. The Frankfurter Hof was bustling with activity; he could almost sense the pulsating beat of this unofficial but real heart of the *Buch Messe*. Famous publishers from all over the world, renowned literary agents, alert foreign-rights representatives were streaming in and out of the elegant lobby or clustering in friendly groups all over the place. He quickly identified several princes of that unique international kingdom—a party of exuberant Italians, a self-effaced Japanese, a few deceptively shabby Englishmen and some aloof, contented Germans. Three American publishers passed by, animatedly discussing what seemed to be the hottest deal at the current fair, the new Forsyth thriller. "A million dollars for a ten-page outline, would you believe that?" a bald man in a bow tie and a modish velvet jacket was saying. "I told his agent he must be out of his mind. Nobody in Frankfurt will pay you that price, I said to him. Why don't you come back when you cool off a little?"

"And what happened?" his younger companion asked eagerly.

The third man in the party smiled. "I bought it," he said softly. "For one million." The three of them burst out laughing.

Several middle-aged men emerged from one of the reception rooms, faces flushed with champagne, beautiful girls hanging on their arms. They walked past Clint to the lavish grill-restaurant. He watched them thoughtfully. Where the hell did all these aging publishers find such stunning girls? He wondered how many of them would talk their ladies into their beds before the night was over. Well, publishers were also human beings. At least some of them.

He shrugged and walked into the *Lipizzaner* bar through the small doorway, brushing against the draped curtain of red velvet. The world-famous lounge was crowded, though by a younger, more informal set. They were chatting around the small tables set by the stained-glass windows and the mural fresco representing the Spanish riding school in Vienna. Pre-

24

cious engravings of horses and horsemen wearing eighteenth-century costumes, a battered saddle artfully displayed in a frame on the wall, the dim lights and the green curtains framing the windows—all these bestowed an old-fashioned atmosphere on the pleasant lounge. The center of the action was the bar itself, a marble-topped horseshoe encircling a sturdy column with glass racks laden with bottles. Clint elbowed his way to the bar, safely anchored his left hand on the brass rail and ordered a double vodka martini. He lit a panatela and gulped his drink thirstily, his back to the entrance, when the sudden stir of the people around him made him turn.

A newcomer had just walked in, followed by a group of beaming American and German publishers. He was small and white-haired, and blinked rather shyly when the crowd welcomed him with a murmur of admiration. Clint recognized him immediately. This was tonight's hero, Martin Conrad, a British historian whose best-selling *Goebbels—the Myth and the Madness* was supposed to be the biggest success of the current fair. He had been the guest of honor at the lavish Bertelsmann party, and his face had become famous overnight, projected over and over again on the television screens, gravely staring from giant posters plastered all over his publishers' stands. French, Italian and Japanese publishers were fighting a tough battle for the translation rights of the *Goebbels*, and the vice-presidents of two Hollywood film companies had flown to Frankfurt to bid for the movie rights.

From his place at the bar, sucking his cigarillo and mechanically clinking the ice cubes in his watered down drink, Craig watched the triumphal entry of Conrad and the commotion it created. He tried to imprint a slightly ironical smile upon his face, but knew that he was unable to suppress the envy that burned in his eyes. A wave of bitterness arose in him, and he couldn't avoid making a cruel comparison. There stood Conrad, a made man, a world-famous author, and here he was, Clint Craig, thirty-seven years old, and a failure.

He ordered another drink and enjoyed the feel of the smooth liquid in his mouth. He had started smashingly well, though, with his two nonfiction books about the London blitz and the fall of Berlin. He remembered his excitement when his second book had hit the best-seller lists in Germany, England and the United States: *The New York Times Book Re-*

view had even defined him as "one of the best American specialists on World War II." It had been so intoxicating to emerge from relative anonymity into widespread fame, to be recognized by strangers, to be interviewed and respectfully quoted in the media, even on topics that had nothing to do with his current research. "World War II historian believes that the operations in Vietnam . . ." "Clint Craig joins the signatories of the Civil Rights petition . . ." "Best-selling author sharply criticizes the White House . . ." He had always been interested in politics. His newly acquired fame suddenly provided him with the means of airing and spreading his views. He had started to drift into politics, got deeply involved in the Vietnam issue, joined half a dozen committees and associations, became acquainted with leading political figures. He had been particularly impressed with James Jefferson, "tough J.J.," the junior senator from California. Jefferson's views were close to his own, and Clint was rapidly drawn into the small intimate circle forming around the emerging leader. When Jefferson offered him the position of press secretary, on the eve of his second senatorial campaign, he accepted right away. His political activity absorbing most of his time, he neglected and eventually abandoned his research work. He decided to write novels instead, in his free time. Instead of the gripping, dramatic nonfiction that had become his trademark, he produced a string of hastily written, shallow novels, and his reputation rapidly faded away. His marriage had shown signs of strain even in the good years; now it was wrecked definitely. As his youth was fading he had to admit that both his career and his private life were going down the drain. He had been somebody known and appreciated on his own merits; he had turned into one of those not-so-young campaign boys, busy selling an ambitious politician to the public. Only too late did he decide that politics was not for him, after all, and make up his mind to attempt a comeback as a writer. But the years that had passed were irrevocably lost; he would have to start from the beginning. What a waste, dammit! Had he only persevered, he could be as successful as Martin Conrad today, reaping fame and fortune. He knew he had talent; he knew he was a thorough researcher with a solid sense of history, a flair for the unusual and the sharp instincts of a police reporter. And even so he had messed it all up.

As if reflecting his own thoughts, a familiar voice murmured softly in his ear: "You know that could be you standing in his place, don't you? If you had just listened to me."

Craig slowly turned and stared without surprise at the long thin face of Peter Bohlen, who watched him sleepily through half-closed lids. Bohlen was sloppily dressed as always—an old tweed jacket, dark baggy trousers, a loosely knotted brown tie. He certainly did not look like one of the best American publishers, which he was.

"If you had just listened to me," Bohlen repeated, and although he kept his voice low and muffled, Clint discerned the undertone of biting mockery. "If you had just kept writing your superb war books, instead of running blind after that half-nut senator of yours and producing no-good quickies that nobody . . ."

Criag tartly interrupted him. "That half-nut senator of mine, as you call him, might soon become the next President of the United States."

Bohlen shrugged. "Maybe. Maybe not. You sacrificed your career for Jim Jefferson, and he doesn't care for you anymore."

"I don't know if he doesn't care for me," Craig retorted heatedly, "but I do care for him. It is time that a bold, candid statesman . . ."

"Oh, Jesus," Bohlen sighed. "Don't start all that bullshit again. What have you become, a push-button jukebox? Jim Jefferson is beside the point. I am interested in Clint Craig. You know you could have done the *Goebbels* book much better than Conrad. I asked you to do it, remember?"

Craig shook his head in mock despair. "You didn't ask me for the *Goebbels*," he slowly articulated. "You asked me for a book on Goering. On Goering's treasure, to be precise."

Bohlen paused for a second before answering. The pale eyes beneath the drooping eyelids flashed briefly in recollection. "That's right. Goering's treasure." His voice grew more animated. "That could be a hell of a good book. Think of it! *Reichsmarschall* Goering. A fighter pilot, drug addict, Hitler's heir, the man who robbed Europe of her treasures and carried his secret to the gallows. What a story! Did you ever give it some thought?"

"Yes, as a matter of fact, I did," Craig said, trying to sound casual. "But you didn't call me again since, so I thought you were not interested anymore." He added lightly: "Julie feels that we should discuss it with Doubleday."

Bohlen's thin-lipped mouth twitched angrily. "Now, don't

pull that one on me, Clint," he rasped. "I don't care what that bitchy agent of yours feels. The Goering book is my idea, and if anybody is going to write it, he is going to write it for me. And you know that."

"All right, all right," Craig said soothingly. It had come off easier than he had expected. He had Bohlen hooked; the old boy was still hot on the subject. "Let's discuss it tomorrow at breakfast then."

"Why not now?" Bohlen asked suspiciously. "You're in a hurry?"

Craig shrugged. "If you wish to talk now, it's okay with me. . . ." He lit a fresh cigarillo and distractedly watched the barman place a clean ashtray in front of him.

"Actually, I did quite a bit of research. I looked into those files you mentioned, in the Army archives in Bethesda. They describe in detail how Goering systematically robbed art treasures from most of the occupied countries in Europe, during the war. I even came across a very odd aspect of the story that nobody has ever touched." He paused, then uttered slowly: "What happened to Goering's treasure."

Bohlen frowned. "What on earth could have happened to Goering's treasure? It was retrieved in all those castles in Germany and Austria, after the war."

"Wrong," Craig said and smiled for the first time. "Only seventy percent of the art objects and only thirty percent of the gold and securities that had been stolen by Goering were ever recovered."

Bohlen tilted his head and looked at him doubtfully. "Is that so?" he said.

"Those are official figures, Peter. But there is something even more amazing." Craig lowered his voice. "You see, there were three people involved in the stripping of Europe—mainly France—of her treasures. One was a shady character, Michel Skolnikoff, who lived in Paris. He was protected by the *Abwehr*, the German Military Intelligence. He confiscated art collections and gold objects for the Germans and stored them in France before shipment to Berlin. When the Allies landed in Normandy, he escaped to Spain. In June 1945, a month after V-E Day, his body was found near Ronda. The corpse was partly burned."

Bohlen was unsuccessfully trying to light his pipe. "Let's sit down," he said, picked up his double Scotch and moved to a vacant table.

Craig followed him, speaking eagerly. "The boss of Skolnikoff, a man named Otto Brandl, was in charge of shipping the treasures from Paris and hiding them in safe places all over Europe. He was personally responsible to Goering. Two months after Skolnikoff's death, Otto was captured in Munich."

"Who captured him?" Bohlen asked. "The American Army?"

Craig nodded. "A special unit of Military Intelligence. The next morning he was found hanged from a beam in his prison cell."

"Suicide?"

Craig shrugged. "Officially, yes." He drained his glass. "Anyway, two out of the three were dead. The only man still alive who knew where the treasures were hidden was Goering himself."

"Who was hanged in Nuremberg," Bohlen said quickly.

"Wrong again," Craig countered, with a note of triumph in his voice. "A couple of hours before his execution, Goering was found dead in his prison cell. Poisoned. There was a suicide note by the body, but nobody ever established with certainty that Goering wrote it. That was very strange, to say the least. You see—he had been searched thoroughly that very evening. No poison capsule had been found either in his clothes, or anywhere else in the cell."

Bohlen leaned over the table. Gone was the sleepy, slightly contemptuous expression that he had been wearing the whole evening. His eyes were gleaming with interest and his motheaten brows had joined together in a frown of intent concentration. "Are you . . ." He cleared his throat. "Are you trying to say that . . ."

"I am trying to say that the three persons who knew where the bulk of Goering's treasure was hidden met an unnatural death. It's worth a closer look, don't you think?"

Bohlen didn't answer immediately. He sat very still, lost in thought. Finally he spoke. "Let me get it straight. You suspect that somebody was after Goering's treasure. You don't believe that Goering and Brandl committed suicide. This man—or maybe it was a group of men—murdered Brandl, Goering and . . ."

"Skolnikoff."

". . . and Skolnikoff, yes. Any evidence, Clint?"

Craig shook his head. "No evidence. Just a hunch."

Bohlen succeeded in lighting his pipe and puffed a dense cloud of bluish smoke that hovered, trembling, in the dim light. "Still, it could be only a coincidence, and you know it. What if Skolnikoff was murdered for money or revenge, and Goering and Brandl really committed suicide?"

Craig frowned. "Maybe. But I don't believe in coincidences. Especially when such a fabulous treasure is concerned."

"Any idea who might have done it?"

Craig shook his head again. "No. It could be a man, an organization, even a government. A lot of money was involved, Peter. The bulk of the wealth of Europe: gold, silver, gems, paintings, statues. Worth hundreds of millions of dollars, maybe even more."

Bohlen whistled softly. "And those three people—why do you think they were killed?"

"I believe that they were forced to talk and disclose the locations of the caches. After they divulged their secrets, they had to be silenced."

A young literary agent from New York popped up at Bohlen's side. "Hi, you two. Peter, do you have a moment? I've got a fantastic manuscript, and I want you to be the first to . . ."

"Not now, George, for God's sake," Bohlen rudely snapped. "Don't you see I'm busy? Tomorrow, okay?" He turned his back on the intruder, who hastily withdrew, a hurt expression on his face. The publisher leaned toward Clint. "Have you got an outline on that?"

Craig shook his head. "No, and there isn't going to be any. I don't want anybody stealing my story."

"You call that a story?" Bohlen scowled. Craig instinctively felt that his publisher had decided to go along, and was already bargaining, trying to play down his interest in the idea to get a better deal. "There is no story here," Bohlen went on, "just a guess based on a probable coincidence. You might be taking me on a wild-goose chase."

Craig didn't answer, but leaned back in his seat and let his eyes wander over the crowded lounge.

Bohlen eyed him speculatively for a long moment. "How much?" he suddenly grumbled. He pushed his drink aside and locked his sharp eyes with Clint's. "How much do you want for that book?"

It was after three in the morning when Clint Craig stepped through the automatic glass doors of the Frankfurt Hof and walked into the cold drizzle that noiselessly descended on the sleeping city. The hotel doorman, a fat tiny Hindu, his round face puffed with fatigue, was pacing to and fro under the portico, miserably attempting to warm himself by rubbing his plump, dark-skinned hands. "Taxi, sir?" he inquired wearily.

Craig shook his head. "No, thank you, I'll walk."

The Hindu stared at the coatless American who walked away down the deserted street, indifferent to the cold and rain. But Clint didn't care, not now. In the inner pocket of his blazer he felt the slight pressure of the thick folded paper, the contract he had just signed in Bohlen's suite. It stipulated that Clint Craig was going to write a nonfiction book entitled *Goering's Treasure* for Bohlen and Sherf Inc. of New York. The advance against royalties would be sixty thousand dollars, payable half on signature, and half on acceptance of the manuscript. For this particular book, Peter Bohlen was to act as his agent for the world rights, for a commission of ten percent.

Bohlen had insisted on one more condition, even though it was not added to the contract: Craig would cancel any other project he had under way, and would immediately start his research on the *Goering*. The subject was hot, Bohlen had pointed out; he wanted to set a crash production plan, and he needed the manuscript as soon as possible. Craig had accepted; he was getting infected by his own enthusiasm now, and was ready to start working that very minute.

He took a deep breath and let the drops of rain stream down his flushed face. He had made the first step; he was back in business. The check for thirty thousand dollars was safely tucked in his wallet. It was up to him to make the most of this break.

Yet now that he was alone, old doubts assailed him. It had been too easy, too quick. He was not as confident as he had pretended while presenting his idea to Peter. What if his publisher was right? What if the odd succession of deaths was nothing but a coincidence? He might research and dig and travel all over Europe—and find nothing. He could enjoy a temporary well-being with Bohlen's money; but if he failed, nobody would ever commission a book of his again. And even if he had guessed right, and there had been a conspiracy to kill the treasure keepers, the chances of discovering any solid evidence thirty-five years later were very thin.

But if he did succeed—the optimist in him retorted—he would be credited with one of the most sensational pieces of investigative journalism in this century. "Cheer up, Clint," he said to himself. "If there is a secret and if it is humanly possible to crack it, you will."

A couple, a man and a woman, silently walked past him. The man seemed to be drunk, and his bulk was unsteadily swaying; the woman, a fading blonde on high heels, held him tight with her right hand while her left tried to protect her hairdo with a folded newspaper, soaked with rain. A cab coming from the opposite direction slowed down as it approached Clint, hoping for a fare. Clint shook his head. What he needed now was a big, steaming cup of strong black coffee in the all-night open *Büfett* of the railroad station. Then he would go to his *pension*, pick up his still-packed suitcase, and head straight to the airport to catch the first flight to Paris. Paris, where it all had started.

He saw his tall, slim reflection in a hi-fi shop window and smiled. "Famous author starts dramatic investigation," he fantasized. "Craig flies to Paris, the city whose treasures were robbed forty years ago by *Reichsmarschall* Goering and his henchmen."

Chapter Two:

October 19:

FILE

"Okay, guys, turn on the lights. Frank, take camera one. All the others, please move back. You are a damn nuisance in this room." David Crawford, the television director attached to Jefferson's staff, paced forward to the far end of the spacious room where the lights converged. Moving awkwardly, he took funny wide-spaced steps to avoid treading on the cables lying on the carpet. He passed in front of the two television cameras, focused from different angles on the stacked bookcases. Senator Jefferson, in an open shirt that made him look younger, stepped into the beams of light and casually propped his elbows against one of the shelves. Crawford busied himself around him. "Move a little to the side, sir. For this set we are going to use camera one, which is just in front of you. I don't want it to take you straight *en face*, but a little from the side—that makes it more casual. Don't forget: the implied idea of this set is that you are inviting the audience into your home, where you live, and work, and move freely, so you must be casual." He checked the directional microphones. "We'll give you the cue right under the camera, so you will not have to shift your eyes. If you stand this way, in half profile, it would be the best. You shifted your eyes too much in the previous set. People don't like that. They want you to look them straight in the eye."

Jefferson nodded. "I am sorry. Maybe we worked too much this morning. How many did we do?"

Crawford looked at the pad in his right hand. "Six two-minutes and four one-minute commercials. But only half of that material can be used. Maybe you'd like to take a break?"

"No, no, it's okay."

"Fine then."

He retreated with the same uneven stride and turned back to the crowd of fifteen-odd people, mostly men in shirtsleeves, packed at the other end of the room. "Silence, everybody, here we go. And stop moving—we don't want your footsteps recorded." He checked the image in the camera monitor. "Holy shit," he angrily whispered to Frank Knopf, the cameraman. "Why can't they just clear the room? Every senior staff member thinks that he should watch J.J. taping his commercials, and nobody wants to admit that he is not a senior member and get out of here." He turned to the candidate. "Okay, sir, we're all set. Wait for a few seconds after the cue." The tiny red light on the camera began to glow, the camera started to whir softly and three low beeps came from the recorder.

Jefferson composedly looked into the camera. "Last week, when I was campaigning in a small city up north, an old gentleman came to me and asked: 'Jimmy Jefferson, what makes you run?' I told him what." Jefferson grinned. "And I want to tell all of you what makes me run."

He paused briefly, and a solemn expression settled on his features. "I believe that this is one of the most important campaigns in the history of our country. America is no longer what she used to be. Most of all, she lacks leadership. A wise man once said: 'Who is a leader? The one who understands that reality is an ever-changing kaleidoscope, and is able to shape and reshape his policy . . .'" He seemed to hesitate, then stopped. "No, I think I blew it." He wiped his forehead. "Can we do that again, David?"

Crawford shook his head. "Who the hell needs his wise old man," he ferociously muttered to no one in particular, then stepped forward. "I suggest that we take a break, sir. You're too tense, and that quote of the wise man rings out of place."

Jefferson looked at him thoughtfully. "No problem. I can drop the wise man"—he smiled—"and rearrange it. We can go on."

"No," Crawford insisted. "You are also sweating too much, and that ruins your makeup. I suggest that you get made up again and relax a little, okay? We're putting too much strain on you this morning."

"All right," said Jefferson, and moved out of the lights.

Crawford turned back. "Where is Lisa? Lisa?"

The makeup girl raised her hand from the corner where she had been sitting quietly. "Lisa, look, I want you to freshen his makeup. Especially under the eyes—get rid of those wrinkles; they make his eyes look smaller. But don't go too heavy on him; I want this tan to come out on the screen. It makes him look fit."

The short girl nodded and followed the senator into the adjoining small room, which had been transformed into a dressing room. Jefferson sat on the upright chair facing the mirror, and the girl started to clean the makeup from his face. "It will take just a moment, sir," she murmured, engrossed in her work.

A young man appeared at the door. He was of average height, with unruly sand-blond hair, a square forehead and a thin, hollow-cheeked face. He looked casual in an open-necked polo sweater, yet his thick horn-rimmed glasses gave him the air of a young scholar. "There is a man at the gate who wants to see you, J.J. He says it's urgent."

Jefferson raised his hand, palm up. "Not now, Ralph, I can't. There are many people who want to see me—so what." He sounded slightly irritated.

"He said you would receive him."

Jefferson threw him an oblique look. "Is that so?" His tone was ironical. "What's his name?"

"He said you might not recall his name, but if I told you that he was Chuck, from Unit Thirty-two, Section Four, you'll remember."

"Chuck, from Unit Thirty-two . . ." Jefferson slowly repeated, and suddenly his face lit up in recollection. "Of course, I do remember him. Yes, I'll see him right away. Bring him to my study." And turning to the makeup girl: "Lisa, would you excuse me? I'll be back in a few minutes." He quickly walked through the crammed corridor, giving friendly nods to his aides and the Secret Service people, went down the stairs to the lower level and entered his study. He circled his large desk and sank into his swivel chair behind it. Now that he was alone, he stretched his hands, yawned and rubbed his eyes.

There was a knock on the door. "Come in," he said and got up.

The door opened and a tall willowy man walked in. He was wearing a gray suit and a dark blue tie. His silver hair was cropped in an old-fashioned crew cut, and his wrinkled face resembled aged leather. He looked a few years older than the senator.

"Chuck?" Jefferson asked with slight hesitation, stretching out his hand.

35

"The one and only." The silver-haired man smiled and shook hands. "Remember me?"

"Well, I wouldn't have recognized you in the street, no," the senator admitted. "How long has it been, thirty-five years?"

Chuck nodded. "I would have recognized you anywhere. You didn't change at all."

"Oh, yes I did," the senator sighed. "We all do." He motioned to one of the leather-upholstered armchairs in front of the desk. "Will you have a drink, or some coffee?"

"No, thank you. Nothing for me." Chuck looked nervous. "I was sure you wouldn't remember my full name. Charles Belford. But I doubt if you ever heard it in full."

"Charles Belford," Jefferson repeated. "Yes, those were . . . exciting days, to say the least." He looked straight into his guest's eyes. "What have you been doing all these years, Chuck?"

"Well, I moved in and out of a few jobs, and finally decided that what we did in the army was the best thing for me, so I came back to the service."

"Military Intelligence? Or the OSS?"

"No, the OSS had been disbanded already. I joined the new team of Allen Dulles, and stayed there."

"CIA then," Jefferson said.

Chuck nodded. He obviously was trying to overcome his inner tension. "Now, Jim—" He smiled awkwardly. "May I call you Jim?"

"Of course," the senator said. "I am still Jim, although some prefer to call me J.J." He chuckled softly.

"Well . . . I want to make clear that my visit here is purely private. I came on my own initiative. I didn't want to call you, because calls may be traced, and I want to ask you not to mention my visit to anybody. Is that all right with you?"

The senator nodded gravely, but a puzzled look came into his eyes. "Of course, Chuck. It's just between you and me."

The CIA official seemed more at ease. "I would like you to know that I follow the campaign very closely, and I respect very much what you are doing. I don't agree completely with all your views, of course, but . . ."

"That's natural." The senator smiled.

Chuck leaned forward. "I came to see you, because we were army buddies once and I am concerned with your safety."

"My safety?" Jefferson was puzzled. "I am well protected, as you know. There are all those Secret Service guys and a team of private agents from Pinkerton's."

Chuck shook his head. "I might be exaggerating, but after your famous speech and the commotion it created, it seems to me that there are some circles, or even institutions, that would do anything to get you out of the way."

"Which circles?" Jefferson sharply asked, his eyes narrowing.

Chuck seemed unhappy, yet he had gone too far to stop. "I might be revealing a secret, but I gather that you would have guessed it anyhow." He took a package of cigarettes from his pocket and lit one with quick, nervous gestures. "For the last seven years, since the first major confrontation between us and OPEC, we have been keeping the headquarters of that organization under close surveillance."

Jefferson nodded. "Yes, I've guessed that, as you said."

"Now, on the last day of the convention—August fifteenth—at the end of your speech, there was an overseas call from Washington to the office of the OPEC chairman."

"Shazli," Jefferson said. "I know him."

"The call originated in the office of William Murphy, the president of American Oil. Have you met him?"

"Just seen him on TV once or twice. I know about his position, of course. Very close to OPEC, and cooperating with them all along the line."

"Uh-huh. Now, we don't know what was said in that conversation." Chuck smiled apologetically. "We have no right to tap those phones, because OPEC is not considered to be an 'object of national security.'" He sounded bitter. "Yet the next evening, Shazli received in his office the four men who are considered to be his private cabinet—Nusserat, Badran, Abd-el-Krim and Baghdadi. And six days later Shazli came to New York and met Murphy in secret."

"In secret?" Jefferson frowned.

"Yes. Shazli was flying to the South American oil conference in Caracas. He changed planes at the airport. He had more than an hour to wait. He was seen going out of the international terminal and entering a black limousine. The limousine stopped at the TWA terminal and picked up William Murphy there. He was wearing a hat and dark glasses."

"And where did they go?"

"Nowhere." Chuck smiled wryly. "They just drove around

for about thirty minutes, and then Shazli returned to the airport and took his plane to Venezuela."

"What do you make of it?" Jefferson asked.

"Well, we don't know what was said at this meeting, of course. But the secrecy worries me. Why did they have to take such elaborate steps to assure secrecy, when they meet quite often and quite openly? You may say that I have a one-track mind, and you may be right. But I was assigned for a couple of years to the White House security section, and I see assassination plots everywhere." Now that he had unburdened himself, Chuck looked more relaxed.

Jefferson leaned back and raised his eyes to the ceiling. He was silent for a long while. Finally he looked back at Chuck and shook his head. "No. It doesn't make sense. I don't know William Murphy . . ."

"He is a mean character, and your election might be quite a blow to him."

Jefferson shrugged. "Maybe. As I said, I don't know him. But I know Shazli personally, and I have read a lot about him. He is too clever a man to get involved in a murder plot. He wouldn't risk it. Never."

"So why this secret meeting?"

"I don't know," the senator said slowly. "I don't know. Maybe they wanted to coordinate their future moves?"

"But there were no future moves," Chuck exclaimed. "Nothing. OPEC didn't react to your speech; William Murphy refused to comment. Something must be brewing there."

"Did they meet again later?"

Chuck produced a small notepad from his pocket and flipped through the pages. "There was another phone conversation on September tenth; then they met during the monthly conference of the major American oil importers with OPEC. They had a private dinner. Since, there have been quite a few phone communications, almost daily."

"Yeah," Jefferson grunted. "And you have no lead whatever."

"No, Jim, nothing."

"Well." Jefferson brought his hands down on the armrests and rose. "I guess we'll have to wait and see. I appreciate that you came to warn me. This is quite a risk for you, Chuck, and I am very grateful to you."

Belford got up too. "I just wanted to make sure that you took more precautions. Maybe you should tighten the security

38

measures. This country is sick of violence. We can't take it anymore."

"You are right," Jefferson agreed. "Still, I believe that I am as well protected as is humanly possible. Will you keep me posted if anything new develops?"

"Of course," Chuck said, and shook the senator's hand.

"Thank you. Thank you indeed." Something suddenly crossed Jefferson's mind. "Oh, by the way, Chuck, now that you are here . . ."

The CIA man stopped by the door.

"May I ask you something?" Jefferson spoke very carefully, as he put his hand on Chuck's shoulder. "A certain matter may develop in which I could need the advice, and maybe even the help, of a man of your experience. I can assure you that it would be of the highest importance to this country, and only in the best interests of America. May I get in touch with you if I decide to go along with that plan of mine?"

Chuck stirred uneasily. "Frankly, I don't know. I don't want to get mixed up in politics. I must hear first what it's all about; then I'll decide."

"Certainly," Jefferson said. "I wouldn't ask you to commit yourself to something you don't agree with. It might be a solution"—he corrected himself—"*the* solution to our problems. How can I get in touch with you?"

Bedford hesitated a second, then jotted some figures on his pad, tore off the leaf and handed it to Jefferson. "That's my private number. Have somebody call me at home."

Jefferson looked at the number. "Fine. The man who'll call you is Ralph, Ralph Dowden. He is my campaign manager, a very reliable young man. And thanks again."

When Chuck Belford was gone, Jefferson returned to his desk and took up the phone receiver. "Mary? Will you tell David that I won't do any more commercials this morning? No, nothing happened—I just don't feel like it. Fix another session for tomorrow, okay?" He listened for a second. "Oh, hell, screw the Daughters of the American Revolution." As the dry laughter of his secretary cracked in the receiver, he hurriedly corrected himself: "Sorry, I didn't mean that."

He leaned back in his chair, his eyes wandering around the room, lost in thought.

In the plane bound for Paris, Clint did not look even once through the porthole on his right. He was deeply engrossed in the voluminous file on his knees that bore the inscription, in bold characters: Goering.

His research assistant in New York had done a thorough job. She had collected all she could lay her hands on concerning Goering: photographs, press clippings, documents, photocopies of whole chapters in books dealing with Nazi Germany, the integral text of entries in various encyclopedias. He had added the facts he had gathered in Bethesda. And the character that emerged from the heap of papers and photographs was, indeed, fascinating.

Clint's eye focused for a moment on the family portrait of Goering's parents. The stern, respectable father, Bismarck's commissioner in South-West Africa, and later German ambassador to Haiti; the pretty mother, who had been for years a mistress of an influential Jew—Hermann, Ritter von Epenstein—in whose castle, Veldenstein, the child Hermann Goering had been raised. Did that secret relationship, Clint wondered, sow the first seeds of anti-Semitism in Goering's mind? Did that make him become one of the most devoted supporters of the extermination of the Jews during the Second World War, as witnessed in his letter of July 31, 1941, to Heydrich, charging him with organizing "the final solution of the Jewish question in the German sphere of influence in Europe"?

He leafed further down the file. An early photograph of Goering showed him in a pilot's uniform, during the First World War. That had been Goering's finest hour, when he had gained fame as a redoubtable and yet chivalrous ace, and had risen to succeed, as commander of his squadron, the legendary Baron Manfred von Richthofen. He had been a man of honor in those faraway years and had left his country, disgusted with the humiliation of former army officers by the civilian population after the defeat of Imperial Germany. And in Sweden, where he worked as a commercial pilot, he had madly fallen in love with the beguiling Baroness Karin von Kantzow, who had divorced her husband to marry him.

How could such an intrepid man of integrity, a war hero, a passionately romantic youth, change so deeply and become one of the most ruthless Nazi leaders, a man whom a distinguished historian would define one day as "one of the cruellest political criminals of all time"? It seemed to Clint that the year 1922, in which the dashing twenty-nine-year-old pilot had married his beloved Karin, had also been the turning point in his life. For by the end of that same year he had

40

joined the small Nazi party in Munich and taken command of Hitler's storm troopers, the *Sturmabteilung*. Wounded in the groin in the Munich *Putsch* in 1923, when Hitler had failed to seize power, he had escaped to Austria and Sweden. The pain from his wounds had been unbearable; his doctors had stuffed him with morphine, and he had become an incurable drug addict. For a while his addiction had pushed him beyond the limits of sanity; twice, in the years 1925 to 1926, he had been committed to the Swedish mental hospital at Langbro.

Yet shortly afterward he was back in Germany, climbing the hierarchy in the Nazi party, concentrating tremendous power in his hands. He had become a member of the *Reichstag* in 1928 and president of the *Reichstag* in 1932. As prime minister of Prussia and its minister of the Interior in 1933, he had Nazified the Prussian police, established the notorious Gestapo, and set up the first concentration camps for the opponents of the regime. That same year Hitler had become chancellor of Germany as Goering, by brutal political maneuvers, using the *Reichstag* fire, had got rid of the Communists and the Democrats and handed dictatorial powers to the Führer. A photograph of that same year showed Goering in the uniform of commander of the *Sturmabteilung*. His head was still impressive: a large, clear forehead, dark wavy hair, purposeful eyes, a determined jaw. Still, his chest was already covered with an excessive array of decorations, medals and badges, and his girth was thickening. These external changes augured his metamorphosis in the years to come into a soft, obese, effeminate figure that would remind the historian Rebecca West of the fat women patting their sleek cats in the late morning hours in the doorways of the ill-famed streets of Marseilles; his childish delight in flamboyant uniforms and jewelry was to transform him into a rather ridiculous figure, clowning in specially tailored attire, colorful suits and even togas and sandals.

And yet he was the most loved and admired of the Nazi leaders, after Hitler; even as a fat, spoiled sybarite he had continued to collect offices of state, becoming the commander in chief of the German Air Force—the *Luftwaffe*—and Hitler's official successor, *Reichsmarschall des Grossdeutschen Reiches*.

Clint quickly perused the documents describing Goering's part in the *Anschluss* with Austria, and in the building of Germany's Air Force. During the war he had never come close to the battlefield, supervising from afar the operations of the *Luftwaffe*. More and more, on the pretext of ill health, he would plunge into the pleasures of Karinhall.

Karinhall. The enormous baronial estate he had established in Schorfheide, north of Berlin, and had named after his first wife, who died in 1931. In the sumptuous rooms of his palace he had concentrated the major part of his collection of art and treasures, plundered from all over Europe. Tapestries, statues, priceless golden objects, rare jewelry, exquisite wines, paintings stolen from every country. He had stolen thirteen hundred paintings, worth fifty million Reichsmarks, from Jews who were sent to the gas chambers; he had put his hands on most of the fabulous treasures that Alfred Rosenberg, another Nazi leader, and the mysterious Otto Brandl had looted in France. The *Einsatzstab* Rosenberg, slyly named "Action Staff," had stolen, mostly in France, about twenty-two thousand objets d'art including five thousand paintings. Some of them had gone to adorn the monumental rooms of Karinhall; many had been given by Goering as "presents" to Nazi dignitaries. Most had been hidden in salt mines, castles, inconspicuous farmhouses. According to one top-secret German document, the concealment of the treasure had been code-named "Operation Phantom." Between 1940 and 1942 alone, Goering had visited France twenty times, skimming the cream of Rosenberg's plunder, supervising the dispatch to Germany of Otto Brandl's best finds. In Paris, special exhibitions were set up for him in the Musée du Jeu de Paume, and there he would select the paintings to be sent to his private collection or to Hitler's residence. In three years 158 railroad cars laden with 4,174 crates of objets d'art had been sent by Otto to Goering. Hundreds of other trains transported other highly valuable goods according to Goering's orders.

Clint thoughtfully examined a photograph of Goering, proudly presenting to Hitler a painting stolen from French Jews. Standing against the background of a splendid Gobelins tapestry, Goering was grinning broadly, clad in his new *Reichsmarschall* uniform made of dark-blue fabric with white lapels and red-striped trousers. Hitler, bent toward him, was contemplating the big, gilt-framed painting held by two SS officers, while a group of photographers was snapping pictures of the event for posterity.

Nothing could stop Goering in his crusade of plunder. Not the nervous memoranda of worried jurists, nor the pleas of museum curators nor the childish complaints of Rosenberg, who felt plundered in his turn by his senior colleague. With his almost unlimited power at the helm of the Reich, with his hundreds of caches all over Europe, with Otto Brandl and Michel Skolnikoff devotedly toiling for him in Paris, Goering had realized the biggest robbery in history.

But all three of them, Goering, Brandl, Skolnikoff, had met mysterious deaths. And with them had died the secret of their treasure, the bulk of which had vanished without a trace. How did they die? Where was the treasure?

Clint turned the last page of his file, and buckled his seat belt as the futuristic shape of Charles de Gaulle Airport appeared in the flat fields of the Ile de France, down below.

A shrill, loud ring echoed in the deserted landing as Clint Craig pressed the brass bell button and consulted his watch. It was three-thirty, and Tailbot should be expecting him. When a minute passed and nothing happened, he rang again. Almost immediately he heard heavy footsteps and an angry, high-pitched voice: *"J'arrive, j'arrive, un moment!"* The door opened and there stood big fat Ernestine, a little bit older perhaps, but healthy and irascible as ever. She scowled at him, while wiping her plump red-skinned hands on her wet apron. She must have been doing the dishes when he rang.

"Bonjour, Ernestine, remember me? Clint Craig."

She peered at him with her shortsighted eyes, and her voice grew slightly less belligerent. "Monsieur Craig? *Bonjour,* monsieur. Is monsieur expecting you?"

He smiled at the old-fashioned turn of speech. "Yes," he said. "Monsieur Tailbot is expecting me." He followed the maid through the tiny vestibule and into the large sitting room. A soft afternoon light was filtering through the lace curtains. The room looked exactly the same as it had twelve years ago, when he had stepped in for the first time. He was a young postgraduate student then, working on his Ph.D. thesis in Paris, looking forward with trepidation to his first meeting with Pierre Tailbot, whose books he knew almost by heart. Madame Tailbot was still alive at that time; she had served him a cup of strong *café filtre* and pleasantly chatted with him to relieve him of his tension, while her husband was busy with another of his students. As he moved about the familiar room now, long-forgotten memories emerged from his past. He was about to sink into one of the cozy armchairs beside the fireplace, when the door at the other end of the room opened and Pierre Tailbot stepped in, his face beaming with pleasure.

"Clint! What a pleasant surprise." He warmly pumped his hand. "When you called this morning, I still didn't believe that you were in Paris. Come, come into my study." His stoop when he walked was more pronounced now, and made him look even more insignificant. Pierre Tailbot was a tiny bald man in his late sixties, with a triangular face, thin-lipped mouth and a big aquiline nose. He looked very much like a retired clerk. Nobody would guess he was the best contemporary historian in France, until he saw the lively black eyes, sparkling with intelligence, and heard the deep, cultivated voice forcefully expounding his sweeping theories in the packed auditoriums of the Sorbonne. His *History of the Occupation* and *Paris Under German Rule* had been translated into many languages. The detailed book he wrote on the robbing of France by the Otto organization had won him the French Academy award for contemporary history. And if there was one man in Europe who could help Clint with his current research, it was Pierre Tailbot.

"Of course I shall help you," he said pleasantly, removing a pile of papers from his desk, the better to see Clint who stood in front of him. "Take this chair." He pointed. "Just dump the files on the floor, it's all right." He raised his hands, palms up, in mock apology. "Better an overstuffed study than a clean desk, right? I am working now on the private letters of *Maréchal* Pétain from the last year he spent as head of the Vichy regime. What a puppet he had become in the hands of the Germans!" He sighed. "As De Gaulle used to say, *la vieillesse est un naufrage.* Old age is a shipwreck." He changed the subject. "And you? What you have been doing all these years? There were those excellent books of yours and then—silence. I heard you turned to politics?" He eyed Clint with mild reproach.

Clint shrugged. "Well, I am trying to get back to serious research now." He paused. "I was in the U.S. Army archives in Maryland last week, and I came across some very strange facts. I would like you to hear my theory." He described in detail his findings and his ideas, although now, in front of his former teacher, he felt less confident than he had last night in Frankfurt. Tailbot listened quietly, occasionally nodding when Craig mentioned a name or a fact known to him. Craig interrupted his narrative only once, when Ernestine came in bringing coffee in two big earthenware mugs. When Clint had finished, Tailbot didn't say a word. He was taking short sips of his coffee, his eyes half closed. His left hand, which held the saucer under his mug, was trembling slightly. Clint let his eyes wander around the room, over the heavily stacked bookcases and the racks laden with yellow and pale-blue files. This was only a part of Tailbot's private archives. Clint remembered that in the adjoining, much bigger, room special shelves had been built along the walls and in the center to store the professor's files.

"It's a strange story," Tailbot finally said. "Highly improbable, and yet—not impossible. You know that I spent five years of my life researching that specific subject—the robbing of France by the Nazis; and there are some facts that seem to support your theory." He got up, walked to one of the bookshelves and took down a fat volume. "That's my book about the Otto organization," he said, and expertly leafed through it. He put his bifocals on the tip of his nose, buried his head in the book, grunting and muttering to himself, then raised his eyes. "Yes. Take this Otto Brandl for example. A strange man. He had two masters: the *Abwehr*—the Military Intelligence of the German Army—and Goering, in Germany. He came to Paris six months after the Germans conquered it, and established his headquarters at the Square du Bois de Boulogne, in the sixteenth *arrondissement*. He built a very powerful organization—at certain times he had five hundred people working for him, mostly French. Thieves, thugs, people with criminal records. First they 'confiscated' the art collections of Jewish and left-wing families who had been deported to the concentration camps. Later they started to clean out museums in Paris, Tours, Lyon—all over the country. The operation soon developed into an all-out robbery of works of art, gold, securities, precious stones, antique furniture, silverware, rare china, furs, perfumes—anything of value. The goods arrived in huge quantities in Paris, where they were stored at the warehouses of the Northern railroads, the *Chemins de fer du Nord*. A part of the loot was shipped to Switzerland. Otto himself used to go to Geneva, to sell the goods to Swiss merchants. They were very obliging and didn't ask questions. The money, in Swiss francs, served to finance unconventional operations of the *Abwehr*, in France and abroad."

Clint quietly placed his empty mug on the desk.

"But the bulk of the take, the precious paintings, the statues, the gold—those went to Germany. Otto had them

45

packed and shipped to hiding places all over Germany. Some selected items were sent to caches abroad, in Spain and Portugal. Trains laden with such treasures used to leave France very often; in the last year of the occupation they left the Gare du Nord every day. Only Otto and Goering knew what was in each crate—they had a system of code numbers—and where it went."

"And Skolnikoff?"

"Yes, Skolnikoff too, of course." Tailbot chuckled. "Some gangster, that one! He was of Russian origin and had been in Paris for years. He knew practically everybody. When the war started, he was nothing but a small-time crook and peddler. He even had no regular papers. One night he was arrested by the Gestapo. On the spot, Skolnikoff offered to trade his knowledge about the art and gold collectors in France. He was released almost immediately. He became Otto's main informer, as well as the supplier of the German Army with rare goods and articles. Soon he amassed a huge fortune. He was living with his German mistress, Hélène, in a sumptuous house at rue de Presbourg, protected by the SS, leading the most fastidious life while the people of Paris walked around hungry. German generals and SS officials were waiting in line to be invited to his lunches and dinners, and gorge themselves with caviar, *foie gras* and champagne. The food was served on golden plates by a house staff of ten cooks, servants and waiters." Tailbot shook his head sadly. "And do you know, Clint, who was the guest of honor at Skolnikoff's table? His black poodle, Peggy, with a napkin around its neck, gulping its smoked salmon and Beluga caviar while the Nazi generals were smacking their lips and praising the cuisine of Skolnikoff."

"It sounds insane," Clint agreed.

Tailbot shrugged. "It was insane. A crook, traitor, a thief, becoming a kind of uncrowned prince of Paris, looting the country, building a fortune of billions, delivering all the fat of the land to the Nazis." He sighed.

"Look, here he is." He pointed to a photograph in the book. Clint leaned over the table and examined the snapshot of a rather insignificant-looking small man, dressed in a suit twice his size. Under the shadow of his soft-brimmed hat, round, suspicious eyes looked at the camera, and the small mouth was curved in a forced smile. He had almost no chin and his Adam's apple bulged in the scrawny neck.

"His accomplices," Tailbot went on, "supplied him with

precise information about any item of value they spotted, and he would alert the special squads of Otto. He also supervised the shipments, particularly those to Spain and Portugal. During the war he even went there, twice. When it became clear that Germany was going to lose the war, Goering and Otto diverted some of the most valuable shipments to Spain, preparing their escapes. Skolnikoff almost made it, you know."

"What do you think about their deaths?" Clint asked. "Isn't it strange that Otto and Skolnikoff died so conveniently? And Goering poisoned himself?"

"Now that I think of it, it does seem strange," Tailbot admitted. He got up and replaced his book on the shelf, brushing the dust off the nearby volumes. "But I never examined that particular angle." He chuckled. "I must confess that I was more interested in the lives of Otto and Skolnikoff than in their deaths."

"Could I borrow your book about Otto . . ." Clint began.

"Of course you can, but I have something more valuable for you. Come." He preceded Craig into the archives room, and took hold of a wooden ladder that was leaning against the wall by the door.

"Let me help you," Clint said.

"No, no, I can manage myself. Old but not dead yet." He laughed softly. He carried the ladder to the opposite corner, climbed up it and started checking the labels on the files that lay on the uppermost shelf. A cloud of dust rose around him, and the tiny particles gleamed like gold as they glided through the pale ray of sunshine. The old man seemed embarrassed. "I never let Ernestine touch this room," he explained. "She puts everything in order, as she says, and then it takes me months to find my files. Oh, here they are." He took two files that lay close to the bottom of the stack and carried them down. "You see, Clint?" he said proudly. "These are the complete files of Otto Brandl and Michel Skolnikoff. You'll find here everything you need, including the American Army report about Brandl, which I obtained by special permission. I also filed my personal notes here, so the files are almost complete."

"Almost?"

"Well, I guess you should do some prying of your own."

Craig nodded. "I must to go Spain and Germany, of course."

"I don't have anything about Goering. You should go to

Nuremberg and visit the Court of Justice. Maybe they still have some archives there."

Clint started leafing through the documents. "I don't know how to thank you."

"Don't thank me, just bring those back to me. I am becoming an insecure old man, and I don't like to part with my papers. Why don't you photocopy the documents you need and return the files?"

"I shall do that," Clint promised.

He emerged from the house into the golden Indian summer that enveloped the city, and felt a sudden pang in his heart as the enchanting Paris of his youth flashed briefly through his memory.

He hurried through the lobby of the Royal Hotel, eager to start working, when a casual glance at the newsstand made him stop dead in his tracks. The last afternoon edition of *France-Soir,* the Paris evening paper, carried a banner headline: HUNT FOR GOERING'S TREASURE. He grabbed the paper, threw a few coins on the counter and felt his way to a vacant armchair, close to a group of noisy Japanese. Under its fat headline, *France-Soir* announced in small characters: "Sensational revelations about the caches of Goering's treasure and the strange deaths of its keepers, soon to be disclosed in a new book." A wave of anger swept Clint as he read the short article. In a press conference held in Frankfurt this very morning—the special correspondent of the paper reported—Peter Bohlen had declared that he was to publish, very shortly, a new book by the well-known historian Clint Craig. This book would bring to light "stunning revelations" about the hunt for Goering's treasure. The publisher pointed out that "Mr. Craig was adding the last touches to his manuscript," which, when published, "will carry the effect of a bombshell."

Clint furiously elbowed his way through the throng of tourists that lingered in the lobby, and hurried to his room. He threw the files on the bed and grabbed the telephone. The red message light was blinking but he ignored it. "Give me the Frankfurter Hof in Frankfurt," he almost shouted into the mouthpiece.

"Do you have the number, monsieur?"

"No, I don't have the number." He strove to regain control of himself. "Just a moment—sorry, I think I have it." He fumbled nervously through his pockets and unfolded a couple of tiny slips of paper. "Yes, here it is. Two-oh-two-five-one. I don't remember the area code. It's person-to-person, for Mr. Peter Bohlen from New York."

His publisher was not in the hotel, but finally they succeeded in getting hold of him at his stand at the Book Fair. As soon as he heard the calm voice of Peter, Clint exploded. "What the hell do you think you are doing?" he shouted angrily. "Are you out of your mind?"

Bohlen sounded slightly amused. "Take it easy, Clint. I thought that a little publicity wouldn't do any harm."

"You call that a little publicity?" Craig almost choked with anger. "You have told the press a huge pack of lies! I haven't even started my research yet. You promised them goods that I cannot deliver."

"That was not what you said last night, Clint."

"Oh, Jesus. I told you it was only a hunch. And how do you want me to work with all the press breathing down my neck? And what if I don't find anything?" He ran his fingers through his hair. "And who the hell is going to help me after that cheap, vulgar, dishonest publicity stunt?"

Bohlen didn't depart from his tranquillity. "Why don't you calm down, Clint? Relax, okay? I just wanted to dissuade any other writer who might have planned a book on Goering. You know that there is a World War Two revival now." He chuckled contentedly. "I thought you would be happy to learn that we aroused tremendous interest. I already have several firm offers from German and British publishers, and that Italian girl from Mondadori is following me around like a watchdog. You and I have made quite a lot of money this morning. Cheer up." He paused for a second, and Clint could hear in the receiver the beehive hum of the huge Hall Five. "Excuse me now. The German television is coming for an interview. Try to make a great book, and be good."

"You sonofabitch," Craig lashed back. But the line was already dead.

It took him a while to cool off. He checked his messages with the operator. They were all from journalists who had learned that he was in Paris and wanted to interview him about his book. Yesterday he would have willingly accepted; today he felt that public exposure was the worst thing that could happen to him. He decided not to return the calls and instructed the operator not to transfer any further calls to his room. He took the small, exquisite Empire desk that stood in

49

the corner alcove of his room and placed it in front of the large French windows that overlooked the magnificent Tuileries gardens. He discarded his jacket, undid his tie, dumped the blue Otto Brandl file on his desk and set to work.

Otto seemed to have been born in the *Abwehr*. Since his earliest youth this mysterious Bavarian, whose real name nobody seemed to know, had been working for the German secret services. First in Cologne, later in Belgium, he had concentrated in his hands many of the spy networks operating in France. Between 1935 and 1939, using his real-life profession of engineer as a perfect cover, he had traveled continually between his rear base in Brussels and various French cities, collecting intelligence and building his system of informers, agents and personal friends. When the war had started and France was occupied, he was among the first to come to Paris, where he built the huge Otto organization. He was a strange man indeed; tall, handsome and silver-haired, a ladies' man and a *bon vivant,* he had become a regular patron of the black-market French restaurants and cabarets that flourished under the Occupation. He always had a smashing model, actress or dancer, covered in furs and diamonds, hanging on his arm. But the suave man of the world sometimes turned into a vicious Mr. Hyde; he could be terribly cruel and violent, and once had beaten one of his subordinates almost to death over a minor disagreement. The violent streak in his character made even the most hardened criminals who worked for his organization fear Otto and obey him totally. He was a high official in the *Abwehr,* a close friend of the Gestapo chief of *Gross Paris,* and the most trusted confidant of Goering. At the end of the war he had returned to Munich in his native Bavaria, and was planning his escape abroad when he was captured by the American Military Intelligence, and died in his prison cell.

Craig leafed impatiently through several reports that described Otto's activities in Paris. At the bottom of the file he discovered a sheaf of papers in English, held together with a big paper clip. Those were the reports of the American Army about Otto's capture. Somebody in Military Intelligence must have had a fair notion of Otto's importance; the report described how the Brandl family residence had been put under surveillance, and how Otto had been finally discovered, when a young sister carrying a bag full of food was followed to a small apartment in the quiet Brugspergerstrasse by the Isar river. He had not resisted arrest.

50

A second document, a routine stenciled form, attested that Otto Brandl, born on January 7, 1898, had been imprisoned in the Stadelheim jail on the outskirts of Munich on August 6, 1945. The last paper was the photocopy of a typewritten report about Otto Brandl committing suicide by hanging, in his prison cell that same night. The report was dated August 7, and carried the name, serial number and signature of the Military Police NCO who was on duty in the prison that night, First Sergeant Jeffrey Oates.

Clint reached the last paragraph in the report—and froze.

It read: "Officer in charge of the questioning of Otto Brandl: Captain James T. Jefferson, Military Intelligence, U.S. Army."

Dumbfounded, Clint reached for the telephone.

Forty-five minutes later, he succeeded in locating Senator Jefferson at his campaign headquarters in downtown Washington. The senator was having a quick snack in his office between appointments. The familiar voice was confident as ever.

"Clint, how are you, you son of a gun?"

"I am fine, Jim, thanks." He disliked calling him J.J. "How are things going?"

"Well, they are looking better and better, to everybody's surprise but mine. In the last Gallup poll we gained another two points, and I need only another four percent to close the gap with Wheeler. They seem pretty nervous in the White House. Where are you?"

"I'm in Paris, Jim, in the Royal Hotel, doing some research for a new book. I am trying to find out what happened to Goering's treasure at the end of the war."

"Yes, I heard something in the news broadcast. It sounds pretty fascinating. Well, I certainly regret that you are not here. You could have written the best *Making of a President* that ever was."

Craig felt deeply embarrassed. "I am sorry to interrupt," he apologized, "I'm sure you are pretty busy now. But I have just run into something rather puzzling." He paused. "It has to do with you."

"Me?"

"I just read a report about the death of a German called Otto Brandl in Stadelheim jail, in Munich. That happened in August 1945. The report says you were in charge of his questioning."

"I was in charge of his questioning?" Jefferson sounded surprised. "What was the name of the fellow again?"

"Otto Brandl. He committed suicide, hanged himself in his cell."

There was a long silence. "I . . . I am afraid I don't remember," Jefferson said.

"You should remember," Craig insisted. "It was quite an important case. This man Brandl was very close to Goering. I have his files here, in front of me. It is rather odd, Jim, but your report about his interrogation is missing."

"Did I interrogate him?" Jefferson asked again.

"Yes, it seems so. And there is another matter. The account of his suicide was drawn up by a First Sergeant Jeffrey Oates. Remember him?"

"No . . ." Jefferson's voice was muffled. "I really don't recall."

"Anyway, Oates drew up the report. But according to regulations, the report on a prisoner's death should have been countersigned by you. You were the authority in charge. But the report in front of me is not countersigned. That's strange, Jim."

For the first time in the conversation Clint detected an undertone of strain in the senator's voice. "Dammit, Clint, how do you want me to remember such details? When did that happen, thirty-five years ago? What you say rings a bell somewhere, but it's very vague. I have other matters on my mind, as you can guess."

Craig ignored the sarcasm. "I am sorry to insist, but it's quite important, Jim. You see . . ."

"For Christ's sake, Clint, don't you understand the pressure I'm under?" Jefferson sounded angry. He paused for a second and quickly regained his calm. "Look, if you could send me a copy of that file, it might trigger my memory. But really, how can I humanly recall something like that, from nineteen forty-five? We had many such incidents, with all those jails crammed with Nazi criminals. Why don't you wait a couple of weeks, until the campaign is over?"

"Well . . ."

"I wish you were here with me now. God, I need a guy like you in this campaign. You surely could help. Keep in touch, okay?"

Jefferson hung up the phone, pushed his unfinished sandwich aside and got up. He walked to the window, which offered a fine view of Capitol Hill. He stood there motionless for a long while, his arms crossed, a tiny nerve twitching and jumping under his left eye. So that was it. Shazli and that oil magnate Murphy were up to something. What did Chuck say? "Something is brewing." They didn't plan an assassination. They had just dug deep enough to find the one secret in his past that could destroy him. And they had put on it the one man who was totally devoted to him, Clint Craig, whom nobody would suspect of having changed sides. How did they do it? Did they buy him? Or were they using him? He returned to his desk and pressed the intercom button. "Get me Ralph," he said. A moment later the phone on his desk buzzed.

"Ralph? You have that number I gave you this morning? . . . Yes, right, Charles Belford. Call him at home and set up a meeting somewhere, a bar, a hotel lobby. There are a few questions I'd like you to ask him."

He restlessly continued to pace. No, Chuck might get some information, but he wouldn't be of much help. He must think of something else.

He suddenly had an idea. His face pale and drawn with concern, he picked up the phone again. "I want to put in a call to Paris, Mary," he said to his secretary. He gave her the number. "This is urgent."

It was almost midnight in Paris when Clint Craig took his last sip from his tiny cup of espresso, paid his check and got up to leave. He had had a long, leisurely dinner in his favorite Paris restaurant, Chez Maitre Paul in the Latin Quarter. He had really needed that break. After the last hectic twenty-four hours, he had felt a physical need for a couple of hours to unwind, put some order in his thoughts, plan his next moves. He was still astounded by the discovery of Jefferson's involvement in Otto Brandl's death. Their conversation over the phone had left him even more puzzled. He had the distinct feeling that Jim Jefferson had not told him the truth. Even though more than thirty-five years had passed, he couldn't have simply forgotten such a dramatic event as the suicide of Goering's treasure-keeper while under his responsibility. So why did Jefferson lie to him? Why hadn't he countersigned the report about Brandl's death? Why was the interrogation report missing? A strange question sneaked into his mind: had he stumbled upon something big, much bigger than he had expected? Could Jim be in any way involved with the mystery he was investigating?

These questions had continued to trouble him during the taxi ride over the Pont Royal, along the picturesque Seine embankment and up the boulevard Saint-Germain. But then he had entered the small restaurant and been warmly welcomed by the blond *patronne*, somewhat heavier and wrinkled with age, but as pleasant and ebullient as he always remembered her. He had let his present worries drift far away. Madame herself prepared for him the specialty of the house—eel in wine sauce—and the eternal Philippe, the wine waiter, had seriously discussed with him the last years' vintages before they settled on a dry Sauvignon Blanc. The dinner in the half-empty restaurant had been pleasant and relaxing. He had let the fatigue of his body slowly take over and blur his senses with a velvety feeling of sweet drowsiness.

He went out in the crisp Parisian night. Rue Casimir Delavigne was deserted. The white illuminated shape of the Théatre de l'Odéon loomed straight ahead, and a refreshing wind blew from the Luxembourg Park. He walked unhurriedly down the street, but the sudden roar of an engine made him turn. A black Citroën, all lights blazing, darted toward him at terrific speed. Instinctively he dived toward a nearby house, crashed heavily against the wall, lost his balance and fell. He felt the blast of hot air from the left-side wheels of the car as the Citroën climbed onto the sidewalk and rumbled past him, missing him by inches. When he slowly got to his feet, the Citroën had already disappeared around the nearest corner. He didn't notice the number of the black car.

Less than twenty-four hours after he had started his research, somebody wanted him dead.

Chapter Three:

October 20—October 21:

LOVE

"I wouldn't jump to conclusions if I were you," Pierre Tailbot remarked. He did not look at Clint. He was absorbed in preparing his own cigarette, rolling long, thick strips of black tobacco into thin paper, expertly wetting the edge with his tongue, shaping the oblong white cylinder with his delicate, pale fingers. Satisfied, he raised his eyes and noticed that Clint was watching him with interest. He smiled. "An old habit I picked up during the war, when I served with the Free French, with De Gaulle. He was a heavy smoker then, always had a cigarette dangling from the corner of his mouth." He closed the tin box containing his tobacco. "That's the best tobacco we have, black, strong—not like the tasteless weeds they use in the factories. This tobacco"—he tapped the lid of the box—"comes straight from the plantation. A cousin of Ernestine brings me a big box every month. It reminds me of a song that was popular when I was young: '*J'ai du bon tabac dans ma tabatière.*' You know, De Gaulle himself used to sing that song. He very dearly loved his little daughter, Anne, who was retarded, and would sing and dance in front of her to amuse her. Did you know that De Gaulle had a retarded child?"

"You still admire him very much," Clint said with compassion.

"Oh, yes," Tailbot said and lit his cigarette. "He was a great man. But the young generation—they don't even understand him. The great leaders are gone, Clint. We live now in a world of dwarfs, and people tend to forget what real giants looked like." He let his eyes wander over the ample foliage of the Boulogne forest trees, which autumn had painted in glorious shades of red and gold. They were having coffee on the open-air terrace of the Cascades restaurant, overlooking a small lake. There was nobody else on the pleasant terrace.

55

The Cascades was officially closed at this early morning hour, and waiters in white aprons were just starting to set the tables outside; but they had got used to the little old gentleman's morning strolls in the park and had some strong coffee ready for him, as a special favor. Clint had phoned him early in the morning, and Tailbot had suggested that he join him for his promenade.

"This is going to be another fine day," the historian remarked now, contentedly puffing on his cigarette. Then he suddenly shook his head. "Where was I?" An embarrassed smile hovered on his thin lips. "I am sorry, I digress. That's old age, Clint. We lose the thread of our thoughts. What were we talking about? Yes, the attempt on your life. As I said, don't jump to conclusions."

"I didn't . . ." Clint started.

The old man nodded. "Oh, yes, you did. You would not admit it, but you suspected that Jefferson might be involved in that matter. It could be anyone else, you know. After the press conference of your publisher all the world knows what you are after, and there might be quite a few people who would sleep better if you disappeared from the scene."

"What kind of people? Nazis?"

Tailbot shrugged. "I don't know, but I wouldn't be surprised." His face became thoughtful again. "Still . . . when I come to think about it, I must admit that all these Nazi secret organizations seem to exist only in the imagination of writers and moviemakers. Important Nazi criminals, if they are still alive, must be in their late seventies now, Clint. They should be more concerned about living their last years in peace. They don't plan the revival of Nazi Germany, and don't try to kill people in the streets of Paris, believe me."

"That brings us back to Jefferson then."

"No, not necessarily." The old man's eyes suddenly twinkled. "But if I were you, I would be very happy after this attempt on your life."

"Why?" asked Clint.

"Because it confirms that your theory is right. It proves that there is somebody who wouldn't stop at murder to make sure that the secret of Goering's treasure remains untouched."

It was early afternoon when Clint completed his projects for the day. He made two sets of photocopies from Tailbot's files and brought the originals back to his apartment. He kept one set in his room and left the other in the safe-deposit box of the hotel. After a short tour of the various buildings that had once housed the offices of the Otto organization—just to familiarize himself with the places—he took a cab to the Ministère de la Culture. The recommendation of Pierre Tailbot carried a lot of weight in the ministry, and the curator of the national museums—*les Musées de France*—agreed to see him immediately. He was an affable old gentleman with a rebellious lock of snow-white hair and the dreamy eyes of an artist. When informed of the reason for Clint's visit, he busied himself in his dossiers, alerted secretaries and assistants, harassed the various services of the ministry by long, impatient phone calls, all the time sighing, shrugging helplessly and rolling his eyes upward to demonstrate his annoyance with the inefficiency of his colleagues. But finally a sullen-faced girl brought him the document he had asked for—the complete list of the still-missing pieces of art stolen by the Germans from the museums of France. He looked sadly at the list before passing it to Clint, and his lips soundlessly formed the famous names: "Sisley . . . Corot . . . Rodin . . . Renoir . . . Mirò . . . Picasso . . . Paul Klee . . ." He raised his eyes. "What a tragedy, monsieur," he said softly, handing him the list, as if he had just reread the names of dearly loved relatives killed in a horrible accident.

"Are you sure that these pieces were stolen and not destroyed?"

The curator nodded mournfully. "I know that there are other views on the matter," he conceded. "You may be referring to my predecessor, Rose Valland, and that marvelous book of hers, *Le Front d'Art*. She maintains that the Germans burned six hundred paintings by Klee, Picasso, Max Ernst and others, in the Tuilèries gardens in 1943. But I checked that matter thoroughly. The Germans burnt only valueless canvases from the Louvre attics. There was not even one good painting among them. Believe me, I know what I am saying. All these paintings are still hidden somewhere, and one day we'll bring them back where they belong. After the war a fantastic art collection was discovered in a salt mine near Alt Ausee. The Americans found there several paintings by the Van Eyck brothers and the famous 'Madonna of Bruges' by Michelangelo. Who knows? Maybe there are other salt mines to be explored in Germany and Austria."

Clint murmured some words of thanks and took leave of the sad-eyed old gentleman. He dropped into a nearby travel agency and booked a flight to Málaga for the following morning. Paris looked more beautiful than ever, in the mellow afternoon sunlight, and he decided to take a stroll through the Marais district. Maybe it was not safe for him to walk the streets alone; but everything seemed normal, nobody was following him, and his initial vigilance slackened as the hours went by. He was even able to joke about the black Citroën when he called Peter Bohlen from the phone booth of a small café. Peter didn't find the story funny at all. "It worries me," he admitted. "I guess it was all my fault. I shouldn't have alerted the press yesterday. You were right and I blew it." His concern grew when Clint told him about his amazing conversation with Jefferson. "Look, if there is something there, you may have got the scoop of the century. But it scares me. This project might be too big, Clint. You should either abandon the whole thing, or hurry up and find as much as you can before the sixth of November."

"Why the sixth of November?"

"Why? Because if your hero Jefferson is elected President on that day, and if he is involved in that affair—he would do anything in his power to seal your mouth. I wouldn't like to be hounded down by a President of the United States."

"Well, I'm not quitting, if that's what is bothering you."

Peter had sighed. "Yes, I know you. Stubborn as ever. At least let's keep in touch. Call me daily, from wherever you are. I am leaving tomorrow, flying back to New York. Don't get lost somewhere. Life can be dangerous, you know."

But life didn't seem dangerous at all, this afternoon. The streets were full of cheerful Parisians, enjoying the unexpected boon of an extended summer. And the Marais, with its magnificent palaces and aristocratic residences of the sixteenth and seventeenth centuries, offered a resplendent image of what Paris had looked like at the peak of its glorious past.

He never knew what made him take the rue Bourgeois east, past the Renaissance facade of the Musée Carnavalet, across the rue de Turenne. But he suddenly looked around and found himself standing on the Place des Vosges, the small square where he had spent his most blissful hours and which stirred now, at first sight, a load of painful memories. They had used to come here so often, he and Denise, before the marriage, and the child, and the bitterness. He had been very deeply in love then, for the first time in his life. Later, when the disappointment had come, and the pain, he had started to doubt if real love could ever exist. Since, he had only used the word in his novels, cynically padding it with a few stereotyped scenes and silly descriptions of locked eyes, outstretched hands and burning lips.

He shook his head to get rid of the sentimental memories that had no more place in his life. The Place des Vosges looked as he had always remembered it: peaceful, serene, with its beautiful French garden and its four fountains, surrounded by thirty-six ancient mansions. Time had no meaning here, and the past seemed so close, almost at hand's reach. Cardinal Richelieu, one of the most powerful men in French history, had lived here in the seventeenth century; in the neighboring residence the illustrious writer Victor Hugo had spent sixteen years of his life. And on the very place he stood now, many a deadly duel had been fought between French noblemen ready to shed their blood for the love of a lady of the court.

A girl walked into the square. She was tall, slim, and her rich golden hair fell naturally on her shoulders. The soft afternoon breeze ruffled it playfully, blowing loose blond strands across her face, but she didn't seem to care. She wore a simple yet stylish white dress that moulded her full breasts and long body. She seemed at ease in her high-heeled shoes. He liked the way she walked, with a graceful motion of her hips. She stopped briefly in the center of the deserted square, looking around her, spotted a simple iron chair by the equestrian statue of Louis XIII and dragged it to the northern corner, not far from where Clint stood. The legs of the chair made a crissing sound on the fine gravel of the walk. The girl sat down in front of the corner house with the peeling, rust-colored facade. Its narrow wooden shutters were wide open, and a strip of white curtain was fluttering from one of the French windows. She took a large sketchbook and a few pencils from her slack shoulder bag and started to draw with quick, expert motions.

Clint slowly walked around the square, savoring its tranquillity to the full. A nun came out of the Musée Victor Hugo and hurried in the arcaded passageway. He smiled to himself. Nuns usually walked two by two in the streets; the Parisians used to say that the sight of a nun walking alone was a good omen. He completed his tour of the square and stood by the fountain, idly watching the silvery jets of water spurting from the mouths of stone lion heads. The girl was still there, absorbed in her work. He approached her and peered over her shoulder. "May I look?" he asked in French.

She turned back. She had limpid blue eyes and a generous, sensual mouth. She wore almost no makeup and her skin was fresh, slightly tanned. Her nose was delicately upturned and she had a tiny beauty spot on her left cheek. "If you wish," she said. She had a slight foreign accent.

Her drawing was almost completed: a part of the facade, the arched doorway, a silhouette in one of the windows, all of that framed in the foliage of two big chestnut trees.

"Why this particular house?" he asked politely.

She didn't raise her eyes. "This was the house of Cardinal Richelieu." She added a touch to the window. "And under this very window took place one of the most famous duels in the history of France."

Her accent was definitely American. *"Vous êtes Américaine,"* he said, in mock accusation. She smiled at him, and her lovely face lit up. "You too," she said in English, and gracefully brushed back the loose wisps of hair from her face.

"You don't look American," he said frankly. He felt at ease and in the right mood, so he added: "Looking at you, one can imagine why they fought the duel under this window."

Irony slipped into her voice. "Come on," she said. "That was very exaggerated, very French—and completely untrue."

"Untrue?"

"Sure." She nodded seriously. "The particular duel I have in mind had nothing to do with a lady. It was intended as an act of bravado, to protest the royal edict forbidding dueling in France. Two groups of noblemen came here in sixteen twenty-seven and fought a duel under the windows of Richelieu, who was the gray eminence of the French court."

He looked at her with interest. "And how did that end?"

"Very badly," she said, and closed her sketchbook. "The Marquis Bussy d'Amboise was killed, Monsieur la Berthe was wounded, and the angry Richelieu had the counts of Montmorency and des Chapelles arrested, tried and beheaded."

"How do you know all that?" he asked, genuinely impressed.

"I studied French history and art at the Sorbonne. For five years." Her long fingers brushed against her forehead again, pulling back the rebellious silken strands.

"And this sketch is for your studies?"

"No, not at all. I want to do a piece for an American women's magazine." She rose and slung her Hermès bag over her shoulder. An exquisite scarf, its pattern colored in autumn shades, was loosely tied to the bag's strap. "I want to call it 'Romantic Paris,' and illustrate the romantic episodes in the history of Paris with a few stories and sketches."

He fell in step with her. "And what's your next stop?"

She looked at her small gold watch. "I think I still have time to go to the Quai aux Fleurs. You know the place?"

"Sure," he said, slightly puzzled. "But I didn't know of any romantic story connected with the Quai aux Fleurs."

"Have you never heard of Abélard and Héloïse?"

He shrugged. "Vaguely."

"Well, that's the story. And now, if you'll excuse me, I have to go."

A sudden impulse made him take a step after her. "May I come with you?"

She hesitated, and for a brief moment her face looked strangely distressed. "I don't know . . ." she mumbled, looking away and playing with her hair again. "I feel better by myself."

"Please," he said. "In Paris, they won't let you be by yourself for five minutes, and I can keep the crowds away." He quickly added: "My name is Clint, Clint Craig. I'm a writer."

"Craig." She looked impressed. "Yes, I know who you are. I mean, I know your name, but I haven't read your books."

"That's all right," he consoled her, smiling. "I've read them all, and I enjoyed them very much. Take my word for it."

She couldn't help laughing. "At least you are objective."

"And humble," he added, parodying a deep sigh. "I know, my modesty will kill me." He looked at her laughing eyes. "So, may I come?"

She held his eyes for a second, then nodded perkily. "Okay. My name is Jill. Jill Hobarth." She glanced at him, as if awaiting his reaction.

"I am glad I met you, Jill," he said pleasantly.

They left the placid little square and turned south, toward the rue Saint-Paul. "Is it far?" he inquired.

"Five minutes walk. It's just behind Notre-Dame, on the Ile de la Cité."

A couple of minutes later they emerged on the lively Quai des Celestins. Nearby, the twin towers of the Notre-Dame cathedral rose majestically over the muddy waters of the Seine. As they approached, they could distinguish the hideous statues of mythological monsters, griffins and devils perched on top of the ancient cathedral. They crossed the river by the

Pont Louis Philippe. A glass-roofed boat, crowded with tourists, lightly glided under the bridge, leaving behind a trail of white froth. The Quai aux Fleurs curved gracefully by the riverside. A multitude of wooden stands and kiosks stood on the river bank, laden with fresh flowers, and stocky women in blue smocks lovingly rearranged their colorful merchandise. "I was here a couple of times," Clint observed. "On Sundays they transform the whole street into a bird market. There are thousands of birds, trilling and chirping all over the place."

Jill pointed at the dilapidated facade of an old house. On the wall over the porch were affixed two busts carved in stone, a bearded young man and a woman in a nun's headdress. An inscription on a small marble plaque read: *Ancienne habitation d'Héloise et d'Abélard, 1118.*

"Héloise and Abélard," Jill said dreamily. "One of the most tragic and poignant love stories in the history of France."

They sat on a bench facing the house, and Jill busied herself with her pencils and sketchbook. "It is also a story of jealousy and revenge, and utter devotion," she went on. "When I first heard it, I was deeply moved."

He kept silent, and she spoke intensely. "Pierre Abélard was a brilliant young philosopher who came to Paris in the year eleven hundred, studied at the Notre-Dame cloister, and became one of the most outstanding thinkers of his time. At the age of forty he moved to the house of the canon Fulbert, and became part-time teacher of Fulbert's niece, Héloise. She was seventeen years old, and breathtakingly beautiful. They fell madly in love, and a few months later Héloise discovered that she was pregnant."

"In the twelfth century? That must have been an unpardonable crime."

"It was. Abélard did the only possible thing—he eloped with Héloise to his sister's home in Brittany, where a baby was born, a boy. They named him Pierre-Astrolabe. Abélard wanted to marry the girl, but she refused; she maintained that an outstanding man of science shouldn't burden himself with a wife. However, they swore never to part. After a while they came back to Paris. Abélard returned to teaching and writing, and soon became immensely popular. To such a point that many of his colleagues, blinded by jealousy, started to plot against him. He was forced to stop teaching at Notre-Dame."

He cast a sideways glance at Jill. She was meticulously

reproducing the passionate faces of Héloise and Abélard in her sketchbook, forehead furrowed in concentration.

"But somebody else was planning his revenge: the canon Fulbert, still fuming over the seduction of his niece. One night he sent a group of thugs after Abélard. They assailed him and brutally castrated him."

"What? I can't believe it."

"That's how it happened, though," Jill said. "News of the maiming spread quickly, and Abélard became the laughing-stock of his enemies. He was dishonored and deeply humili-ated; he decided then to take the vows, and became a recluse. Héloise herself joined an order and entered a convent. They continued to correspond in secret. But this was not the end of Abélard's sufferings. His rivals, and even Pope Innocent the Third, who had been his student, persecuted him until he died. Héloise had his body transported to her convent. Twenty years later, when she died, she was buried in the same coffin according to her last wish."

Jill had stopped drawing and her eyes had a faraway look. "There is a legend about her death." She faintly smiled. "They say that when the coffin was opened, Abélard's corpse opened his arms and embraced the body of his beloved."

"That's embellishment, of course," Clint observed.

She nodded. "Yes. But what follows is true, though. Al-most five centuries later, in the year sixteen hundred and thirty, a prudish nun heard about Abélard and Héloise and was revolted. She exhumed their coffin, had their skeletons separated, and reburied them in two coffins in two different cemeteries. However, eighty years later another nun read the story. She was from the La Rochefoucauld family, very ro-mantic by nature and a compulsive reader of love stories. She reunited the two coffins and buried them side by side. And even that was not the end. After the French Revolution they were exhumed again. A special coffin was built for them and their remains were put in it together; but in order to preserve decency, a thin partition of lead was installed to separate them. In this common coffin they were finally buried in the Père Lachaise cemetery. And *that's* the end of the story."

He kept silent for a moment. "Incredible," he murmured. "Love beyond death." He eyed her curiously. "And you, Miss Jill Hobarth, are a very romantic young woman."

She was startled. "Why do you think so?"

"You had to see your face when you were telling that story. You were living it."

A group of people had gathered behind their bench and were watching Jill's drawing. She snapped her sketchbook shut and thrust it into her bag. "And you?" she said. "Have you ever been deeply in love?"

He felt profoundly embarrassed. "Yes, I think I was . . . once."

"And . . ."

"It ended differently," he said, his face taut. "The love turned sour, and all that is left is a little daughter of five, whom I love very dearly."

There was some unexpected tenderness in her eyes, and she shifted uneasily. Dusk had fallen over Paris, and the last flower merchants were locking their stands. She got up and said with forced cheerfulness: "Well, it's time to go."

He cleared his throat. "Now that I have imposed myself upon you, maybe you'll allow me to make amends and invite you to dinner."

"Yes," she said spontaneously. "Yes, I would love that."

"This way . . . Héloïse."

"No," she said, and the same strain he had noticed before flashed in her eyes. "Don't call me that."

What's the matter with you, Clint Craig? an inner voice furiously lashed at him as they crossed the small bridge onto the aristocratic Ile Saint-Louis. *What do you think you are doing? You are on the most important assignment of your career, on the verge of a fantastic discovery, and instead of sitting on your ass and working, you behave like a college kid and pick up girls in the streets of Paris. Abélard and Héloïse,* the voice mocked, *love beyond death, and you make a fool of yourself for a girl you don't even know?*

He knew the voice was right; he knew he shouldn't do what he was doing, and yet, when he looked at the slender girl gracefully moving by his side, he felt a strange excitement. There was something radiant about her, a genuine spontaneity, an inner fire that burned intensely and lit sparks in her eyes. She was intelligent, without airs, and seemed to have discovered the real France, the true spirit of Paris—not like all those silly American girls he had met here before, blabbering about food, perfumes and fashion shows.

There were quite a few models from the famous fashion houses in the Orangerie, the exquisite restaurant on Saint-Louis island. He noticed the looks directed at them and felt a twinge of foolish pride when he realized that she was among the most beautiful women in the place. The maître d'hotel, obviously impressed with Jill, ushered them with great pomp to a nice table by the window. They ordered a light dinner— he didn't care about the food, not tonight—and were soon engrossed in a candid, easy-flowing conversation. She wanted to know how he became a writer—and he told her about his hardships as a penniless youth, his military service with the Green Berets ("before Vietnam"), his ambition to make it and work his way through college.

"Was Paris as hard?" she asked sympathetically.

"No, not really. I had gotten my master's degree from Stanford, I had a scholarship, I had written pieces for a few magazines. I could devote quite a lot of time to my research. I was working on the lightning German offensive against France, in the summer of nineteen forty."

"You seem to have a fascination with Germany and the war," she observed, when he told her about his nonfiction books.

His face became pensive and he did not answer right away.

"Maybe you are right," he finally conceded. "Maybe it has to do with my father. He was killed in Germany in one of the last battles of the war. I never knew him. He had been a bomber pilot in the Pacific. In nineteen forty-three he was transferred to Europe, and on his way, during a home leave in California, he met my mother and married her. When I was born he was long gone. He died barely a week before V-E Day. Therefore the war with Germany became very closely associated with the memory of my father."

"Your mother remarried?"

"Yes, she did." He didn't feel like talking about his mother, so he changed the subject. "And you? You worked your way through college too?"

"Oh no." She smiled self-deprecatingly. "I am the classic poor little rich girl, whom her parents send far away to the most expensive schools, because she is a nuisance at home . . . and interferes too much with their quarrels." A bitter note crept briefly into her narrative. "I was sent to Radcliffe, then to Geneva, finally to Paris. I stayed here for a long time—five years—and loved it. Tried to return to America last year, bit it didn't work."

"What didn't work?"

She sighed and smoothed her hair with what he already regarded as a familiar gesture. "Maybe . . . maybe I got too influenced by the French in the way I was handling my emotions." She looked at him earnestly. "I don't know how it was with you, but a girl, an American girl, who grows up in Paris, becomes very vulnerable. The French worship love, total all-consuming love. Most of their songs, poems, plays, immortal books, are centered around love. Any girl here is conditioned to dream of and aspire to *le parfait amour*—the perfect love. There is nothing more important. And it should be a love of total devotion, with no limits, no reservations."

"Like Abélard and Héloise." He smiled.

A hurt look came into her eyes. "Don't make fun of me," she said. "I am serious. There is a famous song of Edith Piaf, where she says to her lover: 'I'll deny my friends and my homeland, if you ask for it.' One grows up in this atmosphere, and one is affected—or infected—by it, even without realizing it. And I grew up here."

"And how did America . . ." he began.

"Well, I came back home and fell in love with a guy in New York." She looked out the window, then took her unused fork and ran it over the tablecloth, idly watching the four parallel tracks it left in the soft whiteness. "We were thinking of getting married. But he didn't love me the way I loved him." Her voice grew insecure as she seemed to grope for the right expressions, anxious to convey her exact feelings. "Maybe I was demanding too much, I don't know. He loved me in his American, efficient sort of way; he had his plans, his business, his career, which were extremely important to him. I just had to fit in somewhere. I couldn't stand it. I wanted to be number one, to be the center of his life as he was of mine. He never felt that way. He loved me very dearly, but was unable to give me what I gave him."

"Total devotion," Clint murmured, then leaned forward over the table. "You should not blame him for that." He smiled. "It took so long for the American man to get used to the idea of women's liberation, and here you were, trying to pull him back into a world where a woman is predominantly a love object."

"Oh no, not at all," she said heatedly, and tossed her blond hair back. "On the contrary. I can very easily fit into the common American image of a free and liberated woman. I have my fields of interest, I write, I publish my essays and my articles, I can easily get a teaching job in a college, and I am definitely not the sort of woman who thinks that her role in life is summed up in staying home, raising children, being desirable and waiting for her husband to come back from work. But I demand something more. I believe that being liberated should not stop me from being a woman. I didn't want Burt"—she blushed slightly—"I didn't want this man just to share his life with me, and accept my equality, my competence and my efficiency. I wanted him to be also very deeply infatuated with me; I wanted him once in a while to stop being so efficient, stop thinking and start feeling. And feeling very strongly, very passionately." She blushed again and put her fork down in the middle of the crisscross patterns she had been scratching on the tablecloth. "I don't know why I am telling you all this, and getting so excited." She looked deeply embarrassed. "It reminds me of my discussions with Burt."

Clint did not speak. This lovely girl, who was practically a stranger, had bared a very painful and intimate memory; he did not want to hurt her by an awkward remark.

She sighed. "Maybe I am too romantic, as you said before. Anyway, it didn't work. Burt and I, we decided to split, and each went his own way. And I came back to Paris, a few months ago, to recover and . . . and cry a little bit." Tears welled in her eyes.

He softly touched her hand. "Now, Jill, let's not talk about that anymore, okay? Let's go."

She tried to smile. "Where?"

"Come," he said.

He took her to a cabaret on the Left Bank, which he knew from his student years. On a small stage, in a modest setting, a madonna-faced girl dreamily sang love ballads from the Middle Ages. The crowd, mostly young intellectuals and artists, joined her in the refrain, in an improvised chorus. Then the lights went out; a single spotlight focused on a young poet with long jet-black hair and intensely burning eyes, who read his passionate poems. A trio, two girls and a boy dressed in black body-stockings, performed a short pantomime. "Like it?" Clint whispered to Jill.

She nodded. "That's the real Paris."

Echoing her words, the traditional Parisian *chansonnier* came onstage and launched a brilliant, witty satire on topical subjects. While the audience was warmly applauding, they finished their small glasses of cognac and went out. They dropped into a few other cabarets and savored the intense songs, the passionate monologues, the sharp witticisms of talented young artists. Clint noticed that Jill's preferences were quite similar to his. He felt a genuine, spontaneous closeness growing between them. The crisp night was full of stars; it carried about it the magic of a dream. Somewhere, he didn't exactly remember where and when, he took her hand and didn't let go anymore.

It was very late when they descended the steps to Badel's cellar. She had heard that Badel's private club was the best discotheque in Paris but had never been there. They had a couple of drinks in a small alcove, cut in the very rock. "Feel like dancing?" he asked her.

She nodded and he led her to the dance floor, where a few other couples were swaying to the music with the easy abandon of the wee hours. He enjoyed dancing with her. She had good control of her body and adapted well to the beat; there was something very natural in the supple, relaxed way she moved on the floor. But when the lights dimmed and a sensual slow song replaced the hot rhythms, she came into his arms, soft, exciting, incredibly beautiful. He held her close, buried his face in her silken, fragrant hair and felt his body tighten against hers. Her eyes were closed when he kissed her, and her full lips slowly parted under the pressure of his mouth. Then her fingers dug into his hair at the nape of his neck, and her body clung to his.

"I don't want to let you go tonight," he murmured. His voice was hoarse, unsteady.

"No," she whispered softly. "Don't let me go. Keep me with you, Clint."

In the cab that drove them back to his hotel, she buried her head in the hollow of his neck, breathing heavily. But when he undressed her in the privacy of his room and his febrile hands felt her perfect body, her firm round breasts, her velvety thighs, she metamorphosed into a hungry, passionate animal, scratching his back, biting his shoulders, pulling him deep inside her. He let himself sink into total oblivion. When it was over, and she lay quietly on her back, he softly kissed her cheek and tasted the warm saltiness of her tears.

They slept and awoke and passionately made love again and again, yet with a growing tenderness. He felt as if in a dream. It was the most fulfilling night he had ever had.

He woke again when the pale rays of dawn painted the room with eerie light. He pulled shut the heavy velvet draperies. She slept deeply, cuddled like a small child. He tiptoed to the bathroom, careful not to wake her, showered and slowly dried his body. He critically examined his reflection in

68

the mirror: the wavy, deep brown hair, the large forehead, the sharp black eyes, the strong jaw, the powerful shoulders. He knew he was not bad-looking, but still an uneasy feeling gnawed at his heart. Jill could have any man she wanted; why did she choose him? Why didn't she go for somebody her own age? She was at least ten years younger than he. Was she really attracted to him, or did she just need a man, any man, after having bared her loneliness and reopened the wounds of her recent love affair? He soundlessly moved back into the room. Her bag lay upside down on a chair, most of its contents spilled onto the cushion. Ashamed, yet curious, he opened her purse and in the half-darkness leafed through her passport and French identity card. Afterward he came back to the bed and lay quietly beside her, his eyes staring at the ceiling, his lips tightly compressed.

When she woke up, stretched her hands and lovingly nestled into him, he looked the other way and tried to keep his voice casual.

"Why didn't you tell me," he said, "that you were Jim Jefferson's daughter?"

Chapter Four:

October 21—October 23:

DEEP

Jim Jefferson plunged into the dark opening of the underwater cave and lit his torch. The powerful white beam transformed the blurred black shapes in front of him into a dazzling canvas of vivid colors, swarming with life. Under the growth of red and white corals, a school of striped groupers lingered peacefully; tiny goby fish were busy cleaning parasites from the groupers' heads with their suction disks. Farther down, an inflated porcupine fish swayed behind the protecting branches of some fire corals, looking like a big milky lampion hanging on invisible strings. As the cave narrowed, Jefferson pressed his hands tightly against his body and swam close to the bottom, careful not to touch the low coral ceiling with his air tanks. He slowed the motion of his flippers and glided smoothly forward, until the water ahead of him became a shade lighter and he emerged from the deeper opening of the cave.

A sea-urchin colony nestled at the foot of a big rock. He drew his Tres-Mares knife from the sheath fastened to his right leg, and neatly sliced a fat urchin in four pieces, raising a small cloud of white sand. Within seconds a horde of fish assembled around him, attracted by the smell of the urchin's flesh. They hurled themselves on the broken shell, devouring its white contents, the bigger fish driving the smaller away or snatching the prey from their mouths. In less than a minute the urchin was swallowed and the fish dispersed. He readjusted his mask and slowly swam away. He was always fascinated by this lightning onslaught of the big fish on a vulnerable prey. Once he had witnessed from afar a pack of sharks tearing to pieces one of their own that had been wounded. Life was the same everywhere: everyone's sharks lurked in the darkness, ready to devour at the first sign of weakness.

He continued to descend, and spotted some delicate fanlike

boughs of black coral on his right. He looked at his depth gauge; he was down to 140 feet, approaching the danger zone. Far above him, a small light was diffusing a dim glow. That was Powell, a soft-spoken Cruzan who was his constant companion on the island. When they dived, Powell would always stay behind, to let Jefferson be by himself; yet at the smallest hint that something was wrong, he would be by his side in seconds. That's how Powell had saved his life two years ago, when Jefferson had run out of air at 155 feet; he was choking, his vision became blurred and his eyes were about to pop out of their sockets, when the huge black body of Powell appeared at his side. He fed him fresh air from his mouthpiece all the way up to the surface.

He knew scuba diving could be dangerous. One of his fellow divers had been killed in a stupid accident; his friend Harold Holt, the Australian prime minister, had drowned while exploring the unique underwater scenery at the Great Barrier Reef. And then there had been Emily's accident. Still, he continued to dive with a passion that others could not understand. He was a very tense, self-controlled man, working under permanent strain, watched by others and closely watching himself. He didn't drink, didn't play cards, had no patience for television. But under water, in that colorful, unspoiled world of silence, he was able to relax, to switch off his brain and feel free. He would let himself be carried by the currents far below the surface, plunge to the black depths or ascend by a slight movement of his flippers, and feel as if he were effortlessly flying in a strange, private world of his own.

Tonight's dive was a luxury that normally he couldn't have afforded; the campaign was entering its last stage and every day, every hour counted. But lately, since Clint's call, he had been restless and his performances were poor. During today's rally with the campaign volunteers in Florida, word had come that his next-morning appointment with Governor Anderson had been canceled; he had decided on the spur of the moment to fly to St. Croix for a dive and a relaxed dinner in his tropical garden.

He stopped his ascent at one hundred feet and lay suspended in the water, to depressurize. Water had seeped into his mask, so he turned on his back, tilted the mask gently upward and blew through his nose. The air removed the water, and a few bubbles slowly rose to the surface, gradually expanding. The sight of them brought to his mind Emily's

71

death, barely a couple of hundred yards from here; and once again he had to face the cruel question that would haunt him as long as he lived. Why did she die?

It was Emily who had initiated him to diving, and it was at her insistence that they had bought the house on the hill shortly after their marriage. She had always been so competent, so resourceful under water; the slowing of brain function, which occurs in great depths, seemed never to affect her. And whenever he visualized her, confidently moving in the deep, he would come again to the terrible conclusion: It had not been an accident. It had been suicide, and he was to blame.

He had never really been in love with her, either when he had first met her at UCLA or when he had courted her during the war years. He had felt a deep affection for her and had enjoyed her company, her quick brain, her refined taste; still he had to admit that he had always looked at her with the hungry eyes of a poor boy, who saw in the daughter of the rich and powerful senator Hobarth a means to climb the ladder and achieve his own dreams. He had never known real passion for her; as the years passed and Emily grew into a bony, hollow-chested woman, indifferent to his aspirations, he had slowly drifted away.

But the romantic streak deeply buried beneath his rugged purposefulness had never died; and he had secretly craved the taste of real, overwhelming love. That was why he had lost his head completely at the age of fifty-one, when he had met Rosalynn Ross. He had been introduced to her at a party after the New York premiere of a new play in which she had superbly performed. His attraction to her had turned into an obsession, as he discovered that her talent and her beauty were matched by a sharp intelligence and a fiery, passionate nature. He had called her the next morning and had waited for her, every night, to come offstage. He started to neglect his work and did not show up in the Senate for weeks. Soon he had become deeply infatuated with Rosalynn, and had not hesitated to plunge headfirst into an affair that rekindled the dormant fire in his heart and made him feel young again.

But here he had made his terrible mistake. He should not have told Emily about Rosalynn. But he did, in his candid, straightforward way. And Emily, the cold, stern Emily, had reacted in an outburst of bitterness and pain that he had never anticipated. Only too late did he realize that he was all she cared about. Her world had suddenly shattered and she became a desperate woman, unable to overcome her humiliation. Life at home turned into a living hell. Their two sons were on their own already; Bɪyan was married and Dean was completing his studies in Massachusetts. But Jill, whom he loved most, was only eighteen, and only too vulnerable. They had hurriedly sent her to Geneva, then to Paris, to keep her away from home.

Finally, his self-control and his political ambitions had prevailed over his emotions. He had stopped seeing Rosalynn and had tried to restore his crumbling marriage. Strangely enough, it was in those years that he started to feel a genuine strong attachment to Emily, after realizing how deeply and truly she did love him. But Emily was a broken woman. She never fully recovered; she started drinking heavily, and the best psychiatrists in the country could not cure her successive depressions.

For a while, though, their life had resumed a semblance of routine, and he had been tempted to believe that the worst was behind them. Until that morning, in Washington, when Powell had called him from Christiansted and told him of her "accident."

The investigation and the autopsy didn't reveal a thing. She had been found drowned, with a rupture of the lungs caused by an air embolism; her air tanks were missing. The faint traces of nitrogen in her blood had made a few experts suspect nitrogen narcosis, that feeling similar to drunkenness that occurs at great depths and may induce the best diver to break all rules, discard his air regulator, throw away his air tanks and drift carefree to his certain death. Still, the findings were inconclusive and the cause of Emily's death was never definitely established. There had been the usual rumors, of course, but nobody in the small circle of intimates who knew about her ordeal ever accused him of being responsible for her death. Nobody but himself. And he had to carry that cross, in secret, till his dying day. Oh, Emily, Emily.

During the first year after her death, he had often felt the urge to sell the house in St. Croix and never return to the place where she had died. But oddly enough, such a step seemed to him like running away from her memory. The house and the diving had been Emily's idea. The underwater scenery at the foot of the hill was the best in the Virgin Islands. And the death of Emily so close by . . . He could imagine her wry smile and her slightly ironical voice: "Come on, dear, you won't stop diving because somebody had an ac-

73

cident here? Ever heard of any good diving hole where there have been no accidents? Don't be silly, Jim."

Don't be silly.

He slowly exhaled and followed the expanding, mushroom-like bubbles, all the way up to the surface.

Ralph Dowden was waiting for him on the pier. "Hey, what are you doing here?" Jefferson was surprised, but pleased all the same.

"I arrived in Miami just after you left, so I thought I might as well follow you down here."

"Fine. You'll have dinner with me tonight." Jefferson liked the quiet efficiency of his young chief of staff. "But no politics, okay?" He turned back. "Powell, will you take care of the equipment? And join us for dinner on the terrace."

The black man flashed a smile and waved. Jefferson wrapped a huge bath towel around his body and walked barefoot to the car.

"If you don't want us to talk politics during dinner, let's talk now," Ralph suggested pleasantly.

Jefferson nodded. "Did you see Chuck?" He slammed the car door shut and started the engine. The Secret Service car moved ahead of them.

"Yes, I did. He looked into the matter. You were right, J.J. Murphy owns a majority of the stock of Bohlen and Sherf. He has been a silent partner in that company for the last eight years and is the one who put Bohlen in the president's chair. They have known each other since the war. They were both in Germany then. Murphy was with the OSS."

"The OSS? How come I didn't run across him? We were practically in the same unit."

"I asked the same question. Chuck says it's only natural, because of compartmentation rules and so forth. He didn't know Murphy either, and met him only years later, in the CIA."

"Yeah," Jefferson grunted. "Anything else about Bohlen?"

The car climbed up the winding hill road amid lush tropical vegetation.

"Murphy owns his stock through a subdivision of a subdivision of a company of his called American Communications. That is quite an empire. They own a TV network, a number of radio stations, magazines . . ."

"Yes, I know about that," Jefferson said impatiently. "I had Murphy checked. He's as powerful in the media as in the

74

oil business. Most of our trouble comes from his papers. The ones we know of, I mean."

Ralph looked at him sideways. "Let's not exaggerate, Jim," he suggested.

Jefferson shrugged. "Well, what matters now is that Murphy is behind that publisher. He must be masterminding the whole project." He was lost in thought for a while, his eyes fixed on the narrow strip of asphalt that lay ahead. "Anything else?"

"Yes. They are bringing King Omar of Saudi Arabia to Washington."

Jefferson didn't say a thing. But Ralph could tell, by the familiar forward thrust of his chin and the tightening of his lips, that the candidate was worried.

"He has come to New York for the Palestinian debate in the UN assembly, and has been invited to the White House."

In front of them, the Secret Service car stopped briefly at the villa gate. Jefferson slowed down. "The Palestinian debate is eyewash, of course, nothing but a pretext. They must be dead worried by the last poll, so they throw in everything they can. Omar will make a few statements about his deep friendship with the United States; he will promise oil to supply our needs . . ." The car went through the checkpoint and crawled onto the driveway. "That's another trick of Shazli," he murmured. "I know that fox. Very clever."

"What do you think we should do?"

They left the car in the driveway and walked on the spacious terrace that offered a magnificent view of the Caribbean. Ralph could sense that the computerlike brain of his boss was already at work, analyzing and sorting possible countermeasures. Jefferson suddenly stopped. "That State Department study dealing with economic retaliation against the Arab countries . . . Remember?"

"No . . . I don't think so."

Jefferson turned to him and spoke earnestly. "Six months ago, the State Department prepared a secret study about possible reprisals against the oil sheikhs if they continued their blackmail. The report recommended several measures: freeze Arab assets in America, stop issuing visas to Arab students and businessmen, order American firms to cease any further business with the Arabs, cut off shipments of spare parts, suspend military and technical assistance."

Ralph frowned. "That is a boomerang. It will never work.

And they will never carry it out. Why, the State Department is afraid of its own shadow!"

"Of course. But all the same, this is a study ordered by the American government. I think Tim Carruthers has a copy in Washington." Jefferson's eyes became narrow slits burning with cold fire. "Get the report and leak it to the press. It will put the President and Wheeler in a tight spot. Omar will have to protest, they will have to apologize and the public won't like that."

Ralph nodded eagerly. "That will do it, J.J. It's a good idea."

Tommy Hendrix, a big blond guy who worked in Jefferson's press office, came toward them. "Telephone for you, sir. Overseas call." He was wearing a T-shirt with the inscription in big characters: "I AM A VIRGIN," and in very small ones, "islander."

Jefferson tapped him on the chest. "Are you?" he sneered. The boy flushed.

The candidate crossed the sitting room and went into his den. He took the phone. "Jim Jefferson."

"Daddy?" the voice sounded troubled and unhappy. "It's me, Jill."

Clint Craig went quickly through immigration and customs at Málaga—there had been very few passengers on the Iberia morning flight from Paris—and rented a small white SEAT at the Hertz counter. He drove west along the Mediterranean. The Costa del Sol was still full of tourists enjoying the sunny Spanish autumn. Crowds of German and Scandinavian vacationers lazed on the white sandy beaches of Torremolinos, or wandered in the small shops selling leather goods, dolls and lace. At the Mijas crossroads, he saw two cheerful Swedish girls riding down the mountain on the famous "burro-taxis"—a couple of donkeys herded by an old, wrinkled-faced Andalusian. One of the girls flashed him a dazzling smile and waved her hand to the passing car. He instinctively compared her to Jill—Jill, whose passionate face and smooth, lithe body had haunted him since he left her in the early morning. Their last conversation still rang in his ears. When he asked her about Jefferson, she had been surprised but had not lost her composure. "How did you know that Jim Jefferson was my father?" she inquired.

"By putting two and two together," he lied. "I worked for your father. I knew his wife's maiden name was Hobarth, I knew that he had a daughter named Jill, and I knew that she was away in Europe when I met Jim."

She had nodded gravely. "I didn't tell you I was J.J.'s daughter for the same reason I decided to call myself Jill Hobarth. At Radcliffe everybody referred to me as Jefferson's daughter or 'the Jefferson kid.' I hated that. I wanted to be judged and liked, or hated, for what I was, and not for being somebody's daughter. So I decided to take my mother's name." She quickly added: "Not because I dislike my father. On the contrary, I love him dearly. I was always very close to him; we have a lot in common. Since my mother died we've become even closer. I don't like my brothers."

"Didn't you know that I had worked for your father?"

She had propped herself on her elbow, holding the bed-sheet close to her breasts. "Of course I did. He mentioned your name, many times. But why should I have told you about him? You would have treated me as your former employer's daughter, and . . ."

". . . And we wouldn't have ended in my hotel room."

"No," she said seriously. "Maybe we wouldn't have."

He had looked at her sharply. "It's funny, though, that I should run into you, of all people, just when I'm in the middle of some research in which your father is involved."

"Really? What kind of research?"

He had told her about Goering's treasure, and about her father's report, closely watching her reactions. But she showed only a mild interest. "And I am flying this morning to Spain, to look into Skolnikoff's death," he had concluded.

"Are you coming back?"

"Yes. I'm keeping the room. I'll be back tomorrow night, or the day after."

She quickly asked: "Will you call me?"

He had hugged her close and kissed her bare shoulder. "Of course, Jill, as soon as I land."

He was troubled from the moment he had left her. He was a grown man now and did not believe in coincidences, not this kind of coincidence. Could she have followed him to the Place des Vosges and played her little comedy in front of him, and given him that bullshit about Abélard and Héloïse just to worm herself into his bed? What were your orders, he wanted to scream at her, did your father tell you to spy on me and find what I was after? Did you also set up the attempt on my life the other night, did you send some of your friends, or maybe it was you driving the black Citroën?

And yet, when he recalled the details of last night, when he remembered the tenderness in her eyes, her passionate embrace, her tears, he did not know what to think.

He almost ran into a peasant's cart on the outskirts of Marbella. His hands were clutching the wheel like petrified claws, his knuckles white with pressure. At San Pedro Alcántara he branched off to the right, and started the long climb to Ronda in the Andalusian mountains.

Two hours later he saw the steep cliffs of Ronda in the distance. A deep canyon, flanked by almost vertical slopes, divided the city in two; clusters of red-tiled, whitewashed houses perched on its very edges, as if suspended in the sky over the Guadalevin valley.

He left his car at the Plaza de España and crossed into the Ciudad, the old city, by the Puente Nuevo. The stone-paved streets, bordered by coquettish white porches and wrought-iron balconies, were deserted. It was siesta time, and the Andalusians had retreated into their cool patios and behind their wooden shutters for the afternoon nap. The peaceful city had a soothing effect on his nerves. He wandered alone in the empty alleys, wishing he had come here as a tourist. Ronda was a historical monument. Miguel de Cervantes had stayed in the Animas inn, and here Ernest Hemingway had written *Death in the Afternoon.* Considered the cradle of modern Spanish bullfighting, Ronda was proud of its bullring, the oldest in Spain, and of the sober and daring style of its *toreros.*

At the Plaza de Campillo he met two skull-shaven kids playing barefoot in the shade. He had some trouble making himself understood with his Spanish learned in California, but finally one of them nodded and led him to an isolated house on the very edge of the ravine. *"Está aquí."* The kid grinned. *"La casa de Juan Romero."* He gave the children a few coins and they ran away, their carefree laughter echoing in the empty street. The house was quiet. Pots of flowers were neatly arranged on the balconies, and strings of small red peppers hung on the wall, drying in the afternoon sun. A skinny dog lay by the porch. It slowly opened its eyes at his approach, rose on its hind legs, stretched and regretfully sneaked down the street. Clint knocked on the door. After a short while, it was opened by an old woman. She was dressed in black, and her white hair was done in a tight bun. She eyed him suspiciously.

"Señor Romero?" he inquired.

She nodded. "Will you come in?" He followed her into the cool obscurity of a big room. It was sparsely furnished with a big wooden table and upright chairs. A crucifix was hanging on the wall. The tile floor was spotlessly clean. "Siéntese," the woman said, pulling out one of the chairs, then turned back and disappeared into the dark corridor. In a few moments she was back, followed by a man who looked to be in his late sixties. He was bald, fat, and dragged his left leg. His dangling white moustache had yellow edges, probably from smoking. His wrinkled skin formed loose pockets beneath his brown eyes. He ceremoniously shook hands with Clint, and painfully slid into the chair in front of him.

"My name is Craig," Clint said. "I am American, and I came to see you because I am writing a book. I would like to ask you some questions about a man who rented this house from your family thirty-five years ago. He died here. His name was Michel Skolnikoff."

Romero didn't react to the name. He slightly turned his head and glanced at his wife, who quickly left the room. Clint heard the sound of running water and of pots and dishes clinking in the kitchen.

Clint pulled a tin case from his pocket. "Do you smoke?"

The old man took a cigarillo with his leathery fingers and examined it carefully, feeling it with his fingertips as if wondering what to do with it. Finally he stuck it in his mouth, and bent forward toward the flame of Craig's lighter. While puffing on it, he looked at Clint. "We told the police everything we knew about the *francés*," he said. "It was a long time ago."

"Tell me what you remember," Clint said.

The old man didn't seem to like the cigar, but continued puffing at it. "Why don't you ask the police?" he suggested.

"I have nothing to do with the police and I don't want to have any business with them." Clint knew how much the Spanish people feared and mistrusted the police. "I know I shall be taking your time, and I am ready to reward you for that."

There was no answer and an awkward silence descended upon them. Clint sensed a growing uneasiness. Romero was hostile; he would not talk. The old man shifted on his chair, moved his bad leg and grimaced in pain. "Does it hurt?" Clint asked sympathetically.

The old man seemed surprised by this mark of interest.

"Sometimes," he mumbled. "I have got used to it. It's been forty years that I am living with it."

"You were wounded?"

"Gored. By a bull in Málaga."

"You were a bullfighter?"

For the first time Romero smiled, a shy, sad sort of smile that revealed tobacco-stained teeth. "I wanted to be. I succeeded only to become a *banderillero,* you know"—he raised his hands over his head, to mimic the sticking of the *banderillas* in the bull's back—"and I got gored. The bull attacked me and hit me here"—he pointed at his hip—"and here, in the belly. I lost a lot of blood."

"You must have been very disappointed that you could fight no more," Clint said softly.

The old man nodded gloomily. "Oh yes," he said, "oh yes. Does my name mean anything to you? Do you know who Romero was? Pedro Romero? He founded the 'Ronda school' of bullfighting. He was born here, in this street, more than two hundred years ago. And you know how many bulls he killed? Five thousand and six hundred. Yes, señor. And he died in his bed, at the age of eighty-five. What do you say to that?"

Craig nodded eagerly. "And you are of the same family?"

"Yes, señor, the same family. You know what is the '*estoque a recibir*'? No? You know how the *toreros* use to kill the bulls? They wait for them to get tired, they make them stand still, and then—they hit." He was making sweeping gestures with his hands, fighting an imaginary bull over the table. "But Romero devised a different style. He was a brave man. His style was to let the bull attack him, and to 'receive' him with his sword in the middle of his attack. Like this, understand? That's the way he killed his bulls, in fair fight. He didn't slaughter them like a butcher."

"A brave man," Craig conceded.

"Yes, a very brave man." The old man's eyes twinkled and he tapped Clint's forearm. "Would you like a glass of Amontillado?"

"With pleasure," Clint said, and sighed inwardly. The ice had been broken.

Night was falling when he left Romero's house. Over a few glasses of pale sherry the old man had talked for a long while. He told him about the first visits of Skolnikoff in Ronda, during the war. The "Frenchman" had been looking for an isolated house, where he could live "quietly." He had

80

finally rented the Romero house, and they had moved in with relatives, in the same street. The Frenchman had come and gone several times, traveling all over Spain. Finally he had settled in the city, but not for long. After a few months, his body was discovered at the bottom of the ravine. He had been partly burned, but was easily recognizable. The dead man looked as if he had been tortured before he was killed.

All that was not new to Clint. But as he had suspected, there was more to the story, which the Romeros had not told the police. The old man took him to the cellar and showed him some big holes dug in the ground. When they had returned to the house, he explained, they had found these holes. There was nothing in them except empty crates and bits of wrapping paper. Somebody had been in the cellar after the death of the Frenchman—probably the same night—and had dug out some heavy objects that had been buried there.

Clint asked him if he suspected who the mysterious killers were. Yes, he did, Romero said. During the week before the Frenchman's death, a foreigner had come to the city and had asked several people where the Frenchman lived. He could not give a description of the man, and the people who had seen him had died long ago.

On one particular point, however, the old *banderillero* was positive. The foreigner knew Spanish well, but his accent and his clothes had made everybody who met him reach the same conclusion: He was American.

Clint spent the night in a big hotel in Fuengirola, full with noisy tourists. He had a light meal brought to his room overlooking the sea. After dinner he called Peter Bohlen in New York to tell him about his findings. Peter's excited voice boomed in the receiver.

"That's it, Clint! By Jove, you are on the right track. That book is going to be a blockbuster!" He chuckled. "If you don't get killed first, of course."

"Very funny." Clint told him about Jill Jefferson.

"Frankly, I am not surprised," Bohlen said thoughtfully. "I was sure Jefferson was after you, since you phoned him. Remember what I told you when you called me from Paris? You've got to hurry, Clint, and to wrap this story before the election. This man has no scruples. He might destroy you if he is elected."

"I know, Peter, I am aware of that. I'm flying tomorrow to

Paris, and then I'll proceed to Germany. I must go to Munich and Nuremberg."

"Yes, sure. And another thing, Clint. Stay away from that girl. She means trouble."

"Of course, Peter, don't worry."

He stood for a long while on his small balcony, staring into the moonless night. Some people were strolling on the beach. Clint could not see them, but their voices sounded very clear, carrying on the gentle Mediterranean breeze. A child asked something, his mother answered and they both laughed. The carefree laughter stirred a faraway memory and he suddenly felt a pang of jealousy. In his childhood, he had always envied his friends who went with their parents to the movies or to the beach. He had grown up as a lonely, withdrawn boy. After the death of his father, his mother was rarely at home, more anxious to find a new husband than to take care of him. He never forgave her; even today the bitterness was still there. Nevertheless, today he was more inclined to understand her, to try and see things her way. She had been a young, unexperienced girl when she had met the dashing Air Corps captain; she had fallen in love with him and had married him a couple of weeks later. But after three months he was gone, never to come back. When the war was over, and she had received the official notice from the Pentagon, she had suddenly realized that she was a widow with a baby to raise. She must have panicked, fearing that life might pass her by; she had done all that she could to get a second chance. He had turned into a burden, an obstacle to a second marriage. He must have felt it, with that strong intuition little children have. He had gotten used to staying at home alone, with his books and magazines about the war, worshiping a father he had never seen.

His mother had finally remarried when Clint was eight, and his stepfather had turned out to be an unexpectedly good-hearted man, who had treated him very kindly and encouraged his passion for reading. But the wounds of his childhood had never healed completely. He had been unable to open up to his stepfather, although he had tried; he had grown up a loner. In college he was too busy working in his free time to go to parties and taste the real pleasures of a student's life. And his deep need for human warmth, for love and understanding, had never been quenched. Only when he had met Denise, in Paris, and had fallen in love with her, had he tasted real happiness for the first time in his life.

Denise. He would always remember the first time he saw her, in that night of violence and fire, back in May 1968. He had arrived in Paris only a couple of weeks earlier, when student riots erupted in the courtyard of the Sorbonne university, spread like brush fire all over Paris and swept the whole country. In the most serious threat ever to President de Gaulle's regime—he resigned a year later—the students' insurrection turned the streets of the Latin Quarter into a battlefield. The young people's resentment against an authoritarian system had been quickly building in the campuses and the smoke-filled café cellars of the Left Bank. When it exploded, it triggered a miniature urban war, the students blocking the streets with barricades made of stones, uprooted trees, overturned cars—and the special detachments of French police, shielded and helmeted, attacking them with gas and heavy clubs.

That night Clint had gone to the boulevard Saint-Michel, curious to see the action for himself. The scene reminded him of photographs from the World War. The sidewalks were strewn with debris: broken glass from the shopwindows, shattered flowerpots that angry residents had thrown at the police, broken branches, smashed garbage cans. Most of the paving stones had been removed, to serve in the construction of barricades. A few cars and trees were burning in the middle of the large boulevard, partly concealing from view the foreboding dark-blue mass of the antiriot police companies, preparing for the assault. Hundreds of students stood on the huge barricade, a few of them wearing motorcycle helmets, others chanting slogans or feverishly preparing their supplies of bottles and stones to throw at the advancing policemen. The air was heavy with smoke from burning vehicles and the faint, acrid smell of tear gas. On top of the barricade, her face illuminated by the flames of a burning police van, he had seen the girl.

She was tall and very slender, wearing a loose tan sweater and brown corduroy jeans that clung to her long legs. Her short auburn hair was ruffled and the white skin of her hollow-cheeked, triangular face reflected the reddish glow of the dancing flames. The most outstanding features in her small face were the eyes: enormous doe eyes, shining with excitement. She was shouting and brandishing her small fists at the police. A burly, fierce-looking young man with long black hair and drooping moustache stood by her side, occasionally putting his arm around her waist with a familiarity that made Clint dislike him immediately.

Clint stood on the sidewalk, watching the scene among a crowd of Parisians who had assumed the role of audience in the showdown between students and policemen. But when a police officer on the far side of the street shouted an order, the showdown was quickly over. The police attacked in closed ranks, brandishing their heavy clubs and hurling tear-gas grenades. The defenders of the barricade quickly dispersed, except for a handful of boys who bravely tried to oppose the far superior assault waves. They were soon overwhelmed, and police batons mercilessly clubbed the exposed heads and bodies.

Suddenly he saw the girl, alone, in the middle of the street. The white haze of tear gas was advancing toward her, and she gazed bewildered at the approaching policemen. Her boyfriend was nowhere in sight. Impulsively, Clint broke out of the crowd, caught her by the hand and dragged her to a porch a few seconds before the policemen swept through the place. She had inhaled some of the gas and was now choking and coughing while tears streamed down her cheeks. But when she could finally speak, she rasped angrily in English: "I'll show that rat! I'll show him! To bring me here and then run away at the sight of the first cop. What a coward!"

"Let's try to find him," he suggested.

"I don't want to find him," she countered belligerently. She did not seem surprised that he answered in English, too furious to pay any attention to him. He then offered a second suggestion—to find an open café where she could tidy up and calm down. She glanced at him and shrugged indifferently. They found a small bistro in one of the quiet back streets, and she slowly simmered down. Her name was Denise Berger, she was a New York girl, studying modeling and fashion design. She had been living with François—the boy with the moustache, an art student—for a few months. "But I am not going back home," she stated categorically, "not after tonight."

For a second, Clint had toyed with the idea of inviting her to spend the night at his place, but on second thought had given it up. The girl did not seem to care very much about him; he was just a nice guy who had happened to be there to help her get out of trouble. He finally escorted her to the home of a friend she knew. "May I see you again?" he asked when they stood in the dim entrance of a decrepit house at rue de l'Echaudé. She cocked her head and looked at him, for what had seemed to him the first time. "Yes, why not?" she said, and disappeared into her girl friend's apartment before he could even ask for her phone number.

But he would not capitulate so easily. The next morning he was back in the old house. A plain but cheerful redhead in a floating nightgown opened the door, still sipping her morning coffee from a tall mug. Denise? She hesitated. She was getting ready to go; François had just called. He started to feel very foolish standing at the door, when Denise entered the tiny vestibule. Her hair was neatly brushed, her fresh face was made up, and she was looking lovely. She stared at him with surprise. "What are *you* doing here?"

He had rehearsed his line. "We decided to meet again, so I came to take you to lunch."

"Lunch? No kidding?" She looked embarrassed. "Why, it's only nine in the morning."

He feigned surprise. "Is it? Wonderful, we'll have time for a walk. It's a beautiful day outside." Sensing that she was going to refuse, he added quickly: "Don't say no, please. You can go back to François this afternoon. And this is my only chance to get to know you better."

The redhead discreetly retreated, and Denise slowly said: "You don't waste time, do you?" The mention of François's name had made her blush.

He tried to smile, to conceal his growing uneasiness. What the hell was he doing here, forcing himself on a girl he did not even know? She had made up with her boyfriend, she was going back to him, and here he was, looking at her hungrily, playing Casanova at nine in the morning. "I am sorry," he said. "I should not have come." It was his turn to blush. "I happen to like you, I wanted very much to see you again, and I was afraid I would miss the only chance I had if I did not come this morning. Please excuse me."

He woodenly walked down the stairs and up the rue de l'Echaudé, calling himself all the names that came to his mind, furious with himself, with the girl and with that moustached bastard who had nothing better to do in life but to call her and apologize. Only when he had reached the boulevard Saint-Germain did he hear the quick clicking of high heels, and a small hand gently tapped his shoulder. He turned back, to find himself facing Denise, who was smiling mischievously, her head cocked in what was becoming a familiar mannerism. "I'll have that lunch with you, if the invitation is still open," she said. "By the way, what was your name?"

That was how it all started. They spent a pleasant morning together and had their lunch in a tiny Vietnamese restaurant, and she went back to François, but not for long. A couple of weeks later she left the art student. At that time Denise and Clint already were seeing each other almost daily. But she did not go to bed with him before she had left François; and she insisted on living with Roxanne, the redhead, for quite a while before moving to his apartment. "I don't change men like I change clothes," she had said, and he had liked that. Finally, in midsummer, she climbed, out of breath, to his small flat in the very attic of an old building behind the Pantheon. And for Clint that was the beginning of the two most beautiful years of his life.

As he stood now on his hotel balcony in Fuengirola and stared into the darkness, he felt, almost physically, his old scars reopening and bittersweet recollections emerging from the depths of his memory. He tried to recall the sweet intoxication of a first young love in Paris. He had been deeply in love with Denise. She was pretty in an elfin sort of way, had an alert mind, a passionate temper and, most of all, an inborn sense of beauty. She had made him discover the real, unspoiled Paris, the lively markets, the glorious palaces, the ancient taverns, the small shaded squares, the Montagne, the Marais, the Place des Vosges. . . . He was convinced that her talent for discovering and conceiving beauty was a guarantee of her future success as a fashion designer, even though her natural grace and her slim, almost boyish body could make her a top model. They had married a week before sailing back to America, laden with hopes and great expectations. And back home, things had started to roll downhill.

Somewhere down the beach a man spoke in German and a girl laughed. Clint tried to light his half-consumed cheroot and the flame quickly flickered and died in the breeze. Oddly enough, the first cracks in their marriage had occurred when they were still very much in love. Their relationship was badly shaken by the different turn that their careers had taken. His first two books were a success; her fashion collections were a disaster. And for no apparent reason. Denise was a victim of the unpredictable trends that govern the world of fashion. She miserably failed, over and over again. After a couple of years no manufacturer would even glance
86

at her sketches. She gradually lost her confidence and her good temper. She could not help envying Clint his success, and resenting his newly acquired fame. She would stay at home, alone, for weeks, bent over her drawing table—and already knowing deep in her heart that it was hopeless—while Clint was traveling around the country or abroad, lecturing, starring in television talk shows, taking his first steps in politics. She had slowly sunk into a bitter frustration, had started to neglect herself, put on weight—and the slim, exquisite young girl sadly metamorphosed into a plump, short-tempered woman. They had gradually drifted apart. Even the birth of little Laurie could not save their marriage. When the child had been born, Denise had switched all her interest to the household, as if in her kitchen she was seeking refuge from her failure. The once original, imaginative fashion designer would not talk with her husband of anything but maids' wages, recipes and grocery prices. Clint had always loved Denise as a wife and a companion. But somewhere along the road, the companion had faded away.

The cheroot in his mouth tasted bitter and he tossed it over the balustrade, following the glowing redness of its tip until it disappeared in the darkness below. Sometimes he would blame himself, too. If he had stayed at home more, if he had helped Denise overcome her crisis, shown her some real compassion . . . But he was too busy with his new idol, Senator James Jefferson. When Denise had filed for divorce, he had not argued.

During the last three years he had experienced again the bitter taste of loneliness. And when he had finally met Jill, who was so different, who could be his second chance—she had turned out to be a spy planted in his bed.

He left the balcony doors open, undressed and lay on his back, letting the night wind caress his skin. He spent a restless night and was up at the crack of dawn. His flight for Paris left in the late afternoon. He landed at Charles de Gaulle Airport after dark, determined not to see Jill Jefferson ever again.

But when he was back in his hotel, in his room, the fresh, vivid memories of the night with Jill hit him painfully. Everything reminded him of her. The large bed, the curtains he had drawn when she slept, the chair where she had left her bag; the jacket that he had worn that night still carried the faint smell of her perfume. He could not help it, he craved that girl. Hating himself, yet unable to resist, he dialed her number. "I'm back," he said, "please come."

When she knocked on his door he held her, and kissed her, and stroked her hair in the darkness, and again felt the tears on her soft cheeks. His fingers trembled when he undressed her, and he caressed her body with his burning lips, and whispered in her ear words that he should not have said, ever.

Much later, when he lay quietly by her side, he told her that he was going to Munich tomorrow. When she asked in a small voice, "Please, Clint, don't leave me here, take me with you, will you?" he held her close against him and murmured: "Yes, my love, I will."

In the morning when he packed his suitcase, he noticed that the set of photocopies from Pierre Tailbot's file had been tampered with.

He did not ask Jill if she had touched his files the day before, when he had left her in his room and had flown to Málaga.

He did not have to.

Chapter Five:

October 23—October 24:

SHARK

Off went the cannon, blast after blast. White puffs of smoke mushroomed over each of the three field guns at the far edge of the lawn, and uniformed artillerymen swiftly moved behind them as they fired successively. When the last discharge of the twenty-one-gun royal salute faded away, the Marine band struck up the monotonous concords of the Saudi national anthem. King Omar, resplendent in white robes and headdress richly embroidered in gold thread, and the President of the United States in a dark formal suit stood immobile by the presidential helicopter that had brought the visiting monarch to the White House. After a short pause the band played "The Star-Spangled Banner." It was a perfect crisp and sunny autumn day in Washington, and only a gentle wind was rustling in the low shrubs. When the last notes of the American anthem died away, Omar turned to the President and hugged him. He then walked along the line of dignitaries, warmly shaking their hands. He reached Vice-President Wheeler, who stood slightly off the receiving line with his pretty wife. Omar opened his arms and embraced him closely.

Ali Shazli, moving a few yards behind the king and the foreign minister, smiled with satisfaction. He had staged every detail of that ceremony like a skilled dramatic director, setting up the biggest show of his life. The long embrace with Wheeler was of utmost importance, he had told the king last night in his suite at the Waldorf Towers. He had to give enough time for the television cameras to focus on this display of intimate friendship, and to allow the photographers to take as many pictures as they wanted. Every American should see this embrace on his television set or in his morning newspaper, and grasp its meaning: Wheeler was Omar's close and intimate friend; Wheeler was the right man to do business with that powerful leader of the oil nations; Wheeler should be elected.

The king moved farther down the line and stopped again, as rehearsed, to pump Bill Murphy's hand heartily and to pat his shoulder affectionately. Bill, who stood amidst five or six presidents of big oil companies, had to be shown some special attention. It would promote his chances of future appointment as Energy Secretary.

Shazli threw a quick look toward the grilled fence, where a crowd of children and young men—he had had some brought over from the Saudi diplomatic mission in New York—were enthusiastically waving American and Saudi flags, and chanting slogans. He removed a speck from the sleeve of his superb light-gray suit. At his insistence, all the members of Omar's entourage—except the king himself—had come to the ceremony in suits and ties. The king had been reluctant on that point, and wanted his ministers to wear galabias, like him. With the help of his public-relations adviser, however, Shazli had carried his point. The American people, made oversensitive to U.S.–Arab relations by the issues of the election campaign, should not get an image of the Arabs as alien, strange-looking people, but as serious, well-dressed businessmen, looking very much like their own.

The President and Omar made their short speeches, assuring each other of everlasting friendship. The public warmly applauded; then the two leaders linked hands and walked into the White House. The receiving line broke and the crowd lingered for a while on the pleasant lawn, to the martial melodies of the band.

Shazli was pleased. Everything was proceeding according to plan. Omar's visit should boost Wheeler's prestige and make Jefferson's slogans look obsolete. Of course, if Bill Murphy's scheme bore fruit, Jefferson would be dealt a mortal blow a few days before the election. The operation bound to destroy him was well under way. But Shazli's golden rule was never to put all his eggs in the same basket. Last week, when Jefferson's popularity climbed another two points, swiftly gaining upon Wheeler's, Shazli had called his inner council and suggested organizing an official visit of Omar to Washington. After their agreement he had flown to Riyadh and spoken to the king. Murphy had taken care of the rest with Wheeler's help. The impressive ceremony on the White House lawn was proof that the visit had achieved its goal.

Shazli was walking briskly toward the building to join the

other ministers in the first informal chat in front of the cameras when somebody tugged on his sleeve.

He turned back. Hussein Al-Majid, the press secretary of the Saudi embassy, stood in front of him, a miserable look on his sharp features. "Will you come with me for a second?" he whispered in Arabic. "It's urgent."

"I can't right now," Shazli said. "I must go in."

"Please, just for a second." Al-Majid seemed distressed. "This is a serious matter."

They broke away from the crowd. Shazli glanced at his watch. "Now, what is it?" he asked impatiently.

Al-Majid took from his pocket a page from a newspaper and unfolded it. It was the front page of today's *Evening Star*. The huge banner headline read: "SECRET U.S. PLAN TO BOYCOTT ARAB OIL POWERS," and in smaller characters: "State Department advises economic war against oil sheikhs."

For a second he lost his breath. The palms of his hands became damp with sweat as he quickly perused the article and his eyes spotted the proposed measures: freeze assets . . . refuse visas . . . suspend military aid . . . forbid business deals. . . . He clenched his teeth and his lips blanched in fury. "When did this come out?" he rasped.

"Fifteen minutes ago. I also heard it on the radio, on my way here. It will be in tonight's news and in all the other papers tomorrow."

"Any official reaction?"

Al-Majid shook his head unhappily. "They said the State Department refrained from comment."

"It must be true, then." He felt an upsurge of helpless wrath. His beautiful plan was going to pieces. Still, he had to keep his head cool. "Not a word to anybody there"—he motioned with his head to the White House. "Not yet. Get back to the office and find out who gave this to the newspapers, and if it's true . . . No, I have a better idea. Get hold of Murphy. He is here, in the crowd. Know him?"

The press secretary nodded.

"Show that to him and ask him to meet me at the embassy, as soon as the ceremony is over." Bill would easily identify the source of the article through his newspapers.

He walked quickly to the White House, seething with anger. He made an effort to compose his features, and was pleasantly smiling when an aide ushered him into the Blue Room. He found his colleagues casually talking with American personalities while press photographers took pictures, their flashbulbs blinking. The President and King Omar were sitting on a sofa, chatting and smiling. An interpreter crouched behind them and translated in a low voice.

Shazli sat woodenly on a chair, simmering with impatience. He sipped his orange juice, his eyes aimlessly wandering over the room. When the meeting was over, he was the first to get out. "I shall be at the embassy," he threw at the king's aide-de-camp, who waited outside. "Ask His Majesty not to answer any questions from the press before he sees me." The ADC nodded, his face faintly puzzled.

Bill Murphy was waiting for him at the embassy, in the press secretary's office. Al-Majid had discreetly moved to another room. The newspaper was spread on the desk. "What a mess," Murphy said.

"Did you find out what it's all about?" Shazli asked.

Murphy shook his head angrily. "A goddam nonsense, that's what it is. The State Department made a study, six months ago, of possible retaliation against the Arab states, then buried the report in its archives. It was not intended to be implemented and nobody would have found it in a million years."

Shazli lit a cigarette. "But somebody did."

"Yes, somebody did, all right. Your friend Jefferson, Ali, the one you didn't want to . . ."

Shazli raised his hand. "Let's not start it all over again, Bill, okay?" He propped his elbows on the desk and rubbed his eyes with the palms of his hands. "How do you know it was Jefferson?"

"I got it from my network. As soon as your man got in touch with me, I called a few of my news editors. The leak did not come direct from the Jefferson campaign headquarters. He used a more subtle way. There are two guys, Turner and Roscoe, one here and one in Los Angeles. Jefferson has been using them for years, when he wants to plant something in the media. They did it this time, too. It's Jefferson all right."

"What bothers me is that the report is genuine," Shazli said. "No matter what we say and what the White House says, nobody can deny that this is an authentic State Department report. You understand, of course, that the king's visit will be a failure."

Murphy nodded. "I wish he hadn't come."

"Well, let's see what we can salvage. We'll draw up a

formal protest by King Omar, in the strongest terms, of course. Bill, try to get hold of Wheeler. See that he prepares a statement of apology or whatever for the President to issue. We shall also need some kind of denial from the State Department. Maybe we'll succeed in arranging a conciliatory meeting between the king and the President for tonight, before the reception."

"I'll suggest to Wheeler that they publish a joint statement," Murphy said. "That bastard Jefferson! What a dirty trick to play on us."

Shazli drew a deep breath and idly fingered a pen in the small tray in front of him. "We played a trick on him; he played a trick on us," he remarked softly.

Al-Majid popped his head in the door. "Jefferson just made a comment on the report," he said eagerly.

"What did he say?" Shazli raised his eyes.

Al-Majid read aloud from his pad: "I am pleased to learn that the State Department, genuinely worried about the oil blackmail employed against this country . . ."

"Oh, fuck him!" Murphy roared and strode out of the room.

Al-Majid retreated, too, on a cue from Shazli. The OPEC chairman leaned back in his chair, his features concentrated in thought. Finally he picked up the phone. "Get me Ahmed Abd-el-Krim," he said to the secretary.

He reached the Algerian oil minister immediately. Abd-el-Krim was in Washington, like the oil ministers of the other Arab countries. That had also been Shazli's idea: to have them all come over to the big party that the king was throwing tonight in honor of the American President. He wanted them to mix with members of the United States government, columnists, commentators, congressmen, and of course to be photographed with the American leaders. Abd-el-Krim had scoffed at the idea. *"L'offensive du charme,"* he had snapped. He had come to Washington all the same, and that was what really counted.

He sounded surprised over the phone now. "Ali? I was just going to call you."

"I guess it was for the same reason that I called you."

"The newspaper?"

"Yes. Can I see you in your embassy?"

There was a pause. Shazli sensed that he had thrown Abd-el-Krim off balance, as much by calling him first as by offering to come and see him. He was the senior of the two, and there was no secret about their rivalry. Shazli's offer to come to Abd-el-Krim was a subtle gesture of flattery, and Abd-el-Krim couldn't refuse it. If he stalled him off now, it would be because he was trying to figure out what Shazli was really up to.

"*Markhaban*—welcome," Abd-el-Krim said finally. "I'll have some tea with peppermint leaves made specially for you."

Half an hour later, the two men met in the Algerian ambassador's office, which had been hurriedly vacated for the occasion. Shazli talked about the White House ceremony, and complimented Abd-el-Krim on the excellent tea. Then he tackled the subject of his visit. "This report is going to be exploited by all the media, and do us a lot of harm," he said. "There are going to be accusations and denials and counter-accusations. . . . Nothing good will come of it. I am afraid that the visit of His Majesty King Omar has misfired."

"It was your idea," Abd-el-Krim said quickly.

"It was my idea," Shazli repeated slowly, "and you agreed to it. Now, as you know me, I believe in the policy of the stick and the carrot. We gave the Americans a carrot—King Omar's visit, and his promise of a steady oil supply—and somebody threw that report on us. Maybe we should use a stick now, frighten them a little."

"What do you mean?" Abd-el-Krim was overtly suspicious.

"Why not show them what could happen if Jefferson gets elected?" He did not look at the Algerian, but poured himself another tiny cup of tea. "Why not give them an example of what could happen to their oil if Jefferson tries to come and get it?"

Abd-el-Krim could not conceal his astonishment. "*You* are talking about using the stick?" he asked.

Shazli nodded and looked candidly at his rival. "That is why I came to you," he said. "You have always urged our council to adopt a tougher line toward the West. You suggested once we do something about the oil wells, remember? I want to ask you to assume command of this . . . this operation. Nobody else should know, of course. It should be carried out by some new movement, called, let's say . . . 'the Sons of Arabia.' . . . What do you think?"

It was only now that Abd-el-Krim saw through Shazli's game. The razor-sharp mind of the OPEC chairman had already digested the State Department report and foreseen the inevitable results. The moderate policy that Shazli had sup-

94

ported, the visit of Omar that he had staged, had failed; he would be harshly criticized by the more radical Arab leaders, and there would be an outcry for a more militant policy, maybe even for the election of a new chairman. Therefore he had moved quickly, outflanking the radicals, suggesting the use of violence, and—supreme effrontery—he was directing him, his main critic, to carry it out! He was pulling the carpet from under their feet, and nobody, not even the Libyans, could accuse him of softness anymore. Abd-el-Krim felt trapped. "You are a fox," he said aloud, baring his anger, "a real sly fox."

Shazli smiled as if he did not hear him. He looked at his watch, got up and embraced him. "You'll do it, then. I knew I could count on you. Only take care that our friends don't do any damage that we could not repair, if we wished."

He stopped at the door. "By the way, Murphy told me that our special project concerning Jefferson is progressing very well. It will destroy him completely just before election day. Peace on you, my brother."

For a week, the first storm of winter had been brewing over the Gulf of Finland, gathering ominous masses of black clouds over the Baltic, rolling its muffled thunder in the gloomy sky of Leningrad. The ice-cold winds impatiently shrieked and whirled over the murky waters, as if restrained by an invisible hand, till they magnified into a roaring tempest. Finally, one night they rebelled. Like a stampeding herd they lashed through the bare Russian steppes, swept to the east in the plains of the Ukraine and the forests of Poland, cooling the exposed flanks of the Carpathians and at last, exhausted, broke against the jagged Bavarian Alps and dispersed in the valleys of Southern Germany. The early winter storm took the city of Munich by surprise; the Lufthansa employees were shivering in their light uniforms when Jill and Clint landed at Munich Airport in a drizzling rain that soon turned into sleet.

The gloomy weather matched Jill's mood. During the flight, she had tried to act the cheerful, happy girl and had miserably failed. She was bound to fail, she bitterly said to herself. She was not a comedian, she did not know how to disguise her feelings, and then . . . everything had turned out so differently from what she had anticipated. At the beginning it had been a task she willingly undertook, even a sort of game. How could she guess that she was playing with fire, with her own unshielded feelings?

When her father had first called her, earlier this week, she had immediately agreed to his request. He had seemed very upset, and there was a ring of real anxiety in his voice. He had told her that Clint Craig, who had been for years his close assistant and confidant, was now in Paris, in the Royal Hotel; for some obscure reason Clint had got involved in a scheme to smear him, and block his way to the presidency. Jefferson suspected that the conspiracy against him was masterminded by the OPEC chairman, Shazli. "Clint just phoned me from Paris," J.J. had said unhappily. "He said he was writing a book about the disappearance of Goering's loot thirty-five years ago."

"Yes, I saw something about it in the papers." Nothing more than the banner headline, actually, but she had recognized Clint's name.

"He said he wanted to ask me a couple of questions," Jim Jefferson had continued, his voice trembling with contained anger, "questions to do with his book. His book!" he spat with bitter irony. "You had to hear those questions. This guy is not after Goering's treasure; he is after my political career."

"But why, Father? It doesn't make sense. You always said that he was the best man on your staff."

"I don't know," he had admitted, sounding perplexed. "I don't know. Maybe somebody has tempted him to join a conspiracy against me, or . . . perhaps they merely use him as an instrument, to frame me. Either way, that's bad, Jillian." He was the only one to call her so, occasionally.

"You said they wanted to frame you," she had slowly repeated. "Frame you for what?"

There had been a pause; then J.J. had slowly said: "They want to implicate me in an alleged murder of a German prisoner, a former Nazi official, in nineteen forty-five."

"Murder!" she had gasped in dismay. The shock left her speechless for a moment. "But . . . but you had nothing to do with it, Daddy, tell me!" She almost cried, ardently hoping for an outright denial.

"Of course not!" he had shouted angrily into the phone. "I just happened to be in charge of the prisoner, that's all!" She had been so relieved, so grateful, that she had ignored his immediate apologies for being so short-tempered. Then he had asked her to help him—to befriend Craig and find out what

96

he was after, who was manipulating him, why was he determined to destroy him.

She had said yes, of course—"You can count on me, Father." She worshipped J.J. and was ready to do anything to help him become President. Still, she had not planned her moves to the last detail when devising a way to approach Clint Craig. She did not know how she was going to make him talk about his research. The idea of sleeping with him had not crossed her mind—although, if she had given it any thought, she would probably have assumed that it could happen. But not the way it did.

It had been fun at the beginning. She had no trouble following the young man through Paris, until he came to the Place des Vosges. Then she had had a quick inspiration, and had taken her sketchbook out of her bag. He had accosted her and talked to her, exactly as she had wanted him to. She had noticed already, while following him, that he was handsome in a romantic sort of way. The large forehead, the unruly mass of dark hair, the inner fire in his eyes, reminded her of a portrait of young Byron. Still, it was not his looks that had troubled her; she had acquired, long ago, a quasi-immunity to men's outward appearance. But there had been something surprisingly warm and candid in his eyes, in the way he spoke, and when he had asked to join her she had hesitated. She was not prepared for the possibility that she might like him. But she did, and found herself telling him the story of her life over dinner. And it had been so good, so natural, to stroll with him across the Left Bank in that crisp Parisian night, to share the pleasure of the artists' performances in the small intellectual haunts; she had loved dancing with him, being close to him, and then that moment came when she felt that he attracted her, he aroused her and she wanted him. For a while she had stopped thinking, letting her feelings take over, until she realized that she was in his bed, clinging to his warm body, and had soundlessly cried in despair. Could this man be an enemy? A man who was determined to destroy her father?

Yesterday morning, after Clint had gone to Málaga and had left her alone in his room, she had almost broken down. She had wanted to drop the whole thing, run away, never see Clint again. But she had found the papers in his room; she had seen the report about Captain James T. Jefferson. And she knew she had to go along. She must have sounded terrible over the phone when she called her father in St. Croix,

97

because he immediately had sensed that something was wrong and had asked her to come home. "Forget about that nonsense, Jillian," he had said softly. "Hop on the first plane and come over. Your place is with me, here. I shouldn't have sent you to play spy games." But she knew that she had to stay and continue playing the game, even though it was not a game anymore. Clint now knew who she was, and certainly suspected what she was after. She had not lied to him about her use of her mother's name; that was the truth. But he would have been the last fool on earth to believe that he had met her by sheer coincidence. What did he think of her, now that he knew? Did he let her come with him on purpose, with the devious intention of outwitting her father? No, he could not be so ruthless. Maybe he was really attracted to her; maybe he did mean all those things he had whispered in the darkness last night. Oh God, what a mess! Over and over again during the flight, she had felt the urge to take him by the hand, to tell him the whole truth about her father's anguish, about her acting, about what she really felt toward him now. She almost did it once, during a long pause of awkward silence, when he had suddenly turned to her and had gently, lovingly, caressed her face, looking into her eyes. But she feared his reaction. He might have seen in her confession another trick conceived by her devious mind. So she kept quiet, aware that a deep abyss lay between her and this man, who had suddenly become so dear to her.

She averted her face and looked through the cab window. The rain-swept dome of St. Peter's Church appeared in the distance, looming against the low, leaden sky.

Stadelheim Prison was a rectangular tawny building surrounded by a high gray wall. At the end of the war it had been quite isolated, a few miles away from the city of Munich. But suburbs had mushroomed all around the booming Bavarian capital, and the prison had become incongruously stuck in the very midst of a residential district. It was still in use. Because of its location, however, the German authorities sent to Stadelheim only petty criminals sentenced to short terms of imprisonment. A young, willowy woman was patiently waiting outside in the drizzle, holding a plastic umbrella in her left hand. A little girl with large brown eyes stood beside her, clutching her skirt. She reminded Clint of Laurie and he felt a sudden pang in his heart.

When did he last see his little daughter? Three, four months ago?

The guard at the gate, a bluff, red-faced man, looked at him warily. Clint stated the purpose of his visit. He had a lot of trouble explaining what he was after, and only following long and tedious negotiations was he finally admitted to the warden's office. The warden, a Herr Goerke, was neat, priggish and icily polite. It seemed as if somebody had years ago painted a prudish smile on his long pale face and had forgotten to rub it out. No, he was sorry, but he did not know anything about the use of the jail during the American occupation. No, he was sorry, he had not heard about a Herr Otto Brandl committing suicide in the prison. No, he was sorry, but Herr Craig could not visit cell 35. It was an isolated cell in the eastern wing of the prison, and it was occupied now by a prisoner who had been caught peddling drugs. No, he was sorry, but Herr Craig could not even look inside through the peephole. It could have a very demoralizing effect on the prisoner.

Clint walked out into the icy rain, utterly exasperated. The visit to the Stadelheim jail had yielded nothing. The only useful bit of information that he had obtained from the prim warden was that the records of the prison, from the years when it had been used by the American Army, had been transferred to the U.S. Army compound at Fürstenfeldbruck, about twenty miles west of Munich. The transfer had taken place in 1955, when the jail was handed over to the German Federal authorities.

Although dusk was already settling, it was barely past four in the afternoon. Clint called the Fürstenfeldbruck base from a nearby *Weinstube,* and arranged with a Lieutenant Hutchinson, in charge of public relations, to meet him at the main gate. Then he hailed a cruising cab and set off. He was glad to be alone. Jill had told him that she wanted to rest in the hotel and later visit the museums of fine art—the Alte and Neue Pinakothek. But he guessed that she wanted to call her father to report about today's progress. He lit a cigarillo. Maybe he had done the right thing in taking her with him, he mused. Had he refused, J.J. would have found a way to sneak another spy into his bedroom. Better the spy you know than the one you don't. *And maybe,* he said to himself, *you are just trying to justify your weakness in your own eyes, Mr. Craig.* Well, the hell with it. He had become infatuated with that girl and wanted her close by for as long as it lasted.

Lieutenant Hutchinson, U.S. Army, was a towering, soft-spoken Black from Charleston, West Virginia. In a kind, almost apologetic tone he rebuked Clint for arriving without prior notice. "I spoke to Captain Foote, who is in charge of our archives, and he is expecting you. But I doubt if he will let you see any papers without clearance from Washington."

"Let's meet him and see where we stand," Clint said noncommittally. He kept the taxi waiting, pinned the visitor's pass on his lapel and got into Hutchinson's jeep. He shivered in his light raincoat, which offered no protection from the bitter cold, and unhappily listened to the lieutenant's clichés about life in Fürstenfeldbruck and army life in general.

The archives section occupied a whole wing in the camp headquarters. "We keep here the records of all the U.S. Army units in southern Germany," Hutchinson proudly said, before introducing him to Captain Foote.

The chief archivist, a sturdy young man with a sallow face and oily yellow-white hair, peered uneasily at Clint through his thick glasses. Clint explained the reason for his visit. He had the distinct feeling, though, that Foote was not listening. While he was speaking, the captain restlessly moved on his seat, nervously fidgeting with his pencils, pads and paperclips, arranging them on his desk in an ever-changing order. Once or twice he cast him a suspicious shortsighted glance. As soon as Clint had finished, the captain spoke in a low, uncertain voice. "I am afraid I cannot help you, sir. I cannot give you any information without consulting Army headquarters. I don't have the authority to show you any documents without written clearance."

Clint felt he was losing ground. This man was in a state of mild panic. Captain Foote had never been in such a situation before and did not know how to handle it. So he preferred not to handle it at all.

"And how long will it take to get such clearance?" Clint asked politely.

"Why, I really don't know, sir. A week, two weeks?" Foote sneaked a quick look at Hutchinson, as if asking for his help.

"I understand," Clint said in the same respectful voice. "Now, there is no reason for me to wait in Munich for two weeks, without even knowing if you have the papers I am looking for. Could you just check in your archives to see if you have any file about this man Otto Brandl, who died in Stadelheim Prison?"

"Why don't you try the Army archives in Maryland, sir? If

there is such a file, they must have a copy there. They have copies of everything prior to nineteen seventy-five."

"You are right," Clint conceded, "but I am here now, and carrying out my research in Germany. Why go back to the States for a simple verification?"

Foote looked bewildered. He started rearranging his pencils again, and finally yielded. "Let me check that, sir."

He disappeared into the back rooms. Clint and Hutchinson waited in silence. Fifteen minutes later, the little captain was back. "Yes, sir, we have a file on Otto Brandl."

Clint felt that he had to move very slowly now, very carefully, not to scare Captain Foote, who was frightened enough. "Now, look," he started, and fumbled in his attaché case. "I have received already, by special permission, a few documents concerning this Otto Brandl." He took the copies of the reports about Brandl's imprisonment and death and spread them in front of Foote. "What I want to ask you—and you will not be breaking any rules by telling me—is, do you have any other documents about this affair? In my file there was no report by the officer in charge of the interrogation." He omitted Jefferson's name on purpose. "Maybe you have it. Or maybe there is another report by the man who drew the account about Brandl's death. First Sergeant Jeffrey Oates."

Foote seemed a little more at ease now, having seen material proof that Craig had been authorized to examine and copy Brandl's file. "Just a moment," he said, and disappeared again.

He was back almost immediately. "No, sir, we have no report by the officer in charge of the interrogation. As far as First Sergeant Oates is concerned, we have a note dated August eight, nineteen forty-five, which is . . ."

". . . Which is two days after Brandl's death," Clint interjected.

"Yes. It says that First Sergeant Jeffrey Oates was killed in a car accident that same day. His jeep overturned and caught fire. First Sergeant Oates died instantaneously, and his body was burned beyond recognition."

Clint froze in his seat.

"Burned beyond recognition," he slowly said. "Do you understand what that means?"

He was sitting across from Jill in the pleasant obscurity of Trader Vic's restaurant. A long, sleek candle in a silver candlestick was casting wavering shadows on Jill's pale face, making her look haunted. "I understand," she whispered. "That means that there is no real proof of his death."

He drew a deep breath. "And that leaves your father as the only surviving witness, Jill."

This time, she did not ignore the allusion. "That story might ruin my father. Are you aware of that, Clint?"

"I knew your father very well. I trusted him more than anybody else in the world."

"But you want to find the truth." She was watching him closely.

"Yes." He nodded.

She bit her lip. "And you believe that he is the man who had Otto Brandl killed, and that he is the man who went to Spain and murdered the other man, Michel . . ."

"Michel Skolnikoff," he completed. He paused. "The truth is I don't know what to believe, Jill. I am sure that the same man was behind the murders of Skolnikoff and Brandl. I have only one name—your father's. I called him and he said he didn't remember! How could he forget something like that?" He realized that they were playing their foolish game again, pretending to discuss his research but actually probing each other, watching each other, each trying to discover the other's intentions. *Why don't you call him and ask him, he wanted to shout at her; why don't you phone dear tough J.J. and ask: Father, did you do it? Were you involved in Brandl's killing? Were you in Ronda, in Romero's cellar?*

But instead he just said: "I hope to reach some more conclusive evidence in a later stage, maybe in Nuremberg."

She took a sip from her glass. "When I was at the Pinakothek today I saw a painting that frightened me." Her voice was low, almost inaudible. "It was 'Don Quixotte,' by Honoré Daumier, the French painter. But the Don Quixotte in the painting had no face, Clint; it was just an oval shape. I can't forget that empty face. I feel as if we are traveling over Europe looking for an unknown man, for a face to fit in that picture, and . . ."

". . . And you are afraid that we'll find your father's face," he said gently.

Her cheeks suddenly flushed with anger. "I don't believe it and I'll never believe it. I'll never believe that my father had anything to do, ever, with such a despicable crime. And I don't care for all the proof and the evidence and whatever you find in your research, Mister Writer." She covered her face with her hands and got up, overturning her glass as she ran away. The crystal glass rolled on the tablecloth and broke into a thousand splinters on the floor tiles. Craig jumped to his feet, threw a few bills on the table and hurried after her, followed by the amused stares of everybody present.

He caught up with her at the street corner, where she was trying to hail a cab. He grabbed her by the arm amd pulled her to him. Her whole body was shaking, and he hugged her close. She tried to resist, then suddenly burst into low, uncontrollable sobs. "Don't," he whispered in her ear, "don't cry, please." He tightly wrapped his arms around her, trying to protect her from the sleet. He kissed and caressed her wet face, and she slowly calmed down. "Come," he softly said. There was no taxi in sight, but he looked around and saw the entrance to a beer cellar. "Come," he repeated. He took her by the hand and she followed him, docile. They went in and down the steps. The place was warm and bustling with typical Bavarian gaiety. Groups of men, their faces red with alcohol, were laughing, shouting and trying to sing to the tunes of a Tyrolean band playing on a small stage. Plump waitresses in dirndls and white, generously open blouses were circulating among the big wooden tables, carrying huge clusters of beer steins in each hand. Clint made Jill sit down at the far side of a half-empty table, and ordered two brandies from a passing waitress. The alcohol warmed her up and some faint color returned to her pale face.

"Are you all right?" he asked with concern.

"Yes, I'll be okay in a moment," she said.

"I am sorry. We shall not discuss that matter anymore, all right? Not tonight."

The men had linked arms and were swaying together to the rhythm of a merry waltz sung by a buxom matron. A smiling young man beckoned to Jill to join the human chain, but she shook her head politely. She still seemed depressed, and Clint did not want to take her back to the hotel, not yet. He tried to think of a way to amuse her, to take her mind off the sordid riddle they were attempting to solve. Suddenly he remembered something he had read in a tourist guide. He said in a tone of forced gaiety: "Would you like to see the most unique discotheque in the world? It's here, in Munich."

She shook her head. "I don't feel like dancing, Clint." She paused. "What's so unique about it?"

"It is built into a huge tank of sea water, about two

103

hundred thousand gallons. And they have forty big sharks from Florida swimming inside." He added, "We don't have to dance, you know. We can just have a drink and look around."

"Okay." She nodded.

This time they had no trouble getting a cab. The old driver knew the place, smiled and smoothly drove his car through the deserted streets.

The Yellow Submarine was indeed built like the hull of a submarine. It was designed in a round shape, like the interior of a huge barrel, and split in three levels. At the lowest level was a dancing floor, swept by multicolored lights and surrounded by small tables. The upper level was partitioned into small, intimate booths. Big portholes fixed in the wood-and-brass walls offered a picturesque view into small, brightly lit aquariums, where tiny exotic fish swam among colorful rocks.

The main attraction was the middle level, where the bar stood. It was surrounded by huge bay windows made of thick glass. The windows afforded one of the most spectacular views Clint had ever seen: a pack of enormous steel-gray sharks, swimming in never-ending rounds, impossibly close, horrendously present, barely a few inches away from the dancing youngsters and the indifferent bartender.

Jill, too, was fascinated by the appalling sight. "It's frightening," she murmured, and moved closer to Clint, instinctively seeking protection from the monsters in the glass cage. For an unknown reason, one of the larger sharks was trying to attack the spectators in front of him. Again and again it would swim toward the glass, dorsal fins upright, porcine eyes dully glinting, crescent-shaped jaws slightly open, baring the razor-sharp teeth. Its snout would hit the glass and it would turn around, with an almost imperceptible motion of its tail, return and attack again.

Suddenly all the sharks stirred. Something had happened that drove them frantic. They started to hurl their huge bulks to and fro, madly excited; their heavy tails whipped the surface of the water into a white froth. The color of the water slightly changed as a reddish substance poured from above, slowly diluted in the tank. Clint understood. "Blood," he whispered to Jill. "They have smelled blood. They are going to be fed."

At that moment, several big chunks of raw red meat were thrown into the water. They had barely touched the surface when the sharks were upon them, a wild, mad pack of demons, darting through the water, turning on their backs and exposing their off-white bellies as their jaws snapped on the prey and tore it to pieces. Jill shivered. "I can't look," she said, disgusted. "It gives me the creeps." She carried her drink to a small table by the bar, and looked over the parapet at the dancing couples on the floor below.

Clint approached the glass window, fascinated by the sickening spectacle. He did not pay attention to two men who flanked him on either side and looked as engrossed as he in the pack of demented sharks. All of a sudden, he felt something sharp thrusting forward in the left side of his back, and at the same moment the two men at his sides crushed against him, immobilizing him completely. A very low voice hissed in his ear: "What you feel in your back is a long, sharp knife, Mister Craig. If I push it a couple of inches more, you'll be dead, good to be thrown to the sharks." The knife slowly moved, and he felt its sharp tip tearing through his clothes. He tried to turn back, but a third man, the one who held the knife, was forcefully leaning against his body. From the corner of his eye he could see Jill's profile, bent over the parapet, looking down. "Don't move," the voice growled low, "and don't scream."

He knew he had to obey; to everybody around they looked like a group of friends absorbed in the gory sight beyond the glass. Before he could even open his mouth the knife would pierce his heart. Beads of cold sweat popped out on his forehead, and a chill ran up his spine. "You'll die, Mister Craig," the voice said, with a strange, indefinable accent. "You'll die if you don't stop what you're doing. Lay off the Phantom operation. Go back to your country." The knife scratched his skin. Death seemed so near.

But he did not think of death. He thought of Jill, sitting there only a few yards away, indifferently looking down. His old doubts assailed him again. Did she move away on purpose, to let them assault him? Could she have contacted the killers when she was alone this afternoon and ordered them to follow her and Clint until she gave them the sign to attack him? Could she be so treacherous?

The pressure on his back suddenly eased and the pain subsided. "This is the last warning," the voice hissed. He was brutally shoved forward, lost his balance and collided with the thick glass. He quickly straightened up and pivoted on his

105

heels, but the men were already at the exit, three dark shapes quickly walking away.

Jill had not moved from her place. He was left all alone against the greenish window, staring woodenly as the sharks completed their bloody feast.

Chapter Six:

October 24—October 25:

POISON

The Cessna took off into the limpid blue sky, and Bill Murphy, who was the sole passenger, impatiently unbuckled his seat belt. His eyes briefly contemplated the concrete towers of Houston that were quickly dissolving in the distance; then he shifted his glance to the pile of newspapers on the table in front of him. For urgent trips around the country he would always use the company's Westwind, a swift, compact jet that was as fast as any you could get on the market today. But when he was not in any particular hurry, and felt like occasionally taking over the controls himself, he would use his private Cessna. The Cessna was also fit for landing at Eagle's Ranch, although the airstrip was short and bumpy and abruptly ended at the edge of the ravine.

Murphy could have the airstrip asphalted and extended, of course. North of the runway there was nothing but rocky land strewn with low bushes. Nevertheless, he had kept it the way it was, and for one very definite reason: he deeply enjoyed the sensation of danger, the tightening of his body and the feverish beat of his pulse as he would land on the uneven runway and the plane would dart toward the brink of the abyss below, to stop finally a few yards short of death.

This was another danger, another challenge he had to defy and overcome. He had lived in danger most of his adult years, and was attracted to it as a moth is drawn to the flame. Nothing on earth could match the thrill of playing the riskiest game and winning it; there was no sweeter sensation than to overcome one's own fear. He was old enough to know that courage was neither a God-given gift nor a durable one. It had to be tested and proven, time after time. During the war, on the eve of the landing in Normandy, he had traveled to Newbury in the south of England, to brief the officers of the 101st Airborne Division on secret objectives in

107

France. They were going to be dropped at dawn, and the men were silently assembling around the black Liberators and gliders. As he walked to the underground operations room, he was wondering how many of them were going to die that night. His companion, the lean, sinewy Colonel Bartholme, who was the division operations officer, had divined his thoughts. "We are going to lose many of them," he had said, "our bravest soldiers." He had paused a second to light a half-chewed black cigar. "You know what makes paratroopers so brave? Let me tell you. They have to jump every week, over and over, and every time to overcome their fear once again. When you have jumped a few times you stop loving it. You've seen people killed, legs broken, parachutes that won't open, all kinds of accidents. You dread it, and you do it all the same. That's real bravery. A brave man is not the one who is insensible to fear. It is the one who is afraid—and yet manages to dominate his feelings and take that little step forward."

Bartholme had been hacked to pieces by machine-gun fire only a few hours later, at Sainte-Mère-Église, but Murphy still remembered every single word the soft-spoken Virginian had said that night. Only years later was he to realize that his own life had closely followed that same pattern. In a way, he had also been jumping from a plane into the blackness of night over and over again: when he had set out, as an undercover OSS agent, on his perilous missions in occupied Europe, in Italy, in France, in Holland, even in Germany; when he had kept risking his life, after the war, in the small team of hand-picked agents that Allen Dulles had chosen to form the nucleus of the Central Intelligence Agency. His assignments had carried him to Prague and Warsaw at the outbreak of the Cold War; to Greece, as the communist battalions of Colonel Markos were already launching their decisive assault on Athens; to Hong Kong, which had become the front of a merciless secret war between spies of East and West, after the outbreak of the Korean war. He had learned to live on the fringe of society, unprotected by its laws, defying its rules, acting by a different scale of values and morals. He had run for his life in the most law-abiding cities in the world; he had savagely killed and had gotten commendations for his ruthlessness.

He had finally surfaced from his shadow world in 1954, two years after the election of Eisenhower. The whole world was changing, recovering at last from the fear and misery of

Hitler's war and its aftermath, engaging in a quest for co-existence and well-being on both sides of the Iron Curtain. Empires were built no more by sword and cannon, but by money and enterprise. And he wanted to build an empire.

Yet in this new world he had set out to conquer, he did not—or maybe could not—part with his old methods. He continued to operate in utmost secrecy, concealing his goals, disguising his moves, shielding his operations by layer upon layer of camouflage. He had surrounded himself with phantom companies, bogus societies, straw people; each and every one of his investments or acquisitions was carried out through a chain of intermediaries, so that nobody could ever assess his real wealth or pinpoint the properties he controlled. He soon became the most elusive, the most secretive among his peers, second only to Howard Hughes. The first time his picture appeared in newspapers was in the mid-seventies, almost twenty years after he had come out into the open. The fact that nobody knew what he did own, which company, factory, shipping line, oil well, was his—gave him a feeling of immense power and immunity. Even today, when he was world-known as the president of the huge American Oil, very few people were familiar with all the other enterprises under his control.

Another distinctive trait he had brought over from his nebulous past had greatly contributed to his success: his taste for the dangerous game, his readiness to take the greatest risks and to play things his own way, against the rules. When he had decided to establish himself one day as an oil king, he knew that he could never do it the conventional way. Every oil well in the world was already controlled by a powerful company. Therefore, he had to develop a different approach. Soon he reached the conclusion that as long as the existing order prevailed he would be banned from the exclusive club of the oil tycoons. He could grab his share only if a new order came to replace the old, an order in the shaping of which he had played a part. Which he did. Secretly, efficiently, ruthlessly.

When in 1958 Brigadier Karim Kassem set out to overthrow King Faisal of Iraq and down the Iraqi monarchy in a bloodbath, he was following detailed intelligence reports about the strength of the forces loyal to the king. These reports, which Murphy had obtained thanks to his close ties with the CIA, enabled Kassem to score a swift and total victory. A year later, Kassem gave a company nobody had heard of, American Oil, the concession of prospecting and exploiting the petroleum reserves of the highly promising Khangin region.

When the Algerian *Front de Libération Nationale* finally took over Algeria from the French, only a handful knew that for years they had been fighting with arms and ammunition supplied by a discreet company established in Liechtenstein. But when they had to negotiate contracts for foreign know-how and investments in the Sahara oilfields, American Oil got the best share. The same process repeated itself in Libya, when Colonel Qadhafi ousted the aging, impotent King Idris, and in Bahrain when the cousin of the ruling Sheikh Tawfik, the young Gamal Rif'at, carried out his coup. Thus it turned out that whenever a civil war or a coup occurred in the Middle East in the last twenty years, Murphy was lurking close behind the scenes, smuggling arms, providing funds, supplying top-notch information.

To the strong, established regimes he had to find a different approach. His discreet emissaries, many of them former CIA experts, conceived and directed the private services of many a monarch. When the Arab lobbyists in Washington, frustrated by the powerful Israeli influence in the United States, needed a channel to the media to expound their point of view, Murphy put at their disposal his newly acquired papers and broadcasting networks. More than once he was at the right place, in the right time, to render even more unconventional services—a secure route for a greedy minister to smuggle hashish into the United States, fair teenage girls and sleek narrow-hipped boys to satisfy an ambassador's secret vices, a discreet bank account in Switzerland for a high official concerned about his future. And he always got fairly reimbursed for his services. When the Suez Canal was closed after the Arab-Israeli war in 1967, and oil had to be shipped by the long route around the Cape, the supertankers of American Oil were the first to be granted adequate facilities at the big oil ports of the Persian Gulf. And when the Israelis conceived an alternative route by laying a pipeline from the Red Sea to the Mediterranean, they did not even come to suspect that the real investor behind the very respectable consortium of European banks that financed the pipeline was American Oil again, skimming the cream from both sides.

He had blundered a few times in his career, of course, the worst fiasco being his support for the Venezuelan rebels. Their revolt failed, and Murphy had to hastily withdraw his

110

surviving envoys from Caracas and Maracaibo. But thanks to his obsessive concern for deception and compartmentation, he succeeded in surviving the political storm that erupted in Washington. Accusations were made against American imperialists and American capital and American warmongers; nothing was said about American Oil. Once again, Murphy had managed to keep out of the scandal. He had learned his lesson, though, and decided to keep away from treacherous South American politics. He concentrated all his zeal in the Middle East, gradually becoming the closest ally of the Arab oil interests in the United States.

He had built his empire, all right: a huge, powerful, widely ramified conglomerate of money, oil, press and shipping, which he controlled from his offices in Houston, Washington and New York, or from the isolated Eagle's Ranch, his mountainous retreat perched atop the southernmost ridge of the Rockies, overhanging the Rio Grande.

And this empire—the fruit of his labor, the basis of his reach for political power—was threatened now by one man, a candidate for the presidency of the United States. A man he hated from the depth of his guts. A man he had to destroy. James Jefferson.

He angrily threw away the *Houston Post* whose headline proclaimed: "J.J. snatches two more points from Wheeler." He reached for *The New York Times* and leafed through its A section. An article on the editorial page drew his attention. It was signed by the well-known columnist William T. Brewster, and was headed: "The rise of James Jefferson—a strange phenomenon in American politics." He perused it quickly with pinched lips, and his eyes focused on the concluding paragraph:

"James Jefferson is a unique phenomenon in postwar politics, in the sense that he is a well-established liberal advocating a strong-hand—some say warmongering—policy. What makes this phenomenon even more puzzling for political scientists in this country is that Jefferson's open exhortation for a military solution of the oil crisis has had almost no effect on the support he draws from liberally motivated minorities and regions in the nation; he still benefits from the support of Blacks, Jews, intellectuals, and his popularity is high in California, New York and Massachusetts. There is no doubt that the hostile attitude of the liberal press in this country has had very little—if any—effect on J.J.'s image. The steady rise in Jefferson's popularity leads to a disquieting conclusion: after years of weak leadership the American people yearn for a strong President, and at the present moment, James Jefferson fits that concept."

Murphy put the paper down, and a stubborn expression settled on his face. That fellow could write whatever he wanted; the fight was not over yet. As a matter of fact, it was only beginning. He looked through the plane window. They were flying now over a low mass of black clouds. The dazzling white fire of lightning flashed over and over again, bathing the dark skies in an eerie glow. He got up from his seat, stepped forward and spoke to his pilot, the taciturn Nat Andrews. "Move over, Red," he said, "let me take her down for the landing."

The red-haired Texan protested mildly. "It's quite tricky down there, Bill. It must be raining heavily and the visibility . . ." He stopped in midsentence, realizing the futility of arguing, shrugged and let Murphy slide into the pilot's seat.

He landed her at the first attempt, and just for the fun of it let the Cessna drift an extra couple of yards toward the brink. He heard the pilot's muffled gasp, and chuckled inwardly.

A light-green station wagon came from the direction of the ranch, its windshield wipers furiously struggling against the pouring rain. His wife, Jo Ann, was driving. He got into the front seat and kissed her lightly. She was wearing a black sweater and gray pants; a quiet, subdued expression was painted on her prematurely aged face. "Peter Bohlen called," she said quietly before he started asking his routine questions. "He asked me to tell you that the man—that's what he said—is in Munich, on his way to Nuremberg."

Clint startled her when he suddenly appeared by her table at The Yellow Submarine, pale as a ghost. There was a curious look in his eyes and his mouth was bitter. "Come," he snapped, "we are going back."

She put her drink down. "Is something wrong, Clint? You look strange." He did not answer, but turned and walked toward the stairs. She was offended by his sudden bluntness, but she got up and followed him. In the cab he spent half a matchbox unsuccessfully trying to light his cigarillo; finally he

112

cursed furiously under his breath, rolled the window down and tossed it away. When they reached their hotel room he did not spare her a look, but quickly undressed and got into the large bed, sweeping aside the foil-wrapped chocolate mints that the maid had left on the pillow. He did not try to make love to her, or even kiss her when she slipped under the eiderdown and came to nestle beside him.

He lay immobile, his back to her, torn by contradictory feelings and unable to make the only logical step. *You should put on your clothes,* he said to himself, *and get the hell out of this room, or send her away. She is the enemy, Jefferson's remote-controlled device programmed to spy on you and eventually destroy you.* The scene in The Yellow Submarine flashed through his mind in vivid detail, followed by that gray morning in Paris when he had discovered her real name, and that night of agony in Málaga when he had decided not to see her again, ever. And yet, he was unable to resist the over-whelming attraction he felt toward Jill. That particular look in her eyes, the soft caress of her lips. She could not be acting, dammit. He could not find the courage, or the indifference, to tell her to go away, even if her presence at his side might bring him to his death.

He knew that he was trapped and there was no way out. For a moment he tried to justify himself in his own eyes by pretending that it was better that way; at least he knew who the enemy was. If he sent Jill away, Jefferson would certainly find a way to plant another spy close to him, and then he would not even know the man's identity. He sighed. That was nonsense, and he knew it. It was a good excuse to give Peter Bohlen, but he should not be fooling himself. The plain truth was that he badly wanted that girl, whatever her game, and he was going to keep her with him, whatever the risks.

For a while Jill lay quiet on her side of the bed, pained by his rudeness. Was he still angry about the scene at Trader Vic's? She lovingly caressed his bare back, and her hand brushed against a small wound. He gasped, and she felt sticky blood on her fingertips. "Did you hurt yourself?" she asked, and he turned to her and said savagely: "As if you don't know!"

"No, I don't. What happened, Clint?"

He turned away again, sinking into a hostile silence. He did not talk to her anymore, and she withdrew to the edge of the large bed, puzzled and hurt. He had been so kind to her, back there in the cold, wet street; what had made him so bit-

113

ter, so cold? For a long time no sound came from his side of the bed, and she assumed that he had fallen asleep, when suddenly he grabbed the phone. "I want to call the United States," he said to the operator. "The city of Carmel, in California." He gave the area code and the number. "It's a person-to-person call for Mrs. Denise Craig."

She felt a twinge of jealousy. Was he trying to humiliate her in his own way? The mention of his ex-wife infuriated her. But then the call came through, and left her even more confused.

"Denise? It's me, Clint." She heard a faint voice, but could not make out the words.

"Yes, I'm okay. And you?"

A pause. "I am calling from Munich, Germany. Tell me, is Laurie at home?"

The voice said something.

"But she is all right, is she?" He stirred impatiently on the bed. "Look, I don't want to worry you without reason, but I am somewhat concerned about her . . . and about you, too. Somebody might try to hurt you."

He fumbled for the light switch and nervously lit a cigarillo, propping himself on his elbow. "No, I can't explain over the phone. . . . No, definitely no threat was made. . . . I am all right, I swear, safe and sound. . . . It just so happened that I had an unpleasant experience. Somebody may—I say *may*—be after me, and I am afraid they might try to hurt you or the child."

He sighed as the voice blabbered excitedly. "Yes, it might be connected with my research. . . . Yes. . . . Yes. . . . Well, the papers were exaggerating, as usual. All I wanted . . ." The voice didn't let him finish. "All I wanted . . ." he started again. Finally he seemed to lose patience. "Will you listen to me and stop being hysterical? Jesus, I am sorry, Denise, I didn't mean to be rude, I'm just a little edgy, that's all."

He listened, exhaling some white-gray smoke. "No. I told you already, nobody threatened you or the child. All I wanted is to ask you to be more watchful for the next couple of weeks. Don't let her far out of your sight. . . . Yes, a couple of weeks at most. I guess everything will calm down after the election." He suddenly shot a glance at Jill, and her blood ran cold. The election? What did he mean by that? Was her father right, after all? Was Clint really trying to destroy him? If not, why was the election so important?

114

"Maybe you could take her to your mother, and stay there for a . . . Yes, yes. . . . That will be fine. . . . Yes, I will. I promise."

He was nodding restlessly, as if he was trying to urge her to finish. "Okay. I promise. Yes, I háve your mother's number. Take care. Bye now, bye."

He switched off the light immediately, and put out his cigarillo. She moved to his side. "Clint, is something wrong? Tell me, please."

Just for a second he turned to her, and hesitantly touched her face with his fingertips. "Nothing is wrong," he said. "Go to sleep now."

She did not, and neither did he. They lay side by side, each immersed in his own thoughts, fighting his own torment, as the night hours slowly crept by. Jill stole a quick glance at the dark head resting on the pillow beside her. In the stillness of the night, all of it suddenly seemed unreal. Could it be that three days ago she did not even know this man, and would have passed him on the street without sparing him a second look? At moments, their relationship seemed so intimate, so close—and then a word, even a hint, would transform it into the most fragile thing in the world and each of them would hastily retreat into his own shell. Where did their genuine attraction end—and their game of deception start? She had phoned J.J. this afternoon, to tell him about Clint's findings in Spain. She was convinced that Clint, too, was making his own contacts with his partners without her knowledge. That was a dangerous game, and her affair with Clint seemed to be doomed from its very start. And yet, she was willing to pay that price if it could thwart the plot against her father.

There had never been anybody in her life as close to her, as beloved by her, as Jim Jefferson. Since her early childhood back in Santa Monica, she had always been her father's girl. And it was not only because he treated her with special attention, brought her the most unusual presents, put her to bed and told her stories whenever he was at home, or surprised her with unexpected outings to the county fair, an amusement park or her favorite ice-cream parlor. It was much more than that. They had been cast from the same mold, they were both stubborn, romantic, lovers of art and literature, endowed with boundless curiosity and soaring imagination. It was J.J.'s imagination—and not her mother's money, as people used to think—that had made him the computer king of the West

Coast; he had anticipated long before the others the advent of the computer age and was the first to build a huge electronic industry. It was his imagination—and not his skill for politicking—that had made him foresee the future changes in American society, and emerge as a leader with whom so many Americans could identify.

Her mother and brothers were completely different. Although a senator's daughter, and later a senator's wife, Emily Jefferson never cared for politics. Neither did Dean and Bryan, Jill's older brothers. J.J. had said once that they were rich people not only by their money, but by their mentality as well. They were passionately interested in sports and hobbies that took most of their time; they were very conscious of their social status and refrained from associating with people of a lower standing in society. They belonged to a closed circle of rich, important, blasé people, indifferent to what happened elsewhere and determined to keep it that way. She had to admit that her mother had dared to breach the sacrosanct rules of the Hobarths by marrying a penniless commoner; yet Emily had not become a Jefferson, but had very soon withdrawn to the traditional Hobarth way of life. Even for Jill's grandfather, becoming a senator had not been an attempt to solve national issues, but rather another tournament he could win with his money.

She was only thirteen when a traumatic experience made her realize that their family was split into two rival factions. She had been secretly writing poetry, and kept her notebook in a locked drawer in her desk. One summer day, when she came home she found her drawer open. The notebook was missing. She had run breathless to her mother's room, but her parents were not at home. Her attention was attracted by shouts and laughter coming from the back of the house. She found her brothers with a bunch of kids their own age— Dean was almost fifteen and Bryan sixteen—bellowing with laughter by the pool. Bryan was standing on a chair, mimicking the passionate gestures of a poet and loudly declaiming a love poem out of her own notebook, his voice booming in exaggerated pathos. For a second she stopped dead in her tracks, then she walked to him, trembling, her face deep purple. "Give me that!" she cried, seething with anger. But he just laughed and tossed the notebook to Dean, who ran around the pool, jumped on a table and continued the recitation, triggering another wave of laughter. And so she scurried back and forth around the pool, in tears, while they threw the

116

notebook to each other, reading aloud her verse, mocking her, exposing her most precious secret. She had never been so humiliated in her life. Finally the inevitable happened: the notebook had fallen into the water, and only then did they let her fish it out, while they went away.

Her mother and father had found her sitting by the pool, bitterly crying, trying to dry the pages on which her poems were quickly turning into unintelligible smudges. Her mother had angrily scolded Dean and Bryan. There had been a severe punishment, as far as she remembered. But all that Emily Jefferson had found necessary to tell her was: "I did not know that you write poetry, Jill. You did not have to hide it; that's perfectly natural at your age."

Jim Jefferson, on the other hand, had hugged and consoled his "little Princess Jillian" until she had stopped crying. He had taken her to her room and had stayed there half the night helping her to copy the poems into a clean notebook, meticulously restoring words and phrases out of the stains of diluted ink. Then they had read her poems together, discussed them at length, and her father had soberly analyzed the influence of English and American poets on her verse. It had finally turned out to be an enchanting night, as she and J.J., their eyes shining with excitement, had talked for hours about a subject that was so dear to both of them. He had brought several books from his study and had read to her, and she had gone to sleep with a happy smile on her face. Yet she was to remember her father's casual remark about Dean and Bryan: "Let them be. They just don't understand those things." And she knew that night that she and J.J. were a breed apart, very different from her mother and the boys.

Her father's affair with Rosalynn Ross, and the family drama that ensued, had strongly affected her. Her parents had tried to conceal their bitter clashes from her knowledge. But she had overheard a little, and guessed the rest, even before they decided to send her away from home. She understood her father; Emily Hobarth was certainly not the type of woman this passionate, ardent man needed by his side. On the other hand, in teenaged Jill's idealistic conception of the world, gratitude and loyalty played an important part. Emily Hobarth rebelled against her family to marry Jim Jefferson, and he should not have forgotten that, ever. Her mother's death a couple of years later had been a terrible shock to her. For a while she refused to accept her father's phone calls to Paris, and returned his letters unopened. He had finally flown to France and had spent a week with her. For the first time, he had talked to her openly about Emily's death. He had candidly admitted that her mother had broken down and started drinking when she had learned about his affair with Rosalynn Ross. Still, J.J. had said, there had been a genuine reconciliation between them, even a new kind of warm, honest love. And then, all of a sudden, when she seemed to be recovering, the strange accident had happened. Since then, he had not known a single moment of peace.

Her father's frankness, his obvious pain, had rekindled Jill's affection for him. He had succeeded in convincing her that his guilt in her mother's suicide had been less than she had believed. Or maybe she had wanted to be convinced. She was not eighteen anymore; she had begun to understand the cruel complexity of life.

It was not because of her mother that she had taken the Hobarth name. But she had kept it as a tribute to her memory. Furthermore, as the prestige of her father grew in America and abroad, she became determined to prove that she was able to succeed on her own merits. When she had gotten her first assignment from a prestigious American magazine as Jill Hobarth, expert on French art and literature stationed in Paris, she had felt an overwhelming satisfaction. She had done it. She was able to pull herself up by her own bootstraps. Her happiest year had been the one before last, when she had stopped cashing the checks her father sent her regularly, and had made her own living. But then she had come back to New York and met Burt, who was a very successful television producer, very competent in his job, very good-looking, and very efficient in bed. And he just could not understand what else she could want.

Clint stirred beside her, and looked at the luminous dial of his watch, interrupting her train of thought. He turned to her and lightly touched her bare shoulder. "We must get up, Jill," he said evenly. "We have to catch the first train to Nuremberg."

It had snowed all night, and the old city of Nuremberg, huddling behind its medieval walls, looked like an enchanted kingdom. Jill contemplated with fascination the centuries-old houses and churches, picturesque vestiges of the ancient Free Imperial City. The Hauptmarkt—the main square—was extraordinarily peaceful, covered with virgin snow and dominated by the old Frauenkirche, a fourteenth-century Gothic

118

church displaying a triangular facade topped by a little tower. The view reminded Jill of a tourist brochure she had seen earlier in the Grand Hotel, about the Christmas toy market that every year transformed the main square into a magic children's world. "Germany is a winter legend," Jill murmured. "Who said that? Heine?"

Clint did not answer, and she stealthily glanced at his drawn, tired face. He was remote and reserved this morning, and had barely talked to her during the train ride from Munich. In the Grand Hotel, by the railroad station, he had busied himself with the telephone and, after a few phone calls, had dryly suggested a short walk to the old city. While they strolled along the picturesque streets, she noticed that he was rather high-strung and kept looking back over his shoulder. Even now, on the Hauptmarkt, he seemed more interested in the few passersby who hurried about than in the marvels of Gothic architecture before them.

The big clock on the Frauenkirche chimed twelve. She looked up at the old church. Under the brightly painted clock, red-robed mechanical figures were emerging from a trap door and slowly passing in front of a bigger effigy before they disappeared through a second aperture. This was the *Männleinlaufen*, the mechanical clock built in the early sixteenth century, that represented the seven Electors paying homage to Emperor Charles IV.

Clint did not wait for the ceremony to end. "Come," he said to her, his voice a little softer. "We have an appointment to keep."

The taxi carried a pleasant smell of pine, thanks to a conifer-shaped air purifier that hung under the steering wheel. The sallow-faced young driver carelessly gunned his car through the slushy streets, and took the way east, past the railway station and the Opera, until he reached the drab Fürtherstrasse. He stopped in front of a stolid dark-gray building topped by a typical Nuremberg roof and poorly embellished by two onion-shaped green domes crowning its round towers. A small sign affixed to the wall carried the inscription *Justizgebäude*. The two identical porches were adorned by statues of two men and two women, protected by a net from the disrespectful practices of the city pigeons. The building as a whole, although very large, looked rather insignificant. Jill noticed, however, that Clint seemed profoundly affected by its sight. "In this house," he murmured, briefly glancing at her, "were tried the vilest criminals in history."

They walked in. A uniformed janitor gave them detailed instructions, and they climbed the large wooden staircase to the second floor. A big painting on their left represented Samson slaughtering the Philistines with a donkey's jawbone. They walked through a large hallway whose arched ceiling was supported by massive marble columns. On the third door on their right was pinned a small visiting card bearing the name Werner Lischke. Clint knocked and moved aside, to let Jill enter first. A small man with an open face, clear brown eyes and sparse gray hair got up from behind his desk. "Fraulein Hobarth? Herr Craig?" He smiled warmly. "Come in, please. I have been expecting you."

They sat on simple wooden chairs facing him. "I must apologize"—he raised his hands, palms up—"that we have not a small library, or a museum, even not the tiniest cubicle in this whole building, commemorating the Nuremberg trial. Nothing!" He had a clipped German accent, but his English was good and fluent. "The clerks in this building don't even know where the courtroom was. All we have got is a set of about twenty photographs, in my office, which we show to the visitors lucky enough to get here." He reached over to the shelf behind him for a thin folder coated in peeling plastic. He handed it to Jill. A faded inscription in German and English was stamped on the black cover: "Nuremberg trial, November 20, 1945—October 1, 1946. Photographs from the trial of the major Nazi criminals by the International military tribunal in Nuremberg."

"That's all we have got," he repeated. A thoughtful expression settled on his face. "You will not believe how quickly people forget. Try to ask young people in the streets of Nuremberg. Many of them don't even know that there has ever been a Nuremberg trial. The same here, in this building. Young people come here every day, sit in the same courtroom, without even suspecting that the most dramatic trial in history was held in this building. When they showed this American movie . . . *Holocaust,* on television a couple of years ago, millions of Germans were deeply shocked. They didn't know." He sighed.

"And you?" Clint asked straightforwardly. "When did *you* get shocked?"

"Me?" Werner Lischke did not seem to take offense. He smiled sadly. "I got my shock on the twentieth of November, nineteen forty-five."

120

Jill glanced at the inscription on the folder she was still holding, then back at him. "You mean the same day . . ."

"Yes, Miss Hobarth. The same day that the trial opened. I was a young advocate, doing my training in the office of Mr. Brunow, Gunter Brunow. Our office had been appointed by the tribunal as referee on German law, in connection with any legal points that could arise during the trial. You know, of course, that the accused were represented by German lawyers. That's how I came in that courtroom, to assist at the trial." His smile turned bitter, and the pale skin stretched on his high cheekbones. "I was a young German, raised in the Nazi propaganda, firmly believing what I was told, trained in the Hitler Youth. . . . And all of a sudden, to be faced with such horrors. My whole world crumbled to pieces."

"You mean that you discovered the truth through the trial?" Clint asked.

"Some truth." Lischke nodded. "Some truth. We saw here the first movies about the concentration camps, the heaps of corpses, the ovens, the gas chambers. The whole courtroom was sobbing and crying, even—you won't believe it—some of the accused. But their tears were crocodile tears." He paused. "Well, I may say that the Nuremberg trial shaped my whole life. I decided to stay here—I am originally from Hanover—and devote my life to the study of the trial and its proceedings. My official position here is legal adviser to the penal court, but most of my time is devoted to historical research."

He walked to the window and stared outside. "You had to see this place when the trial started. All around, heaps of black ruins, a stench of dead corpses—they said there were about six thousand bodies buried in the bombed houses—and an angry crowd of Germans who wanted to lynch Goering, Streicher, Rosenberg. And the Americans"—he shrugged—"they had turned this courthouse into a fortress. There were five Sherman tanks in the courtyard, infantry positions, machine-gun nests all over and even in the corridors of this building. There were wild rumors of an imminent Nazi uprising, and the Allies were very nervous. Could you imagine—a Nazi uprising in nineteen forty-five, with four huge occupation armies controlling this country?" He came back to his desk but did not sit down. "Well." His voice suddenly became practical. "I should not be wasting your time. Let me show you the courtroom and the prison block—and then we'll talk, all right?"

"Fine," Clint said, quickly glancing at Jill. She nodded and smiled at Werner Lischke. She liked his open manner and his candid sincerity.

"Let's go, then."

He led the way through the arched hall to a big wooden door bearing the inscription *Schwurgerichts Sitzungssaal.*

"It all happened here," he said in a low voice. "In courtroom six hundred. It was too small, so somebody suggested to hold the trial in the opera house, but the British objected. They refused to have the Nazis tried in what they called a 'music hall.' They feared that the trial might be considered as a parody of justice." He reached for the handle. "We must be very quiet inside," he apologized. "There is a trial going on."

Room six hundred was half empty. It was a big rectangular room, its walls and ceiling covered with brown wood panels. The big doors were framed in portals of green marble, crowned with oval shields representing various symbols of justice. The shield over the door on the left showed Adam and Eve under the tree of knowledge. The room was illuminated by tall narrow windows and several fluorescent lights. The judge sat on the bench, under a big crucifix. An aging bald man was sitting in the box of the accused, flanked by two policemen.

They sat in the back of the room. "For the purpose of the trial, they had built a big gallery here," Lischke murmured, pointing to the high ceiling. "That was for the press and the movie cameras. The box of the accused was bigger, of course; they had twenty-one defendants sitting there. There were to be twenty-three, but Robert Ley committed suicide at the beginning of the proceedings and Bormann was tried *in absentia.*"

"Where was Goering sitting?" Clint asked in a whisper.

"On the extreme left, first row," Lischke said. "I'll show you the pictures later. The prisoners would come through this door, right behind the box of the accused. Behind it there was an elevator that took them to an underground gallery connecting the courtroom with the prison block. The elevator is still there, by the way. There were plenty of American Military Police around here, all of them armed, in brown uniforms and white helmets."

The judge said something and the public, mostly old people and a couple of teenagers, laughed loudly. The accused shifted uneasily on his seat.

"What did he say?" Jill asked. "What is this man being tried for?"

Lischke's face broke into a tight smile. "This poor devil is accused of running a not very orthodox massage parlor. You can imagine the sort of humor that may provoke."

They rose and quietly left the courtroom. Clint was smiling.

"What is so funny?" she asked.

"I find it very reassuring," he said cheerfully. "It's comforting to find out that the same courtroom where mass murderers were once tried is used today for pimps' trials."

"Let's hope it always will be," Lischke said softly.

They went into the courtyard, Lischke flashed his pass to the guards at the door and they walked into the former maximum-security block, where Goering and his cronies had been jailed thirty-five years ago.

It was like penetrating into an eerie world of ghosts. Their steps echoed on the stone floor of the disused prison, and the gloomy darkness of the empty, cold passage inspired a feeling of anguish. The electrical supply had been disconnected long ago, and their only light came from the heavy lantern Werner Lischke carried above his head. He did not turn back, not once. The yellow flame in the lantern would flicker now and again as he swung it to point at one of the solid iron doors along the walls and announce: "Ribbentrop . . . Keitel . . . Kaltenbrunner . . . Rosenberg . . . Streicher . . . Jodl . . . Frick . . . Frank . . . Sauckel . . . Seyss-Inquart . . . Goering."

Eleven cells, Clint counted. Eleven names. The most odious Nazi criminals had spent their last two weeks in that death row before they were hanged in the nearby *gymnasium*, on October 15, 1946.

They stopped in front of Goering's cell. In the dim light of the lantern it was impossible to discern anything inside. "He died here," Lischke said. "On the night of the execution, barely a few hours before being hanged. At ten forty-five the guard at the door noticed that he was behaving strangely. He was lying on his bed, his body shaken by violent spasms, his legs kicking. He seemed to be choking. The guard started to shout, and very soon the officer on duty and the prison physician were there. But it was too late. He died from a massive dose of cyanide."

"Suicide," Jill said.

Lischke hesitated for a split second. "Yes. Of course. Suicide."

They went out into the courtyard. The clouds had dispersed and the snow was already melting in the bright sunshine. They returned to Lischke's office, and he had some coffee and sandwiches brought from the canteen. Jill left her food untouched.

Clint was pensive, and studied Lischke's face over the rim of the cup. "You had a moment of doubt before," he observed, "when Miss Hobarth asked you about Goering's suicide. You were not so sure it was suicide. Why, Herr Lischke?"

Lischke did not answer immediately. He ran his fingers through his sparse hair and leaned back in his chair. "I am not so sure it was suicide, that's right," he admitted. "For one main reason: I still don't understand how Goering got the poison."

"But they said he had a capsule . . ." Jill began. "I read somewhere that he had left a note explaining that he had the poison capsule hidden in a container of pomade."

"Nonsense," Lischke countered impatiently. "He had no cyanide capsule, neither on his body, nor anywhere in his cell. During the trial I became quite close to some of the security officers of the prison. Do you think they did not fear he might kill himself? They were obsessed with the idea that Goering might commit suicide and 'cheat the tribunal.' So they searched his cell and his clothes daily, with the utmost care. He could not possibly have concealed a capsule of poison."

He paused briefly. "The version that my colleagues have come to accept was that the capsule was smuggled to him during the last forty-eight hours of his life. They believe that he got the poison from another prison inmate, SS General von dem Bach-Zelewski. Every time he crossed the path of Goering in the hallway, Zelewski would greet him very respectfully, and the last time they met he insisted on shaking his hand."

"That means nothing," Clint said.

"Of course. But Von dem Bach-Zelewski himself boasted to the commission of inquiry that he had provided Goering with a capsule of poison. In nineteen fifty-one he even produced a capsule identical to the one which was found under Goering's bed."

"And you don't accept that?" Jill asked, frowning with surprise. She seemed engrossed in Lischke's account.

"No. Believe me, Miss Hobarth, I checked everything thoroughly. I reconstructed Goering's schedule to the very minute. He had been searched twice after he met Von dem Bach-Zelewski for the last time. He did not have the capsule. And another thing: if Zelewski really had smuggled the poison to him, why did he wait until fifty-one, six long years, to produce another capsule? Why did he not show it to his guards the same week, the next week? For a simple reason. He did not have one. I believe that a few years later somebody provided Zelewski with an identical capsule for him to show the Americans, to definitely establish the version of suicide, and put an end to the rumors concerning Goering's death."

Clint eagerly leaned forward. "You say 'somebody provided Zelewski.' Who? Do you suspect anybody?" He glanced at Jill, who swiftly lowered her eyes.

Lischke shrugged. "No, I don't. I am sorry. I could never pinpoint any particular person or group who could have done that."

"Herr Lischke," Clint said. "Let me offer a theory I have." He took a deep breath. "I believe that Goering was murdered or forced to kill himself, which amounts to the same thing. I believe that his death was connected with the treasures he had stolen and concealed all over Europe—the notorious 'Phantom operation.' Let me give you an account of my theory, and I shall be very grateful for your comments."

Lischke looked at him with interest. "Why, certainly," he said. "Please, go ahead."

Clint spoke at length, describing his thesis in detail; he did not omit a concise account of his own findings in Paris, Ronda and Munich. Lischke seemed deeply intrigued, but once Clint had finished, he shook his head. "It is a fascinating theory, I must admit, Herr Craig. It sounds very logical too. But I can't accept it."

"Why?" Clint asked eagerly. "Do you see any errors, or any inconsistencies in my conception?"

"No, no, on the contrary. You have done your homework well, and I must congratulate you for that. Your errors are very minor. You did not mention that Rosenberg also played a part in the plunder of the art treasures of France. Did you know that he had created a special command—*Einsatzstab* Rosenberg—that stole more than twenty thousand objets d'art in France alone? They also reaped the art treasures of the East: icons, paintings, rare artifacts. The most famous was the magnificent amber room which had been given to

Czar Peter the Great of Russia by the Prussian King Friedrich Wilhelm the First, in the seventeenth century. It was a whole room, overlaid with carved pieces of the finest amber. It was virtually priceless. Peter had it set in his palace at Tsarskoye Selo, near Leningrad. Rosenberg had it dismantled in nineteen forty-one. It was never seen again."

"I know about it," Clint remarked. "I just did not mention it."

Lischke shrugged. "Well, this whole aspect is irrelevant, as most of Rosenberg's take finally found its way to Goering's art collections." He took another sip of his coffee. "No, there are no real flaws in your theory, Herr Craig. It just seems too fantastic to me. I could not imagine how anybody could secretly contact Goering despite all the security measures in Nuremberg, squeeze from him the information about the hiding places of the treasure, and finally get him killed."

"Maybe this somebody, this American I am looking for, had promised Goering to save him from the gallows?"

A peculiar expression settled on Lischke's features. "Is there any evidence that makes you think so?" he quickly asked.

"No. Why?"

"It is strange that you speak of such a promise. Because if there ever was something which we all felt at Nuremberg, it was that Goering was convinced he would not hang."

"What do you mean by that?"

Lischke got up and started pacing around the small office, speaking earnestly. "You had to see Goering in Nuremberg, Herr Craig. The man was calm, confident, sure of himself to the point of insolence. He would often laugh and joke; he never showed any sign of fear. It was a strange phenomenon. You only had to see the others. With the exception, maybe, of Albert Speer and Von Papen, who did not risk their heads, most of the others were obviously frightened, and some had lost all human dignity. But Goering—he behaved as if nothing would happen to him. He fought back the American prosecutor, Jackson, as an equal. He even transformed the courtroom into an instrument for his Nazi propaganda. I remember an incident, when he was loudly talking to . . . to Ribbentrop, I believe, and an American soldier touched him on the shoulder, to make him stop. He looked at him angrily and brushed his shoulder, at the place where the fingers of the American had touched him. He seemed very sure of himself. Let me show you!"

Lischke bent over the desk, reached for the black folder and leafed through the collection of pictures from the trial. Goering could be seen in most of them, sitting in his corner, giving evidence in the witness box, listening to the prosecution speeches. He was neatly dressed in his *Reichsmarschall's* uniform. Once he could be seen wearing a light summer suit and a tie. He looked thinner and healthier than usual. His large, heavy-jowled face was groomed and his dark hair was neatly combed. In all the pictures he was either smiling or serenely surveying the courtroom. The other defendants in the box of the accused looked gloomy and depressed.

"You see? He looks as if he knows for sure that he will save his neck. There was even a rumor at the beginning of the trial that before he surrendered to General Stack, of the Seventh American Army, he secretly had met an American emissary who had promised him that his life would be spared. But as I told you before, there were so many rumors drifting about in Nuremberg . . ."

"Was he as calm even after he had been sentenced to death?" Jill asked.

"Oh yes, definitely. He had appealed for clemency and expected that his appeal would be accepted. As a matter of fact, his appeal was rejected by the Allied Control Commission in Berlin barely two hours before he committed suicide. But he did not know that! Colonel Andrus, the chief of security of the prison, had the cable about the rejection in his pocket when he was called to witness Goering's last convulsions."

"That's really strange," Clint said. "But you have to admit that what you say actually corroborates my version."

Lischke shrugged. "Maybe. But frankly, I still can't believe it."

Clint idly leafed through the photographs of the trial. He had seen hundreds of them before, and yet, he had not given a thought to the aloofness displayed by Goering. But something in Lischke's words bothered him. Lischke doubted if anybody could get to Goering, through the security measures in the prison. But somebody did get to him, so there must have been a way!

He turned to Lischke again. "Do you have any logbook, where the visits to Goering's cell were recorded?"

"Yes, of course," Lischke replied. "The security system in the prison was very tight. Each visitor who came to see an inmate had to sign the logbook of the prison, and was then escorted to the cell of the prisoner he was going to visit. The guard on duty at the cell door would record the time and length of the visit in a second logbook, make the visitor sign it, and then have him escorted back to the exit."

"May I see the logbook for Goering's cell?" Clint asked.

"Of course. I have all the originals here. The copies are in the archives of the four Allied powers. If you'll excuse me for a moment, I'll get the logbook for you."

Five minutes later Lischke was back, carrying a fat oblong notebook bound in green cardboard. Clint bent over the desk and went through the logbook page by page. He noticed that several people had visited Goering's cell quite frequently: Colonel Andrus, the chief of security; Major Airey Neave of the British Army, who had served the indictments; Dr. Hoffmann, the prison physician; an officer of the British MI-6, Derek Hamilton; two Russian officers, Korolenko and Zagarov; a special agent Jones of American Military Intelligence; Major Kevin Sheppard, the secretary of the tribunal.

"You know who Kevin Sheppard is, of course," Lischke said. "He became a justice in the Supreme Court of the United States. He lives in Washington now; I think he is retired. He can tell you quite a few things about the case."

Craig nodded. With growing interest he scanned the pages, and turned the leaf of October 14. And all of a sudden he became very still.

The next leaf had been torn out, long ago.

The record of October 15, 1946, the day Goering died, was missing.

Chapter Seven:

October 25—October 26:

SHOT

Dusk was falling when they came back to the Old City. The cab driver entered the ancient part of Nuremberg through the Haller Gate, and turned to the right at Maxplatz. Sommerweg was a peaceful narrow street which offered a view of the beautiful *Weinstadel*. "*Schön, ja?*" The elderly driver smiled, lovingly motioning at the half-timbered medieval building. "Once this was lazar house, for lepers, *später* wine storehouse, *und jetzt*—hostel for students." He slowed down, looking for a parking place. Jill pointed to a beautiful covered bridge that lay over the still waters of the Pegnitz River. "What is the name of this bridge?" she asked the German.

"*Henkersteg*," the driver readily answered. "Hangman's bridge."

"Very appropriate," Clint grunted without looking at Jill. His thoughts were far away, trying to pierce the secret of that night, the fifteenth of October, 1946. The night when Master Sergeant John C. Woods of San Antonio, Texas, who was reputed to have hanged more than three hundred convicted American soldiers in fifteen years, passed the noose around the necks of the Nazi criminals condemned to death at the Nuremberg Palace of Justice. All but one. Hermann Goering. In the private collection of Werner Lischke there was a picture of Goering lying dead on top of his coffin, shortly after his alleged suicide. His thin lips were parted in a last rictus, and his right eye was half open. Somebody had tucked an Army blanket under his head and thrown a shirt over his chest. An oblong slip of paper, carrying the name "H. Goering" in block letters, was placed on top of the shirt. Beside him lay the coffin of Ribbentrop. The picture had been taken before the eleven coffins had been hauled onto military trucks and carried to the death camp of Dachau. The horrible ovens, where so many thousands of innocent victims had been burned, had been set alight for a last time that night. In a strange act of poetic justice, the bodies of the Nazi criminals had been cremated in the Dachau ovens, and their ashes had been secretly thrown into a river.

Clint sighed. The freshly stirred memories of the Nuremberg trials, the war, the death of his father, had opened old wounds and upset him deeply, more than he wanted to admit to Jill. Yet he had to return to reality and proceed with his investigation. The ashes of Goering, carried by the unnamed river to the sea, had taken with them the secret of his death. There was no record of the people who had visited the *Reichsmarschall* during his last day on earth. Lischke had been as puzzled as he when he found out that the crucial page was missing from the logbook. The enigma was still unsolved.

The cab stopped, and the driver pointed to a house surrounded by a pleasant courtyard. "This is number thirty-two, *mein Herr*."

Clint raised his eyes and spoke to the driver. "Will you wait for us here? We shall be back in about half an hour."

"Yes, good." The friendly driver nodded vigorously, and swiftly ran around the car to open the door for Jill.

Clint got out of the car and contemplated the house. A rectangular copper plaque affixed to one of the gateposts carried the inscription: *Dr. Julius Hoffmann*. The narrow gate was open and he let Jill pass before him. This was going to be their last visit in Nuremberg, and maybe in Germany. Their last effort to solve, here, at least a part of the mystery.

Dr. Hoffmann, who had been the prison physician during the Nuremberg trial, lived in a small, tidy cottage, built in pseudomedieval style. The house was quiet, and a single light burned on the porch. They climbed the three low steps and Clint rang the bell. Almost immediately quick footsteps were heard inside and the door opened. An old woman dressed in black appeared in front of them, a grave expression on her pale face. She was tall and very thin, but her throat was abnormally swelled, probably as a result of a malfunction of her thyroid gland. "*Guten Abend*," she quietly said.

"Good evening," Clint answered. "Do you speak English?"

"A little." She looked puzzled.

"We would like to see Doctor Hoffmann," Clint went on. "My name is Clint Craig. I am a writer from the United States, and this is Miss Hobarth."

The woman stood in silence for a moment, then sadly shook her head. "I am afraid this is impossible," she said.

"Why? Is the doctor busy?"

"Come in, please." She led them into a small vestibule, furnished with a brown leather sofa and a couple of chairs. A coat rack stood in the corner. She did not invite them to sit down.

"Herr Doktor Hoffmann died a week ago," the black-clothed woman said. "I am sorry if you came specially. You should have telephoned first."

"Oh, I am sorry." Clint was embarrassed, groping for words. "I didn't realize, Mrs. . . . Mrs. . . . ."

"I am Mrs. Stahl. I am the housekeeper."

Clint nodded. "I understand. Was the doctor very ill?"

Her expression did not change. "Not at all. He was old but very healthy. He had an unfortunate accident."

"An accident?" He quickly raised his eyes. "What kind of accident?"

"The electricity," she said, seeming in difficulty to find the right words. "He tried to repair a short . . ."

". . . A short circuit?" Clint helped.

"Yes, a short circuit." Pain flashed in the brown eyes. "He was alone at home, and something was wrong with the electricity, so he tried to repair it. He got a very strong electroshock. We found him in his study. He was still holding an electric wire. His fingers were burned, black." Her voice broke, but she did not cry.

"I am very sorry to hear that, Frau Stahl," Clint said softly, and Jill nodded sympathetically. "May I offer you my condolences?" He bowed courteously, but his brain was already dissecting the information and flashing signals of doubt through his mind. Another accident. Another coincidence.

He cleared his throat. "Excuse me for asking, but was this a habit with him? I mean, did he used to repair things that went wrong in the house?"

"No," she said, and a slight look of annoyance came into her eyes. "He never did. He was such a careful man, he would always call an electrician or a plumber. Nobody could understand how that happened." She paused, her eyes still glued to Clint's face. "May I help in any way?" she offered, in the same even voice.

"No, thank you, thank you indeed. Excuse us for disturbing you. We had no idea . . . Good-bye."

"*Auf Wiedersehen,*" the housekeeper echoed and softly closed the door behind them.

As they walked out through the small garden, Jill murmured: "That is someone who will never tell how Goering really died." Clint, immersed in thought, did not answer.

Darkness had already settled. A soft glow came from the far end of the street, where the Weinstadel and the Henkersteg were artfully illuminated. The cab was parked in the deserted street, right in front of them. The driver was not in it. They saw him standing at the corner, contemplating the old buildings. Clint called him softly and waved, and the old man returned his wave and hurried back. Jill shivered slightly. Clint opened the back door of the car to let her in.

The shots echoed sharply in the stillness of the night. The first bullet grazed Clint's right arm, and he gasped in dismay. Instinctively Jill threw herself on him and violently shoved him to the right, falling on top of him.

The second and third bullets hit her in the back, and she slowly collapsed beside the car.

There was no fourth shot.

Clint was back on his feet, but he only glimpsed the shadows of the two men as they quickly ran down the narrow street, their footsteps echoing in the distance.

Inspector Helmut Brandt was surprisingly young and impeccably dressed in a dark brown suit, light beige shirt and rust-colored tie. His straight honey-blond hair was neatly brushed back, his moustache recently trimmed, and his manner was courteous. The only disconcerting thing about him was the fixed, penetrating stare of his pale green eyes, which did not for a moment leave those of his interlocutor, seeming to probe deep into his mind. He closely watched Clint Craig, who sat in front of him, his face unshaven, his eyes bloodshot, his right shirtsleeve cut above the elbow, where a dressing had been applied to his wound. They were sitting in the office of the chief administrator of the Nuremberg municipal hospital. It was past midnight, but the inspector looked fresh and alert. Now and again, a policeman in green uniform would knock on the door, bend over the inspector and respectfully whisper in his ear; occasionally, the telephone would ring, and Brandt would pick it up, listen and say a few words in a soft voice. But even then his eyes would not turn away from Clint's face, would continue to observe him attentively, watching for his slightest reaction.

"Could you be so kind and tell me again what did you do since you arrived in Nuremberg?" he asked politely.

"How many times must I repeat that?" Clint exclaimed in

exasperation. "You asked me and I told you. I have nothing to add, for God's sake!"

"Please, tell me one more time." Inspector Brandt looked unperturbed.

Clint breathed deeply and ran his fingers through his hair, disarraying it further. "We arrived in Nuremberg at half past nine from Munich, we checked in at the Grand Hotel, I called the Palace of Justice and fixed an appointment with Herr Lischke for twelve thirty, then we went for a stroll in the Old City. At twelve o'clock we took a cab to the Palace of Justice, spent the afternoon with Herr Lischke, and left shortly before six P.M. The cab took us to Dr. Hoffmann's house, at Sommerweg."

"Didn't you call Dr. Hoffmann before you left?"

Clint sighed and angrily shook his head. "I told you I didn't. If I had, I would have known that he was dead and wouldn't have gone there."

"Did you tell Herr Lischke that you were going to see Dr. Hoffmann?"

"No. I told you that before."

"Did anybody know that you were going to see Dr. Hoffmann?"

"Nobody."

With a slight gesture, Inspector Brandt touched the tip of his moustache. "So you just decided on the spur of the moment to see Dr. Hoffmann."

"No. I intended to see him, but didn't tell anybody about that."

"Not even Miss Hobarth?"

"I told you that before."

"And you just came out of the house, and somebody shot at you?"

"Exactly." Clint could hardly control himself. Jill had been in surgery for two hours already, and all he wanted was to see her, to be assured that she would live. They had told him before they wheeled her into the operating room that her chances were good, but then they always said that.

"You have no idea who shot at you?" the inspector continued in his flat voice.

"Listen," Clint exploded, "would you stop throwing these stupid questions at me? I gave you all the answers two hours ago. Am I the criminal, or those thugs who ran away half an hour before your policemen deigned to appear?"

"We are doing our jobs the best way we can," Inspector

Brandt calmly answered. "This is a strange affair and I am trying to solve it." He leaned back in his chair. "Do you have any enemies, Mr. Craig?"

"Not that I know of," he said.

"Nobody threatened you, in Munich, or here, or in France before you came?"

He managed to keep his face impassive. "No."

"And no attempt was made on your life before?"

"No. I told you that."

"But do you have any idea who might want to kill you?"

Clint shrugged. "No, no idea." He paused, then asked aggressively: "How do you know they were after me, and not after Miss Hobarth?"

"Oh, they were after you all right. She was hit by mistake, no doubt about that."

Clint stared at him, amazed. "By mistake? What do you mean by that?"

The inspector spoke with authority. "We checked the trajectory and the impact of the bullets. We also established exactly where the man with the gun was standing."

"There were two of them," Clint said quickly.

"Yes, but only one fired. We found all the bullets, and they were all fired from the same gun, a Beretta nine millimeter. When you went out of Dr. Hoffmann's house, the killer was standing under a big oak tree, slightly off the entrance—barely three meters, which is approximately nine to ten feet. I still cannot understand how he missed you. You were—how is the American expression—you were a sitting duck. Any child could have killed you with the first bullet from such a distance."

"Well, he hit my arm."

For the first time, Brandt's face changed its expression and his pressed lips twisted in contempt. "That was as good as missing you." He paused. "Anyway, Miss Hobarth was on your left side, away from the trajectory of the bullet. Now, when this man fired at you, she hurled herself upon you, and pushed you down, to the right. In doing so, she also fell to the right, and crossed the trajectory of the second and the third bullets. That's how she was hit."

"So, if she had just stood where she was . . ." Clint began, all blood draining from his face.

"If she had just stood where she was, she would not have been hit. By the way, you would not have been hit either.

134

The second and third bullets were fired even more to the right than the first one. It's a strange affair, indeed . . ."

But Clint was not listening anymore. The door had opened, and the stout, blond nurse who had escorted Jill into surgery looked in. A big smile flourished on her large warm face. "You can see her now," she cheerfully announced. "She will be all right."

Clint didn't spare a look for the inspector, but darted out of the room and along the corridor. The blond nurse hurried after him, laughing and shouting directions. A moment later he entered Jill's room, his heart pounding like a sledgehammer in his chest. The room was plunged in shadow. A single light burned on a small white table by the door. The figure on the bed lay immobile, breathing heavily, her arms sprawled. From plastic bottles hanging over her head, plasma and glucose were dripping into thin transparent tubes connected to her veins. A stock man in a white blouse was bent over her. He straightened up and came into the light, and Clint recognized the surgeon who had talked to him before. "I am Dr. Ruecke," the man said. "I operated on her. We extracted the bullets. She will recover quickly. No vital organs were damaged."

"Thank you, Doctor," Clint murmured and made a step toward the bed, as the surgeon went out and softly closed the door behind him.

The figure on the bed stirred. "Clint?" she whispered in a small voice, slightly slurred. He swiftly moved to the bed and crouched beside her, his head almost touching the pillow. Her hair was fanned on the whiteness of the sheet. Her face was deathly pale, and her open eyes were unfocused, the pupils still dilated under the effect of the anesthesia.

"Clint . . ." she murmured again.

"Don't talk," he hushed her, and hesitantly touched her face. "The doctor said you would be okay. In a couple of days they will let you out of here, as good as new." He smiled, but felt a strange sensation of choking, and his eyes grew damp. He bit his lip. "I am getting sentimental," he whispered in silly apology.

"I . . ." she began.

"You saved my life," he said slowly, caressing her face, while the cold account of the inspector rang over and over in his ears. "You almost got killed to save my life." He drew nearer, careful not to touch the plastic tubes hanging about her, and buried his head against her neck, detecting the faint

135

fragrance of her perfume beneath the strong odors of antiseptic. His lips touched her ear. "I love you," he whispered, so spontaneously that he was himself surprised. She did not move and he said again, very softly: "I love you, Jill."

The door opened and the blond nurse stuck her head in. "You must go out now, Herr Craig. She must rest. You'll come again tomorrow, all right?"

He pressed his lips to the cold cheek and went out. The bright light in the corridor made his eyes blink. Or maybe it was not the light.

From his hotel he called Jefferson's campaign headquarters in Washington. It was late evening, but Ralph Dowden, the chief of staff, was still in the office. When he heard Craig's name he sounded reserved, but his reticence turned to genuine concern as Clint told him about Jill. "Do you want me to connect you with J.J.?" Ralph asked. "He's in Minnesota. I can get hold of him in minutes."

"No." He did not want to talk to Jefferson, not now. "I just want you to give him the news. Carefully. Tell him that he has nothing to worry about. Jill's wounds are light; she'll be out of the hospital in a couple of days. I think they can talk over the phone tomorrow. She has been admitted to the hospital as Jill Hobarth, and the police promised to keep the newspapers off the story for the time being, but I did not want to take any chances. I don't want Jim to learn about the shooting from a newscast."

"I certainly appreciate that, Clint," Ralph said a little more warmly.

His next call was to Peter Bohlen. By the exclamations on the other end of the line he could tell that Peter was deeply worried. "I warned you that this thing was too big for us," Bohlen said finally. "You may get killed, Clint. It's not a joke. Those guys mean business."

"Well, I mean business too," he said softly but stubbornly. "They just chose the wrong approach, Peter. I don't like to be pushed around, and I won't chicken because a couple of gunmen who don't even know how to shoot straight ambushed me in a deserted street. All these attempts are the best proof that I'm on the right track. I am flying back tomorrow. I have some work to do in Washington. I'll call you as soon as I know what my schedule is."

Early in the morning he was back in Jill's room at the hospital. She was propped up in bed; her soft hair combed, and there was just a tinge of color in her cheeks. For a moment he stood awkwardly by the door, not knowing where to put the huge bunch of red roses he had bought on his way, until a nurse came in with a big vase, and with the warning that he had just a minute, as the doctors' morning round was about to start.

He tenderly kissed Jill, and told her of his talk with her father's aide. "You'll call him today, promise?" She nodded. There was a strange radiance in her eyes that he had not seen before. He took her hand to conceal his confusion. "I . . . I shall have to leave you here, Jill. I know it's a disgusting thing to do, but I have no choice, really. I must check a few details, back in Washington."

She said nothing, just watched him with her big, clear eyes.

"They'll take good care of you here, and you'll be safe. Safer than in my company."

"I didn't complain," she murmured.

"No, that's true, you didn't." He paused again. "When you feel better—let's say in a week—you can join me. Will you?"

She smiled faintly. "Do you really want me to join you?"

"Oh yes," he said fervently. "Yes, I do."

"I shall join you." She still had difficulty in talking and her voice was very low. "I'll join you, but not as a watchdog."

Her frankness surprised him. "Do you trust me now?"

She nodded.

He bent over the pale, distraught face, and kissed the full lips. Her mouth was dry but warm, and its response sent a current through his body.

"Take care," she murmured. "Please, Clint, I want you alive."

An hour later, in a drizzling rain, he took off from Nuremberg Airport.

The three series of explosions occurred almost simultaneously. The first swept the Al Hamra oil field in Libya. The oil wells exploded in quick succession, spurting upward huge red and black flames. Roaring columns of fire, rising in the black night like flaming geysers, swayed and whirled in the sirocco winds, devastating everything around, burning cars and cisterns, transforming millions of dollars' worth of equipment into heaps of scorched, twisted metal. Reaching higher and higher, the flames joined in a formidable firestorm that raged over the field, an awe-inspiring sight visible from afar.

The second explosion shook the oil port of Ras-At-Tannurah in Saudi Arabia. The enormous reservoirs were the first to blast, like giant Molotov cocktails, and the tremendous heat wave rolled inland, melting pipes, loading installations and an electrical power plant on its way. When the wall of fire reached the oil wells, they detonated one after the other like firecrackers; hundreds of workers, screaming with panic, stampeded toward the nearby hills.

The third explosion destroyed the offshore oil rigs of Bir al Nabi in the Persian Gulf, off the coast of the small emirate of Bahrain. Two giant oil rigs, rising above the sea like mythological monsters, collapsed into the warm waters of the gulf. The petroleum, freely gushing to the surface, ignited immediately, and in a matter of minutes the entire bay seemed to be burning. The southernmost rig caught fire at its very underwater base, and a strange glow spread around, turning the sea into a boiling kettle of liquid flames. The superstitious fishermen, awe-stricken at the sight of the burning sea, saw in the explosion a vengeful act of the wrathful Allah.

Five minutes after the third explosion, anonymous callers assailed the phone lines of the world news agencies in Algiers, Tripoli, Jiddah and Baghdad. They said they were spokesmen of a new underground organization called the Sons of Arabia, and gave a detailed account of the fires devastating the oil fields. "This is our answer to the cynical threat of the warmonger Jefferson, to take the oil fields by force. This is only a foretaste of the destiny that awaits the major world oil fields, if this maniac attempts to carry out his abject scheme. Not one drop of oil will reach the West, which will quickly collapse, victim of its own folly."

The chairman of OPEC was the first to condemn, in harsh terms, the sabotage of the oil fields and to urge the countries affected by the explosions "to seek and punish the perpetrators." A carefully worded paragraph in Shazli's press release stressed, however, that the deplorable outburst of violence had erupted after several irresponsible statements issued by "certain Western politicians." He also warned that "those politicians" would have to answer for any shortage in the oil supply that may occur in the near future, owing to the sabotage of the oil fields.

The first news flashes about the explosions reached the east coast of the United States at 9:27 P.M., in the middle of a television debate between Vice-President Lawrence Wheeler and Jim Jefferson. The debate was taking place in front of a live audience in the Washington studios of NBC. It had been running for about half an hour, and Jefferson clearly had the upper hand. The two candidates faced each other on a round platform with the appearance of an arena. In order to enhance the impression of a duel between the two candidates, the directors of the debate had decided to skip the traditional panel. There were no journalists or representatives of the public on the platform. Only a moderator was present in the "arena," occasionally intervening to make sure that both debaters had equal opportunities to speak.

Jefferson was engaged in answering Wheeler's statement that American foreign policy had increased the prestige of the United States, as it was based on respect for the rights of the individual and the rights of the nations to govern themselves.

"I don't know where our prestige has increased in the last eight years of the present administration, which Vice-President Wheeler so eloquently praises," Jefferson was saying, his leonine head slightly bent forward, his eyes unwaveringly focusing on the camera. "Mr. Wheeler mentioned the Middle East. Did our prestige increase there after the catastrophe in Iran? Did we move our little finger to help the Shah, who had been our faithful ally for years? And even if we assume that the regime of the Shah was corrupt and had to be overthrown, why didn't we help his successor, the liberal, democracy-loving Bakhtiar, when he turned to us for help? The Shah had left the country; Prime Minister Bakhtiar was trying to carry out a peaceful revolution, to bring back democracy to Iran. He needed our help. But we"—he took a deep breath, his face grave and sad—"we refused to assist him, and let Iran fall like a ripe fruit into the hands of a medieval dictatorship that almost drowned the country in blood. Was *that* respect for the rights of the nations to govern themselves? Was *that* respect for the rights of the individual? Or just another proof of the weakness and the shortsightedness of the administration Mr. Wheeler is so proud of?"

Wheeler controlled himself well, but the tightening of his mouth and the angry spots burning on his cheeks showed that he was upset. "We all know that the Iranian crisis could not be solved by military intervention, and you certainly did not support such a measure yourself, Mr. Jefferson." He paused. "The Iranian question is a case apart. But why do you disregard the other areas of the world? You cannot deny that we have succeeded in restoring our position among the nations of Africa."

"Africa, yes." Jefferson sadly shook his head. "Let us speak

139

about Africa. I don't know where in Africa our prestige has increased. All I know is that Angola, Mozambique, Ethiopia fell into Communist hands. I know that Libya and Algeria have drawn closer to the Soviet Union. I know that Cuban soldiers, masterminded by Moscow, waged colonialist wars all over the continent, while Mr. Wheeler's government tried to restore diplomatic relations with the Castro regime."

In the control room, one floor above, Ralph Dowden and Jefferson's television director, David Crawford, were closely watching the monitors. "Excellent, excellent," Crawford was repeating, clenching his fists in enthusiasm. Ralph Dowden, who had been more reserved at the beginning, also seemed affected by the contagious fervor of his friend. "A beaut," he murmured. "Give it to him, J.J., the audience is with you . . . Hey, what's going on there? That's against the rules!"

While the cameras were showing a close-up of Jefferson's pugnacious face, a thin man in a dark suit had moved toward the platform and handed Wheeler a typewritten sheet of paper. The Vice-President quickly perused it, and there was definitely a new confidence in his manner as he raised his eyes toward Jefferson, at the very moment that the candidate was concluding: "And I didn't speak, as you noticed, of the oil issue."

"Oh yes," Wheeler's voice lashed coldly. "Why don't we speak of the oil issue indeed? You suggested, and I quote, that we 'take the oil,' didn't you, Mr. Jefferson? You brushed away the argument that the oil-producing countries might sabotage the oil fields and cut the supply of oil to this country. What would you say if I informed you that those oil fields are on fire now, and that the organization responsible for the fire accuses you, Mr. Jefferson?"

The audience gasped in dismay. "The son of a bitch," Dowden hissed, "the fucking son of a bitch!"

On the monitor, Jefferson looked bewildered. "I don't know anything about that," he said uncertainly.

"It is a flash that just arrived over the agencies' wires, Mr. Jefferson," Wheeler mercilessly went on. He waved the sheet at J.J. "You can read it if you wish. Millions of gallons of oil are burning at this very moment, all over the Middle East, because of you, Mr. Jefferson."

The beads of sweat that popped out on Jefferson's perplexed face appeared clearly on the close-up shot. "The bastards!" Dowden cursed furiously. "I knew they would go to close-up on him now."

"As I was saying before"—Jefferson's voice was unsteady—"I have been assured by the best experts in this country that the worst oil-well fire can be put out in a matter of weeks, maybe months . . ."

An angry murmur buzzed over the audience, and the cameras quickly focused on a few irate faces. "What a disaster," Dowden groaned, shaking his head. He looked as if he were going to burst into tears at any moment. "That's the vilest punch below the belt I ever saw. Why, this motherfucker Wheeler is breaking all the rules and nobody says a damn thing!"

Crawford cut him off rudely. "Calm down, Ralph. You know we wouldn't have missed such an opportunity either. We give it to him—he serves it back to us."

"We lost it, do you hear me?" Dowden raged. "Tonight, at this moment, we lost the damn election!" He removed his thick glasses and rubbed them furiously.

In the car on their way back from the television studio, Jefferson leaned back in his seat, immobile, his eyes closed. The radio, tuned to an all-news station, was broadcasting up-to-date information about the oil-field fires. Reactions were flowing in from all over the world—condemning the new underground organization, but blaming Jefferson as well. Only one oil expert played down the sensational news, pointing out that the sabotaged oil fields were very small, and had a negligible effect on the oil supply of the Middle East. The mood tonight was not one of moderation. An excited night editor of the New York *Daily News* described tomorrow's front page and main headline: "We'll run a huge photograph of a burning oil field—I think the Saudi is the most dramatic one. The headline will be 'Oil Fields On Fire' and in smaller characters: 'Arabs Blame Jefferson.' "

A breathless reporter called the station about a spontaneous demonstration that was just getting underway in front of Jefferson's campaign headquarters. Jefferson still did not react; but a nerve started twitching under his left eye, and he tried to conceal it by pretending to rub off the makeup from his forehead and cheekbones with his fingertips.

Ralph Dowden had worked himself up to a state of mild hysteria. Now he cracked. "I think that we lost the election, J.J.," he said in an almost inaudible voice, looking down at his tightly clasped hands.

Jefferson turned slowly and looked at him, then reached over and patted him on the knee. His features were drawn, but the twitching had stopped and his voice was firm. "Not yet, my boy, not yet," he said soothingly.

He waited for a couple of minutes to let Ralph calm down, then bent closer to him, so that Crawford and the driver would not hear. "Remember Chuck Belford?" he whispered in his ear. "I need him. Tonight."

"But it's almost ten now," Ralph protested. "Where shall I . . ."

"Get him. By hook or by crook." He tapped the driver's shoulder, to stop the car. "Find him, Ralph. Now."

Rosalynn Ross bent over her dressing table and critically examined her reflection in the brightly lit mirror. Her forehead was clear, and the makeup artfully concealed the tiny wrinkles that had started to crawl over her skin at the edges of her temples. But the sensitive areas under the eyes and over the upper lip were still smooth. She knew that when pouches started forming under her eyes and small wrinkles began crawling over her upper lip, she would not be able to play young women anymore. The newspaper critics could substitute for "strikingly beautiful," adjectives like "eternal" or "refined and gracious"; somebody would inevitably crown her "the Grand Lady of American Theater," and she would be downgraded with all the due honors to the category of middle-aged actress. Still, she was lucky, as that would happen to her a good many years after most actresses of her generation. She smiled at her image. The big green eyes were still ardent and eloquent, the high ivory cheekbones unwrinkled, the mouth ripe, the teeth pearly and healthy. Her body was still supple and her voice musical and clear. Well, she chuckled inwardly, if the worst came she could always get a face-lift and fool them for another couple of years.

She dipped a small cotton pad into the delicate bowl of liquid cleanser and carefully started to remove the makeup from her face, concentrating first on the soft skin under her eyes. She no longer remembered who had given her that fine china bowl that had belonged—or so they said—to Sarah Bernhardt. It had been during her first tour of Europe, but that was so long ago. She was barely twenty-five then, happy with her success but still unsure of herself, eager to taste life to the fullest, right away, while she was still young; she never believed in those days that twenty years later she would still be on the stage, and still playing the leading roles of young, attractive heroines.

She noticed the reflection of Doris in the mirror, moving noiselessly in the spacious dressing room, carefully folding her costume and lovingly rearranging the big bunch of red roses in the crystal vase. She is getting old, Rosalynn sadly reflected, as the small, bony woman bent too close over the card that had come with the flowers. Doris had always been proud of her fine eyesight and would not wear glasses in other people's presence. "Who sent them, Doris?" she asked, daubing another pad in a pot of eye cream. "Is it a duke or a prince?"

Her assistant straightened up. "It is the Rotary Club of Cooksville, Maryland," she said. "You sent them an autographed photograph last week and tonight their president was in the audience with his wife. You had to see them applauding; one could almost believe that they understood the play." Doris was an expert in watching the audience, able to report, row by row, who was present, how he or she was dressed and when they applauded.

"But they didn't fool you, of course." Rosalynn smiled. Behind her, Doris shrugged and started preparing the clothes Rosalynn would wear on her way home. "And how was I tonight?" Rosalynn asked. It was a ritual question, which always got a straightforward answer.

"Nothing special," came the verdict. "You didn't try too hard, and you were sloppy in the second act. But you know me"—Doris made a deprecating gesture with her hand—"I don't like Pinter. I can't get used to him. The first act is always fine, but when he takes off in the second act . . ."

She was interrupted by the ring of the telephone. It stood on a small table by the sofa. Doris picked it up. "Miss Ross's dressing room," she said dryly. She listened in silence, then covered the mouthpiece with her hand. "It is for you," she said in a strangely quivering voice.

"You know I can't take it now," Rosalynn said, irritated. "Tell them to call later. Who is it anyway?"

But Doris would not budge, holding the receiver. "I think you'll take this call," she said softly.

Rosalynn frowned and slowly pivoted on her stool. Doris stood upright, very pale, clutching the phone with both hands. Rosalynn noticed that the hand cupping the mouthpiece was trembling. "Give me that," she said impatiently, and took the receiver from Doris. "Hello?"

"Lynn?"

She recognized the voice immediately. Even if she had

143

failed to identify the voice, she should have known by the way he addressed her. There was only one man in the world who ever called her that.

"It's you," she said, with a sharp intake of breath.

"It's me," he admitted wearily. "And I want to see you very badly."

She slowly recovered from the initial surprise. "You want to see me very badly," she repeated, and bit her lip, striving to control herself. A wave of anger and frustration was rising in her and she wanted to scream at him and slam down the receiver, to hurt him as he had hurt her by his silence. But she checked herself and asked in a cool, even voice: "And you have been waiting for three years to tell me that, of course."

"Please," he said, and for the first time she became aware of his terrible distress. He had never begged before, not even when he had courted her and had waited for hours in his car by the stage door. "I know there is no apology for what I did. One day maybe I could explain . . ." He paused, and she could hear his breath. "Please, let me see you. I need you. I must talk to you."

"About what?" she asked warily. "What is so urgent?"

He seemed to hesitate. "Lynn, I can't take it anymore. My daughter is in the hospital with two bullets in her back . . ."

"What?" Her hand jerked and covered her eyes. "Oh, my God!"

". . . and they are trying to destroy me, hunting me like a pack of bloodhounds."

"Who are they? Whom are you talking about?"

He ignored the question, or maybe he was not even listening. "Lynn, I must see you. I must talk to somebody, and there is nobody else but you."

She nodded sadly, as if he were watching her from the phone. She made a few hesitating steps toward her dressing table, twisting the telephone cord in her fingers.

"Lynn? Are you there?"

She made up her mind. "Come to my place in half an hour. I have a rented apartment in Washington for the season." She gave him the address. "Be careful," she added uneasily, "somebody might see you."

"I don't care," he snapped angrily. "I don't care if they see me, Lynn."

"But I do, Jim," she said softly, and slowly replaced the receiver on its cradle. She shot a quick, wary glance at Doris,

144

but the old woman had hastily started to rearrange her clothes in the wardrobe, her back upright.

They did not kiss; they even did not touch each other. The thin, silver-haired man with the wrinkled face, who had escorted him to her apartment, turned away, avoiding her eyes, as soon as she unbolted the door. She only heard Jefferson saying, "Thank you, Chuck, and bon voyage," as the stranger quickly walked to the elevator. Jim stepped in and stood awkwardly in the anteroom. The black and white eyebrows cast a shadow on his eye sockets, and the impetuous chin was drawn in. "Come," she said simply, and he followed her into the living room. He had not changed much; only the gray hair had turned white at the temples, and his shoulders had sagged slightly. He stood by the window, crossed his arms and unfolded them again, eluding her searching look. All his self-assurance seemed to have evaporated as he had crossed her threshold.

"Why don't you take off your jacket and undo your tie?" she said softly. He nodded gratefully and started fumbling with his buttons. She took the jacket and their hands briefly touched. He raised his eyes. She could not look at him that way, could not stand the defeat that was etched into the leonine face; the steel-blue eyes had lost their sharpness and were gleaming dully. She gestured toward a comfortable Danish armchair. "Let me pour you a drink," she said. He raised his hand in mute objection, then dropped it and slowly sank into the armchair. She was back, with two glasses of cognac. She handed him one, and sat on the small stool before him. "Thank you," he said, rather formally, sipped the fragrant liquid and retreated again into his awkward silence. It pained her to see him so. This strong, tough man had never needed other people, and now he did not know how to open up to her, to strip himself of his shield.

"How is Jill?" she asked gravely.

He nodded. "I talked twice to the hospital today. They said she would be all right. She has been operated on and she is recovering."

"You *talked* to the hospital?" she asked in disbelief. "You did not go to visit her?"

"She is in Nuremberg, in Germany." Noticing the surprise in her eyes, he went on: "She was in Europe, in Paris. I called her last week and asked her to do something for me. She got involved in an accident." He sighed. "It's all my

145

fault, and I am the only one to blame. I shouldn't have sent her."

Rosalynn frowned. "I don't understand. She got mixed up in an accident? What kind of accident? I mean, people don't get shot in the streets, just like that."

"I am the only one to blame," he repeated stubbornly, and she understood he wouldn't talk about it. Not yet.

"But it had to do with the election?"

He took a sip from his drink. "Oh yes. Every bloody thing that is happening lately has to do with the election." Then he added, in a low voice: "They are determined to destroy me, Lynn, at all costs. They are panicked. They won't stop at anything, not even the dirtiest tricks. There is a whole conspiracy against me. They are spending millions to dig up an old story that might bury me. Tonight they blew up three oil fields in the Middle East and put the blame on me. Tomorrow they'll crucify me in the papers as the villain who has cut the lifeline of the free world."

She stared at him in amazement. "I didn't know about the oil fields," she said. "Was it made public already?"

"Oh, yes," he smiled bitterly, "and how! Wheeler announced it in the middle of the television debate, tonight."

"I was at the theater," she whispered. "But I don't understand something. This conspiracy—who is behind it? Wheeler?"

He shook his head. "No, I don't think so. OPEC and a couple of oil companies are pulling the strings. I am a threat to them. Wheeler is just their sort of man. He is a decent guy." The bitter smile flashed again. "I mean, as decent as any politician can be, which is not much."

"That includes you," she said quickly.

"That includes me," he admitted. He looked down at the amber liquid in his glass. "I am not a saint, Lynn; I never pretended to be. I have also pulled quite a few tricks in my career. But not that kind." He ran his fingers under his collar and undid another button. "Sometimes I feel I am suffocating." He threw his head back and she noticed how exhausted he was. Deep furrows descended from the corners of his mouth to his chin, and the skin under his eyes was puffed and sagging in small pockets. "I am campaigning all over the country, flying from one city to the other, cheering up campaign volunteers, planning the next stages of the campaign. . . . I am supposed to provide this huge party—and maybe the whole nation—with a new, clean leadership." The bitter smile appeared again on his lips. "But I can't tell them the truth, Lynn. I can't tell even my closest assistants that on the other side of the fence, a bunch of bastards are striving to expose me as one of the biggest criminals in the world." An unmistakable note of despair slipped into his voice. "And I can't stop them, Lynn. I am helpless. Do you understand what that means?" He furiously drove his fist into his open palm, and repeated hoarsely: "I am totally helpless."

She did not ask him what the plot was about. She knew Jim Jefferson. He would uncoil slowly, gradually. He was a lonely man, making his own decisions, unable to confide in others, to rely on others. She must let him unburden himself in his own way, in his own time.

She shivered. "It's getting cold," she said. "Would you light the fire, Jim? The logs are by the fireplace."

He seemed grateful for the opportunity to do something. He knelt by the fireplace, and she liked the expression on his face as he deftly sorted the chunks of wood and built the fire. He looked better now. The flames caught, hesitantly at first, then spreading over the pile, and the first cracklings were heard as the pleasant smell of burning pinewood wafted into the room. He suddenly said, without turning back: "Only God knows how I missed you, Lynn, how many times I wanted to call you. I just couldn't. I'll never forgive myself for the death of Emily. It haunts me till this very day. She didn't die by accident, Lynn. She killed herself because of my affair with you. Every time I reached for the phone to call you, I would see Emily's face, before the funeral." He abruptly stopped, then blurted: "You and Jill are the only women I care about in the world."

She came to him and knelt by his side, stretching her long hands to the fire. He did not look at her, embarrassed by his own confession. After a long silence she touched his shoulder. "Jim, why did you have to go into all this? Why did you decide to run for President?"

He slowly got to his feet and picked up his glass. "You are an ambitious woman, Lynn, and if I tell you that I am running because of sheer ambition, you'll understand. There is ambition, of course." He slowly nodded to himself and started pacing around the room. "But it is not only that, Lynn, I love this country. I am worried about it. I feel it is disintegrating, falling to pieces. I always think of the decline of the Roman Empire. That's what is happening to us, now."

147

"And you can stop it?" she said coolly, without turning back.

"At least I should try," he stated forcefully. Somewhere beneath the surface, the old J.J. was emerging again. He left his unfinished drink on the big dining table and dragged his armchair beside the fire, close to the place where she squatted on the carpet. "Believe me, Lynn, I know that I can do something for this country." His face clouded. "But lately I have got the feeling that I shall not be able to hold out until the election. I'm out of breath, and they keep hitting below the belt. I don't know what to expect next."

She moved closer to him and sat at his feet, her back to him, her head lightly resting against his knees. He gently touched her hair. "As a matter of fact," he admitted, "I know exactly what will come next." She did not answer. He was struggling with himself now, willing to share his secret with her and yet fearing the exposure, even before somebody so close, so dear, who knew so many of his secrets.

She sat immobile, her eyes riveted on the burning logs.

"I want to tell you a story," he finally said. His voice was uncertain, and he cleared his throat. "It happened in Munich, in August nineteen forty-five."

Chapter Eight:

October 27—October 29:

MUMMY

"So you are Clint Craig. I can't tell you how pleased and honored I am to meet you. I knew you were very gifted, but I did not know that you were so handsome. I have read your books and I think they are excellent indeed."

Clint was flattered and agreeably surprised. He warmed up immediately to the charming old gentleman who was cordially shaking his hand. Justice Kevin Sheppard was about seventy-five years old, with china-blue eyes, snow-white hair, rosy cheeks and a kindly smile. He had an upright carriage, and looked very dignified in his pin-striped suit and polka-dotted bow tie. For some reason he reminded Clint of the kind, human image he had had as a boy of Uncle Sam, until the day when he had seen a poster—or was it a cartoon?—of the goatee-sporting, angry-eyed old man in his tails and funny top hat, spanking a screaming child on whose sombrero was printed the name of some South American republic.

"Come in, come in, Mr. Craig. Let me show you the house." Kevin Sheppard dismissed the gray-haired Black butler and proudly led the way into his vast Georgetown mansion. Clint looked around him in wonder. The spacious, high-ceilinged rooms, tastefully furnished in late eighteenth-century style, looked like museum galleries. On the walls hung oil paintings signed by renowned masters, colorful Gobelins, sketches and aquarelles. A great many statues, of classical as well as early modern schools, were mounted on marble pedestals and bore witness to the taste of their owner. Light filtered softly through the voile curtains on the windows, and glowed from small spotlights affixed to the walls. Sophisticated devices for maintaining a constant level of humidity were installed in all the rooms.

Clint contemplated with admiration the splendid collection amassed by the old judge. He had landed at Dulles International Airport barely an hour ago, feeling utterly exhausted, his nerves on edge after the dramatic events of the last twenty-four hours. Still, the display of art and beauty in Sheppard's house was so magnificent that for a short while his present concerns seemed to retreat to the back of his mind. "Here I keep my gold collection," Justice Sheppard was saying, a note of pride vibrating in his soft voice. And with reason, for the sight of the gold objects, displayed in a succession of tall glass showcases, was enthralling indeed. Early pre-Columbian statuettes, breast plates and rings, antique Egyptian jewelry, Persian plates and figurines, together amounted to one of the most valuable collections Clint had ever seen. The old man sadly tapped the showcase where the Persian plates stood. "There are only four cups needed to make that set complete," he sighed. "Unfortunately, Jean Rigaud got them first. Do you know him? He lives in Paris, Place Vendôme." Clint shook his head and Sheppard explained: "A very good collector, Rigaud, one of the best." He chuckled. "For the last thirty years we have been fighting over the most beautiful gold pieces in the world. He got some, and I got some. . . . I outbid him in the battle for those plates in London, but that treacherous dealer had sold him the cups before the auction even started." He looked lovingly at the ancient reddish gold. "Isn't it a crime to spoil such an exquisite set?"

"Well, one cannot have it all, sir," Clint said.

The justice looked at him and shrugged helplessly. "I know, my friend, believe me, I know. But that is my weakness, and I admit it. If I ever had to confess my vices before my Creator, I would admit that all my life I was irresistibly attracted to art, good art, the best of art. And I don't like only to contemplate it, but to possess it, to be able to say it is mine. I am an old man now, and I know how ephemeral life is, believe me. The only thing that lasts—the most sublime achievement of man—is beauty, in its purest form. All the money I have ever had I have spent on paintings, statues, art objects. Look around you. Isn't it glorious? To live your last years on earth, surrounded by the very essence of human genius?"

Clint smiled warmly. He liked the old aesthete, quietly living in his museumlike house, surrounded by his beloved masterpieces. "But I am forgetting my manners," Justice Sheppard said briskly. "You must be exhausted after your long flight, and you must have other matters on your mind.

Come, let's sit and relax in my den. We'll have some coffee and you'll tell me what I can do for you."

Half an hour later, having followed Clint's account of his voyage and findings with undisguised fascination, the old man put down his empty cup. He did not speak immediately. He sat upright in his armchair, his white head bowed, his right hand softly beating a tattoo on his armrest. Finally he raised his head and looked at Clint. His face was grave. "Your theory seems fantastic, Mr. Craig," he slowly articulated, "but I wouldn't rule it out. It might be true. I didn't know Brandl and Skolnikoff, but I did know Hermann Goering. When I was secretary of the International Tribunal in Nuremberg, I visited him quite a few times in his cell and had long conversations with him. I wanted to understand that criminal mind of his, to find out what made him act the way he did. He was the only real leader in the group, the only one who was worth something even when divested of his power. The others were just a despicable bunch of criminals. But Goering? He almost cut to pieces the American prosecutor Robert Jackson, and had it not been for that brilliant Englishman Maxwell-Fyfe, he might have succeeded in eluding quite a few counts of the accusation. Slippery as an eel, he was. I was very interested in him."

"Why?"

"I wanted to write a book about him." He quickly corrected himself. "No, not about him, but about the functioning of a criminal, highly intelligent mind. I wanted to take Goering as an example."

"Did you write that book?"

"Oh yes, I certainly did. It was not really a book—a long essay, rather. It was published in the early fifties." He dismissed the subject of his book with a gesture of his hand. "But that is not the point. If I try to think now about your theory, and match it against my experience—I must say that on one cardinal point you are absolutely right. Goering was sure he would not die."

"Did he tell you so?" Clint asked quickly.

Sheppard seemed surprised by the question. "Oh yes, definitely, many times."

"Why?" Clint asked. "I mean, why was he so sure?"

The old man shook his head. "He did not tell me why. But time and again he said in so many words that he was convinced he would not be executed. Later somebody told me

151

that Goering was in a kind of euphoria, because of all the drugs he was taking. You know that he was a drug addict."

Clint nodded, and the justice continued. "That was nonsense, of course. In prison he stopped taking drugs, he had lost weight and was in full possession of his mental capacity." He paused. "I saw him after he was sentenced to death. He still believed that his life would be spared. I was baffled by his suicide. Still, maybe . . . maybe somebody had secretly informed him that his appeal had been rejected; so even before Andrus came to tell him about it, he swallowed poison. But frankly, this is a very nebulous affair."

"Do you remember other Americans who visited his cell?"

Sheppard considered the question for a moment, then slowly shook his head. "No, my recollections are quite fragmentary. At the time, of course, I knew practically everything, and I had collected all the documents for my book, but . . ."

"Did you keep copies of the files?" Clint interrupted. "Did you make a copy of the cell logbook, where the names of Goering's visitors were recorded?"

Sheppard sunk into deep reflection again. "Oh yes, I certainly did. I had copies made of all the documents concerning Goering." He smiled. "It was easy for me, as I was the tribunal secretary. I believe they also photocopied the visitor's logbook for me. It must still be somewhere in my cellar, with all my documents."

"May I . . . may I see it?"

"Why, of course," Kevin Sheppard said kindly. "I shall be delighted to let you see all my documents and notes. Unfortunately, it can't be done today. I told you over the phone, I am leaving for a short vacation in the Caribbean. But if you come back in . . . let's say in ten days, I shall have my files ready for you."

"Maybe your secretary . . ." Clint began. He could not afford waiting for so long."

"No, no," the justice said with finality. "Nobody but I would know where the files are and what is in each of them." He rose. "Your visit was a sheer pleasure, Mr. Craig. I shall be back in ten days, and I am looking forward to meeting you again. You must find the truth about that sordid affair, and I'll do all I can to help you."

The skinny fair-haired corporal in the U.S. Army Archives at Bethesda, Maryland, looked like a teenaged boy, but actually was efficiency itself. He flashed a quick look at Clint Craig's credentials, and in big block letters swiftly wrote on a pad the subject of his inquiry, while his left hand was already dialing an internal extension. Even before Clint had finished speaking, the young virtuoso was repeating his request over the phone. Five minutes later, a pretty Black girl in army uniform brought Clint an old file in regulation khaki cardboard: the personal file of 4647899 First Sergeant Jeffrey Oates, U.S. Army, Military Police, deceased.

"The file does not contain any documents of a private or business nature," the girl chanted. "All such material has been removed and returned to the family of the deceased. The documents left have been classified, and you can take notes or make Xerox copies of everything you need. We have the appropriate equipment and shall be glad to assist you." She flashed him a mischievous smile, hinting that she did not take her recitation very seriously, and walked away, sensually swaying her full hips. Clint followed her with his eyes, then smiled to himself and slowly untied the straps that held the file together.

The contents of the file were more or less what he had expected: a few forms and questionnaires, filled out in a laborious handwriting; promotion orders; a letter of commendation for exemplary conduct during a mutiny in a military prison in Rennes, France, on September 17, 1944; several reports from Oates's commanding officers praising his seriousness and devotion; an account of the accident in which he was killed, filled in by a Major Haggerty. The only useful information the file yielded was the address of First Sergeant Oates in New Orleans, Louisiana, and a photograph of a youth, handsome in a rather arrogant sort of way, trying to look tough in a Military Police uniform. A crescent-shaped scar, half an inch in length, was visible under the youth's left eye; mention of it was also made under the "distinguishing marks" heading in two of the forms in the file.

Clint noted down the address: 2560 Sycamore Drive, New Orleans. It crossed his mind that they did not yet have area codes in the forties; he only hoped the name of the street had not been changed. The helpful corporal at the inquiries desk said yes, of course, we can have the photograph duplicated for you, disappeared in an inner room and was back in no time with a couple of photographs and a receipt for $3.70.

Two hours later, Clint was buckling his seat belt on an Eastern Airlines flight bound for New Orleans. The plane landed at the New Orleans International Airport at half past seven P.M. After a short hesitation Clint checked in at the nearby Skyways Inn. He showered, changed and was out again in the warm, sticky Louisiana night. The first cab in the file lazily crawled toward him. He was relieved that the driver nodded knowingly when he gave him the Sycamore Drive address.

Only when he leaned back in the pleasant darkness of the cab's interior did he realize that there was not one good reason for his visit that he could give the Oates family, if they still lived there. He had come here on a hunch, unsubstantiated by any solid evidence. He could not say to Jeffrey Oates's closest relatives: "I suspect that Jeffrey did not die in that accident," or "I believe that your beloved son faked his death." He had to play it by ear, and find a way to win those people's confidence, without stirring painful memories or hinting at a horrifying possibility that would give them nightmares for the rest of their lives.

He felt the accumulated fatigue pervade his whole body. He closed his eyes, hoping to doze for a couple of minutes, but he could not; he was too tense, and numberless questions tortured his mind. The radio was on and a country singer was sweetly purring an election song, ending with the line: "Wheeler's the man for you and me." A couple of weeks ago the election would have been all that counted for him; now it seemed far away, on another planet. He did not really care who was going to win, as long as they let him complete his research on time. He had got so deeply involved in the thirty-five-year-old mystery he was trying to unearth that nothing else seemed to matter. Money and fame, which had tempted him in Frankfurt, seemed trivial now. The truth about Goering's treasure was all that counted. And the identity of the man who stole it.

He looked out of the car window. Jim Jefferson's face floated toward him on a huge billboard, towering by the roadside. "JEFFERSON IS YOUR MAN" read the slogan under the smiling face.

The home of First Sergeant Oates was a decrepit old wooden house with a peeling whitewashed facade, identical to scores of other two-story houses that stood in a long line down the obscure street. Overflowing garbage cans clustered on the sidewalk; one of them was overturned, and its rotten contents were spilled on the pavement. As the cab stopped, a couple of scavenging cats smoothly retreated from the heap

154

of trash and melted in the black shadows. The stairs rasped faintly as Clint walked up to the southern-style porch. For some reason this neighborhood, at this hour, reminded him of his own childhood in San Diego, when he would emerge out of the darkness and breathlessly climb the porch while a gang of children ran after him, mockingly shouting: "You have no father! Where is your dad? Little orphan Clint!" He would call for his mother, but she was never home, and the scoffing children would go on chanting their insults under his window while he cried, alone in the house. Children could be so cruel sometimes. Mothers too.

The outer door was open and a bare yellow bulb diffused a dim light in the shabby living room. Somewhere in the back, the radio was playing. Clint hesitated on the threshold, knocked on the bare wooden wall and called: "Is anybody home?"

"Coming," a woman's hoarse voice replied, and bare footsteps rustled on the floor tiles. A fat, short woman in a long, untidy dress came from the dark corridor and into the circle of yellow light under the lamp. She was in her late forties. Her long oily hair fell in loose gray stands over her shoulders. She had a bulbous nose and heavy masculine jowls. Her eyes were slightly glazed and Clint's nostrils picked up a faint smell of marijuana wafting from the interior of the house. "What do you want?" she asked, but there was no hostility in her voice.

Clint flashed his most charming smile. "Excuse me for bothering you. I am looking for the Oates family."

A quick smile bared nicotine-stained teeth. "I am the Oates family," the woman replied.

Clint was momentarily confused. "You—and nobody else?"

"Well," the woman said with the easygoing nonchalance resulting from a first joint of grass, "Mom and Dad are dead, Beth and Ron have gone, Jeff was killed and I am the only one left. Rosie. Sweet, rose-cheeked Rosie."

"I am Clint," he said lightly, trying to adapt himself to her mood, and casually leaned against the doorframe. "Nice to meet you, rose-cheeked Rosie."

Her giggle rang again and he decided that, besides grass, there was also a good measure of booze in sweet Rosie's belly.

"Clint," she said, "Hi, Clint. I once knew a guy called Clint. He was from up north, from Maine. Bangor, Maine," she added gravely. "Where do you come from?"

"California," he said, still wondering how he was to continue this conversation. He realized that Otto Brandl and Stadelheim jail and even Goering's treasure were not the subjects sweet Rosie would care to discuss. "I'm a writer."

"A writer? No kidding?" She tilted her head, eyeing him doubtfully. "A real writer? You write books?"

"Uh-huh." He nodded.

"Whaw, ain't that something?" she said in awe. "I like to read sometimes, when I'm on a night shift. I'm a telephone operator, see, and sometimes the nights are real quiet. Real quiet," she repeated, her plump hands making graceful, flying motions to show him how quiet the nights were sometimes. "They don't allow us to bring any liquor there, and I bring books. I like books about sex, and love, and Mafia. Bestsellers. Did you ever write a bestseller, Clint?"

"I'm writing one now," he said, expecting her to ask about what, but she did not. "Oh, I am tired," she mumbled. "Let's sit down, okay? Out there, on the porch." She did not wait for his answer, but sailed to the corner of the living room, and came back dragging two dilapidated rattan chairs. "There," she said. "Sit, sit down, California Clint." A black cat came soundlessly from inside the house and sat at her feet, its yellow eyes suspiciously staring at him.

"I need a drink," she said. "Care for a drink?"

"I'd love that, Rosie."

"What's your poison, stranger?" She seemed to have read the complete book of *Playboy*'s party jokes.

"Whatever you drink will be fine with me."

"I drink bourbon," she said. "Straight. No ice, no water. There's no ice anyway." She chuckled again. "The refrigerator broke down."

"Straight bourbon will be perfect."

She disappeared inside, and was back immediately with a half-full quart and two unmatching glasses. She filled the glasses almost to the rim and handed him one. "Here we are, all set now, aren't we?"

"That's just wonderful," he stated. "Real southern hospitality. Cheers."

She took a large gulp from her glass, and he suddenly grasped that if he did not get a couple of answers from her now, she might very soon be "unavailable for comment," as they used to say in newspaper jargon.

"You know, you too may be in my book," he said.

156

Sweet Rosie's eyes widened with surprise. "Me? You're kidding. How come?"

"Well, I'm writing a book about a unit of American soldiers who fought in the World War, see? About them, and their families, and friends, and their girls. Your brother Jeffrey was among them."

"Jeff. You are writing a book about my brother Jeff?"

"About him too. All the soldiers I write about have been killed in the war, so I go to their homes, and talk to their families, and they give me their photographs and letters and . . ."

"Jeff never wrote home," she said, her face sullen. "Never. And he sent no photographs either. I even don't remember how he looked. I was a kid when he was killed." She started to cry softly, with the easy sentimentality of the drunk.

"How come?" he asked. "All the soldiers write home."

"Jeff didn't," she said stubbornly and took another gulp from her glass. "He quarreled with Mom and Dad and they said he was a dis . . ."—her speech was already slurred—"a disgrace for the family and he ran away from home, and enlisted, and we didn't hear of him again, nothing, and then a letter came that he was dead. Father said he didn't care, but Mom cried and I did too. I sat on the porch and I cried. I loved Jeff, he was so handsome and he called me his sweetest Rosie." The tears were streaming down her cheeks and she refilled her glass.

"Why was your daddy so angry with him?" Clint pressed on.

"Because of that girl," she said, bobbing her head vigorously. "Because of that Mexican girl, the daughter of the Carranzas. He was crazy about her, my brother Jeff was. He wanted to marry her and Dad said it was a shame on the family, that his son should be running around with a Mexican whore." She stretched and yawned. "Got some grass, Clint? I had only one joint, before, and I'd love some more." She closed her eyes and shook her head. "Oh, how I'd love some more."

"No, I don't have any right now, I'm sorry," Clint said.

She shrugged. "Okay." Suddenly she smiled. "Then I'll have another bourbon. It's very good, you know?"

He ignored her question. "What happened to the girl?"

The bottle was shaking in her hand as she refilled her glass. A couple of drops fell on her dress. "The girl? Isabel? I dunno. She went away. After Jeff died, she went away. She never came back. Or maybe she did, but I dunno." She

157

grinned at him and leaned toward him. Her open mouth reeked of alcohol. "You are a nice man. I like you. I like the way you call me sweet Rosie. I like to be called that. I am sweet, rose-cheeked Rosie." She started to giggle again.

"Did all the Carranza family go away, too?"

She scowled at him mockingly. "I won't tell you. I won't tell you if you don't call me sweet Rosie, and promise to be nice. Why are you asking all these questions?" She drank thirstily, and some of the bourbon spilled on her double chin. Down in the street, two Black boys walked past the house. They wore T-shirts and sneakers. The taller of the two was carrying a big music box.

"I'll be nice," he solemnly promised. "Tell me, sweet Rosie, where are the Carranzas now?"

"Where they always were." She almost choked laughing. "In their restaurant, the same they always had on Bourbon Street. Carranzas' tacos. The lousiest tacos in New Orleans. Wait, I need a drink, just one more. I think I have some more bourbon inside." She started to get up, but swayed and slumped back in her chair.

"Let me take you inside, sweet Rosie," Clint said, passed his head under her limp arm and half carried, half dragged the drunk woman inside. Her head rested on his shoulder, and she was mumbling unintelligible words. The radio was still playing; he fumbled in the dark until he found the volume knob and turned it off. He found the bedroom and carefully put her on the unmade bed. Rosie's eyes were closed and she was breathing heavily. In a second she would be snoring.

On his way out he stopped in the living room, took a few bills from his pocket and stuck them under the cheap glass ashtray on the dining table. He owed at least that to sweet drunk Rosie.

Carranzas' tacos perhaps were not the worst in New Orleans, but they certainly were the worst he had ever eaten. He sat at a small table by the window, munching the tasteless dough, and idly watched the crowd of noisy tourists exploring the lively French quarter. Families with kids stood by the striptease joints, stretching their necks to catch a glimpse of a nude damsel. A young couple, holding hands, stopped on the sidewalk in front of him and pointed excitedly at the wrought-iron balconies above. Somebody opened the restaurant door and a few measures of jazz drifted in. He turned his head. Two teenagers had just walked in. The girl was definitely Mexican and the red-haired boy seemed to be of Irish descent. They sat by the counter, laughing, and the girl spoke in quick Spanish to the middle-aged waitress. Rosie's story came back to him. That's how Jeff and Isabel must have looked thirty-five years ago, when they dropped in at her father's restaurant for some enchiladas. He tried to visualize the stormy scenes in the small living room at Sycamore Drive, with the father shouting obscenities and young Jeff bowing his head, fists clutched in anger. The story did not surprise him. He knew well those poor, ignorant southern families, who had been conditioned to believe that they were here to protect the purity of the white race from being soiled by Blacks or Latin-Americans. Fifty years ago they not only screamed at their kids, but went out at night, hooded, to burn crosses and lynch Blacks in the countryside. He could understand the feelings of Jeffrey Oates when he ran away from home, determined never to return, dreaming of a different life for him and the girl he loved, if he only had the means. . . .

He got up and walked to the cashier's booth, where a dark man approximately his own age was sorting credit-card slips. He paid his check and asked conversationally: "Are you Mr. Carranza?"

"One of them." The young man smiled. "We are four brothers and two sisters."

"Isabel Carranza is your sister?"

Carranza started. For a moment he seemed dumbfounded. Then he slowly spoke, studying Clint with a cold, hostile look. "She was my sister, yes. . . . How—I mean, why do you ask about her? Who are you?"

"My father knew her," Clint lied. "He grew up with her boyfriend, a guy named Jeff Oates."

"I see." The hostility in the Mexican's eyes softened, but it was still there.

"My father used to say that Isabel was one of the most beautiful girls he had ever seen," Clint said. "He used to speak a lot about her and Jeff."

The young man scowled. "But Jeff was killed, wasn't he?"

"So you knew him!" Clint exclaimed with a smile.

"No, I didn't. I was in my diapers when he . . . when he was my sister's boyfriend. I don't remember her either. I only heard about Isabel from my elder brothers. I am the youngest child in the family."

Clint frowned, puzzled. "What do you mean, you don't remember her?"

Carranza looked at him suspiciously. "It must be a long time since your father was around here," he observed.

"Oh yes, we moved to California, during the war."

The young man slowly nodded, then resumed his work. "That's why you don't know the rest, then. My sister left this country after Jeff was killed, and went back to Mexico, to Guanajuato. She married an American there, a rich guy. Jerome. Cyrus Jerome. He bought a hacienda in the mountains and named it 'Hacienda Isabel' after her."

"And you never went to visit her?" Clint asked in disbelief.

Carranza's face clouded. "My sister died more than twenty years ago, in childbirth." A note of mild apology slipped into his voice. "That's why I was so surprised when you asked about her. She's been gone a long time, so to speak."

"I am sorry," Clint said. "I didn't realize."

"That's okay," Carranza said and looked over Clint's shoulder at the next customer. "Excuse me now, there is somebody waiting. Enjoy your stay."

Before returning to his hotel, Clint stopped at the airport and booked a seat for the early morning flight to Mexico.

The sun was already setting when he reached the first ridge of barren hills surrounding the city of Guanajuato. He nervously changed gears and the small rental car left the main highway and started the climb up the steep mountain road. He was high-strung, conscious that he had wasted a whole day, a luxury he could not afford, not now. There had been a delay in New Orleans and his flight had landed in Mexico City only in the early afternoon; the formalities at immigration had taken longer than expected, most of the car rental agencies had no cars available, and he had set out quite late on the 226-mile drive to Guanajuato. Furthermore, he was constantly tormented by the thought that he might well be embarking on a wild-goose chase after all, that no answer was waiting for him in the little Mexican town, no solution to the mystery he had sworn to unravel. Yet this trip to Guanajuato was his last chance. All his former endeavors had ended in blind alleys. Sure enough, there had been an American in Ronda when Skolnikoff was killed; sure enough, Otto's death had been very strange; Goering's firm belief that he would survive was puzzling, as puzzling as his suicide. But all those events could be mere coincidences, and scores of historians before him had accepted them at face value.

But on the other hand . . . the attempts on his life had

160

been real; his arm was still bandaged and Jill was still in the hospital; somebody had supplied poison to Goering, and somebody had torn that leaf from the visitors' logbook; Dr. Hoffmann, the prison physician, did not die in a routine accident while fumbling with live wires, which he had never touched before. Somebody had deliberately murdered him, a few days before Clint came to Nuremberg, to prevent him from speaking about Goering's death. And Jeffrey Oates did not die in that car crash. But could he prove it? Could he find the real Jeffrey Oates? Was he the mysterious American who had married, here, Isabel Carranza? The sergeant must have been a member of a conspiracy that had involved several people, for he had disappeared from the scene more than a year before Goering died and the rest of his treasure had been removed from its hiding places. If Jeffrey Oates was alive, and living in Mexico under a new identity, he should be able to name his partner or partners in the wartime plot. Everything depended therefore on his visit to the Hacienda Isabel, the last stop in a trip that had carried him around half the globe.

Night fell all of a sudden, as it did in this part of the world, and Clint turned the headlights on. His car was alone on the narrow mountain road. Now and then, a small group of Mexicans would emerge from the darkness, walking barefoot along the road or riding their small mules. They were dressed in white shirts and trousers, and wore big sombreros embroidered with silver thread. It was Saturday night, and they were coming down from their tiny hamlets to the bigger villages for a modest fiesta and a couple of drinks. The car passed a pueblo nestled on the mountain slope, and he saw them in the main square: a group of men in white, singing to the accompaniment of a small mariachi band who played trumpets and guitars. Some of the men were holding big bottles of local beer in their hands; others would spread some salt on the outstretched back of a hand, swallow a small glass of tequila in a single gulp, jerking the head backwards, and lick the salt with gusto. Women, their hair black as a raven's wing, would watch them from their windows, and laugh softly.

The road curved sharply to the right, and then suddenly a myriad of lights appeared in front of him, down in a valley enclosed on all sides by steep dark mountains. Guanajuato. He stepped on the accelerator. The car darted downhill, past the illuminated ruins of the old quarter and the abandoned mines of gold and silver that had made the small city, centuries ago, the crown gem of Spanish Mexico. He crossed a few illuminated squares, then was suddenly engulfed in a subterranean street running under the very foundations of the ancient town. Huge underground archways loomed on his left, and in the darkness he discerned the gaping mouths of black tunnels leading to the bowels of the strange city. A river must have flowed here, ages ago; the water marks were still visible on the stone walls. He shivered slightly. The underground gallery looked like the set of a Hollywood horror movie.

But the weird ride ended as abruptly as it had started. He was out in the open air again, climbing uphill. In front of him emerged the brightly lit contours of the magnificent Santa Cecilia Castle, which had been transformed into a luxurious hotel. He wearily walked to the front desk. No, the clerk apologized, they had no rooms; the hotel was fully booked. Maybe the motel, out of town . . . Clint pressed a few bills in his palm and the memory of the young Mexican started functioning all of a sudden. Oh yes, he remembered now, they had a room available, as the other gentleman had not showed up. He handed Clint a heavy brass key. Yes, he knew Hacienda Isabel. It was up in the mountains and he would gladly give him directions in the morning. Yes, the hacienda belonged to the Jerome family.

He had an overcooked meal in the big dining room, furnished in early colonial style. Pine logs were merrily crackling in the big stone fireplace, and a pleasant scent floated about the room. The waiter suggested an after-dinner cognac, but he shook his head and got up. He was restless and preoccupied. From his room he tried to phone Jill in Nuremberg, and Peter Bohlen, but the switchboard operator was unable to put the calls through. He smoked a cigarillo on the balcony, contemplating the flickering lights of the city. The elegant facade of the Teatro Juárez, built as a miniature imitation of the Paris Opéra, was flooded in bright illumination. He mused over the odd adventure that had brought him here, from the cliffs of Ronda and the sleet of Munich, to a strange city in central Mexico. Finally he undressed and went to bed.

He slept fitfully, his thoughts tormenting him even in his dreams. The faces of Bohlen, Jefferson, Goering, Sheppard, and old Juan Romero, the young Jeff Oates appeared over and over again in a strange nightmare, until they all merged into an oval, featureless face: the blank face of Don Quixote Jill had seen in the Munich museum. The face slowly dissolved and he found himself in Washington, in front of the White House, and somebody told him that he was too late, the election was over and he would never find the treasure. "Who was elected?" he asked. "Who is the President?" The man laughed at him, and he woke, bathed in cold sweat. Down in the city, the bells of San Francisco church struck five.

He was up almost immediately, and when the sun rose in the east, he was halfway up the mountain, his eyes burning in expectation as the little car panted on its climb to Hacienda Isabel.

Hacienda Isabel was a huge ranch, where fighting bulls were raised to die one day in the arenas of Mexico. As he drove past the big corrals, followed by the bloodshot eyes of the black monsters, Clint remembered the sad, disillusioned Juan Romero, the old bullfighter from Ronda, whose dreams and flesh had been hacked by the sharp horns of a frenzied *toro*.

The ranch house was a beautiful one-story structure, gleaming in spotless white. Its spacious marble-tiled veranda offered a panoramic view of the Guanajuato valley. Somewhat to the right, emerging from the sea of low gray clouds, loomed the monument of Christ—a gigantic statue of Jesus, standing on top of the steep Cubilete hill, his arms outstretched. It was as big as the famous "Corcovado" overlooking the city of Rio de Janeiro. Clint left his car in the drive, close to the garage where two cars were standing: a Volkswagen van and a small sports convertible. At the foot of the steps leading to the house he was met by a dignified, silver-haired majordomo, dressed in a tight black Mexican suit and an immaculate white shirt.

"Good morning," Clint said cheerfully in Spanish and the majordomo bowed ceremoniously. "My name is Clint Craig. I come from the United States and I would like to speak to Señor Jerome."

The Mexican studied him oddly, and was about to speak when a clear woman's voice lashed coldly from above: "What do you want?"

He raised his eyes. A young woman stood at the top of the stairs, looking at him in overt hostility. She was in her early twenties and strikingly beautiful. Her long black hair was dressed in a bun on top of her head. Big almond-shaped eyes, black as well, burned with an intense internal flame in the smooth-skinned oval face. Her nose and chin were small and delicate, but her protruding red lips lent to her whole face an expression of wild sensuality. She was wearing a tight riding suit of tan velvet that enhanced the lines of her statuesque body, her round breasts and her full hips. In her left hand she

163

held a flat Spanish hat that matched her clothes. She wore riding boots over her breeches. There was something proud and lovely in her carriage, and yet her mouth was tautly drawn and her nostrils quivered with sustained fury. "Who are you?" she asked again, this time in English. "What do you want?"

Clint was taken aback by the rude welcome. "Is this the hacienda of Mr. Jerome?" he asked courteously.

"Yes, it is," the girl snapped.

"May I talk to him?"

"No, you may not," she said dryly. "Cyrus Jerome was murdered at the exact spot where you stand, six years ago. Mrs. Jerome died twenty-three years ago. I am their daughter. Do you have any other questions?"

The terrible disappointment hit him painfully. "I am sorry," he said. "I am very sorry. I only wanted to clarify a certain matter with Mr. Jerome. I think I knew him once, a long time ago."

"You knew him, did you?" Her mocking voice, her tilted head, her slitted eyes clearly indicated that she did not believe him. "And where did you meet my father?"

"In Europe," Clint said. "In Germany." He could not understand the reason for the girl's hostility.

"He has never been in Germany," the girl said quickly. She slowly walked down the steps and stood in front of him, watching him intently. "What did you want to ask him?"

"Miss Jerome," Clint said, trying to pick the right words. "I realize that my presence here is not welcome. I understand that both your parents are dead, and you don't wish to talk about them. I am sorry to tread on such a sensitive and painful subject. But please, believe me, it is very important. I came especially from Europe to meet your father. I am a writer; my name is Clint Craig." She did not seem to care, so he took out his passport and showed it to her. "I think that what I am trying to do is important for your father's country, and in a way, for justice as well. I believe that your father was known by a different name when he was young. Do you have any photograph of him?"

"No, I don't," she said aggressively. "And now, if you have no more questions . . ."

"Wait." Clint took from his pocket the photograph of First Sergeant Jeffrey Oates, in army uniform. "Please tell me, was this your father?"

She did not even look at the picture. Instead, she suddenly smiled, but it was a wicked, weird kind of smile. "I have no picture," she said again. "But if you insist, I can take you to see my father."

"What?" Clint stared at her in dismay.

The majordomo, who had listened in silence to the exchange, paled and raised a trembling hand. "No, Señorita Consuelo, not that, please!"

"Don't tell me what to do, Esteban," she spat at him furiously. "Well, will you come with me?"

Her smile made Clint's blood run cold, and he murmured: "I don't understand."

"You will come, then," the girl whispered, and triumph glinted in her eyes.

Clint nodded.

"Come!" She purposefully strode to the sports car, and switched on the ignition. The engine roared. Clint had barely got into the car when she stepped on the gas, and the convertible darted forward with a strident screeching of tires. Clint glanced back and saw Esteban running to the van.

The car tires screeched and screamed all the way down the sharply curving road. Consuelo Jerome drove as if possessed, ignoring the traffic signs, taking crazy risks, forcing peasants walking on the road to dive in panic into the roadside bushes. They crossed the city, scaring a few early morning risers, rattled up a badly paved street, and finally stopped in front of the cemetery. *Panteon Municipal* read the inscription over the grille gate. Consuelo got out of the car, pushed the gate open and entered the cemetery with Clint following. She went past a red uneven rock stamped with a cross, went around an obelisk-shaped monument and stepped into the arched doorway of a low chapel. A big crucifix hung on the opposite wall, over an altar laden with massive candlesticks. In the middle of the chapel there was a round, dark opening, and stone steps led to the crypt below. Consuelo went down the circular stairs, and Clint quickly followed.

The crypt was plunged in semidarkness. Clint stopped for a second, till his eyes gradually got used to the obscurity. He made a few steps forward, and all of a sudden he halted, thunderstruck. He was staring at the most horrifying sight he had ever seen, a sight that surpassed in horror any horror chamber he had visited. All around him, on both sides of the narrow gallery, stood hundreds of corpses, their mouths gaping, their hollow eyes seeming to focus on him. Most of them were naked; a few wore rags and shoes. An uncontrolled shiver ran through his body. Could such a ghoulish reality exist—or was he having a nightmare of terror? His saliva dried in his mouth and his pulse throbbed madly in his temples. God, was that real? In the twentieth century? A kingdom of the dead, in the heart of Mexico?

"Come!" the girl's voice commanded.

His body stiff, his mind in turmoil, he walked, terrified, among the upright corpses. There were men, women, little children, their yellowish bodies desiccated like mummies. They had their hair, their teeth, their sex organs; hideous expressions were stamped on their faces.

Consuelo was waiting for him at the end of the gallery, her face a mask of fury. She pointed at a withered corpse, standing in a kind of niche in the wall. "Here is my father, Cyrus Jerome," she whispered savagely.

Clint raised his eyes in aversion. His look slowly moved up the naked body. He beheld the petrified legs, the shrunken penis, the sunken belly, the scrawny neck, the gaping mouth, the crescent-shaped scar in the dead tissue, under the dried left eye.

He had found him at last. All that remained of First Sergeant Jeffrey Oates.

Chapter Nine:

October 29—October 30:

CODE

Slow steps echoed in the gallery. Clint sharply looked over his shoulder and saw a dark figure walking toward them. He recognized Esteban, the aging majordomo of Hacienda Isabel. The silver-haired Mexican came near them and stood by Clint's side. He did not utter a word, but his sad, reproachful eyes held Consuelo in a grim focus. The girl furiously stared back at him. She was about to speak when her lower lip started trembling. She clenched her teeth, bent her head and quickly walked away, repeatedly slapping her hat on her hip. Esteban's eyes followed her upright figure until she disappeared in the darkness and they heard the tapping of her heels on the stone staircase. *"Pobrecita,"* the Mexican murmured compassionately.

Clint made a step after her, but Esteban gently put his hand on his shoulder. "Don't go," he said softly. "Please wait." There was an innate goodness in the wise brown eyes that studied him in deep concern. "You are pale as a ghost," Esteban said. "Señorita Consuelo should not have taken you here." He sighed. *"Pobrecita,"* he said again, "poor child."

Clint ran his tongue over his dry lips. "What . . ." he started to say and the word came in a rasping sound from his contracted throat. He swallowed and breathed deeply. He was not a man to scare easily, but this ghastly encounter with death had shaken him tremendously.

"You are shocked," Esteban said kindly. "You didn't know what lay in store for you here. Stay a moment with me. If you go out now, you'll bear the horror for the rest of your life. There is nothing supernatural here, nothing that cannot be explained."

"But how did this corpse . . ." Clint began again, pointing at Jeffrey Oates's body.

Esteban raised his hand. "I'll tell you about it, too. In a moment." He started to walk, very slowly, between the two rows of mummies, and Clint followed. "Guanajuato," the Mexican said, "has a very dry climate. The driest in Mexico. The composition of the soil is also very special. No worms. No bacteria. Many of the corpses buried here don't decompose. They bloat, then shrivel, and become completely mummified in three to four years. Their hair, their teeth, sometimes even their eyes are preserved." He pointed to a woman's naked body, whose tongue was trapped between her teeth and whose odd, opaque eyes seemed to be popping out of their sockets. "This woman was murdered. Strangled. That is how they found her in her grave five years later." He resumed his slow walk. "Now, according to our laws the family of the deceased should pay for the burying lot, so his corpse would stay there forever. But the poor families have no money for that purpose. Therefore, five years after the burial, the cemetery workers exhume the corpses and bury them in a common grave to make place for others."

Clint nodded, gradually affected by the calm that emanated from the Mexican.

"This cemetery was inaugurated about a hundred years ago. When they started exhuming the corpses of the poor devils, the workers discovered to their amazement that many of them had been miraculously preserved. The authorities decided to transfer the mummies to this underground gallery. After a few years, the mayor of Guanajuato decided to make this gallery accessible to the public. They named it 'Museum of the Mummies,' and people started visiting."

"You mean that people are paying money to see these . . . these things?" Clint asked in disbelief.

"Oh yes." The Mexican nodded. "You are a writer, aren't you? So you must be a man who observes human reactions and studies the human mind. Didn't you notice that people have a strange attraction to death and horror? They flock here in thousands, from all over the country. This afternoon, when the museum will be open, they will stand in line to see what you saw." Esteban bent and picked up a small white ticket. "Here, look."

Clint examined the small rectangle of paper. *"Museo de las Momias"* read the print. *"Cinco pesos."* He cleared his throat. "I can't believe it. People are paying five pesos to see that?"

"Well, there is a lot to see." Esteban smiled dryly. "These two mummies, here, were among the first to be exhumed. They were a couple of Frenchmen killed in the civil war.

168

Here"—he pointed to the nude fat body of a woman, holding something small in her left hand—"is the corpse of a woman who died during a Caesarean operation. You can still see the incision in her belly. In her hand she holds the mummy of her unborn child. They say it is the smallest mummy in the world."

Clint suddenly remembered that yesterday, at the car-rental counter in the Mexico City Airport, the employee had started to laugh when he had told him where he was going. "You are going to Guanajuato?" he had said. "Why should you go all that way? Look at my friend—he is a real mummy!" The Mexican had pointed at his skeletally thin colleague, and they both had guffawed loudly, slapping their knees. He had smiled politely, thinking that was a kind of private joke. Now he understood what they meant.

"Here is a woman who was buried after an attack of catalepsy," Esteban was saying. "She must have awakened, hours later, in the grave. See how she scratched herself before she finally succumbed to the lack of air."

"It is sickening," Clint said. He suddenly imagined a poor child whose mother had been exhumed, and he would have to come and see her in that ghoulish exhibition, jaw dropping, breasts dangling, pubic hair hanging in loose strands, revealing her withered vagina. Five pesos.

"One of your famous writers visited this place forty years ago. His name was Bradbury, Ray Bradbury. You know him?"

"Yes, of course," Clint said, surprised.

"He wrote a story about Guanajuato. He called it 'The Mummies,' I think."

Clint shook his head. "I have not read it," he said.

A hideous black-haired head, its eyes closed, was exhibited in a glass case beside a few mummies of children. Esteban pointed at it. "This is the head of a murderer, Julio Nieto. He was executed for the assassination of Señor Geo Ross, in eighteen hundred ninety-nine. When the head was exhumed and put here on display"—he sadly smiled—"the primitive Indians started bringing here flowers and small offerings. They thought that was the head of a saint. Some saint! But popular beliefs are very strong, you know. Even today, we find sometimes a bunch of wild flowers lying on top of the case."

Esteban turned back, and again they approached the niche where the corpse of Jeffrey Oates stood. "Today they won't bring new corpses here anymore," he said. "They cremate them. And Señorita Consuelo could pay, of course, for her father's lot. But she had seen him murdered, in front of her. She loved him very dearly, and she swore to find his murderer one day. So she had him buried, and exhumed, and put here. As a reminder."

"A reminder that one day she would kill his murderer?" Clint asked.

Esteban shrugged. "She has a very fiery temper. A hot-blooded woman, like her mother." He raised his hands and sighed again. "What can I say? She is an orphan, very lonely in that big hacienda. All she speaks of is revenge. Sometimes I am afraid, very afraid for her. This is not a sane thing to do." He motioned at the mummy. "She might get crazy."

Craig nodded thoughtfully. "How was Señor Jerome killed?" he asked. There were no marks of violence on the body.

"He was shot at the back of the neck," Esteban side, and turned away from the yellowish mummy. They went out of the crypt.

The sun was shining in a deep blue sky and big acacia trees were peacefully rustling in the morning wind. Clint rubbed his eyes. He thought of Dante's description of returning from Hades, from the world of the dead.

Esteban walked beside him. He seemed to hesitate, then finally asked without looking at him: "Did you . . . did you recognize the body? Was that the man you were looking for?"

"Yes," Clint said. "His real name was not Cyrus Jerome. He was called Jeffrey Oates and he was believed to be dead for thirty-five years."

Esteban stopped and looked at him in amazement. "But this is impossible!" he said. "He never said anything, and I knew him since he came to this country, in forty-five!"

"He kept his secret," Clint said.

Esteban halted by the cemetery gate, his face an image of distress. "What are you going to do now?"

"I don't know," Clint admitted. "I wanted to talk to Consuelo, but she wouldn't talk to me. I don't know why."

Esteban wanted to say something, but checked himself and kept quiet. Clint gave him a long look. "I guess I should go back to the hacienda to pick up my car, and then I'll return to my hotel."

"Where are you staying?"

"In the Castillo de Santa Cecilia."

"No need for you to come back to the hacienda," Esteban said quickly. "Go back to your hotel. I shall drive your car

170

down there. Maybe . . . maybe the señorita will talk to you later."

Clint nodded. "All right." Esteban motioned toward the van, inviting him to get in, but he shook his head. "No, I'd rather walk back."

The Mexican smiled in understanding. "Yes, some fresh air will do you good. *Hasta luego!*" He climbed into the van.

"Good-bye," Clint called after him. "And thank you—*gracias,* Esteban."

He did not feel like returning to the hotel right away.

He strolled by the Granaditas fort and reached the lush Union garden, shaped in the form of a slice of cheese. He dropped into a popular restaurant, elbowed his way to the crowded counter and had the same meal as the Mexican workers: a chunk of fried fat, called *ciçarron,* dipped in hot chili sauce, and a bottle of beer. He felt good to be here, among real people, to hear their laughter, smell the sweat of their bodies; it made quite a contrast with the monstrosities he had left in their underground cave. Yes, he reflected, he should be grateful to Esteban. The old Mexican had dispelled the mystery of the crypt and led him back to the firm ground of logic. His reasonable explanation had swept away the primitive fears that had assailed him when he had first seen the gaping mouths and the twisted corpses. His shock down there had been so tremendous that he had not even grasped the importance of his discovery: he had found Jeffrey Oates.

"Señor Craig?" The clerk at the hotel desk smiled with relief when he entered the lobby an hour later. "Somebody is waiting for you. This way, please."

He looked for the severe black suit and the silver hair of Esteban, but it was a feminine figure in tan velvet who rose from a colonial armchair in the far corner and came toward him. Consuelo Jerome stopped in front of him, and he found to his great surprise that her face was flushed with embarrassment and she failed to find the right words. "I . . . I am sorry for what happened this morning," she stammered, trying to avoid his eyes. "Esteban told me about your conversation. He thinks you are a good man . . ." She bit her lower lip. "You must understand, we had lately a very unpleasant experience."

"Why don't we sit down?" he suggested.

"No, no, I'll be on my way." She stood awkwardly in the middle of the big lobby, facing him. "As I said, we had a bad experience. Somebody phoned the hacienda several times, asking if this was the ranch of Mr. Cyrus Jerome. Finally, last

171

week, some people broke into my father's room. They tried to steal his papers."

His eyes lit with sudden interest. "Did they take anything?"

"No, I don't think so. They succeeded in breaking the locks of the chest where he kept his papers, but the servants heard them and alerted Esteban. We tried to get hold of them but they managed to escape."

"I see," Clint said. Somebody was moving ahead of him, systematically destroying vital evidence. A week before he came to Nuremberg, they murdered old Doctor Hoffmann; a week before he came to Guanajuato, they tried to steal the papers of Jeffrey Oates.

"Then you came in," the girl was saying, "and also asked about the ranch of Cyrus Jerome. When I overheard you talking to Esteban, this morning in the hacienda, I thought that you were one of those people who broke into our house last week. So I . . . I was not very friendly." She blushed again. "Mr. Craig, will you please excuse me for . . . for . . . ?"

"Yes of course," he said, ill at ease.

She quickly looked up at him. "You told Esteban that my father had a different name once. And you also said that there was a secret in his past."

"Yes, that's true."

"Will you come tonight to have dinner with me at the hacienda?" Her voice was softer now. "I would like to hear from you about my father."

Clint suddenly felt a surge of pity for the unhappy, high-strung girl. "I want to be completely honest with you, Consuelo. I might have to tell you some unpleasant truths about him."

Her eyes glistened with contained tears and she drew a deep breath. "Please come," she said again.

Clint slowly nodded.

They had dinner on the veranda. The starry sky formed a canopy over their heads and the multicolored lights of Guanajuato spread like a carpet at their feet. The candles on their table were protected from the soft fresh breeze by bell-shaped crystal globes. The servants moved soundlessly as shadows, carrying silver salvers laden with exquisite food. Esteban himself, his face beaming, emerged every now and then from the darkness to fill their glasses with chilled cloudy white wine. Consuelo looked very lovely in a long white dress, a *rebozo* wrapped around her shoulders. They started their dinner with small talk. Clint waited for the girl to speak first about her father. He was prepared to tell her all he knew about him, hoping to learn in return about his murder six years ago. The murder was certainly connected with the secret that Oates-Jerome had carried all the way from Stadelheim jail to this Mexican retreat.

But Consuelo did not mention her father. After a while, Clint indirectly hinted at the purpose of his trip; as no comment came from Consuelo, he mentioned it overtly, time and again. Still, she did not react. Furthermore, whenever he spoke her father's name, she would quickly switch subjects and start talking about something else. It dawned on Clint that she was afraid to talk about Cyrus Jerome. There could be no doubt that she worshiped him, and dreaded the moment when she would hear the truth. He suddenly became aware of her solitude. She was a lonely, fragile girl, living withdrawn from the world in her big hacienda, surrounded by tragic memories of a mother she had never known and a beloved father who had been assassinated in front of her. A girl with no friends, no family, burning with an all-consuming lust for revenge. Esteban had been right. The macabre streak that had driven her to expose the naked mummy of her father in the Guanajuato cemetery betokened a wavering mental balance. She sat in front of him, so pretty, so appealing with her sparkling eyes, her glistening red mouth and heavy black hair—and yet she was a haunted girl, lingering on the very verge of fathomless insanity. He was swept by sincere compassion for the unhappy young woman; on a sudden impulse he decided to drop the subject of her father for a while. *The hell with it, Clint Craig,* he said to himself. *Why don't you try to make her happy, just for a few hours? Tomorrow you will be on your way—and she will sink back into her solitude, her morbid pilgrimages to the scary crypt and her dreams of revenge and death.*

He tried to amuse her, to make her laugh. He told her stories from his past, described his student life in Paris, his trips around the world, some memorable experiences he had had as a writer and a reporter. Gradually the sadness disappeared from her face and her eyes livened up. She listened to his stories, enthralled, and her laughter had a spontaneous, candid ring. Halfway through their dessert he leaned back and said: "Consuelo, what about going down to the city? They say that there is nothing more enjoyable than a Sunday night in Guanajuato."

She drew back and her voice was uncertain. "I don't know," she said, nervously fidgeting with the silk tassels of her *rebozo*. "I . . . I have never gone to Guanajuato after dark. I don't know any friends there."

"Well, you know me, don't you?" he said boyishly. "Come on—the night is still young. I'll take good care of you, I promise."

She hesitated for another moment, but finally she smiled and gave in. "All right," she said and laughed, surprised at her own temerity.

They parked the car behind the Teatro Juárez and strolled in the maze of small crooked streets winding up the hill. Soon they were lost in the labyrinth of narrow cobbled alleys twining and twisting between the ancient houses of the old quarter. Some of the sinuous lanes led to tiny, lovely squares, surrounded by suspended balconies and open doors that offered a glimpse into pleasant patios. At times, the alleys would become incredibly narrow, like deep, dark canyons running between blue and white walls. In one of the narrowest streets, Consuelo suddenly pointed up. "Look." She smiled. Two young people, a boy and a girl, leaned over from opposite balconies and their lips met in a kiss. "This lane is called *El Callejón del Beso*," she explained, "the alley of the kiss."

"Yes"—he smiled in return—"and I can see why."

Suddenly her face was very close in the darkness, and her soft, ripe lips hesitantly touched his. He returned her kiss, surprised, but did not say a word. He felt strangely embarrassed.

They emerged on the picturesque Baratillo Plaza. Sounds of laughter and music came from the far end, where people were sitting in an open-air café. A trio of young Mexicans were plucking mandolins and guitars, singing romantic serenades of the nineteenth century. Clint and Consuelo found a vacant table. Consuelo listened blissfully to the soft melodies, a peaceful expression settling over her lovely features. The minstrels were dressed in knee breeches and ruffles, and wore long cloaks ornamented with colorful ribbons. "Who are they?" Clint asked the waiter who came to take their order. "The Guanajuato *estudiantinas*, señor," the stocky waiter whispered. "They are student singers, typical to this city. You see the ribbons on their cloaks?" He chuckled softly. "Presents from señoritas for the beautiful serenades they sang under their balconies."

They sat in the small café for a long while. After the singing was over, they drifted through the lively streets, occasion-

174

ally dropping into a tavern where mellow-voiced *mariachis* sang popular tunes, inviting the public to join in. In another small square, a group of amateur actors was performing *entremeses*—one-act miniplays—written by the great Miguel Cervantes. While enjoying the purity of the style and the old, noble Castilian language, Clint let his mind drift back to the horrid experience of this morning. How could such morbid exhibitions and such refined artistic performances coexist side by side? This strange city was a mixture of startling contrasts.

Exactly like the girl beside him. Gone was the woman with the distorted face and the fire of hatred in her eyes. When they went back to the car Consuelo beamed with happiness. Stars were dancing in her eyes, and she told him, dreamily: "This was one of the most beautiful nights in my life, Clint. Thank you."

The hacienda was plunged in darkness. A single old-fashioned lantern shone above the porch. "I'll see you tomorrow," he started to say, turning toward his car, but she took him by both hands and came shyly to nestle against him. Her voice was almost inaudible. "Don't go now. Not now that I am so happy." She slowly raised her face toward him. The red lips parted invitingly. They kissed and she held him close. He felt that her arms and body were trembling. "Come," she said, and led him by the hand through the big, dark rooms. He followed, puzzled, a flurry of contradictory thoughts rushing through his mind. Was she so hungry for sex? Was this open invitation to him, a stranger, the fruit of a deranged mind? Or did she follow a devious preconceived plan? He could not forget the hateful fire that had glowed in her eyes this very morning. He reluctantly stepped over the threshold of her bedroom. Still, the voluptuous body, the sensual red mouth were irresistibly tempting. And when she slowly took off her clothes in the moonlit bedroom and stood in front of him, her breasts erect, her long legs slightly parted, all her body quivering, opening to him—he reached for her hungrily.

But when she lay beneath him, and he entered her, she was almost immobile, strangely passive. He could not tell if she climaxed, when he could not control his building hardness anymore and his spasms exploded and slowly died inside her. Her breath became even again, and after a few minutes she murmured shyly: "I have made love with a man only once before. Hold me, stay close to me."

He had been completely wrong, he now realized, as he clung to the warm body, drained but strangely unsatisfied. It was not for the sake of sex that she had made her advances, and offered herself to him. It was for a bit of warmth, for his touch, for a fleeting substitute of love. This girl craved someone to hold and to be held by. The burden of being alone, without love, without a man to cherish and care for, was too heavy for her. He touched her face tenderly. Poor, loveless Consuelo.

Clint rolled to the other side of the bed and stared at the ceiling. He understood Consuelo's need for affection and felt compassion for the lonely girl. But nothing else. Nothing like the overwhelming passionate response Jill had touched off in his heart and body. Jill was present in his mind even during his brief moment of abandon in Consuelo's arms. That strange, quickly fading closeness with Oates's daughter only made him realize how deeply, how desperately he had become involved with Jill, how much he longed for her presence and her touch.

He arose, fumbled in his clothes and took a cigarillo from his pocket. He sat on the edge of the large bed, smoking in silence. Consuelo sensed that he was not hers anymore, that he had retreated to his distant, alien world. She lay quietly for a long while, and finally whispered in a miserable voice: "Tell me about my father."

He hesitated. He did not want to hurt her. But he could not back away from his promise. He told her everything he knew. He told her that her father had been a first sergeant in the military police, assigned to guard Otto Brandl's cell. He said there was no longer any doubt in his own mind that Oates took part in the murder of the German, and later faked his own death and escaped with his part of the loot to Mexico.

She listened, speechless, and by the spasms of her huddled body he understood that she was soundlessly sobbing. He reached over and gently touched her shoulder. "You have to learn to live with this, Consuelo," he said. "Your father did commit an abominable crime. But I don't think that he did it out of greed. He did it for one reason only: to start a new life with the girl he loved, Isabel Carranza, in a faraway place. He must have got here first and then secretly established contact with your mother."

"Who . . . who died in the car crash in Germany?" Consuelo asked suddenly.

He shrugged. "We'll probably never know. Germany was in complete disarray then, throngs of homeless people were drifting around, many of them without papers. . . . It must have been a poor wretch they picked at random, maybe a prisoner

176

of Stadelheim jail. So many people disappeared at the end of the war, without leaving a trace."

His voice faded away. Consuelo was not crying anymore. "I loved my father very dearly," she whispered. "Whatever he might have done—for me he was the most wonderful father. But he was unhappy here."

"Unhappy? Why?"

"He said that after the death of my mother he hated this place. He wanted very much to go back to America. That was when I first started to understand that there was a secret in his past, that he could not go back. I was seventeen at the time, and I still remember him speaking with nostalgia of 'the old country.' That's how he called it. And then, one day, when he was reading an American magazine, he thought of something."

"Of what?" Clint asked quickly, suddenly alert.

"I don't know. He was very excited, all of a sudden. He told me that by sheer luck he had found the way to go back to the United States. He went to his study and wrote a letter to somebody in America. Two weeks later, when he went out for his evening tour of the hacienda, he was murdered. He was shot in the back, down by the stairs where I met you this morning."

"And nobody spotted the murderer?"

"Nobody *caught* the murderer," Consuelo corrected, and her voice was suddenly the same as on the previous morning, cold, cruel, loaded with hatred. "But I saw him. I had gone to the small garage, over there. Those days it was not a garage, but a stable. I had a young mare, and went to feed her some sugar. I was standing inside when I saw my father coming back, and this man came from behind and shot him. I wanted to shout, to cry for help, but I was like . . . like paralyzed. Probably that saved my life, for he would have killed me too. Then the man turned, and I saw his face in the moonlight. I saw him very clearly, and I rememebr every trait, every wrinkle in that face. One day I'll find him and I'll kill him."

Clint took her by the chin and looked at her face. The hatred had disfigured the lovely features and transformed them into an ugly, vengeful mask. "Life is not only hatred and revenge, Consuelo," he said gently.

"Mine is," she snapped back.

She got up and threw a robe over her shoulders. "Come," she said. "I want to show you something."

He dressed quickly and followed her to her father's study. It was a small room, tastelessly furnished with heavy Mexican furniture. She pointed to a small chest whose lock had been recently broken. "My father used to keep his papers here," she said. "You can read them; I don't mind. You cannot find there anything worse than what you told me just now. And maybe . . . maybe you'll find something that could help me trace my father's killer."

Craig opened the chest and dug into the heaps of paper inside.

Two hours later he slowly rose from his seat. Most of the papers were of no use to him at all. But two military ID cards tucked in an envelope at the bottom of the chest were in the name of Jeffrey Oates. Those, together with the mummy in the museum, were the first tangible evidence to prove his theory. He had been right all along. Oates was Jerome. Oates had not died in Germany. He had killed, he had stolen a part of Goering's treasure and had lived in Mexico under an assumed name. Until the day when somebody, probably the leader of the conspiracy, had come and killed him.

There were no documents in the chest linking Oates with Jefferson or anybody else. There was nothing concerning the other members of the conspiracy.

Except one item: a slip of paper bearing the date August 9, 1945, and a handwritten inscription: SF 756324, B.S.C. Geneva.

He copied the sequence of letter and numbers into his notebook. He felt that they were the key to the enigma. That's where he would get the answer to all his questions. Geneva.

In Geneva it was early afternoon, but the leaden sky that lay low over the city enveloped it in a premature dusk. The biting October winds were howling over Lake Leman, whipping its dark waters into frothy waves, driving the Geneva swans and ducks to seek cover beneath the bridges of the Rhône River. The few sailboats that had tried to plow their way to the center of the lake had been brutally forced back by the sudden fierce gusts; in the half-empty streets pedestrians hurried, bending low, in quest of more merciful havens.

Ahmed Abd-el-Krim watched the shivering city from the big bay windows of his suite on top of the Hotel du Mont Blanc. He was wearing a long loose gown, the traditional North African *jellaba,* the munching some *amarradin,* his favorite sweet. It was a thick, sticky paste made of apricots that had been dried and pressed in a Syrian mountain village until they acquired a rich amber color and a sourish taste. During the war he had lived for weeks on that paste alone, or on some handfuls of dried dates.

He went to his desk and read again the draft resolution he was going to submit to the OPEC council tomorrow. He made a couple of corrections with his cheap ball-point pen. It was a good resolution. If adopted—and he had every reason to believe it would be—it could inaugurate a new, tougher policy of OPEC toward the West; it could also be the first open defeat of Ali Shazli, and the beginning of Abd-el-Krim's ascent to the leadership of the energy government of the world. And, one day, of the Algerian government as well.

The first round of the showdown between him and Shazli had taken place the previous night, at the meeting of the inner council in Shazli's office. Abd-el-Krim smiled to himself. The meeting had been called at his demand and he had timed it perfectly. He knew that Sheikh Badran, the sleazy Kuwaiti pleasure-seeker, was in Paris, screwing his ballet dancer, and would be unable to attend the conclave; Shazli could count therefore only on the half-hearted support of the Iraqi, Baghdadi. He had also made sure of the steady support of the Libyan, Nusserat. The man was a fanatic, but even fanatics could be useful at times. His strategy planned to the minutest detail, Abd-el-Krim had walked into Shazli's office and presented his draft resolution: OPEC should cut the oil supply to the United States by 25 percent in the forthcoming weeks, "due to difficulties resulting from the destruction of several oil fields in the Middle East." He was convinced that such a measure would deal a mortal blow to Jefferson and serve as a further warning to those in America who still preached the takeover of the oil fields by force. Lately he had started to doubt that Murphy's scheme to compromise Jefferson was progressing as well as reported. The election was only a week away, time was growing short and Jefferson was still there, losing popularity, indeed, but still kicking. Abd-el-Krim had been a soldier; he believed in quick, brutal solutions. The oilfield fires had shaken Jefferson badly; an oil embargo, now, could bring his downfall.

As soon as he had presented his case, Shazli had counterattacked. The resolution was a boomerang, he said. An oil embargo, even though partial, even though resulting from *force majeure*, might trigger an angry reaction in the United States.

179

Some would interpret it as an attempt on the part of OPEC to influence the election; others would present it as proof that OPEC was unreliable, and that King Omar's promises of last week were empty words. Wheeler himself would be badly hurt, Shazli added; he based his energy program on close co-operation with OPEC, and now OPEC was driving a dagger into his back.

Abd-el-Krim had listened to Shazli politely, and had even complimented him on his reasonable attitude. Nevertheless, he said, he would go ahead with his project. Nusserat had supported him, as rehearsed; Baghdadi had mumbled some generalities, as presumed; and Abd-el-Krim had won. For the first time. Shazli's authority had been openly challenged; for the first time, he had lost his temper and had furiously shouted at him: "If you submit your resolution to the council, I shall vote against you!"

Let him vote, Abd-el-Krim said to himself, savoring in advance tomorrow's drama. Let him lose and bite the dust. He does not belong there anymore, he has become too meek, too westernized, a new version of the colonialist lackey.

The phone rang. "Monsieur Abd-el-Krim?" The hotel concierge spoke very reverently. "There is a gentleman here who would like to speak to you. His name is Jean Pierre Maarouf, and he is a Lebanese journalist."

He knew Maarouf quite well. "Yes, put him on the line."

"Monsieur le Ministre?" Like most Lebanese Christians, Maarouf spoke an excellent French. "Here is Jean-Pierre Maarouf, from *L'Orient* daily. Maybe you remember me?"

"Of course I do."

"I just got a telex from Beirut to ask for your comments on an article we are going to publish tomorrow. The main points of the article have been telexed to me as well."

"And the article is about me?"

"You are mentioned in it, yes."

"All right, then come over to my suite. I happen to be free right now."

He hung up, puzzled. Could somebody have already leaked the news about his draft resolution? Who? Nusserat? He was not on speaking terms with the Lebanese. Shazli? But he had no interest whatsoever in heralding his upcoming defeat. Then who? Baghdadi?

There was a discreet knock on the door and the young, handsome Maarouf walked in. He was an athletic, narrow-
180

hipped young man, looking very swashbuckling with his mass of black hair and his deep blue eyes. Abd-el-Krim remembered somebody joking about Maarouf's eyes. They were proof, the joker said, that the Crusaders had some fun in Beirut on their way to the Holy Land. But the young Lebanese did not seem to care. The rumors said that every night there was a different girl in his bed; therefore, as far as the Crusaders were concerned, the account had been settled long ago.

"How are you, *mon cher* Maarouf?" He could not refrain from a jab at the journalist's behavior, which offended his puritanical views. "Still busy enjoying the pleasures of Geneva?"

Maarouf bowed his head with respect, but his tone was reserved. "Good afternoon, *Monsieur le Ministre*."

"Come in," Abd-el-Krim said lightly. He turned, and threw over his shoulder: "It's about the council meeting tomorrow, right?"

"No, not exactly." Maarouf seemed ill at ease. He hesitated a moment, then fumbled in his pocket and took out a sheet of paper. He carefully tore off the lower part and handed it to the Algerian. "Here are, as I told you, the main points of the article."

"Let's see." Abd-el-Krim took the telex to his desk and put on his glasses. He started to read aloud: "TITLE TOMORROW LEADING ARTICLE FRONT PAGE: 'ALGERIAN MINISTER IMPLICATED OILFIELD FIRES' . . . What?" He stared at the printed sheet in utter disbelief. For a moment he was petrified with shock, then straightened up, his face becoming crimson with fury. "What is this?" he yelled hoarsely at the young Lebanese. "Who gave you that trash? What is this, a frame-up?"

Maarouf was pale as a sheet. "I know as much as you, Mr. Minister," he stammered. "I received the telex only half an hour ago."

His lips drawn, his nails digging into the palms of his fists, Abd-el-Krim bent over the telex again. The lines trembled before his eyes.

"MAIN POINTS ARTICLE AS FOLLOWS: SABOTAGE OILFIELDS AL HAMRA RAS AT TANNURAH BIR AL NABI BELIEVED CARRIED OUT BY TEAM ALGERIAN COMMANDOS. LEADERS TEAM SERVED IN ALGERIAN INDEPENDENCE WAR UNDER ORDERS AHMED ABD EL KRIM PRESENTLY OIL MINISTER ALGERIAN GOVERNMENT. CHIEF OF

OPERATION BELIEVED TO BE SAMIR KURIAH CLOSE FRIEND AND CONFIDANT ABD EL KRIM. OUR SOURCES PROVIDED NAMES SEVERAL OTHER AGENTS..."

A list of names followed, the real names of some of the agents that he had picked himself. He cursed venomously and resumed his reading.

"MENTIONED ABOVE ALGERIANS SEEN VISITING RESIDENCE ABD EL KRIM SEVERAL TIMES BEFORE SABOTAGES CARRIED OUT. SAME LATER IDENTIFIED IN BAHRAIN AND SAUDI ARABIA. TWO ALGERIANS ARRESTED BY LOCAL POLICE IN BAHRAIN AFTER FIRE HAVE BEEN RELEASED FOLLOWING DISCREET INTERVENTION BY ALGERIAN AMBASSADOR. RELIABLE SOURCES LINK ABD EL KRIM AND HARDLINERS ALGERIAN GOVERNMENT TO UNPRECEDENTED OILFIELD SABOTAGE."

His knees gave way and he slumped into a chair, his eyes looking fixedly in front of him. His thoughts rushed madly ahead, drawing the inevitable conclusion: he was destroyed. This article will appear in tomorrow's *L'Orient,* to be at once picked up by all the major world media. It will create a worldwide sensation. OPEC will be accused as the instigator of the sabotage; Abd-el-Krim will be labeled a terrorist. The reporters will hunt him down like a pack of mad dogs. No denial will help. And those bastards at *L'Orient* probably have enough evidence to substantiate their accusations. He immediately knew who was the culprit: that filthy harlot's son, Ali Shazli. He had fed the story to the Lebanese, there could be no doubt about that. Abd-el-Krim's eyes wandered aimlessly around the room and fell on the draft resolution lying on the desk. He would never submit it to a vote in the council meeting tomorrow; as far as he knew, the way the Algerian president was making decisions, he might not even be here tomorrow.

Maarouf coughed discreetly. "Mr. Minister, would you answer a few..."

"Get out!" Abd-el-Krim snapped, seething with anger. "Get out of here!"

"But I hoped that you would comment on the article."

"My only comment is that if you print that pack of lies I shall sue your paper for libel! Get out, now!"

The reporter retreated hastily. Abd-el-Krim stepped into the bedroom, removed his *jellaba* and hurriedly dressed. His feverish fingers trembled as he buttoned his shirt. He picked up the phone: "Get me a taxi!" he barked at the concierge, and went out, clenching and unclenching his fists in blind rage. He rode the elevator down and crossed the lobby, muttering to himself, ignoring his bodyguard who rose from an armchair by the entrance, folded his paper and hastened to join him. "Rue des Délices, the OPEC building," he barked at the cab driver, while his bodyguard ran around the car and took the front seat. During the ride, he read once again the telex from Beirut. His sweating hands smudged the print on the crumpled paper. Shazli. The sly sonofabitch, he made him sick.

He emerged from the elevator, ignored the bewildered secretary, and strode into Shazli's office. The chairman of OPEC was sitting at the conference table, presiding over a meeting with the senior executives of ELF, the French government-owned petroleum company. His traditional cup of steaming tea was at his elbow. He quickly rose and smiled nervously. "Ahmed? What brings you here?"

"I must talk to you," Abd-el-Krim said in English. "Now. It's very urgent."

Shazli looked at him thoughtfully, then nodded. "Yes, certainly. You would not have walked into the middle of a meeting if you did not have a good reason." He turned to his guests, spreading his arms in apology. "Messieurs, I must confer for a couple of minutes with Monsieur Abd-el-Krim, whom you know well. Will you excuse us? We'll resume our conference very shortly." The Frenchmen got up, two of them approaching Abd-el-Krim, who shook their hands absently.

Shazli closed the door after them, then turned to the Algerian. "What happened?" he asked, his face showing concern.

"That's what happened," Abd-el-Krim roared, and threw the crumpled telex on his desk. Shazli picked it up and studied it intently.

"And don't tell me that you don't know about it!" Abd-el-Krim snarled furiously.

Shazli raised his eyes. "Oh, yes, I know about it. They called me from Beirut half an hour ago, to ask for my comment. I told them that this was a despicable lie, and a vile attempt to smear you and your country. I said that OPEC had full confidence in you and rejected these odious accusations against an outstanding member of its council."

"That's what you said. Isn't that nice?" Abd-el-Krim thumped his fist on the mahogany desk. "But you and I know the truth, Ali. We know that you gave them the story, you treacherous double-crosser!"

Shazli paled but remained calm. "I understand that you are distressed by this piece of slander," he said softly, "but I would refrain from any accusations, if I were you. And I would certainly use different language."

"Why should I use different language?" Abd-el-Krim's voice trembled with fury. "It's the truth. You gave them the story. You are the only one who could give them the story."

Shazli looked at him, his face devoid of any expression. "How could I give them that story? How could I find out all these details, all those names . . ."

"How?" The Algerian stood in front of him, fuming, his breath coming in quick, short gasps. "It was an easy thing for you to have me followed since our meeting in Washington. And then to spy on my men, the people I entrusted with the mission on your instructions."

Shazli sadly shook his head. "Why should I do such a thing?" he said in a very low voice.

"Why?" Abd-el-Krim almost choked with indignation. "You ask me why? To prevent me from going ahead with my draft resolution, that's why. To get rid of me, that's why. To get rid of a rival, who could defeat you and take your place behind that desk. You have been fighting me since the first time I walked into this room."

Shazli leaned back and closed his eyes, as he always did when he wanted to put some order in his thoughts. "Yes, I have fought you, Ahmed. Since the first time you walked into this room. That's true. And I'll tell you why. Because I thought, and I still think, that the policy you try to impose on us is dangerous for OPEC and for the Arab nations as well."

"Most of all for you," Abd-el-Krim interjected.

Shazli ignored the jab. "Since I assumed this position, the only matter of importance to me has been the benefit of our nations. There were battles that I won; there were others that I lost. You might call me a moderate, or a coward; but I always believed that we should not pull the rope too tight, because any extreme move on our side might turn into a boomerang. I objected to an oil embargo. I objected to steep raises in the price of oil. Sure, they could be very profitable to us in the short run. In the long run, however, they might lead us to disaster."

He rose from his chair, and paced around the room. "My grandfather, may he rest in peace, was a tribal chieftain. A warrior. He had fought all his life, and was known all over the Najd desert for his bravery. He once said to me: 'When you trap your enemy, when you have him cornered, or surrounded, or pinned to a wall—don't try to cut his head off. Leave him an outlet, a way to escape; let him save his life. Because a man who has his back to the wall is a desperate enemy, and he can be very dangerous. He might finally kill you.'"

"What . . ." Abd-el-Krim began, but Shazli raised his hand with authority. "Let me finish. What we are doing now, since nineteen seventy-three, is pushing the West with its back against the wall. We cut the oil supply. We raise the prices. Some of the council members want already to charge fifty dollars per barrel. Why not? The West has no other sources, the West must pay.

"But what you and your friends don't understand, Ahmed, is that the West won't pay infinitely. A democracy does not easily decide to wage war. I read history as a student, in England. If Hitler had not forced England to the wall, she would never have declared war on him. If the Japanese had not bombed Pearl Harbor, Roosevelt might have never succeeded in overcoming the American isolationists." He sighed. "And that is a mistake we are making now. We don't leave the West a way out."

"You speak like Jefferson," Abd-el-Krim hissed.

"Jefferson must be stopped," Shazli said forcefully. "But how did he become so popular? I'll tell you. Because of us. We made Jefferson. He just happens to express the feeling of a great many Americans. We shall stop him, all right. But what will happen next? If we don't change our policy, and don't lower our prices and stop those embargoes—a new Jefferson would arise. Even Wheeler, this pleasant, soft Wheeler we want so much in the White House, even he may have no choice but to make war on us. That's why I preach moderation. We have still our oil reserves for thirty or forty years, let's make the best of them. I'd rather sell a barrel for fifteen dollars for thirty years than raise the price to fifty, and have my country occupied by the Americans."

"We can blow the oil fields," Abd-el-Krim threw at him angrily.

Shazli suddenly turned and came to face Abd-el-Krim, looking closely in his eyes. "You know that this is cheap propaganda stuff. The truth is that the Americans, with their experts and equipment, can put down any oil-field fire in a couple of months."

"I never heard such defeatist language before," snapped Abd-el-Krim with contempt. "You think we cannot resist the Americans? And the Russians—they will just sit idly on their asses?"

"The Americans are still the most powerful nation in the world," Shazli said, lighting a cigarette. "And the Russians?" He sucked the smoke into his lungs and exhaled it slowly. "The Russians worry me. I don't think they would oppose any American offensive. I rather think . . ." He stopped in mid-sentence, his eyes lost in thought.

"All this doesn't change the fact that you destroyed me!" Abd-el-Krim said.

"I did not destroy you," Shazli said, irritated. "And you are not destroyed. Compromised, yes. But not destroyed. I believe you should have to resign as oil minister of Algeria. You can't stay in the cabinet after being charged with international sabotage. Your president must have been alerted already. I guess he will call you in the next couple of hours, ask for your resignation and offer you an honorable way out—like an appointment as ambassador to a South American country. Then, in a couple of years, after the scandal is forgotten, you might make a comeback. Who knows?" The shadow of a smile fluttered on his face. "Maybe I shall not be here anymore, and your way to the top will be all paved."

Abd-el-Krim felt he could strangle the man in front of him with his bare hands. But he just stood there in the middle of the room and glared at him.

"Why don't you go back to your hotel," Shazli asked gently, "and wait for your president's call? It might come at any moment now."

The call from the president of Algeria came to Abd-el-Krim's suite at the Hotel du Mont Blanc shortly after six P.M.

While Abd-el-Krim was discussing his resignation with the president of the Algerian Republic, a PanAm plane landed at the international airport of Geneva. Among its passengers was a tall, aging man with a wrinkled face. Chuck Belford had been granted a leave of absence from the CIA this very morning. In the transit hall of the airport he took out of his travel pouch an English passport, established in a different name, and a plane ticket that had been prepared beforehand. He got his boarding pass at the Aeroflot counter and sat quietly in a remote corner of the hall, waiting for the flight for Prague and Warsaw, with final destination Moscow.

Chapter Ten:

October 30—November 1:

DEPOSIT

The slim-waisted headwaiter daintily minced between the tables and steered them to a quiet booth on the upper level. "Here you are, Mr. Bohlen," he said, exaggerating his French accent. Clint slumped in his chair and exhaled a long breath as he unbuttoned his jacket and loosened his tie. "God, am I exhausted," he moaned and closed his eyes.

A pretty waitress was already bending over Peter Bohlen. "I'll have a Scotch on the rocks," he said. "And you, Clint?"

Clint barely opened his eyes, "What?"

Bohlen smiled amiably. "A drink. Cocktail. What will you have?"

"Oh, whatever." He made a vague gesture with his left hand and his eyelids dropped again.

"The last time we met, you had a double vodka martini," Bohlen said, leaning over the table. "Would you like the same?" Clint did not react, so he turned to the waitress. "Bring him a double vodka martini, on the rocks, with a twist." He studied Clint's face. The pockets under his eyes were puffed with fatigue, his hair was disheveled, and he badly needed a shave. His tan lightweight suit was rumpled and a dark line of sweat and dust had crusted on the collar of his blue shirt. "You do look exhausted, indeed."

Clint blinked a few times and tried to straighten in his chair. He ran his left hand over the stubble on his face. "Look, Peter—" His voice was low and weary. "I did not sleep the whole night, I drove four hours from Guanajuato to Mexico City, I flew another four hours on a crowded plane to New York. . . . Not to speak of the accumulation of fatigue for the last couple of weeks, since I started running around the world. This whole story is insane, and what I am doing is insane."

188

The waitress brought their drinks. "Are you ready to order?"

Clint pushed the menu aside. "Give me something light," he said. "Sole or trout, whatever you've got." Bohlen placed his order and the girl retreated. A group of Wheeler campaign volunteers, wearing their distinctive blue jackets, big Wheeler buttons in their lapels, came into the restaurant and swiftly took over two tables on the lower level. They looked exhilarated.

"What are they so happy about?" Clint asked, slightly annoyed.

"Their man is winning," Bohlen said. "Since the oil-field fires, the polls are on his side. He's got a six-point lead over Jefferson." He paused and watched the noisy campaigners thoughtfully. "This country has never been so excited about an election campaign," he remarked. "I haven't met one person who pretends to be neutral, or not to care. The oil issue has stirred a lot of passion."

"And whose side are you on?" Clint asked.

"I'm neutral," Bohlen said, and burst into his peculiar high-pitched laughter. "Anyway it's going to be a very close race. The winner will carry it by a very narrow margin."

Clint raised his hand to his face and touched the bridge of his nose with thumb and forefinger. Fine grains of dust had settled at the edges of his eyes. He looked down at his glass. "There might be no winner," he said wearily. "Just one runner. I am on the verge of opening a Pandora's box, Peter, and I must tell you that I am scared. I fear that what I find inside might change the destiny of the United States."

The waitress brought their salads and Bohlen poured a generous dose of creamy Roquefort dressing into his bowl. "You said that you got the evidence," he remarked, busy with his food.

"Not yet, not really."

Bohlen looked up at him, mildly puzzled. "That's what you said over the phone this morning, when you called me from Mexico. You said that you had found the evidence."

"I saw the evidence," Clint corrected. He munched a tasteless forkful of green salad. "I saw the body of Jeffrey Oates and I saw his papers. But I believe the real evidence is somewhere else. In Geneva." He took his notebook out of his inner pocket and leafed through it. "Here it is. SF seven-five-six-three-two-four, B.S.C. Geneva." He showed the inscription to Bohlen.

The publisher studied it, frowning. He returned the notebook to Clint, and a cunning smile slowly spread over his face. "And you have got a good guess as to what it means."

Craig shrugged. "It is not difficult. Geneva means Switzerland, which is already a good indication. B.S.C. means *Banque Suisse Centrale*, a small but very discreet bank in Geneva. The letters and numbers most likely refer to a secret account. And there," he suddenly bent forward and slapped his hand flat on the table, "there, I think, lies the solution."

A skeptical expression settled on Bohlen's long face. "How do you know? You found the number of a secret account in a Swiss bank. So what? What if it turns out to be an account that Jeffrey Oates opened in Geneva in nineteen forty-five? Something he left for his rainy days? And if I am right—then you'll be back to square one or almost, and you'll be blocked in the middle of your investigation, with no more leads to follow."

Clint shook his head vigorously. "No, you're wrong. I thought about that possibility. It can't be. The account is not in Jeffrey Oates's name."

"How do you know?" Bohlen repeated aggressively.

"Simple logic," Clint said, yawning and stretching his arms. "Look at the date. August ninth, nineteen forty-five. On this day, Oates was supposed to be dead for twenty-four hours, burned alive in his overturned jeep. But he was not dead. He was already on the run, over the Swiss border, with a forged passport in the name of Cyrus Jerome. Now, he was traveling to Mexico—where he would arrive by boat from Italy at mid-September the same year. On his way he stopped in Geneva and made a bank deposit. In his own name? Highly improbable. He was carrying his loot with him. We know that he came to Mexico with a lot of money. But let's say that he left a part of it in Geneva. Why didn't he ever return to take it? He never left Mexico from the day he arrived. He never told Consuelo anything. He never mentioned any bank account in Geneva in his will. And I saw the will."

He paused a second and took a long gulp of his drink. "The only logical conclusion is that on his way to Mexico, Oates stopped in Geneva and made a bank deposit for his partner, the head of the conspiracy. The man we are looking for."

Bohlen raised his brows. "Don't you have any other clue to the identity of this man?"

"I have a pretty good idea, though," Clint said. The wait-

190

ress came with their main courses and he impatiently waited for her to change their plates before resuming. "I am looking for a man who was extraordinarily clever. A man who was in the OSS or Military Intelligence of the U.S. Army, therefore able to travel freely between France, Spain and Germany. A man who killed Skolnikoff in Ronda and got his part of the treasure, then had Brandl murdered in Munich and whisked his accomplice, Oates, over the border with another portion of the treasure. He moved to Nuremberg, and found his way to Goering's prison cell. He must have been somebody important, at least important enough for Goering to believe that he would save his life."

"And you think he murdered Goering?" Bohlen asked, dipping a fried scallop in a small bowl of tartar sauce.

"I don't know," Clint said slowly. "Maybe he had another accomplice. Maybe Doctor Hoffmann, who attended to Goering that same day, was in cahoots with our man and poisoned Goering, or just provided him with the poison."

"And that's why he was murdered thirty-four years later," Bohlen filled in.

Clint nodded. "The man I look for is somebody who came back to the United States after the war, made an immense fortune, but kept an eye on his former accomplices. A man with enough power and money to have Oates murdered when he grew restless in Mexico, to have Hoffmann electrocuted when I set out on my trip, to have people break into the Hacienda Isabel, and others try to assassinate me."

"The logbook of Nuremberg did not give you any clue?"

"Oh yes, it did. The only American name that appeared a few times was that of a secret agent Jones. He might be the man I'm looking for." Clint tapped on his half-open notebook. "But the solution is here, right here. Give me the name of the owner of this account—and I'll give you the name of the cleverest thief in history." He sighed. "But there is no way I can get to the name behind the account."

Bohlen bent over the table and there was something sinister in his sly smile. "But you have an educated guess, don't you?" he whispered. "You know somebody who has been in American Military Intelligence, who has been present at the scene of at least one killing, who has the money and the power to set up new murders, to have clues removed at the eleventh hour, to send hired killers after you. A man who has planted a spy right in your bed."

"Leave her out of that," Clint snapped.

"Oh, shit, won't you ever change?" Bohlen's voice cracked with dry irony. "You are so incurably romantic that you never miss an opportunity to make a fool of yourself." He noticed the tightening of Clint's jaw and raised his hands in mock surrender. "Okay, okay, let's not talk about her. Let's talk about her father. Dear old tough J.J., who does not even remember Otto Brandl's death." He closely looked at Clint. "You still like him, don't you? You are afraid that you'll find his name behind the bank account, and there will be only one candidate left by Election Day next week."

Clint did not answer, and pushed aside his barely touched plate.

Bohlen sighed and wiped his thin lips with his napkin. "Come," he said. "I know the one man in this country who will get the name for you."

The cab bumped a couple of times on the uneven pavement of Third Avenue, and its shock absorbers squeaked in protest. "Hey, take it easy," Bohlen said. "My friend here is a sick man." The driver scowled in the mirror, but slowed down nevertheless.

"A sick man, that's the right word," Clint mumbled and assumed a half-lying position on the hard back seat. "So you called Denise," he asked for the fifth time that evening.

"Yes, I did," Bohlen patiently repeated. "Your daughter is all right, they are with Denise's mother, no threats were made against them, no suspect characters with knives between their teeth were seen lurking in the bushes."

"Oh, cut the crap, for Chrissake," Clint groaned but there was no anger in his voice. "It's funny, you know"—he sounded slightly surprised—"but now that I come to think of it I suddenly realize that there was nobody hunting me after I left Nuremberg."

Peter frowned. "Are you sure?"

"Yes, definitely. Nobody bothered me in Washington and in New Orleans. In Guanajuato, too, I felt quite safe. That's strange."

The publisher looked out the cab window. "Perhaps they just wanted you to get away from Europe and did not care what you would find in America. It was the evidence still left in Europe that worried them."

Clint shrugged. "It's strange, all the same."

The car stopped by the curb. "Fifty-ninth and Madison," the driver chanted with a strong Polish accent.

Clint looked up at the huge building of steel and tinted glass. All of its seventy floors were brightly illuminated. "No energy crisis here," he sneered. Bohlen chuckled, and with a mock flourish opened the heavy glass door. A discreet inscription, embossed on the glass in sleek gold lettering, announced "American Communications."

"So here is the mother company," Clint said. "And you are still in your dark cave behind the Algonquin? What's the matter, they don't want you here?"

Bohlen smiled indifferently. "Oh, I could move here any time and get a whole floor to myself. I just happen to like my dark cave, that's all."

The night watchman led them to the elevator, and Bohlen pressed the top button. "Will you finally tell me whom we are going to see?" Clint asked. "What's all this mystery about?"

"You should have guessed by now." Bohlen grinned, and Clint did not insist any further.

The elevator opened into a spacious outer office, where two middle-aged secretaries were furiously pounding on their typewriters. Clint looked at his watch. "Ten thirty," he said in wonder. "Funny working hours." Bohlen barely nodded at the women, and strode quickly forward. He opened the door of the inner office without knocking, then moved aside to let Clint come in.

A big bulky man with a bald skull, bushy eyebrows and coal-black eyes rose from his chair and swiftly moved toward them. He was wearing a three-piece gray woolen suit, a blue-striped shirt and a knit tie. There was something feline in his supple, soundless stride. Behind him, Manhattan's ever-changing kaleidoscope of lights filled the big panoramic bays.

"Meet my boss," Bohlen said.

Craig shook the firm outstretched hand. A discreet golden cufflink flashed under the soft gray sleeve. "So you are Bill Murphy," he said.

"That's nothing," Murphy smiled, "but *you* are Clint Craig." He could make his deep, hard voice sound pleasant, Clint noted. But only if he tried very hard.

He watched Bill Murphy while the president of American Oil and American Communications busied himself mixing drinks at the small corner bar. So this was the secretive, publicity-shy king of one of the biggest publishing powers in America. And the huge American Communications company was nothing but a side-product of Murphy's oil and shipping business. That made him a very powerful and very rich man indeed.

Clint had only a fragmentary knowledge of Murphy's career as a secret agent and a businessman; he was as poorly acquainted with his private file. He knew, though, that he had no children, and perhaps this was the key to understanding his secret motivations. On a flight to San Francisco a couple of years ago, Clint had asked the stewardess for something to read. The only available magazine had been a ladies' monthly. The magazine had turned out to be much more interesting than he had expected. Its main feature was a rare interview with Jo-Ann Murphy, the millionaire's wife. She had not disclosed anything about their life at Eagle's Ranch, their secluded retreat in the Rockies. But she had mentioned that they could not have children, and had admitted that her husband had been deeply affected when he was informed that he would never be a father. That was a year after their marriage, the very same year when America entered World War II. Bill Murphy had refused to adopt a child. But since, his OSS career and his business had become his main interests in life. Clint had intuitively guessed that the impotence was Bill Murphy's and not his wife's. A man as tough and egocentric as Murphy seemed to be would have discarded his wife with a snap of his fingers if she were unable to provide him with what he wanted.

The interview had cast some very revealing light on Murphy's character, Clint had thought later. It would be excellent raw material for a psychiatrist—the "what makes Billy run" sort of stuff, the story of the man looking for compensation for his impotence and finding his challenge in the thrills of a dangerous life, first, and later in the building of multimillion-dollar empire.

He smiled to himself. A few years ago, in one of his trash novels, he had portrayed a similar character, a secluded and mysterious millionaire. But his man was taciturn, brooding, smoked big cigars and lived in a Gothic castle transported stone by stone from Germany. And he was, of course, the villain of the story, a murky affair of espionage and of a plot to gain control of the CIA. "Hardly original," the critics had lashed at him, and they had been right of course. The book had been quickly buried and forgotten, or so he hoped.

Murphy brought their drinks. "Peter has kept me informed about your progress," he said to Clint, his penetrating black eyes watching him earnestly. "He thinks that you've got the biggest bombshell ever in your hands."

"And what do you think?" Clint asked quickly.

The question caught Murphy off balance. He did not answer immediately. He sat in one of the leather-covered armchairs, his eyes absently examining the contents of his glass, his left hand probing the protruding edge of his jaw. "This is a dirty business," he finally said. "You must be very careful. So far you have no proof against Jefferson. You might, involuntarily of course, smear a distinguished name and thwart the chances of a good man of becoming President."

Clint looked at him in puzzlement. Murphy was definitely not a Jefferson supporter. Was he so dedicated to fair play—which seemed improbable—or just trying to impress him? "To hear you talking, one would assume that you were a Jefferson fan," he remarked insolently.

Bohlen threw him an alarmed look, but Murphy remained unperturbed. Only his voice grew colder. "I don't want Jefferson in the White House, if that satisfies your curiosity. But we are not discussing my political opinions now. I am talking to you in my capacity as president of American Communications. I can't allow my publishing house—and, needless to say, my papers and other media—to hurl such a catastrophic accusation against a presidential candidate without solid evidence."

"On the other hand," Bohlen interjected, "if Jefferson is involved in the killing, the American people might elect a criminal as their President."

Murphy nodded in agreement. "That would be a terrible disaster. It should never happen." He sank in thought again, then looked at Clint. "I understand that beside that report from Munich, you have not got any hard evidence that Jefferson was in Nuremberg during the trial."

"No," Clint admitted. "I guess you heard about the missing page from the prison logbook, with the names of Goering's visitors on his last day."

Murphy nodded. "Yes, Peter told me. But what about those people who visited him before?"

"There were quite a few," Clint said. "Several people used to visit Goering's cell quite often; a doctor . . ."

"Who was killed," Murphy said.

"Right. There were some others: a couple of Russians, and Englishmen, Kevin Sheppard, and . . ."

"Just a moment," Murphy said quickly. "There should

have been a priest. I read somewhere that the prison priest visited all the condemned in their cells on the eve of the execution."

Clint shook his head. "You are right, but only to a point. Goering denied his religion and refused to see the priest. And that leaves me with only one name. The name of an American agent, a special agent Jones. He came to see Goering quite a few times."

"Special agent Jones . . ." Murphy chuckled. "That reminds me of my days in the OSS. It's like one of those lousy espionage movies where the spy is called 'John Smith.' That was certainly an assumed name."

"Could Jones be Jefferson?" Clint asked eagerly.

"He could, but I doubt it," Murphy said. "If Jefferson was the head of the conspiracy, he would be careful not to expose himself. Jones could be one of his accomplices."

"You were in the OSS once," Clint pressed. "Isn't there any way to discover the identity of Jones?"

"I am afraid not," Murphy said slowly. "Let me explain how it worked. During the war, we—the OSS—and a few officers of Military Intelligence were quite independent when we set out on a mission. On many occasions we did not have a second-line organization to back us and provide the documents, weapons, safehouses, and all the rest we needed. So we had to rely on ourselves. We were issued several virgin sets of documents, to be used for a certain operation and later destroyed. We were to fill in the names on those papers—according to the progress of the mission—and when we did not need them anymore, we burnt them. Those papers could not be tracked, for there were no central records. The same agent could use different names and papers at different places."

"That explains how Jeffrey Oates got his new papers so easily," Clint observed, and turned back to Murphy. "Can't you try, with your OSS contacts, to locate Jones?"

"I could," Murphy said, skeptically raising his eyebrows, "but as I told you, I'm almost sure I'd draw a blank."

Bohlen cleared his throat. "As a matter of fact, Bill," he said respectfully to Murphy, "we came to see you for a different reason. As you know, Clint has just come back from Mexico where he identified the body of Oates. But his most important discovery was the number of a secret account in a Swiss bank, which he found among Oates's papers."

"I did not know that," Murphy exclaimed, surprised. "That's very important!"

"I am sure this account does not belong to Oates but to the leader of the conspiracy," Clint added. He quickly expounded his theory. Murphy listened without interrupting.

Bohlen waited impatiently for Clint to conclude. "Anyway," he intervened, "we both agree that it is of crucial importance to find the name of the owner of this account." He smiled. "When I brought Clint over, I told him you were the only man who could help him get that name."

Murphy's lips stretched in a taut, detached smile, but his eyes had assumed a faraway look and his left hand was rubbing his jutting jaw again. "Is that really so important?" he inquired, not looking at them.

"I think so, yes," Bohlen said. "Clint believes that's the only way to nail our man."

Murphy's eyes focused on Clint, who nodded. Murphy sighed. "I think that can be done," he said tentatively, but his expression was unhappy. "I must admit, though, that I hate doing what you ask for. It's unethical, it's unlawful, and it will force me to contract a debt to a couple of men who are not exactly . . ." He did not finish his phrase, but looked vacantly somewhere above their heads. After a pause he spoke again. "I shall have to use some of my old contacts in the CIA. They have people on their payroll in each and every bank in Switzerland. Those people—usually recruited among the senior staff—keep the agency informed about any secret transactions which might be of interest to us." He consulted his watch. "I shall have to raise several people from their beds, and make them contact their man in the Banque Suisse Centrale in Geneva." He abruptly rose. "You are flying there, of course."

Clint got up too. "I'm all mixed up, really. I haven't stopped running, and flying, since the Frankfurt fair." He shrugged. "Yes, I suppose I should go there in person, but I might crack on the way." He smiled at Peter. "If you hear of a guy who has had a heart attack on a plane, don't be surprised."

Bohlen softly remarked, "I think that this will be your last trip." Clint nodded thoughtfully and rearranged his tie.

"Why don't you get a good night's sleep?" Murphy asked. "We'll book you on a flight to Geneva tomorrow. I'll talk to my friends now, and by your departure I'll have a name, an address, and a contact code for you. Okay?"

"Fine," Clint said. He wanted to say good-bye, but Murphy already had his back to them, bending over the telephone.

But once they were out of his office he stopped dialing, pressed a button, and dialed again a long sequence of digits. The line was clear and soon he heard the phone ringing, far away. It was picked up almost immediately; he recognized the suave voice of Ali Shazli. "Good evening, Ali," Murphy said. "My man just left. I am putting him on the next plane to Geneva."

She laughed, and cried, and laughed again, when she recognized his deep, slightly husky voice over the telephone. "Clint, is that you? Where are you? Oh, I am so happy. I was worried to death." She did not let him say a word, her happiness pouring into the phone, now that the heavy weight of worry and uncertainty had been lifted. He was trying to say something, repeating the same words over and over again. For a split second his lean, tanned face flashed before her eyes, his forehead impatiently frowning, his fingers plowing through the thick brown hair in that characteristic gesture of his when he was getting upset. *It's funny,* she said to herself, *how long did we stay together? Four, five days? And I remember already his small gestures, the little private things that make one so close, so dear. . . .*

His insistent voice on the phone broke her reverie. "What? I don't hear you."

"How are you?" He was shouting. "Your wounds? How are your wounds?"

"Better, much better," she replied. "I am going out for a walk today, for the first time."

"You are going out?" He sounded upset. "Did the doctor let you?"

She burst out laughing. "Now you're talking like my father used to, when I was little. Yes, sir, my doctor said that I could take a walk today, and check out of the hospital tomorrow."

There was a short silence on the line. "I miss you, Jill," he said in a different voice. "I miss you terribly. Maybe I shouldn't be saying that, but I am thinking a lot about you."

"Why shouldn't you?" she asked. "Say it. I miss you, too."

He said something quickly and she made out only the word *Geneva.* "What did you say? What about Geneva?" Her eyes fell on the glistening bud of a red rose standing in a glass

198

half-full of water, all that remained from the big bouquet he had brought her before he left.

"I am flying to Geneva, tomorrow. Can you join me?"

"Of course I can," she exclaimed joyfully. "Where will you be staying?"

"Hotel Richemond, by the lake. Take a cab from the airport. The room is already reserved." He paused, and once again the husky voice was serious, and a little sad, when he signed off: "I can't wait, Jill."

She slowly replaced the receiver on its cradle. Some of her reactions, the beating of her heart, her sudden joy, surprised her. *What is happening to me?*

Impulsively, she opened the drawer of her white-painted bedside table, took out her small mirror and critically examined her face. She was pale, her lips were bloodless, and her eyes still had that unnatural gleam caused by the drugs she had been taking. She had brushed her hair in the morning, but it was still untidy and needed urgent care. She busied herself with her cosmetics, kept in a small Hermès pouch. Looking at her reflection in the mirror, she suddenly realized that she was faintly smiling. Was that because of Clint? Because of that husky voice saying over the phone: "I miss you"? She tried to imagine a similar conversation with Burt, who almost became her husband some months ago. Yes, they could have exchanged the same words over the phone, only his tone would have been different, less earnest, less committed.

An image flickered in her mind, something rather trivial that had happened on her second night with Clint, while they were still at the Royal Hotel in Paris. It was early morning, and the night shadows were slowly retreating from the quiet room. They had made love and she lay, pleasantly drowsing, with her back to him. Something—she did not remember the reason—had made her turn back abruptly, and she had caught a glimpse of his face. He was looking at her intensely, and there was tenderness and concern in the big dark eyes. "Why are you so intense?" she had asked, and he had just smiled, somewhat embarrassed. That had been the first time that she had made a comparison with Burt. Burt had never looked at her that way.

She put down the mirror. Her room was quiet, but the autumn wind was gently moaning outside, tearing the last rust-red leaves off the oak tree that grew by her window. The tree, together with a patch of gray sky and the red-tiled gable of an old Nuremberg roof adorned with its crest of tiny skylights, was the picture she had been contemplating for the long hours she lay sleepless in her hospital bed. That roof intrigued her to the point of mild obsession. What lay under it? An old barn? A medieval inn? A princely mansion? She decided to explore it.

She got up from the bed and opened her suitcase, which the motherly blond nurse, Lotte, had brought over from her hotel. She was giddy and still weak; therefore she dressed very slowly, taking her time. Her back was not healed yet; she felt sharp pains when she stretched her arms to pull her boots on, and while struggling with her white cashmere turtleneck. Finally she was ready to go, in her casual blue suit—a skirt and jacket of soft wool that she had bought in Paris.

She went out of her room. In the corridor a flock of young nurses passed her, laughing, and she felt a little better. She filled out a slip at the ground floor desk, and walked out in the crisp sunshine of the beautiful Nuremberg morning. She immediately spotted the tidy row of skylights on the roof she had seen from her window, and made a beeline for it.

The house stood in a charming small square in the old section of the city, close to the citadel. It turned out to be nothing but a students' hostel, yet its picturesque, half-timbered facade, is dark and mysterious porch, and the old city wall looming in the background bestowed a fairy-tale atmosphere upon it. It reminded her of her first visit to Disneyland, when she was still a small child. She had a vague memory of herself, tightly clutching her father's hand and fearfully stretching her neck to look for the witch in the dark recesses of Sleeping Beauty's Castle. She smiled to herself, recalling the glorious time she had had with her father that day.

She started walking back, and stopped for a moment to study the unusual Gothic roof of a medieval house. A tourist bus was parked beside it, and a thin, effeminate guide was explaining to a group of plump English ladies that the house had once belonged to Albrecht Dürer, the famous German artist. At the left side of the house, Jill saw an open-air café, its round tables and colorful umbrellas gaily spread over the cobblestones of the square. The thought of some fresh-ground coffee tempted her. The Nuremberg hospital was excellent, but coffee was not its most outstanding feature. Suddenly, a soft voice spoke in her ear, echoing her own thoughts: "What about some strong, fresh coffee, Miss Hobarth? Or should I say Miss Jefferson?"

200

She turned back, startled, and found herself staring into the pale green eyes of Police Inspector Helmut Brandt.

Confidently, the young detective took her by the elbow and steered her to one of the more secluded tables before she could even utter a word of protest. A slim young waitress, her heavy coils of light-brown hair worn as a crown over her small-boned face, took Brandt's order of two coffees and some cakes. He looked at Jill with a reserved smile. "The answer to both questions which you are about to ask is yes, of course. Yes, of course we knew for quite a while that you are Senator Jefferson's daughter, but we prefer to be discreet about it and keep it from the press. And yes, of course I have been following you. I looked for an opportunity of having a relaxed conversation with you, since your . . ."—he hesitated—"your friend Mr. Craig had to leave town. And our own meetings in your room were quite unsatisfactory, I am afraid, mostly because of your bad health."

With his forefingers he smoothed down the tips of his moustache. He was elegant as ever, in blue-gray tweeds, a white shirt and a Scots tie made of Shetland wool. She had the vague impression that by his clothes, speech and mannerisms he was trying to build the image of a Scotland Yard supersleuth.

"I don't know what I can add to what I have told you before," Jill said coolly.

He leaned back, his probing eyes watching her speculatively. "Miss Jefferson," he casually asked, "has your father anything to do with the attempt on Clint Craig's life?"

She gasped and instinctively clutched the table rim with both her hands. The question was so brutal, the accusation so monstrous, that she was unable to speak, while her heart pounded in her chest and a tremor shot like a current through her whole body. "My . . . my father?" she stammered finally, choking with indignation. "That's the most disgusting insinuation I have ever heard. How dare you?" She tried to get up, but her head was spinning and she felt a sudden wave of warmth spreading through her body, while sticky sweat broke on her forehead. The inspector leapt to his feet with unexpected agility, and ran toward the interior of the café. He was back in a moment with a big glass of water, and a wet towel which he applied to her forehead and cheeks. She gulped some of the water, and blinked a few times.

"I am sorry," he said, and he sounded like he meant it.

"You paled so suddenly, I thought you were going to faint. I should not have been so outspoken."

She looked at him for a long moment without speaking, trying to regain her breath. Finally she asked in a low, unnatural voice: "Do I have to go through all this?"

Brandt slowly nodded. "I am afraid that you must, Miss Jefferson." The pretty waitress arrived with the coffee, but Brandt did not spare her a glance. "Tomorrow you are checking out of the hospital, and going away. But I have to solve a murder attempt, and maybe even a murder."

"What murder?" she asked, trying to keep her tone neutral.

"Dr. Hoffmann's, the man you went to visit before you were wounded. I spoke to Mr. Lischke at the courthouse, and to the doctor's housekeeper. I don't believe that he died in an accident."

"But what has my father to do with this?" she flared again.

He sighed. "I see that you really don't know. I mean, about the other attempts on Mr. Craig's life."

"The other attempts?" She looked at him in disbelief.

Instead of answering, he opened his black briefcase and took out a portable tape recorder, which he put on the table. "I was authorized by Judge Bauer, president of the criminal court of Nuremberg, to tape the phone conversations of Mr. Craig, after the shooting at Sommerweg. I have here some excerpts from his conversation with his publisher, Mr. Bohlen, in New York. This communication took place on October twenty-sixth at two-fifteen A.M., half an hour after Mr. Craig left your hospital room and returned to his hotel. I'd like to play it for you."

She bit her lower lip. "I don't want to hear it."

"Please," he said in his ever-soft voice, the pale green eyes locked with hers. "I believe that you care about Mr. Craig. Somebody has tried to assassinate him. You must help me find who he is."

"But you already know," she said bitterly. "My father, isn't it?" Yet she did not object anymore when he started pressing and releasing the keys of his tape recorder. "I shall not play the whole conversation," he said without looking at her. "It lasts for seventeen minutes. I just want you to hear some relevant excerpts."

He kept running the tape back and forth. A duo of thin, squeaking voices came out of the machine. Brandt seemed to be quite familiar with the recording, for when he finally pressed the "play" key and Clint's husky voice was heard saying ". . . The Yellow Submarine," he nodded with satisfaction and let the tape run. The volume was quite low, to keep the other patrons of the café from overhearing the recording. Jill's curiosity took over, and in spite of her former objection, she bent toward the table to hear better.

"She went to the table to have a drink," Clint's voice said, "and I stood in front of the bays, to watch the sharks. I did not notice that three people came and took positions behind me and on both my flanks. When I felt them pressing against me, it was too late." Jill listened dumbfounded to Clint's description of the threat upon his life, with the man whispering in his ear while driving the tip of a knife into his back.

An older, dry voice interrupted Clint's. That had to be Bohlen, Clint's publisher. "And where was Miss Jefferson all that time?"

"Jill was sitting there," Clint said, "enjoying her drink and looking down, as if she had moved away on purpose, to let them close in one me." Jill gasped. So that's why he had behaved so curiously, that night in Munich; she recalled his distraught face and his abrupt voice as he came over to her table, his rudeness back in their hotel room, the fresh scar on his back, his impulsive call to his ex-wife as he feared for his daughter's life.

Bohlen's sardonic voice crackled again, "I told you to keep away from that girl, Clint. I told you she was bad news. She was there to spy on you and finger you. Her father must have sent her."

"Peter, you make me sick." Clint's answer was tinged with cold, barely controlled fury. "I know now that I was imagining things in The Yellow Submarine. I trust Jill completely. That girl almost got herself killed trying to save my life."

"She might have been hit by accident," Peter started, but Clint did not let him finish. "I won't listen to that, Peter. Cut this bloody crap!"

There was a long pause. "Okay," Bohlen said. "Let's assume that she did not know that her father wanted to kill you. Maybe he just told her to find out what you were after, while he planned your death. Now, try to be reasonable, Clint. You called him from Paris, on Monday, and told him where you were staying, right? That same evening, by a strange coincidence, the first attempt was made on your life and that car tried to hit you." Jill shivered. She had not known about that. A new, frightening reality was unfolding before her and ugly questions were shaping in her mind.

"And the next day you met, by sheer coincidence, Miss Jill Hobarth." Bohlen's voice was heavy with sarcasm. "She didn't waste any time, did she? Very soon she was alone in your room, going through your papers. And then she flew with you to Munich, and those people threatened you at the discotheque. And Dr. Hoffmann died in Nuremberg, by sheer coincidence, a couple of days before you arrived. But his name was in your papers, and Jill Hobarth had seen it, hadn't she?"

"I don't know," Clint whispered.

"And when you came, the killers followed you and tried to kill you. For God's sake, Clint, don't you see who is behind all this?"

She could not listen anymore, not for one more second. She got up, leaned heavily on the chair to steady herself, and without a word turned her back on Inspector Brandt and walked woodenly toward the middle of the square. He did not rise from his chair—or maybe he did, but she did not notice. She hailed a taxi and managed to say "Nuremberg Municipal Hospital." Later, when she tried to recall the details of that morning, there was a big black hole in her memory. She did not remember the ride to the hospital, nor her coming in, going into her room, picking up the phone, dialing. . . . She did not remember the call being relayed from Washington to some midwestern city where her father was campaigning. But she remembered the voice of J.J., very far away, and herself crying, "Father, was that you? Did you send those people to kill Clint?" And she remembered him gasping, and denying, vehemently, and the concern in his voice as he said: "Jillian, something must be terribly wrong with you there. Could you believe that I would do such a thing?"

And she went on, on the verge of hysterics, the phone sticky in her sweating hand: "I don't know. Daddy, I don't know. I trusted you completely, but now that we found all those things . . . Clint is not after you, but I saw the evidence, and I saw your name, and those people tried to kill him. Daddy, please, tell me," her voice was desperate, "what happened here thirty-five years ago? What did you do?"

And her father's voice came back, very sad, very defeated: "I didn't murder, and I didn't steal, Jillian. I swear."

"Then why are you so afraid of what Clint might find? Why did you send me after him?"

204

"I . . ." J.J. hesitated. "I was sure he was going to frame me . . ." He paused again.

"I've heard that story before," she whispered, and she sofltly replaced the phone in its cradle and buried her face in the pillows.

She did not hear the soft click on the line, as Inspector Brandt switched off the wiretapping device in his cubicle adjoining the hospital switchboard. The girl had behaved exactly as he had expected. She could not have guessed, of course, that Judge Bauer had authorized him to tap her phone as well.

The early Swissair flight from New York landed in Geneva at 9:17 A.M. Fifteen minutes later Clint Craig was in a phone booth in the arrival hall. He took out of his inner pocket the envelope that Murphy's messenger had delivered to him shortly before takeoff, and unfolded the typewritten sheet of paper that was inside. He read the instruction once again and dialed a number in Geneva. "Banque Suisse Centrale," said a woman's voice on the other end of the line.

"Monsieur Louis Chavet, *s'il vous plaît*," Clint said evenly.

"Who is calling, please?"

"Mr. Craig, on behalf of . . ."—he threw a last look at the instruction sheet—"of Mrs. Emerson."

"Hold on, please, monsieur."

With his free hand he took a black Upmann cigarillo from his pocket, tore the cellophane wrapping with his teeth and lit it, using two matches at a time to get a bigger and longer-lasting flame. A series of clicks filled the receiver as the call climbed through the superimposed levels of the bank hierarchy. A throaty woman's voice asked: "Mr. Craig? Here is Mr. Chavet," and the affable voice of the vice-director of the B.S.C. oozed smoothly in his ear. "Monsieur Craig? Welcome to Geneva. How is Mrs. Emerson?"

"She is fine, and she sends her best wishes," Clint said. Mrs. Emerson's name was a recognition password, but from what he knew of the CIA, there was a genuine Mrs. Emerson who had a genuine account in the bank."

"She called me at home last night," Chavet went on. "I understand that you envisage making a deposit in our bank?"

"Yes," Clint said. His instructions were to follow Chavet's hints.

"I shall be delighted to assist you personally. Where are you now, Mr. Craig?"

"At the airport."

"Why don't you come directly to the bank? We are at sixty-seven, rue du Rhône. The information desk will contact me as soon as you arrive."

The taxi moved quickly through the sparse morning traffic. The bells of the Tour du Molard were chiming ten when Clint walked into the spacious lobby of the Banque Suisse Centrale. He gave his name to the bald, cadaverous man sitting behind the information counter, and the clerk immediately picked up his phone. A moment later a small man dressed in a conservative gray suit came from a side door and strode toward him. His big head was out of proportion with his narrow-shouldered, compact body. He had a wide mouth, a bulbous nose, and his short-sighted eyes peered fixedly at Clint from behind the thick lenses of his black-rimmed glasses.

"Monsieur Craig?" He warmly shook his hand. "I am pleased to meet you." He spoke quickly, without pausing, and Clint understood that Chavet was establishing his own alibi while simultaneously giving him the necessary instructions. "We have several kinds of deposits," Chavet was saying. "As far as I understand, you don't want to open an account or to hire a safe-deposit box. What you need is a secret deposit. You can leave whatever you want for safeguard by the bank—an envelope, a package or a box. We shall give you a secret number corresponding to your deposit. Whenever you want to gain access to it you will have to come in person, identify yourself by your passport and give us your deposit number. Very simple, isn't it?"

Clint nodded. "That's exactly what I had in mind."

"Fine." Chavet smiled. "Of course, if you want a certified receipt for the contents of your deposit, we shall be glad to give you one. For obvious reasons, though, most of our clients prefer not to get such receipts. The bank fee will be a hundred and fifty dollars a year, the first year payable upon the rental of the deposit."

"Very well," Clint said.

A fat plain girl came out of one of the cubicles, spotted Chavet and hurried toward him. She held a sheaf of papers. He looked at her, made an annoyed face and signed the papers with a flourish. He turned back to Clint.

"If you have your deposit with you"—he glanced at Clint's briefcase—"we can get straight down to the vault, where you'll fill in the necessary forms. You can also make a de-

206

posit in somebody else's name, with the same conditions. This way, please."

He did not wait for Clint's answer, but turned and led the way down a large staircase to the lower level. The clerks on his way bowed and smiled, and the short vice-director strutted between them like a bantam cock, with the arrogant confidence of an important executive among his subordinates. They passed through several iron grilles and steel doors, protected by armed guards. Finally they entered a small room adjoining the vault. It was furnished with four identical desks, complete with chairs, shaded lamps and wastebaskets. The room obviously was used by visitors to the vault for checking their deposits. An aging guard in the bank's special uniform rose from the corner desk and greeted Chavet with a greasy smile.

"I shall take care of this gentleman, Bouvier," Chavet said. "Will you please give him the forms for a secret deposit, and leave us." The guard placed several printed forms on a desk and left the room. Chavet motioned toward a chair. "Why don't you sit down and fill in the forms, Mr. Craig? While you are busy, I shall attend to some other business I have down here."

Clint sat behind a desk and spread the forms in front of him. He remembered the instructions on the typewritten sheet: "When you are alone, give him the opportunity to see the number of the deposit. No word on this subject should be exchanged between you." He took out of his case the slip of paper on which he had copied the figures and letters he had found in Oates's chest in Guanajuato: SF 756324, B.S.C. Geneva. He held the paper in front of him. Chavet was moving in the room, suddenly very busy rearranging the chairs behind the desks and checking the ashtrays. He stopped for a second behind Clint and peered over his shoulder, then opened the second door of the room, which gave access to the vault, and walked out.

Clint sat behind his desk, absently filling in the forms. He was on the verge of obtaining the most important piece of evidence in his investigation. He knew he should be very excited but he was not. A strange sensation of numbness bordering on apathy had descended upon him. He waited patiently, as if he did not care for what he was about to find out. Maybe that feeling resulted from the sterile atmosphere in that insulated room, belonging to a world so different that it made his whole adventure of the past three weeks seem like the fruit of a sick imagination. And yet, thirty-five years ago Consuelo's father had sat in that same room, perhaps by the same desk, and had filled out the forms for his secret deposit.

The door to the vault opened and Chavet walked in, followed by two guards who carried a heavy rectangular object wrapped in burlap. The guards carefully placed their load on one of the desks and straightened up. "I'll call you when I am ready," Chavet said curtly, without sparing a look for Clint. The two men left the room.

Chavet busied himself with the wax seals fastened to the sacking, his back concealing from Clint the nature of his moves. After a moment he removed the wrapping. An old iron case painted dark green was revealed. The green coat of paint was peeling at places, and powdery rust had settled on the exposed metal. Chavet shot a blank look at Clint. He did not speak, but turned back and snapped open the spring clasps that held the lid tightly fastened to the box.

Clint got up from his place and stood behind Chavet. The Swiss did not look at him. Clint could not help admiring his cleverness. They had not exchanged a single word about the deposit, and no document concerning it had passed between them. Clint had just "happened" to be in the same room while the vice-director of the B.S.C. was checking the contents of an old deposit. Chavet could never be accused of unlawful behavior.

The vice-director gripped the rusty edges of the peeling green lid. With an abrupt gesture he pulled it upward, and the box opened.

Clint gasped.

He had never seen a treasure before.

The stack of golden bars, stamped with the seal of the *Reichsbank*, the official bank of Nazi Germany, glowed dully in the electric light. Beside them, bundles of Swiss francs and dollar bills were neatly piled, filling about a third of the box. Clint could not take his eyes off the hoard. Chavet did not utter a single word, yet Clint noticed that the chubby fingers holding the box lid open were trembling slightly.

A sheet of paper lay on top of the golden bars. It bore the letterhead of the bank. Clint bent over it. It was an old carbon copy of an official receipt. It carried only four typewritten sentences, an illegible signature of a bank employee, and the official seal of the B.S.C.

208

Number of deposit: SF 756324

Date of deposit: August 9, 1945

Total value of the deposit according to the official gold and currency rates fixed by the Confederal board of Swiss banks: 1,027,005 U.S. Dollars (rates of August 9, 1945).

Owner of deposit: James T. Jefferson, citizen of the United States of America.

Chapter Eleven:

November 2:

YALTA

Jim Jefferson received the two telegrams a few minutes before boarding his chartered campaign plane at O'Hare airport in Chicago. It had rained all night long over Lake Michigan and the flat plains of Illinois; the tarmac was still wet and a couple of heavy drops splashed on his face as he got out of the car. The morning air was cool and humid; he shivered slightly in the light worsted suit he had chosen to match the more clement weather of the south. He looked up at the mass of gray clouds that hung low over the city and wondered what the weather was going to be in Atlanta. He had four days left and five more states to tour before he returned to Washington for Election Day. Today he would speak in Georgia and Florida, tomorrow in Texas, spend one day in California, his home state, and rush back for a final rally in New York. These were the most important days of the campaign, as the last appearances of the candidates were bound to make the final impact on millions of voters. Yet his speeches, in Chicago last night and in Boston the night before, had been nothing but poor. He bitterly reflected that he had lost more votes than he could have gained if he had just skipped the speeches and stayed home. He still had not recovered from the setbacks of the last few days. A great deal of his confidence and his punch were gone; the gloomy faces of his assistants and a few whispered remarks he had overheard while passing through the press section of his plane were unmistakable indicators of a forthcoming defeat. And they still did not know the worst.

From afar he saw the correspondents boarding the plane, while the fuel tanker and the mobile generator were pulling away. During the campaign he had developed a habit of stopping a couple of hundred yards from the plane to walk alone on the runway, thus stealing a few moments of solitary reflec-

210

tion at the beginning of another hectic day. The Secret Service agents and the private bodyguards from Pinkerton had grown accustomed to his bizarre morning strolls, and quickly fanned around him as he reluctantly headed for the plane.

The sound of running steps made him turn back. Ralph Dowden had come out of the second car and was hurrying toward him, brandishing a large manila envelope. Jefferson stopped, irritation painted all over his face. "What's the matter, Ralph?" He had grown irascible lately, and the smallest trifle could make him lose his temper.

The campaign manager paused a second to catch his breath. "There are a few cables I thought you'd like to see." Jefferson took the envelope from his hand and leafed through the papers inside. They were the usual stuff: public statements by party bosses, messages of congratulation, thanks, commitments, the last Harris poll showing his rating shrinking by another point—44 percent against 51 for Wheeler, with 5 percent still undecided or refusing to answer. "All this could wait for the plane," he snapped. "What's the hurry?"

"There are two personal telegrams, right on top." Dowden sounded hurt. "They were rerouted from Washington. I thought you might want to answer before you board the plane."

"Where?" He impatiently scanned the sheaf of messages again, and his irritation grew when he discovered the cables, in their Western Union envelopes, exactly where Ralph had said, fastened with big paper clip on top of the bundle. He tore open the first envelope and quickly perused the message. It was from Jill, postmarked Geneva. Geneva? He frowned in surprise and took the text of the telegram in one single glance.

"CLINT FOUND DISTURBING EVIDENCE B.S.C. GENEVA WE MUST MEET YOU IMMEDIATELY PLEASE CONTACT US HOTEL RICHEMOND GENEVA URGENT LOVE JILL."

His heart missed a beat; he swayed slightly. So this was the final blow. They had found it.

The printed text blurred and melted before his eyes. He stood in the middle of the runway, shoulders sagging, eyes unseeing, oblivious to what was happening around him. After a few moments, though, a persistent sound came to his attention. Somewhere in the distance a voice was repeating the same words, over and over again. He slowly realized that it was Ralph's voice, very close, calling his name. "J.J.? J.J.? Something's wrong? J.J.?"

He raised his eyes and noticed the concerned expression on Ralph's face. He sighed and made an effort to control himself, as his trembling fingers tore at the second envelope. In his haste he also tore the telegram it contained. He cursed inwardly and held the two pieces of paper together, trying to concentrate. He first noticed the word MOSCOW, and that jolted him back to reality like an electric shock. He gulped the text hungrily:

"HOSTS AGREE MEETING REFUSE GOVERNMENT OFFICIAL SUGGEST EDITOR IN CHIEF PRAVDA KORCHAGIN SUGGEST NEW YORK OR NEUTRAL CITY I RECOMMEND PLEASE CABLE HOTEL ROSSIA MOSCOW REGARDS CHUCK."

His lungs contracted and he let his breath come out in a long whiff. All was not lost yet. He had abandoned hope of hearing from Chuck. As a matter of fact, he had never really believed in his mission. But the man had made it, offering him a last chance. A chance he should take, not only for his personal sake but for the sake of America as well. For the cable meant that he had been right all along, even more than he himself had believed.

"Let's get back into the car," he told Ralph, and hurried back to the black limousine, which was still parked at the intersection of the runway with the service road. As he opened the back door, he beckoned to the driver; the long-limbed young man got out of the limousine. J.J. slumped on the back seat. Ralph slid in beside him and softly closed the door, his lips drawn up in puzzlement, his glance nervously darting to his wristwatch.

Jefferson read the cables again, closed his eyes and leaned back. Bad news first. Jill's cable meant that Craig had found the deposit. Any moment now, the sensational news could explode in banner headlines all over the world: "Presidential Candidate Robbed Nazi Gold, Stashed It in Swiss Bank." And he would be washed down the drain without even getting a chance to clear himself. Which would not make any difference, anyway. No sane American would vote for a man suspected of hiding a wartime Nazi treasure in a Swiss vault. As soon as Craig reported his find to his publisher and to Bill Murphy, the snowball would start rolling downhill and he would be buried in the avalanche. His only hope was Jill. If

212

she could persuade Craig to delay publication until they met, there was a slight chance that he might avoid the scandal.

But Jill had changed sides. Her bitter words over the phone, when she had called him from Nuremberg yesterday, still echoed in his ears. She had spoken of "Clint," which meant that she had grown quite intimate with him. She had said "I saw the evidence," which meant that she did not trust him anymore. He had tried to call her afterwards, but she had disconnected the phone. The telegram he now held in his hands was another proof that she did not want to talk to him. She could have easily reached him by phone. But she must have guessed that he would pressure her to hush the affair, and she feared she would not be able to resist. Therefore the cable. "WE MUST SEE YOU IMMEDIATELY." We—she and Clint, the other side. Even his own daughter, who had gotten involved in that affair out of sheer devotion to him, did not trust him anymore. Did she also hold him responsible for the attempt on her life?

He shook his head, trying to chase the sudden surge of emotion from his mind. Cool it, J.J., he said to himself. You'd better start thinking what to do next. He quickly made up his mind that the only thing he could do was get in touch with Jill, and make her promise that she and Clint would do nothing before they met face to face.

Now, the second piece of news. He had to use all his willpower and self-control to switch his mind from the sordid German affair and concentrate on Chuck's telegram. He had asked Chuck Belford to undertake a top-secret mission to Moscow on his behalf, a mission that had a chance in a million of succeeding. But Chuck had succeeded! It was like firing a shot in the dark and scoring the bull's-eye. Or maybe it was not a shot in the dark after all, and the Russians were more concerned about the oil issue than they would publicly admit. For it was the oil issue that he had proposed to discuss with them, on election eve. And they had finally agreed.

He had to cable Chuck in Moscow, telling him to accept the meeting with the editor in chief of *Pravda*, and indicate the place where the meeting should be held. New York was very convenient, as he could meet Korchagin without seriously interrupting his schedule. But if he also wanted to gain some political benefit from the meeting—and he certainly did—then New York was the worst possible choice. It was on American territory; it was the seat of the United Nations, always swarming with hundreds of foreign dignitaries, among

213

them scores of high-placed Russians. A meeting between Jefferson and a visiting editor in chief of a Russian newspaper would bear almost no impact on public opinion. On the other hand, a dramatic press report about a top-secret conference between Jefferson and an outstanding Russian figure in a faraway place could carry the effect of a bombshell. The media would focus on it and deal with nothing else until Election Day. And he could be sure of being elected by an overwhelming majority. But where should he set the meeting?

The idea suddenly struck him, so simple, so obvious, that it was almost a spark of genius. Of course. There was only one place in the world where the meeting should be held. It was not easy, though. He would have to change all his plans and jeopardize the crucial stages of his campaign. He had to make up his mind, now, without wasting one more minute. He turned to Ralph, who was playing a nervous tattoo on his armrest with his right fist.

"There is going to be a change of plans, Ralph," he said briskly. "Now listen to me carefully."

The campaign manager looked at his watch. "Look, J.J., why don't you dictate your answers to those cables—if you have any—and get on that plane? We are already twenty minutes late and the press might get upset."

"Let them," Jefferson said with a shrug. "Let them get upset. We are not taking that plane."

"What?" Dowden stared in amazement. With an abrupt gesture, he took off his thick horn-rimmed glasses, and his shortsighted eyes peered at him angrily. "What the hell are you talking about? We're due in Atlanta in three hours!"

"We are not going to Atlanta," Jefferson said. "Something far more urgent has come up."

Dowden shot a look at the telegrams Jefferson was still holding. "What can be so urgent?"

Jefferson did not answer.

Ralph Dowden put on his glasses and drew a deep breath. "Now look, J.J." He was trying to restrain himself. "I know that there are a couple of things that you have not told me. Everybody at headquarters feels that you are in some kind of mess. We understand it is something personal, so we don't ask questions. You are entitled to your private life, I guess. But if it interferes with the campaign, I am not going to take it. So if you want to cancel Atlanta, you'd better fill me in, and now." He blinked nervously a few times, his hand gripping the armrest.

Jefferson nodded gravely. "You are right, and I'll fill you in. But first things first. I want you to cancel Atlanta, and all my other scheduled appearances till the election."

Dowden's jaw dropped and a stunned expression settled on his angular face. "You must be out of your mind," he exploded. "What is this? Political suicide? If we cancel now, you are beaten, J.J. Don't you understand? Didn't you see your rating in the polls? Jesus!" He angrily looked the other way, muttering to himself. "Cancel all his appearances four days before the election." He turned back to the candidate. "You must have gone nuts!"

Jefferson ignored the outburst. "You'll cancel all my appearances," he repeated in low voice. "Tell the press that I am sick, I have food poisoning, the Hong-Kong flu, whatever, I don't care. Tell them the doctor recommended a full rest." While he spoke, he started scribbling some word in capital letters on a small pocket pad. But the low, furious voice of the young campaign manager made him stop. "No deal, J.J.," he said, his voice quivering with frustration. "I am not taking such orders anymore. I'm fed up with being your messenger boy. Either you tell me, *now*, why you want me to cancel everything, and let me make up my mind if I agree with you, or I'll resign as campaign manager this very minute. And I'll go and tell all those correspondents waiting in the plane over there that I have nothing more to do with your fucking campaign." He stared out of the car window, his face sullen and pale.

For a second Jefferson remained immobile. Then he stretched out his hand, still holding the pen, and gently put it on Ralph's arm. "I am sorry, Ralph," he said. "You are right, and I apologize. I'll tell you what happened, and you'll decide for yourself if you stay with me or resign."

He paused. Ralph slowly turned back and studied him warily. "I got two telegrams this morning, as you saw," Jefferson said. "One of them concerns a personal affair, about which I can't tell you. I hope it will not interfere with my candidacy. I said I hope."

"Is it so grave?"

"Yes, it is grave. But I'll cross that bridge when I get to it. Now, let's talk about the second telegram, the one that made me change my plans. Remember that night when I asked you to find Chuck Belford? After the sabotage of the oil wells?"

Ralph nodded. "How could I forget it?" he asked bitterly.

"I had a long conversation with Chuck. I asked him to

take a leave of absence and undertake a mission for me. In Moscow."

"Moscow?" Ralph stared at him, dumbfounded. "What for?"

Jefferson looked out the window. It had started to rain again, and the driver of their limousine, who had been waiting outside, took refuge in the Secret Service car. Yet two of the Secret Service agents, assigned to the candidate's protection, did not budge from their places by the limousine in spite of the pouring rain.

"A few months ago," Jefferson said, "I saw a secret CIA report, indicating that in two years of Soviet bloc will be affected by a serious fuel shortage. The Russian oil fields in Baku and the Rumanian wells in Ploesti will fall short of the demand, and the Warsaw pact countries will start importing oil—several hundred thousand barrels a day in the first year, about a million the second year, and so forth, in ever increasing quantities." With his left hand he tapped his briefcase. "I have the figures here."

Ralph listened, his face still grim, but his angry expression slowly fading away.

"That new reality," Jefferson went on, "is going to make the Soviet bloc as dependent on OPEC as we have become."

Ralph frowned. "I don't see the Russians yielding to blackmail as easily as we do."

Jefferson nodded. "Exactly. They won't give in to blackmail. They would rather opt for a tough solution and try to take the oil that they need by force. But they have to consider the balance of terror between East and West. As long as we object, and honor our commitments, any Russian intervention in the OPEC countries might trigger a world war. But if Russians and Americans got together and decided, by common accord, to share the oil reserves between the blocs, no war would erupt and each side would get the oil it needs."

"By common accord?" Ralph leaned toward him, engrossed in his theory. "You mean us and them dividing the world's oil between us?"

"Yes," Jefferson said firmly. "We have a common interest, don't you see? And if we reach an agreement with the Russians on that matter—who could oppose it?" His voice grew more animated. "I am convinced that we'll get the oil without spilling even a drop of blood. No armed intervention will be necessary. The threat of the two superpowers alone will be

216

enough to make the OPEC sheikhs double the production and cut the price."

Ralph took off his glasses and rubbed the bridge of his nose. "It sounds logical," he conceded. "The Russians should go for it."

"On one condition, though," Jefferson said, looking straight into his eyes. "That Jim Jefferson, and not Larry Wheeler, is elected President of the United States. For if Larry gets into the White House, nothing of the kind will happen. He would rather go down on his knees to satisfy OPEC, and he will pay them any price they ask. On top of that, he will promise them full American protection."

"And the Russians' hands will be tied," Ralph filled in, reflective. He nodded several times, starting to understand what Jefferson was driving at. "They will have to cope with an oil shortage."

"But they can't, don't you see?" Jefferson said forcefully. "They don't play this kind of politics. Sooner or later they will have to move and use force. And if they do, we shall either have to go to war—or admit our impotence. Either way, that's bad for America." He thrust his chin forward. "We need the oil desperately, Ralph. And we are not prepared for a war. It might turn into a holocaust. We must find a different solution. I have always believed in a balance of power. Russia is there, she is strong, she is tough, and she needs the oil almost as badly as we do."

Ralph tilted his head, and looked at Jefferson through narrowed eyelids. "Maybe, but what if we don't try to negotiate with Russia? What if we merely reconfirm our support to the OPEC states? What will Russia do then? Fight?"

Jefferson's voice was very low. "She might just do that, Ralph. The Russians might be tempted to call our bluff, to prove that we are unable—or unwilling—to honor our commitments, if they strike. After the invasion of Afghanistan, they don't take our warnings seriously anymore. They might send a task force to the Middle East—and we shall have to swallow our pride and bow to the accomplished fact." He shook his head glumly. "And if we give in on oil, we shall have to give in on steel, and plutonium, and gold and who knows—all that we need from abroad. We must assure our future. We must establish a new understanding with Moscow."

Ralph was repeatedly nodding, digesting the facts and

weighing the options. "The Russians should be interested in such a solution," he finally said.

"They should also be interested that I become President," Jefferson pointed out, "and that's why they should meet me before the election. We must reach an understanding now."

"Wait a moment," Ralph objected, raising his hand. "Why not wait until the election is over? From the Russian point of view, I mean. Why should they get compromised in a meeting with a presidential candidate on the eve of Election Day?"

"Because . . ." Jefferson started impatiently.

But Ralph had already seen the point. "Oh yes, I see. Of course. Because Wheeler might be elected and they will be stuck with him for at least four years."

"Or maybe drawn into a confrontation over the oil that might trigger World War Three," Jefferson said quickly.

Ralph absently rubbed the window glass with his forefinger, clearing a transparent patch in the layer of condensation. "Isn't that going too far—to ask for their support of your candidacy?"

"I will ask for nothing of the kind," Jefferson snapped, and furiously drove his right fist into the palm of his left hand. "That would be worse than treason." Then, checking his anger, he went on slowly: "I only want to reach an understanding with them. I want to prove to all those people who have been brainwashed by Wheeler's propaganda that if I am elected, there is no danger of war with Russia. On the contrary."

"It makes sense," Ralph agreed, "it makes sense." He looked at Jefferson. "And that's what you asked Chuck to tell them?"

Jefferson cleared his throat. "When he was in charge of White House security, Chuck got to know quite a few of his opposite numbers in Moscow. I asked him to go there unofficially, as a private citizen, and sound them out about a meeting between me and a senior Soviet representative."

"And they agreed?" Ralph asked, suddenly excited.

Jefferson handed him Chuck's telegram. Ralph read it and softly whistled. "Isn't that something?" Then he chuckled. "But you must admit that they are playing it very clever. The editor in chief of *Pravda*. He is a member of the Politburo, isn't he?"

Jefferson nodded.

Ralph's smile widened. "So, as a matter of fact, he is more

powerful than a minister, and fully qualified to negotiate with you. On the other hand, if the talks misfire . . ."

"If the talks misfire," Jefferson remarked, "he can always claim that he had asked to meet me for an interview, on election eve. And nobody could accuse the Russians of mixing in America's internal politics."

Ralph lapsed into a long silence. Then: "That's a gamble, and you know it," he said gravely. "If that meeting succeeds, you are the next President of the United States. If it fails . . ." His voice trailed away.

Jefferson was leafing through the morning telegrams that he had taken out of the manila enevelope. "You saw the Harris poll this morning, didn't you?" he asked, pointing at the figures printed on the yellow sheet of paper. "I don't think I have much to lose."

Ralph eyed him with surprise. For the first time, Jefferson had admitted that his defeat was certain. He was right, of course. He had to take the chance. His last. "Sometimes I wonder what force it is that drives you so relentlessly," he said softly.

"If I told you that it was a mixture of sheer ambition and true patriotism, you would laugh at me," Jefferson said, looking away. "That's the truth, though."

Ralph straightened on the seat. "Okay, J.J.," he conceded. "You've convinced me. I'm with you. What do you suggest we do?"

Jefferson smiled tightly, resumed scribbling on his pad, tore off the leaf and handed it to him. "First, we have to send those cables. Then—you must get to one of your friends, somebody who can keep his mouth shut. I want him to charter a plane, under his own name, right away. A Boeing Seven-oh-seven or something in that category. Nobody should make any connection between the plane and you or me. Got it?"

"Yes," Dowden murmured slowly, hesitantly, but his thoughts already feverishly rushed ahead, and his brian was weighing and dismissing names, pretexts, cover stories, credible explanations for such an urgent request. He must get that plane even if he had to lie his head off. "Yes," he repeated, "I think it can be done." He shrugged. "We have no choice, have we?"

"Good." Jefferson seemed satisfied. "I shall wait for you somewhere in town, or even here, in the Skyways Motel. Have one of the Pinkerton agents rent a room under his name. Another one will rent a car, and I shall come in their car straight to the room doorstep."

Ralph smiled. He knew Jefferson's weakness for cloak-and-dagger scenarios.

"Spread the word that I am sick," Jefferson was saying. "Cancel my tour, send the correspondents home, and come and get me as soon as you have the plane ready. Take care that we are not seen when we board it. Nobody comes with us. It will be you, me and our four Pinkerton men."

"You don't want the Secret Service agents?"

"Of course not," the candidate answered. "They have to report all my moves, maybe even get an authorization to travel abroad. In half an hour, every radio and television network will be blaring stories about my secret trip." He shook his head vehemently. "We can't take them along. The Pinkertons will do. They don't have to report all our moves to Washington."

"All right," Dowden said.

"And nobody in campaign headquarters should know where we are," Jefferson added hastily.

"But there will be the wildest speculations . . ."

The senator made a contemptuous gesture with his hand. "I couldn't care less. Let the press claim for a couple of days that we have disappeared." There was grim determination in his voice, and the steel-blue eyes were alive again, exuding purpose and confidence.

"But where are we going?" Dowden asked.

Jefferson put his finger on the word in the first telegram he had just written. "You and I, son," he said quietly, "are going to Geneva."

At forty thousand feet above the Atlantic, night fell quickly, suddenly enveloping the silvery DC-8 in total darkness. The thick black mass pressing against the tiny portholes was torn only by the pulsating red and green lights at the liner's wingtips, as the roaring engines thrust the plane forward on its course toward Geneva. Jefferson ran his fingers over the stubble that had grown on his face. They had been airborne for more than six hours now. The dull glow of the oval ceiling lights and the rows upon rows of empty seats bestowed an odd, ominous atmosphere upon the vast cabin. His tired eyes wandered over the bright orange and pink upholstery, matched by wall motifs of the same colors. The lively patterns seemed to him incongruous. They suggested

220

summer holidays, young people bound for a vacation in the sun, smiling hostesses serving champagne "with the Captain's compliments." The gay colors definitely did not suit his reflective mood, nor the dramatic character of the mission he had undertaken.

A slight movement behind him made him turn. A middle-aged Pinkerton agent had materialized at his elbow and now handed him a steaming mug of coffee. Jefferson smiled back at him and murmured thanks in a low voice, careful not to disturb Ralph Dowden and the other three bodyguards, huddled in sleep in the seats across the aisle. Ralph had declined the services of a stewardess, fearing a leak that could be disastrous to their mission; therefore they had to prepare their own coffee and dine on cold sandwiches. But apart from that minor inconvenience, the first stage of their plan had been carried out in the best possible way.

Once recovered from his initial shock, Ralph had become his old efficient self again. He had got rid of the Secret Service agents, rented cars under assumed names and arranged for Jefferson to slip surreptitiously into a room at the O'Hare Motel near the airport. Two hours later, he had whisked him out of the room into an unmarked Ford Fairmont, his face concealed by a wide-brimmed hat and sunglasses. The dark-blue Fairmont, driven by a Chicago-born agent, had plunged into a maze of service roads, to emerge finally in a quasi-deserted area of the airport where the Delta Air Lines DC-8 was already warming its engines. The plane had been chartered by a wealthy Chicago businessman who was a devoted Jefferson supporter and had asked no questions. Ralph had also taken care of the immigration formalities, or so it seemed; anyway, he had deftly evaded Jefferson's questions about a possible leak by airport officials. Jefferson had understood that some unorthodox methods had been used, as far as take-off clearance was concerned, but had preferred not to pry too deep. In politics, it was sometimes better not to ask certain questions and not to know certain truths.

Thanks to the meticulous planning of the young campaign manager, secrecy had been well protected. Only one person knew about their departure and their final destination. Before leaving his motel room, J.J. had placed a single phone call to Washington. He had strongly felt the need to share his decision with somebody he could trust. Rosalynn had listened to him in silence; when he had finished, she had asked only one question: "Do you want me to come with you?" He had felt a sudden surge of warmth. That was more than just words of encouragement. "No," he said, but after a short pause had added softly: "Not yet, Lynn."

And now he was on his way to face the most formidable, the most fateful challenge of his whole life. For he knew that his own future, and perhaps even the future of the United States as a free country, depended on the two appointments he had to keep in Geneva.

Geneva. All the roads seemed to converge there. Jefferson suddenly realized that most of the major characters in the drama that his candidacy had triggered were now waiting or assembling in the peaceful Swiss city, as if drawn to the scene of the ultimate denouement. From his Geneva office the chairman of OPEC, Ali Shazli, had spun his web of intrigue around him, forcing him to confront his own past. In Geneva, Clint Craig and Jill expected him, after the discovery of one million dollars in cash and gold kept under his name in the impregnable vault of a discreet Swiss bank. In Geneva, at last, he was to encounter the Soviet envoy Korchagin for a crucial negotiation, the results of which could herald a new era in the postwar world.

He was so deeply immersed in thought that he did not notice the "Fasten seat belt" sign that flashed above his seat. Only when he started to feel the increasing air pressure on his eardrums did he cast a look out the porthole on his right. A multitude of electric lights was twinkling in the darkness, far below. The DC-8 had started its approach to Geneva airport.

Rodion Vassilevitch Korchagin did not resemble the stereotyped image of the typical Russian *aparatchik*. Jefferson expected to meet a thick-set, dyspeptic character with a morbid face and worried eyes, clad in a poorly cut suit and speaking an inadequate English interspersed with communist propaganda clichés. To his surprise, Korchagin turned out to be a slim, athletic man in his early forties, with short-cropped blond hair, an easy smile and big brown eyes twinkling with intelligence. Creases of laughter bordered his mouth, which was the only discordant feature in the otherwise handsome face: Overfull, red, shaped in a cupid's bow, it looked strikingly feminine, sharply contrasting with the determined set of his jaw. He carried about him an air of easy confidence. His English was excellent, with only a faint trace of Russian accent. "I was born in America," he said, smiling and heartily pumping Jefferson's hand. Noticing his puzzled expression,

222

Korchagin quickly explained: "My father was the director of the Russian Pavilion at the New York World's Fair in nineteen thirty-nine, and my mother had a good sense of timing." His smile expanded. "Therefore, I am fully qualified to run for the presidency of the United States."

Jefferson returned his smile, while intently assessing the man in front of him. He understood now that Korchagin had been picked to meet him not only because of his official capacity as editor in chief of *Pravda*. The Kremlin could as well have sent the chairman of the board of Tass, the Soviet news agency, who was also a member of the Politburo. He had met him once in New York, a dull, square-headed and square-minded bureaucrat who was certainly not qualified to carry out a negotiation, but at most might serve as a go-between. Korchagin, on the other hand, seemed to be from a different stock. His youth, his confident manner and flawless English indicated that the Russians had chosen their best available man to represent them in the delicate negotiation at hand.

They had also shown a remarkable efficiency in dealing with the technical aspects of the meeting. Somebody in Geneva—probably the Soviet embassy—had gotten in touch with the Swiss authorities and made all the necessary arrangements. After touchdown, Jefferson's DC-8 had been instructed to taxi to a remote service area, where two unmarked black limousines were already waiting. The discreet Swiss had skipped all customs and immigration procedures. Twenty minutes after landing in Geneva, Jefferson and his party were admitted to a secluded villa at Cointrin. The first man to meet them on the porch had been Chuck Belford. His wrinkled oblong face wore the same shy expression as ever, but a glint of pride had flashed in his eyes when Jefferson hugged him warmly and said, "Good job, Chuck."

A tight-lipped waiter, who did not look like one, had served drinks and cold hors d'oeuvres. He certainly was a KGB agent, like most of the young men whom Korchagin had vaguely designated as "my assistants," and who were scattered all over the big living room, their watchful eyes glued to the American guests. The thought that microphones were planted all over the house crossed Jefferson's mind, but he did not care. He regarded the meeting as an achievement in itself, and would gladly release to the media every word he was going to tell Korchagin that night.

"Shall we start?" Korchagin was by his side, smiling

223

pleasantly. Jefferson nodded and beckoned to Ralph and Chuck. Flanked by two of his men, Korchagin led the way to a medium-sized room on the upper landing. The room was furnished with a rectangular conference table surrounded by eight chairs. Quite naturally, Americans and Russians sat on opposite sides, Korchagin and Jefferson facing each other. As they took their seats, an elderly woman, her gray hair drawn into a tight bun, came unobtrusively into the room and took a seat at the far end of the table. She was carrying a big yellow pad and a pencil. Jefferson looked at her quizzically.

"That's my stenographer, Tatiana Samuilova." The smile seemed never to desert Korchagin's face. "I always take her with me when I am about to interview important personalities."

Jefferson smiled inwardly. The Russians were taking their precautions, building an ironclad cover story about an "interview" from the very start. But he had no intention of letting them have it all their way. He was not going to carry out a negotiation by answering questions and making statements while the other side refrained from any spoken commitments. He leaned forward and said firmly: "This is not an interview, Rodion Vassilevitch, and you don't need a stenographer. We have come here to exchange views and—I hope—reach an agreement. We are both going to ask questions, and we are both going to give answers."

Korchagin was taken aback. "But I was told that . . ."

"I know exactly what you were told," Jefferson interrupted him. He disliked these elusive games. "If our talks reach a dead end, you can pretend it was an interview. I shall not contradict you. But don't play games with me."

For the first time, Korchagin stopped smiling. He took out of his pocket a sturdy pipe and a pouch of tobacco, lit the pipe with slow, deliberate gestures and studied Jefferson's face while puffing laboriously. Finally he shrugged. "If you wish . . ." He turned to the old woman: "*Spasiba*, Tatiana Samuilova," he thanked her in Russian. "It seems that I shall not need your services tonight." He waited for the stenographer to leave the room, turned back to Jefferson and invited him to speak with a polite gesture of his hand.

"I came to talk to you about oil," Jefferson said. "Oil is going to be our common problem for the years to come."

Korchagin raised his eyebrows. "*Our* common problem?" he asked, feigning surprise. "You don't have enough oil to cover your needs. We know that. You are in trouble, and we

224

know that too. But the Soviet Union?" He looked at his compatriots, who quickly smiled and nodded, as if on cue. "We have enormous reserves in Baku. We are even exporting to many of the democratic republics, to Finland and"——he leaned over the table, as if about to share a state secret with Jefferson—"we are even selling huge quantities of oil on the spot market, in Rotterdam."

Jefferson studied him speculatively. Korchagin was making the classical opening moves of a negotiation. He was trying to gain superiority over his opponent, to prove that the other side was in urgent need of an agreement while his own dealt from a position of strength. That would enable him, at the final stage, to dictate his own terms.

Jefferson opened his soft leather briefcase. He leafed through the documents it contained, selected one and placed it on the table. He put on his bifocals, examined the paper closely, then raised his eyes to look at Korchagin. "This is an extract from a report of the CIA." He reached across the table and handed the paper to Korchagin, then half-rose from his chair and, bending over, pointed at some figures with his pen, speaking in the reasonable yet reserved tone of a teacher explaining an important formula to a pupil who has not done his homework. "This column here, you see, gives the total yearly production of oil in the countries grouped in the Warsaw pact. The second column"——he tapped the paper with the edge of his pencil—"represents the yearly consumption of oil in the same countries. This year, as you can see, you still have an excess of seven hundred and forty million barrels, which you can sell abroad. Next year, though, your excess will shrink to barely one hundred and eighty-one million barrels, which is roughly half a million barrels a day. But in two years, your reserves will not be sufficient. You will start importing. Seven hundred thousand barrels a day in the first year, one-point-two million in the second, and so on, in growing quantities. As I said, Rodion Vassilevitch"——he leaned back in his chair—"we have a common problem." Then he added, offhand: "You can keep that paper. I've got a copy."

Korchagin looked briefly at the paper, then handed it back to Jefferson. He took his pipe out of his mouth and studied its glistening stem. Finally he smiled. "With all due respect, Mr. Jefferson, I have no interest whatsoever in that report. The figures are absolutely false, and are not even remotely connected with the truth. As I told you, our reserves are assured for . . ."

He fell silent as Jefferson abruptly got to his feet. His face was red and the steel-blue eyes flashed with anger. "I think this conversation is leading us nowhere, and I don't want to waste my time," he said bluntly. "Ralph"—he turned to the campaign manager—"will you please call the airport and ask them to prepare out plane for immediate take-off?"

Dowden looked at him in dismay, then clumsily struggled out of his chair. Jefferson shot a cold look at Korchagin, whose face had gone ashen. "I told you I did not come all the way to Geneva to play childish games with you, Mr. Korchagin." He removed his glasses and shoved his papers back into his briefcase. He caught a slight glimpse of the alarmed face of Chuck on his right. This was the showdown. He had to force the Russians' hand, even with a bluff about an immediate departure. If they meant business, they would try to appease him, and then they would start talking at last. If not, well . . .

Korchagin was on his feet. "Now, now, Mr. Jefferson," he said quickly. His voice was conciliatory and he was not smiling anymore. "Let's not get excited, please." He half-turned toward Dowden, who was heading for the door. "Mr. Dowden, please wait." Inadvertently, he overturned his pipe and some charred shreds of tobacco spilled on the table, but he did not seem to care. "Please sit down." He turned again to Jefferson. "Let's try to examine together . . ."

"There is nothing to examine," Jefferson snapped, zipping his briefcase. "The figures in this report are accurate, and you know that. I am not used to trickery, Mr. Korchagin, and I shall not take it." He glanced at Dowden, who was standing by the door, blinking unhappily.

"All right, all right." Korchagin spread his hands, palms up, and made an effort to smile. "Let's assume for the sake of the discussion that the figures are correct. Now, can we proceed on that basis?"

"The figures are correct," Jefferson grunted, and slowly sat down. He had won the first round. Dowden hesitated for a moment, and finally returned to his seat.

Korchagin let out a deep breath. "Why don't we have a drink?" he suggested, wiping his glistening brow, and added with disarming frankness: "I think we all need it."

"Why not." Jefferson shrugged, his voice less belligerent.

Korchagin nodded at one of the Russians, who hurried out

and was back in no time, followed by the stern-faced waiter, who carried a big tray laden with ice-cold vodka and tiny caviar sandwiches. Korchagin raised his glass. "*Na zdorovya,*" he toasted, smiling again.

"*Na zdorovya,*" Jefferson echoed, and emptied his glass. The atmosphere had suddenly warmed up, yet he knew that they were not out of the woods yet.

"As I said"—Korchagin grew businesslike again—"if the figures you produced are correct, what would you suggest?"

Jefferson put his empty glass on the table. He had diligently rehearsed his concise exposition. "Today the United States is subjected to a degrading blackmail by the OPEC countries, which are the world's oil suppliers. Tomorrow it will be your turn as well. If you want to get the oil you need, you will have to accept the conditions of OPEC and pay the price they demand. Or take the oil by force."

Korchagin was listening intently.

"Neither you—nor we—can move and take the oil unilaterally. That might trigger a world conflict, which neither of us wants." He paused and looked at Korchagin in anticipation. Korchagin nodded.

"Therefore," Jefferson proceeded, "my country and yours should reach an agreement, to assure a continuous flow of oil in the forthcoming years." He rubbed his eyes with his forefingers. "Forty years ago, when we had a common enemy, the Nazis, we fought against them together. I would not, of course, compare OPEC with the Nazis in any way. But OPEC is gradually becoming our common enemy, and we should take common steps against it. It is utterly humiliating that the two major powers of our time should wriggle their tails at the order of a handful of greedy sheikhs.

"What I suggest, therefore, is to convene a new Yalta summit."

"A new Yalta?" Korchagin exclaimed.

"Precisely," Jefferson confirmed. "At the Yalta conference in nineteen forty-five we divided the world between the major powers. Stalin, Roosevelt and Churchill met as the war was approaching its end, and delimited the spheres of influence of each power. They laid the foundations of a new world order. Good or bad, it has withstood all the crises of the last thirty-five years."

"That's true, I agree," Korchagin said.

"What we need now is a Yalta-type conference, where we

should decide on the repartition of the world's oil between the nations of the world."

Korchagin raised a skeptical eyebrow. "And who are you going to invite to that conference? OPEC, the Third World, the Common Market . . ."

"No," Jefferson said. "You and us, that's all. We'll decide which countries should supply you with oil, which countries should supply us, who is going to take care of the needs of Europe, Japan, China and the Third World. And each of us will have the right to take the oil from his suppliers, by peaceful or . . ."—he held Korchagin's eyes—"or other means."

"You mean military means?" Korchagin asked quickly.

"It will be implied," Jefferson admitted. "But I am convinced that no military measures will be necessary. Nobody would dare to oppose by arms the Soviet Union or the United States, knowing that he cannot count on any outside help. We'll fix the oil price and the production quotas, and we'll inform OPEC. The conference will put in place a perpetual steering committee, which will regulate the oil market. It will meet regularly to adjust prices and quotas."

"Do you have a rough conception of the spheres of influence?" Korchagin asked warily.

"It is to be negotiated," Jefferson said. "But generally speaking, I have some suggestions. There are states that are politically closer to you—like Libya, Algeria, Iraq. There are states that are pro-Western, like Saudi Arabia, the Gulf emirates, Mexico and Venezuela . . ."

"I am not sure that we agree to that repartition," Korchagin quickly said.

"I understand that," Jefferson responded. "That's why I think the conference should be called."

A silence fell upon the room. Korchagin was sucking his extinguished pipe, his clear forehead frowning in thought. "Do you want my answer, now, on the convening of such a conference?" he asked.

"Yes."

"And why do you need it . . . now?"

"I want to make it public," Jefferson said quietly.

Korchagin's eyes narrowed. "But you are not an official representative of your government," he said. "Neither am I."

"I know." Jefferson nodded. "And yet, a joint communiqué signed by you and me will have a strong impact on public opinion in the world."

"And on the American electorate," Korchagin shot back.

Jefferson's face was impassive. "Our elections are our internal problem, as you know."

Korchagin sank in thought again. "Nevertheless, I am only the editor in chief of a newspaper."

"No," Jefferson said. "You will sign the communiqué in your offical position as member of the Politburo."

Korchagin scrutinized his face closely. He cocked his head, and his eyes had a wary, speculative look. "Tell me something, Mr. Jefferson." He bit his pipe. "Why should the Soviet Union take a common stand with a presidential candidate, two days before the election? Your press will crucify us, and you know it."

Belford and Dowden anxiously turned their eyes upon Jefferson. This was the crucial question that they had expected all along; on J.J.'s answer depended the final result of the meeting. The candidate leaned back, and his bushy eyebrows joined in concentration before he spoke.

"It so turns out, Rodion Vassilevitch," he said softly, almost conversationally, "that because of the oil crisis, your country and mine have taken a collision course. Two months ago, the chairman of OPEC visited Japan. In a conversation with the prime minister there he predicted that the Soviet Union might move by force into the Middle East, to assure her future needs of oil."

Korchagin was about to object, but Jefferson authoritatively raised his hand. His voice was firm and cold. "Please, let me proceed. I can give you the names of generals, ministers, and even some members of the Politburo who have repeatedly recommended that Russia take the oil of the Middle East by force. Don't pretend to be surprised, Rodion Vassilevitch. You know them better than I do."

He paused. "My government, on the other hand, out of sheer weakness and an urge to placate OPEC, is ready to promise the oil-producing countries military protection against any aggression. The result will be simple and cruel: In two years time we shall be at war.

"If we want to prevent that war, we should reach an agreement, now. You are only an editor in chief, as you said, but everybody understands that you would not publish a joint statement without the approval of the Politburo. Therefore, if we take that common stand now, we might prevent that war. We shall force our governments—no matter who the President of the United States is going to be—to hold this

Yalta oil conference. To talk first—and shoot later. And if we talk first, I believe there will be no shooting at all."

Korchagin remained immobile for a second, then turned to the left and whispered quietly into the ear of his neighbor, a bald, stocky Ukrainian who had sat motionless through the whole meeting. The Ukrainian nodded. Korchagin rose to his feet, hinting that the meeting was about to end. "Mr. Jefferson," he said candidly. "I believe that your idea to convene a new Yalta on the oil issue is a good one. I believe that my government will approve of that idea. But as far as a communiqué is concerned, I am afraid I don't have the authority to sign it."

"Why don't you consult your government then?" Jefferson asked, as he also rose and pushed back his chair.

Korchagin nodded. "That's what I intend to do." He looked at his watch. "It's past two A.M. already. I believe that in twenty-four hours I shall be able to give you my answer. Will you still be in Geneva?"

Jefferson nodded. "I shall stay here for another twenty-four hours. You can reach me at the Hotel Richemond."

They descended the stairs in silence. At the door, Korchagin vigorously shook Jefferson's hand. "You are a tough negotiator, Mr. Jefferson," he said.

"So you'd better start getting used to me," Jefferson chuckled. "You are going to deal with me for the next four years."

But he was not sure, not sure at all, as he sank into the back seat of the limousine and closed his eyes, ignoring the enthusiastic comments of Chuck Belford and Ralph Dowden. As the car slowly moved forward, he knew that the worst still lay ahead, the moment of truth that now awaited him at the Hotel Richemond.

Chapter Twelve:

November 2—November 3:

HANGING

The knock on the door was discreet, yet Clint awoke immediately and propped himself on his elbow. He fumbled in the dark for the switch of the bedside lamp, found it and reached for his wristwatch that lay on top of the small commode. Beside him, Jill stirred and frowned, as the soft yellow light fell on her face. "What happened?" she murmured, her voice thick with sleep. "What time is it?"

"It's only half past three," he whispered and gently rearranged the cover on her bare shoulders. "Go back to sleep." He slid out of bed, moved quickly to the bathroom, plucked a towel from the rack and wrapped it around his bare waist. "Coming," he said in a low voice, and turned to the door. "Who is it?"

There was a pause, then a muffled voice whispered: "My name is Ralph Dowden. J.J. asked me to get in touch with you."

"Watch out." Clint heard Jill's voice behind him. She had not gone to sleep after all. "Make sure it's Ralph."

It seemed foolish to him, yet after the last few weeks he no longer knew. He opened the door a narrow crack without unfastening the safety chain. Clint immediately recognized the hollow-cheeked, bespectacled face of Jefferson's campaign manager. He had seen his picture several times in the newspapers. "What are you doing in Geneva?" he asked in bewilderment. "How did you get here?" Dowden's blond hair was disheveled. His eyes were bloodshot with fatigue and his brown suit was in urgent need of a valet's attention.

"I . . ." Dowden hesitated. "J.J. told me it was urgent that I talk to you."

"Now?" Clint was amazed. On the small table beside the door lay Jefferson's telegram, which had arrived early that evening, asking them to delay any further action until he presented them with "a thorough explanation in the next few hours." At Jill's insistence, he had agreed and had not returned Peter Bohlen's repeated phone calls. Still, the sudden arrival of Ralph Dowden in the middle of the night came to him as a complete surprise. Throwing a warning glance at Jill, he slowly released the safety chain, but Dowden did not budge from his place. "We can't talk here," he said. "Could you please come with me? I just checked into a suite on the seventh floor." He coughed discreetly and added, obviously embarrassed: "I understand that Miss Jefferson is with you. Could she also come? I'll wait outside."

Clint nodded and closed the door. Jill had heard their conversation and was already on her feet. They dressed in silence.

They had both slept very little that night. Jill had arrived with the first flight from Nuremberg and was waiting in his room when Clint came back from the bank. They passionately embraced and he had repeatedly kissed the pale beautiful face. But Jill's initial joy had quickly turned sour as he broke the disastrous news about her father's secret treasure. She did not cry. She just collapsed in an armchair by the window, her hands hanging limply at her sides, her dead-dull eyes staring unseeingly in front of her. He knew that she had been suspecting the worst for the last few days, and yet, when the final evidence came she was unable to face it. He had stood there, helpless, feeling at a loss before this miserable girl torn between her love for James Jefferson and the ugly secret unearthed from his past. For a while he had feared that she might crack under the pressure. But she seemed to have inherited the tough streak in her father's character. She had come out of her torpor to draft the telegram to J.J., and to plead with Clint to wait after her father's reply had come in the evening. They had not made love that night, just lay for hours side by side, without speaking. She had been cold and distant, and he felt that deep in her heart she resented him for having shattered her father's image. Only in the early hours had she sunk into a restless sleep.

Now she was dressing with quick, mechanical motions, her face bloodless, her lips drawn, preparing for another ordeal as the "thorough explanation" her father had promised was delivered by Ralph Dowden.

They joined the campaign manager in the deserted corridor and exchanged not a single word as he led the way to the small elevator that carried them up to the seventh floor. Dow-

232

den paused by the door of his suite to take the key from his pocket, and motioned to them to come in. The big sitting room was half-dark. A dim light filtered through the brown shade of the single table lamp by the sofa. Clint heard the soft click of the door and turned. To his surprise, Ralph Dowden had remained outside, leaving them alone in the room.

And then Clint noticed a slight movement in the shadows, and saw the tall silhouette of a man standing by the window, contemplating the dark waters of Lake Leman which stretched below. The man turned and took a step toward them. Jill's muffled exclamation died in her throat, and Clint himself froze in his tracks.

The man who stood in front of them was James Jefferson.

"So you found the deposit," Jefferson said.

Clint stared at him in amazement. For a second he lost his speech. When he finally managed to overcome the initial shock, his voice came out hoarse and grating. "You don't deny it, then." Beside him, Jill swayed and buried her face in her hands. He reached for her, to steady her, but she shook his hand away.

"You don't understand," Jefferson said. His face was still in shadow, but his voice belonged to a defeated, desperate man.

"What is there to understand?" Clint murmured. Strangely, he felt that Jefferson's defeat was also his own. Somehow he had hoped for an answer that would prove, beyond and against all evidence, that Jefferson was clean, that the man he had once admired and assisted was not a criminal. "All along the way," Clint said bitterly, "I hoped to hear an explanation from you that would relieve me of that nightmare, and all I hear is you admitting that the damn deposit was yours." He took a deep breath. "Is that why you came all the way from Washington in the middle of the night?" He paused again. "I think you should resign the candidacy, J.J."

"You don't understand," Jefferson repeated. "You were being used. You thought you were discovering evidence against me. You were wrong"—he hesitated—". . . to a certain degree. Jill told you that the whole story was a frame-up intended to destroy me. It was a frame-up all right, but I had brought it upon myself. I didn't tell you the whole truth"—he was speaking to Jill now—"hoping against hope that the deposit would not be found. But now that you've discovered it,

233

I must make a clean breast of my part in that affair. And if you both care to listen to me, I'll tell you exactly what happened that night in Stadelheim jail."

He turned his back on them and stared again at the black waters down below. As he spoke, the painful memories of that terrifying night emerged in his mind, vivid and ugly, and there he was again, a twenty-three-year-old army officer, reliving the nightmare in its smallest details.

August the sixth, nineteen forty-five. The prisoner had been brought to Stadelheim jail in the early afternoon and had been locked in an isolated cell in the maximum-security ward of the prison. Shortly after the arrest, Captain James T. Jefferson had been alerted by a phone call to his office in the headquarters of Military Intelligence, Third Army Corps. He was ordered to report to Stadelheim jail immediately and take charge of the prisoner. He was to interrogate Brandl thoroughly about his functions during the war, and to file his report with his commanding officer within twenty-four hours. Jefferson immediately left his office in the requisitioned Peysing Palace on the western bank of the Isar, and drove his jeep to the suburb of Stadelheim. He remembered the hot, stifling afternoon, the total lack of any breeze, the dead still air and the ominous sea of clouds hanging low over the city, all of them presaging the imminent outbreak of a summer storm.

The jail was almost deserted. A solitary sentry was idling in the *feldgrau*-painted booth by the entrance. A week ago, most of the three hundred SS and Gestapo officials incarcerated in Stadelheim had been transferred to the Ramstein prison camp, because the U.S. military governor had decided it was healthier to put a safe distance between such an assortment of Nazi criminals and the civilian population. Barely a score of prisoners had remained in the prison, guarded by First Sergeant Jeffrey Oates and a skeleton crew of military policemen.

At the entrance to the prison, Jefferson was met by the three men who had made the arrest: a young, bluff lieutenant and two NCOs of his company. Preceded by Jeffrey Oates, who toted a heavy bunch of keys, they had walked through the empty prison wards to the new prisoner's cell. Along their way, the lieutenant briefed Jefferson on the prisoner's background. "Name is Otto Brandl, alias Hermann Brandl, alias Harry or Helmut Steir, sir. It seems that he was a very high official in the *Abwehr* in Paris. He was mixed up in some very shady transactions. Personal friend of Goering. Tried to

234

escape to Spain a couple of weeks before the liberation of Paris, failed, and finally arrived in Munich with his secretary. We arrested him in his apartment at Brugspergerstrasse. According to our sources, he had stripped Paris bare of its treasures. We've been looking for him for almost ten months. At some of his previous hiding places we found quite a haul of jewelry, silver cutlery, and a unique stamp collection that's worth millions. It was stolen from a Parisian Jew."

Jefferson nodded. "Yes, I think I remember a notice about Otto. Had any trouble arresting him?"

"None, sir. It was all very civil. The guy was so amazed that we found him, he didn't even try to resist."

"How did you get to him?"

"A tip from the OSS guys, sir. They wanted to make the arrest themselves, but were delayed for a couple of hours, so we took over."

They reached the prisoner's cell. Jefferson threw a curious look at Otto Brandl. The man was sitting on his cot, his arms crossed on his chest, observing them calmly. He was wearing an elegant blue serge suit over an open-neck white shirt. He was approaching his fifties, a big-boned, rather plump man with an oval face, a double chin and a shock of undulating gray hair, neatly combed. Something in the small black eyes suggested violence, yet he showed no emotion at sight of them. Jefferson signed the forms putting the prisoner in his custody, returned the lieutenant's salute and watched him walk away with his two subordinates. And then he made his first mistake.

"I shall be back tonight with an interpreter for the interrogation," he told Jeffrey Oates when they returned to the first sergeant's office. Oates did not look happy. He hesitated a moment, then asked worriedly: "Could you make it tomorrow morning, sir? I shall be very short of men tonight. All my MPs have got tickets for the Fred Astaire and Ginger Rogers show." The famous duo, on a tour of the U.S. forces in Europe, was giving a single performance in the Palace Cinema in Munich. "Tonight I'll be all alone here, with a lot of work to do, and I won't be able to assist you."

He frowned. "Who said I need your assistance?"

Oates nodded knowingly. "You do, sir. According to regulations, a prison guard should be at hand during interrogation, in case the prisoner behaves violently or tries to escape. Article Thirty-seven in the military prison code, sir."

Jefferson looked at him reflectively. Oates was right; and

after all, what difference did it make if the interrogation was held tonight or tomorrow morning?

"I thought you were also going to see the show," Oates remarked.

Jefferson said disconsolately, "No, I couldn't get a seat. In the office, people were ready to kill each other for a ticket."

Oates's face lit up. "Just a moment, sir. If your evening is still free, I think I can get a seat for you."

"A seat for tonight? Now?"

Oates smiled. "Well, we have our connections, sir." He paused for a moment, and noticing the puzzled expression on Jefferson's face, continued hurriedly: "The truth is that we were allotted tickets according to the number of MPs serving at Stadelheim jail. But most of them, as you know, moved last week with the prisoners to Ramstein, and we kept the whole bunch of tickets. So, be our guest."

Jefferson instinctively felt that Oates was not telling the truth. He definitely had good connections. He certainly could get him seats for the show, and even more than that. But that was not all. Jefferson had heard quite a few rumors about the Stadelheim MPs' involvement in some flourishing black-market operations. For a second the shadow of a doubt crossed his mind: maybe tonight, too, Oates was planning to carry out some unorthodox exchange with his suppliers, and wanted to be alone in his office. Maybe that's why he was trying now to tempt him with a seat for a show. On the other hand, he said to himself, he was not the sergeant's keeper. And the prospect of getting a seat for the show, even if it carried a hint of bribery, was very tempting indeed.

"Fine," he said. "Let's make it tomorrow morning then. At nine o'clock sharp."

Oates nodded happily. "Very well, sir."

"Now about that seat . . ." Jefferson began.

"No problem, sir. Somebody will be waiting for you at the entrance with a ticket in your name."

Oates kept his promise. When Jefferson arrived at the Palace Cinema a few minutes before eight-thirty that night, a soldier appeared at his side. "Captain Jefferson? First Sergeant Oates asked me to deliver this envelope to you." Jefferson looked closely at the soldier, clad in a freshly pressed uniform. His face seemed vaguely familiar. "Didn't I see you somewhere? Wait, weren't you the sentry on duty at Stadelheim this afternoon?"

The soldier smiled, his face beaming. "Yes sir, that's me. I was prepared for another dull evening—and then, at the last moment, such incredible luck. And here I am about to see them movie stars in person." He had an unmistakable Texas drawl. "My folks at home will be green with envy when they open my letter. You can bet on that, sir. Our Jeff Oates, he's quite a guy, sir, I can tell you that."

Jefferson felt somewhat disconcerted as he walked into the cinema filled with exhilarated soldiers. Oates had lied to him, all right. But the lie was much bigger than he had assumed. It was not only his ticket that Oates had obtained at the last moment; it was also the sentry's ticket. It must have been something quite big—and unexpected—that had made Oates deploy such an effort to assure that he would be left alone in the prison tonight. He certainly did not have the seats beforehand, and all those stories about an early allocation or good connections were rubbish. He must have paid a fortune for those seats at the eleventh hour. Now what was he up to?

The lights in the theater dimmed, the heavy red curtains parted, and hundreds of soldiers were on their feet, applauding, stomping, shouting, whistling, as the band struck up the first notes of "Tea for Two," and the most worshipped couple on the screen sailed smoothly onto the stage. He tried to relax and enjoy the show, but somehow his thoughts kept returning to the Stadelheim prison. What was going on there? If it was just a petty black-market transaction there was nothing to worry about. But if Oates was really involved in some dirty business, he had become his voluntary accomplice. Finally he could not stand it anymore. He got up and made his way toward the exit.

He walked out into a diluvial rain. The storm that had been building the whole afternoon had broken at last, and a heavy summer rain was pouring from a black sky to the accompaniment of rolling thunder and dazzling white flashes of lightning. The wipers of his jeep fought an uneven battle with the torrents of water that lashed at the windshield. Rivulets of water steadily trickled into the jeep through every crack in the soaked canvas hood. The thunderstorm had knocked down one of the electrical power plants of Munich, and most of the city was plunged in darkness. The formidable storm, the rain, the pitch-dark streets, made driving very hazardous. It took him more than a half-hour to cross the town and reach Stadelheim. He parked his jeep close to the prison gate. Here, at least, the electrical installation was functioning. The street was deserted. He could make out the shape of a single car, a black sedan, parked farther down by the opposite sidewalk.

The sentry booth was empty. So was the dimly lit hall, cut in half by a long wooden counter where normally a couple of military policemen were on duty, screening the incoming visitors. Nobody was to be seen or heard. Only the acrid smell of disinfectant and unclean human bodies, characteristic of all prisons in the world, hung in the air. Oates's office was deserted too, although a single electric bulb diffused some raw yellow light inside. Jefferson hesitated on the threshold. The prison seemed abandoned. Yet somebody had to be inside. There were at least a dozen prisoners in one of the wards, and nobody would have left them unattended. Something made him head for Otto Brandl's cell in the maximum-security ward. Maybe his subconscious had made the unlikely, and yet not impossible, connection between the arrival of the new prisoner and the strange behavior of Jeffrey Oates. He walked quickly through the empty corridors, his footsteps resounding hollowly in the eerie stillness of the prison.

The iron door leading to the maximum-security ward swung noiselessly on its hinges. He paused a moment, and then suddenly he heard choking, rasping groans that made his blood run cold. They came from the direction of the only cell in the whole wing to be occupied, the cell of Otto Brandl. Instinctively he broke into a run, his heart thumping, a strange fear cramping his stomach. He stopped in front of Otto's cell and gasped, horrified, at the sight that appeared before his eyes.

Otto Brandl was not groaning anymore. He was not going to groan ever again. He was hanging on the end of a rope that had been thrown over a thick wooden beam supporting the ceiling of his cell. His mouth was gagged and his hands were tied behind his back. His head was already dangling at an impossible angle from the limp, broken neck, while his legs weakly kicked the air for a last time, in the final convulsion of a dying man.

The other end of the rope was tightly grasped in the hands of the killer, who looked with boundless amazement at Captain Jefferson.

As if in a dream, Jefferson drew his service gun from its holster and pointed it at First Sergeant Jeffrey Oates.

Every time he tried to remember that scene, later, his
238

memories would emerge in broken bits and pieces, like a quick sequence of hallucinations in a chilling nightmare. The sight of an American sergeant committing a most abominable crime in front of him had shocked him so badly that his mind had refused to register the horrendous experience. A confused succession of details, of things he had seen, heard, or done, would arise from the depths of his memory, things so unreal, so strange, that he could never be sure if they were reflections of the reality or the fruit of his imagination. Did he really jump at Oates's throat, did he hit him with the butt of his gun, did he try to strangle him, overturning the small table on which lay the sergeant's gun and his keys? Did he try, as if in a trance, to lay Otto Brandl on the stone floor, to remove the gag covering his mouth, to untie his hands? Did he endeavor to resuscitate him? Did he really notice red marks on his body, traces of a savage beating? Did he shout at Oates, did he threaten him, did he ask him why he had done it? All those questions remained in his memory enveloped in a misty haze, pieces of a *cauchemar* that would haunt him forever.

The first scene he remembered clearly was himself standing in Jeffrey Oates's office, still pointing his gun at the livid first sergeant with his right hand, while with his left he tried in vain to crank the handle-operated emergency phone back to life. But no sound would spark in the receiver, and then Oates said quietly: "The telephone is out of order. We are completely cut off."

He recalled stepping out of the office, still covering Oates with his weapon, and shouting savagely: "Is anybody here? Is there any American here?" But nobody answered, and his frantic shouts were swallowed up in the crack of thunder and the heavy drumming of the rain outside. And Oates, slowly regaining his calm, spoke again: "There is nobody here, sir. Just you and me. And nobody is going to come here tonight."

For a while he stared at the sergeant, perplexed, unable to decide what to do next. At first he thought of arresting Oates and taking him immediately to the closest military compound. But after some consideration he discarded the idea. The sergeant was a killer, a desperate man. He would certainly take advantage of the storm and the empty streets to escape in the darkness. The second best solution was to lock him in one of the cells and drive away alone to bring reinforcements. He did not care about leaving the prison unguarded for an hour or so. Yet Oates might have an accomplice who would help him escape from the deserted prison. Or he might pretend that Brandl committed suicide, and then it would be the sergeant's word against his. That was why he approached Oates again, pressed the muzzle of his gun to his temple and rasped: "Take a paper and a pen, and write your confession. Now."

Something in his voice must have impressed Oates that he meant to use the gun, for the sergeant started writing immediately. While he wrote, Jefferson peered over his shoulder, and whole paragraphs remained engraved on his memory. "Shortly before Otto Brandl was brought to the prison a man came to see me . . . American, civilian clothes, hat, dark glasses, medium height . . . Offered me one million dollars in gold and cash if I agreed to kill Otto Brandl that very night and camouflage his death as a suicide . . . As I hesitated, he immediately paid me fifty thousand dollars in American bills . . . He told me that nobody would ever know what I did. He said that in case anything went wrong, he would guarantee my escape across the border and my departure to South America, where I could start a new life under an assumed identity. He said that if anybody learned the truth about what I did, I was entitled to offer him the sum of one million dollars as the price of his silence . . ."

At that point Oates put down his pen and slowly turned to Jefferson. "He was dead serious, sir. I can show you the money he gave me. Good old American bills. Why don't you put that gun away and accept his offer? You could live like a prince for the rest of your days. Just put your gun back in your holster and go away. Isn't that worth a million dollars?"

Jefferson was stunned by the incredible offer, but tried not to show it. Instead, he brutally thrust his gun forward and said, "Keep writing!"

Oates continued scribbling: "I made sure that nobody but me would remain at the prison tonight, and at 8:30 I went to the cell of Otto Brandl, tied his hands and feet, gagged him and hanged him on the central ceiling beam of his cell." He signed his name, rank and serial number, and looked up at Jefferson. His calm should have warned Jefferson that something was wrong, that Oates knew the confession would never be used in any trial. But Jefferson was too agitated, too tense. He only suspected that the confession was incomplete, and that Oates was holding something back. But then, the whole truth would be revealed at the investigation.

He shoved Oates into an empty cell and locked him in

with his own keys. He folded the confession and put the sheet of paper in his pocket, then hurried outside into the storm and started the engine of his jeep. That was his second mistake. He should have stayed in Stadelheim jail, guarding his prisoner, with his gun in his hand, until morning came.

He drove slowly in the heavy rain, trying to figure out the location of the closest military camp. Finally he remembered. East of Stadelheim, barely eight miles out of town, were the headquarters of the Sixth Armored Division. He headed that way and took the narrow, winding road that climbed through a range of medium-height hills before descending into the valley. He did not notice that the black car, the one he had seen opposite the prison, slowly moved behind him, its headlights off. He did not notice it until it was too late, when two huge, dazzling lights suddenly splashed in his rearview mirror, and something hit the rear left side of his jeep with tremendous force. His vehicle was virtually flung off the road, overturned several times and plunged into the ditch below. And then everything went dark, and he sank into an unfathomable black abyss.

He regained consciousness in the U.S. Army hospital at Munich. The nurse at his bedside smiled cheerfully. "You have been in a coma for three days," she said with a slight lisp. "You've been very lucky, Captain Jefferson. No fractures, only minor internal lesions." It took him a few minutes to remember the sordid details of that night at Stadelheim. He started mumbling, spurting a long succession of unrelated words and broken phrases, while deep in his mind a terrible doubt was shaping. "My clothes," he finally muttered. "My uniform!"

"You don't need it now," the willowy, gentle-faced girl said. "Relax, please, you are still suffering from shock."

"My uniform!" he roared, and the frightened girl darted away from the bed. In a moment she was back, carrying a rumpled heap of mud-stained clothes. He feverishly searched his pockets, his trembling fingers probing every recess, extracting all the documents, cards, bits of paper he carried on him.

The confession was not there.

"Who . . . who searched my clothes?"

She looked at him with the sympathetic concern doctors and nurses generally show their patients. "Nobody," she said. "Nobody but me. I found your ID in your breast pocket and called your unit to report on your accident."

"And the other papers?" He grabbed her hand, disregarding her cry of pain as she tried to disengage her wrist from his grip. "What other papers did you take out? What did you do with them?"

"Nothing." She shook her head, bewildered. "I did not take any other papers."

He looked at her, his eyes wide open, his throat on fire. "But . . ."

She smiled nervously. "Please calm down, Captain Jefferson. Soon you'll be as good as new, and back with your unit. You must be very popular there. Since your accident, your commanding officer has been calling every half-hour to ask about your condition. Take it easy, now. I'll get you something to calm you down."

"No, no," he mumbled. "I don't want anything. Anything."

The nurse rushed out of the room. He lay on his back, immobile, as the details of the accident gradually came back to his memory. He had been deliberately driven off the road. Therefore, Oates had had an accomplice after all: the man in the black car who had followed him and forced him into the ditch. Did he mean to kill him? Or just to recover the confession?

The girl returned, but she was not carrying any medicine. She was pushing a small trolley on which stood a field telephone. "Here," she said cheerfully, and he felt that he could strangle her for her incessant chirping. "Your commanding officer is calling again. Would you like to talk to him? He'll certainly be delighted." She waved at him foolishly and backed out of the room.

He slowly took the receiver and brought it to his ear. "Jefferson," he murmured into the mouthpiece. But the voice he heard on the other end of the line was not that of Colonel Baird. It wasn't the voice of Lily, the colonel's secretary, either. It was a distant, cold voice he had never heard before, a voice that sent a chill down his spine even before he started to realize what it was saying.

"Captain Jefferson," the inhuman voice said, and a nerve started twitching under his left eye and the palms of his hands went damp. "I congratulate you for your amazing recuperation. I would have preferred you to die in that accident, but you did not, and I had to let you live. I could not afford that anyone suspect you were murdered. It would have ruined all my plans."

"Who . . . who are you?" Jefferson began, running his tongue over his dry lips.

242

"Don't talk. Just listen," the voice warned. "The confession of Jeffrey Oates does not exist anymore. I destroyed it. The morning after your accident First Sergeant Jeffrey Oates discovered prisoner Otto Brandl hanged from a beam in his cell. It appears that during the night Herr Brandl had torn his clothes and made a rope, which he used to take his life. The official inquiry, carried out the same day, reached the conclusion that Otto Brandl's death was a suicide. The next day, First Sergeant Oates had a deplorable accident while he was driving his jeep." The voice chuckled. "Definitely, too many accidents with those jeeps lately. Somebody ought to take them out of service."

The voice went on. "First Sergeant Oates was not as lucky as you. His jeep overturned, caught fire, and he was burned to death. So, as you can see, as far as Otto Brandl's murder is concerned, no murder, no murderer, no confession. Just plain suicide."

Jefferson listened, his moist hand gripping the phone, terror creeping in his mind.

"Furthermore," said the voice, "I want to inform you that this very morning, the sum of a million dollars in gold bars of the *Reichsbank*, and in Swiss and American currency was deposited in your name in the Banque Suisse Centrale at Geneva. You might be interested to know the number of your secret deposit. It is SF seven-five-six-three-two-four. A letter posted in Geneva, carrying only the deposit number, is on its way to you.

"I'd like to point out the following: you have every interest in keeping your mouth shut about the events that took place during the night of August sixth in Stadelheim jail. You have everything to gain by that. A million dollars is a lot of money. You are a rich man now. On the other hand, if you start blabbing about a murder, you'll get yourself in a lot of trouble. First, you would never be able to prove it. You have no evidence. Second, an investigation would establish that you were a willing accomplice to any crime that might have been committed that night. You were seen at the Fred Astaire show at a time when you should have been interrogating your prisoner. The investigating committee will get a tip that a secret deposit in your name was made in a Swiss bank. That will be another proof of your complicity. Nobody would believe that this deposit is part of a frame-up. A million dollars is too much money to be spent for such a scheme. And third, your involvement in such an investigation will gravely compromise you. All your plans for your future will be thwarted. We know that you intend to marry Miss Emily Hobarth, the daughter of the senior senator from California. We also know that you want to start a political career. Any suspicion that you might have been involved in a murder and in theft of German gold will definitely defeat your chances to achieve those goals. Ever.

"I hope you get my message, and I wish you a prompt recovery."

The line went dead.

"Then I made my third mistake," J.J. said. "The worst."

He still had his back turned to Clint and Jill, his eyes riveted to the murky waters stretching before him. They had not budged from their places throughout his narrative. Jill's left hand clutched the straight back of a chair while her right, uncontrollably trembling, covered her mouth. Tears coursed down her cheeks from horror-stricken eyes. Clint stood beside her, his arms crossed, a half-consumed cigarillo dangling from the corner of his mouth. Now and again he would cast a quick look at the dark figure of Jefferson.

"I made my worst mistake," J.J. repeated. "I obeyed the instructions of the man who phoned me."

He went on in a different, soft tone, talking more to himself than to his audience. "When the phone call was over, I felt trapped. I saw no way out. The man was right. I could never substantiate my version. I had not one shred of evidence to prove a murder had been committed. On the contrary. The devious frame-up was conceived and executed so smoothly that it would make me the chief suspect in any investigation. And even if I were acquitted, that ugly affair would stick to me like a shadow, wherever I went."

He paused. "I remember myself lying awake the whole night, on the verge of despair. I was a boy then, barely twenty-three, and nobody could help me. My whole world had crumbled because of something I did not do." He sighed. "Finally, I gave up. I decided to wait another day; maybe I would come up with an idea. But a day passed, and another. I was discharged from the hospital, and I still did not know what to do."

"You could have gone to your commanding officer and made a clean breast of things," Clint said sullenly.

Jill shot a furious look at him, but Jefferson slowly turned to face them, and nodded. "Yes. That's what I should have

244

done. But I told you I was a young man then, and I was badly scared." He passed his hand over his eyes and his fingers dug in the mop of silvery hair. "And yet, even today I can't be sure that they would have believed my story."

He bent his head and some dim light fell on his face. Small beads of perspiration had broken out on his forehead. His skin was taut, the mouth bitter, the creases deeply etched. Yet the bushy eyebrows sheltered his eyes, sunk deep in the dark sockets. "When I was discharged from the hospital," he said, "and when I reported back to work, I knew that the killers of Otto Brandl had won. At least the first round. For I did not tell Colonel Baird that my accident had been a deliberate murder attempt. I did not tell anybody how Otto Brandl had died. And I slowly realized that as time was passing by, the hold of the killers on me was increasing. If I came now to my superiors to tell them the truth, their first question would be: why did you wait? And I had no adequate answer to that."

For the first time he raised his head and looked straight into Clint's eyes. "This is a moment of truth, Clint. I decided to tell you everything." He drew a deep breath. "And when I say everything, I mean also some unpleasant things about me." He paused again. "The letter with the code number of the deposit arrived from Geneva. I did not destroy it. And I'll tell you why, even if Jill will hate me for that. I tried to convince myself that I kept it just as material evidence, to present one day to the court when I finally unmasked the culprits. But deep in my heart I felt there was another reason." His voice broke, and there was a poignant ring in his half-whisper. "I am not a saint. Nobody is. I was a poor man. I was not sure if I would marry Emily. I did not know I would make my own fortune. And I did not want to grow up in life as a parasite, sucking money and fame from the Hobarths. And I must confess something. I felt that if the worst came, I could go to Geneva and come back a rich man. I admit that this feeling was sometimes strangely relieving. And tempting."

He slumped in one of the deep armchairs, as if the avowal of his most intimate thoughts, of a sin he had envisaged, had drained all his energy.

Jill shuddered. "But you did not go to Geneva, Father," she cried. "You didn't! Why don't you tell us you didn't? Oh God!"

"No, I never went there," Jefferson confirmed. "And I did destroy that letter fifteen years later, when I made my first million in the computer business in California. And you know, Clint, that I can account for every penny in my bank account."

"Still, you never tried to track down the criminals," Clint said accusingly.

"Wrong." Jefferson was on his feet again. He took a couple of steps toward Clint. "Wrong," he repeated. "I admit that it took me quite a while to regain my mental balance. Maybe two or three months, until I could think straight again. The war was over; I could get discharged and return home. But I preferred to stay and carry out my investigation. I took long leaves of absence. I asked to be assigned to places and projects that had a connection with Brandl and his death." His mouth curved bitterly again. "And everywhere, I drew a blank."

He started pacing around the room, speaking in short, quick outbursts. "I tried to locate the people who had given us the tip about Otto Brandl's hiding place, before we arrested him. I tried to find out who contacted Jeffrey Oates the day of the murder. I looked for the car that had driven me into the ditch. I made my own investigation of Otto Brandl, to find out why he had been murdered. I went to Paris and to Spain, and followed his trail throughout Germany.

"I discovered the reason for his murder, all right. I found that he had hidden the stolen treasures all over Europe. The Nazis called that 'Operation Phantom.' I understood that those who killed Otto Brandl were after the Phantom treasure. I joined the team of investigators who searched Europe with a fine-tooth comb. I was the one who found in his house the jewels he had brought to his sister-in-law, the set of three hundred pieces of silverware, the embroidered silken linen. I found in Munich the seventeenth-century Gobelins tapestry. I also found the crates of silver in a farm at Fürstenfeldbruck." He shrugged. "But those discoveries were nothing. Most of the caches I found, in France, Spain, Germany, had been swept clean before we ever came there. Somebody had been moving ahead of us, hauling everything away and assembling the biggest treasure ever."

"And you had no indication who that somebody was?"

"Of course I had." The bitterness seeped into Jefferson's voice. "That was the man who called me, the man whom Oates had described as an American, medium height, hat, dark glasses, civilian clothes."

246

"That description could fit anybody," Clint said.

"Why are you so hostile?" Jill exclaimed, red spots of anger burning in her cheeks.

Jefferson raised his hand. "That's all right, Jillian. Let him." He turned back to Clint. "You are right. Physically, the description could fit anybody. But not really. How many Americans could know all those things? How many were able to anticipate Otto's arrest, move all over Germany and France and even Spain when the war had barely ended? There was only one category of Americans who could do it. Secret agents. The OSS guys. I tried to meet them, check their moves, find out who had been in Munich when Otto Brandl was killed. I asked to be assigned to all the places where OSS were sent in great numbers. I was in Berlin, in Hamburg, in Nuremberg . . ."

"So you were in Nuremberg too," Clint said coldly, avoiding Jill's accusing eyes.

"Yes, during the trial. And I found nothing. As you know, they were quite an elusive bunch. Finally, I gave up and came home. I hoped that one day, when I would have enough political clout, I would be able to unearth the files of the OSS agents who had operated in Germany at the war's end, and pinpoint my man." He spread his hands, palms up. "Blank again. When I became senator I asked, under some pretext—I even don't remember what—to see the files of the OSS personnel. But the CIA director informed me very politely that OSS files would remain secret for an undefined period of time, as many of them were employed now in the CIA. He informed me that senators had no right of access to the files without, I quote, 'an adequate reason.' And I had no adequate reason." He ended abruptly. "That's my story."

Spontaneously, Jill stepped forward and hugged him close. For a while she was unable to speak, her head buried in her father's chest.

Jefferson patted her hair gently. "Now, now, Jillian," he said softly. "No need for crying. I told you. Your father is not a criminal. Not a saint either, but no killer and no thief."

She raised her eyes slowly. "When I think . . ." She choked. "When I think of the hell you've been living through all these years . . ." She suddenly turned to Clint. "Well, does that satisfy you?" she managed to say. There was no warmth in her voice. She had crossed the line again.

It took an excruciating effort for Clint to look at them. Excruciating, because he knew what he was going to say. "Your

247

story seems credible, Jim." His voice was hoarse and miserable. "You did not touch the deposit in Geneva, that's true. But how can I know that you did not make up that story? In this affair I was cast for the part of the devil's advocate, and I have no choice; I must play it to the end. How can I be sure that you were not Oates's accomplice? Your accident after the murder was very convenient. It provided you with an ironclad alibi. How can I be sure that there were no other deposits, besides the one in Geneva? You admitted that you were the man who searched all over Europe for Otto's treasure. How can I be sure that you did not move sometimes ahead of your team, and clean out the caches? You were in Nuremberg, too, during the trial. How could I swear that you were not the man who established contact with Goering?"

"So you do want to destroy him," Jill said, her voice a harsh whisper, as if she suddenly realized an ugly truth.

"You don't trust me, then," Jefferson said wearily.

"I don't know, Jim," Clint replied. "I really don't know." He shook his head. "I came to Geneva, hoping to find an answer. I failed." He paused. "Maybe . . . maybe there is one last place where I can get that answer. I'm not sure."

"Find it, then," Jill snapped at him.

For a second, his eyes locked with hers, desperately trying to convey his feelings. But there was no response.

He clumsily pivoted on his heel and left the suite.

Two hours later, he was on the first flight to Washington.

Chapter Thirteen:

November 3—November 4:

CELLAR

Shortly before 11 P.M. Clint Craig walked into the crisp, chilly Washington night. He had slept most of the day since his arrival, in his hotel room in downtown Washington. He had chosen a second-rate, rather shabby hotel, but for once it suited his purposes perfectly. He had only one card left up his sleeve, and now that he was going to use it, he was ready to go to any length to avoid being spotted and followed. Whoever the culprit was—Jefferson or somebody else—he would not allow anyone to stop him from going through with his plan. And his plan could be carried out only at night, for the simple reason that he could not break into a house in broad daylight.

He had decided on this last, desperate move while listening to Jefferson's narrative in his Richemond suite. Jefferson's story had not provided him with the key to the mystery. He realized that the solution lay elsewhere; in the missing page of the logbook of Goering's prison cell. One of the people who visited the Nazi *Reichsmarschall* before his death was the killer, the brain behind the conspiracy. And the only record of those names was an old photocopy in the files of an elderly gentleman. Kevin Sheppard's files, in the basement of his Georgetown mansion.

Of all the people he had met during his frenzied expedition across Europe and America, the white-haired judge had been the most friendly. Clint did not want to break into his house like a common burglar, in the middle of the night. But he had no choice. Sheppard had left for the Caribbean barely a week ago. He would not be back before the election. And Clint had to know the truth before the people of America went to the polls.

The house was dark, like the spacious garden that surrounded it. Clint looked over his shoulder at the peaceful street that stretched behind him. He had taken every possible precaution and was certain that nobody had followed him here. He had no trouble climbing over the tall fence, and moved stealthily toward the massive bulk of the house, keeping mostly in the shadows.

His vague notions about the ways to cope with an alarm system were mostly picked up from detective stories. To his surprise, though, there were no alarm devices on the kitchen window. Could Sheppard be so careless or absent-minded as to disregard that part of the house? For a second he considered checking the other windows too, but gave up the idea. He had not come to test Sheppard's security system that night. He had something more important to do.

He broke the window glass with his heavy flashlight, as the most old-fashioned burglar would, opened the window and heaved himself in. He landed among splinters of broken glass, switched on his flashlight and in a couple of seconds was out of the kitchen and into the corridor that led to the big, dark-paneled dining room. He had only a vague memory of the ground floor of the house, and wandered for a couple of minutes through the magnificent rooms where he had contemplated so many art treasures. Finally, he reached the entrance hall and found the staircase to the basement. His way was barred by a massive oak door equipped with a huge steel lock. One glance was enough for him to know that he would never be able to pick it. There was only one way. "*À la guerre comme à la guerre*," he mumbled to himself, and ran back to the kitchen. In a toolbox in one of the cupboards, he found what he was looking for: a heavy hammer. Back in the basement he swung the tool with all his power, down upon the lock. The solid steel device did not give way so easily. He pounded at it for more than ten minutes until he smashed the heavy lock, and the door yielded to his pressure. He stood in the darkness, bathed in sweat. He directed his flashlight at the nearby wall and found the light switch. He closed the door behind him and turned on the switch. The powerful electric light flooded the basement at the very moment that he turned back, looked at the vast underground hall, and froze.

There were no papers in the basement. No archives, no files, no documents.

There were paintings, and statues, and Gobelins, big vases of Sèvres china, exquisite figurines and other priceless pieces of art. And these were not just beautiful objets d'art purchased over the years by a devoted collector. Clint did not have to go back for the list that he had gotten in Paris from the curator of the *Musées de France*. He immediately recognized the immortal pieces whose descriptions were engraved on his memory: the three statuettes by Rodin, the famous landscape by Corot, the colorful compositions of Sisley, the warm, moving strokes of Renoir. . . .

So here they were, all those stolen paintings, sculptures, tapestries and aquarelles that had never been found. Here was what remained of Goering's art treasure!

And now he knew who had promised Goering that his life would be saved. And who received in return the complete list of the caches where the *Reichsmarschall* had stashed the pieces he had stolen in France.

Justice Sheppard. The former secretary of the International Military Tribunal in Nuremberg. The man who had free access to Goering's cell. The sweet old gentleman, the secluded aesthete, was also a member of the conspiracy. Not for money. Not for gold. Just because of his love of art. What had he said, while showing Clint his collection on the upper floor: "I don't like only to contemplate art, but to possess it, to be able to say it is mine." He had gotten involved in one of the most despicable schemes ever planned, in a bloody enterprise of murder and violence, just to assuage his addiction and to possess, in secret, the immortal works of the great masters.

Frenzied thoughts flashed through Clint's mind, as he took the stairs two at a time. Now he knew why Sheppard had not installed an alarm system on his windows. He did not want anybody, neither the police nor insurance investigators, to pry around if a robbery was committed. He was ready to risk the theft of his art collection, in order to make sure that nobody would ever see the secret treasures he kept in his basement.

And now, finally, Clint had the solid evidence he had been looking for: Goering's art treasure. And he had one of the culprits. Sheppard. The man who could lead him to the other members of the conspiracy. The man who could tell him, at last, what really did happen in France, Spain and Germany thirty-five years ago.

He swept the dark rooms with his torch until he found the telephone. He grabbed the receiver and was about to dial, but something made him hesitate. For a second he looked at the phone, frowning, and finally replaced the receiver on its cradle. He hurried into the garden, climbed the fence again and ran up the empty street. Two blocks away, he found a public phone booth. His fingers were trembling as he fed the coins into the slot, and he stammered for half a minute until he managed to convey to the operator the number and the name of his party in New York.

Peter Bohlen picked up the phone almost immediately. "Clint, is that you? Where the hell have you been? What happened? I was worried to death. I was about to call the police."

Clint tried to control his voice. "Listen, Peter. I'm in Washington. I . . ."

"Washington? What are you doing in Washington? What about Geneva? Did you find the deposit?"

"Forget about that," he said quickly, and hearing the puzzled exclamation on the other end of the line, went on: "I found something much more important. I am in Washington, at Kevin Sheppard's house. Now listen . . ." In a few succinct phrases he described his discovery.

"Jesus Christ!" Bohlen growled. "Are you sure? I mean . . ."

"Of course I am sure," Clint angrily interrupted him. "I saw the paintings, didn't I?"

"But the deposit . . ." Bohlen was still unable to grasp the enormity of the latest development.

"The deposit is a dead end, for the moment," Clint snapped impatiently. "Look, I need you here, as soon as you can arrive, with a photographer. I don't know what might happen, but I need material proof of what I saw. I want you to come on the first plane you can catch. We have to take pictures of every damn piece Sheppard has hidden in his cellar."

There was a long pause. Finally Bohlen spoke again. Some of the urgency in Clint's voice must have affected him at last, for now he was as brisk and efficient as ever. "Fine. I still don't know which photographer I'll get, but don't worry. We'll be on the first shuttle. Now, you get away from that house and don't get near it. If you are seen there, it might cost you your life. Wait for me at the airport."

Bohlen kept his word. It was 8:10 A.M. when he appeared in the arrival hall of the Washington National Airport, where Clint, red-eyed and unshaven, had been pacing aimlessly for hours. Bohlen was followed by a burly man sporting a huge black beard. Two cameras were slung over his shoulders. He glared sullenly at Clint and limply shook his hand. "This is the photographer, Ned Stashek," Bohlen said. "The finest

252

photographer in New York City." Stashek grunted into his beard, and all three of them hurried to the taxi line.

But when the cab reached the Georgetown mansion, it was too late. The Washington Fire Department had not been able to prevent Kevin Sheppard's house from burning to ashes. The fire that had started two hours ago had consumed all the treasures inside the house, and the proof of Kevin Sheppard's crime as well.

Clint stood in the crowd, clenching his fists in frustration as the subsiding flames systematically devoured the charred remains of the priceless treasures and of what had once been a magnificent house. The mansion had been built of brick, concrete and steel. To burn the way it did, it must have been set on fire by experts. The fire had started simultaneously at a dozen or so different points all over the house and the cellar. The arsonists had taken no chances.

Bohlen gently put his hand on Clint's shoulder. "I know how you feel, Clint," he said with compassion.

Clint was shaking his head, his eyes riveted to the blaze. "How did they know?" he groaned. "I was not followed on my way here, I could swear to that. How did they know I found the cellar?"

Bohlen frowned, cocking his head. "It could be very simple, you know. They must have tapped Sheppard's telephone. Maybe he did it himself. As soon as you called me, they knew they had to destroy the evidence, right away."

"No, no," Clint said. He was about to tell Bohlen that he had called not from Sheppard's house but from a public phone, but his words died in his throat. He stared, mesmerized, at the last blackened supporting columns of the house, as they crumbled in quick succession, raising clouds of red, hissing sparks.

And then he knew.

He sharply turned to Bohlen and grabbed his arm. "Peter, I think I know who did it. And how. Excuse me." Before Bohlen could open his mouth to reply, Clint had elbowed his way through the crowd of onlookers. He hailed a cab at the nearest corner and gave the address of his hotel. He pressed some bills into the driver's hand, hurried to his room and grabbed the telephone. "Operator," he said, "I need to call Guanajuato, in Mexico. It's very urgent."

Five minutes later, he recognized Consuelo's voice. "Consuelo, it's Clint," he said quickly, not letting her answer. "I have a lot to tell you, but not now. I am about to find out who killed your father."

He ignored the shocked reply on the other end of the line. "But you must help me. I have no time. I need your answer to two very simple questions. Okay?"

"But Clint, please . . ."

"Don't ask me anything now. We'll have plenty of time later. Now listen. What I want to ask you is the following . . ."

Some moments later he was on his way again. He did not recognize the gaunt stranger who looked at him from the wall mirror beside the door.

Another cab brought him to the Library of Congress. He knew exactly what he was looking for, and avidly leafed through some old volumes. It was about ten when he came out. He had not slept all night, and yet he felt no fatigue. He felt elated and excited and he sensed that nothing could stop him now that he had found the solution.

He spent half an hour on the phone trying to locate Bohlen. Finally he found him at the Statler Hilton. Bohlen had called his secretary late in the morning and had informed her where he would stay, in case Clint tried to get in touch with him. Once again, he did not leave him time to answer. "Peter, I am flying back to Mexico. I must be at Guanajuato tonight. I know exactly where Oates's real papers are hidden. And I know for sure that the name of our man is there. I'll call you when I'm back."

In the streets, the fresh edition of the *Evening Star* carried a banner headline: JEFFERSON MISSING. In smaller characters the paper announced the sensational news: "Presidential Candidate Vanished. Rumored He Will Resign Race for Personal Reasons."

Clint smiled bitterly.

A velvet Mexican evening had descended on the Guanajuato valley. The Hacienda Isabel was dark and looked deserted. The lantern above the porch diffused a milky light over the spacious veranda. Swams of tiny insects hovered around the source of light, irresistibly drawn to the opaque glass, only to burn their wings and drop on the marble tiles below, where they would helplessly writhe and twist until they died. The dry air was filled with the sounds of night: a chorus of crickets and frogs, the rustling of dry grass, the sad moans of night birds. In the corrals far below, a young bull would low once in a while, restlessly stomping its hooves. The drone of a light plane blended with the sounds of nature, then faded away.

The small study of the late Jeffrey Oates—alias Cyrus Jerome—was dark and quiet. Its window was open, and the evening breeze gently played with the thin lace curtains. As the half moon rose into the indigo sky, the open window metamorphosed into an oblong rectangle glowing faintly with a misty light.

The night hours slowly ticked by. It was well past midnight when suddenly the field sounds stopped, as if switched off by magic. Birds, crickets, frogs, abruptly suspended their cacophony. Only the dogs, locked in the entrance hall, stirred in alarm. One of them raised its head, baring its fangs, and uttered a low, menacing snarl.

A dark silhouette appeared in the embrasure of the window. The man climbed on the low sill, carefully parted the transparent curtains and noiselessly slid inside the study. He stood still for a second, to accustom his eyes to the darkness. Then cautiously he stepped into the room.

As he moved forward, Clint Craig rose from the armchair in the far corner of the room, where he had been waiting, immobile, since dusk.

"It has been a long time, Special Agent Jones," he said hoarsely, and pressed the switch of his powerful flashlight.

The dazzling beam focused on the startled face of Bill Murphy.

Chapter Fourteen:

November 4:

CONSPIRACY

For a second, hatred lit the coal-black eyes, shrunk to narrow slits against the beam of the flashlight. With lightning speed Murphy's right hand jerked forward, leveling his heavy .38 Magnum at a spot slightly above and to the left of the source of light. Clint knew, as he looked at the unwavering barrel of the gun, that if Murphy pressed the trigger now, he was a dead man.

But Murphy did not want to kill him. Not yet. The thick voice commanded: "Turn on the lights. Switch off the flashlight."

Clint complied. He stepped back and with his left hand fumbled for the switch on the wall. The ceiling light cast a soft illumination over the small study. Murphy was wearing a thin turtleneck pullover of black clinging fabric that molded his powerful torso, woolen trousers, black as well, and soft-soled moccasins. He faced Clint, legs apart, body slightly crouching as if ready to jump for his throat. "Those papers," he said. He stretched his left hand forward, palm open, fingers spread. "Give them to me."

Clint's mouth was dry, his tongue bitter and pasty. He tried to conceal the shudder that ran through his body. "No papers," he said.

Murphy hissed, "I want those papers, Craig. The papers that Oates left."

"There are no papers," Clint spoke wearily. "Just you and me, Mr. Murphy."

For the first time a shadow of alarm crept into the piercing eyes. "What the hell are you talking about?"

"Oates left no secret papers," Clint said.

"No papers? What do you mean?"

"I mean that you have fallen into a trap." Clint could not

256

keep the vindictive triumph out of his voice. "A trap like the one you set for Jim Jefferson."

Murphy stared at him, speechless. There was a slight hesitation in his eyes, and his left hand rose to touch the jutting edge of his jaw. "A trap?" he said finally, tilting his head back.

"You see," Craig said, slowly regaining his confidence, "my mistake from the start was to believe that the idea of a book on Goering's treasure had been mine. I was so eager to sign a contract that I didn't realize it had been planted in my mind by my good friend Peter Bohlen. When I started my research I was too excited by my findings to understand that I was being used. And that I was supposed to discover exactly what ... certain people wanted me to."

A smile fluttered on Murphy's lips. He backed toward the desk that stood by the window and sat in the upright chair, his gun on his lap, its barrel still pointing at Clint. "And when did you find out that you were being used?" he asked.

"Only this morning," Clint admitted. "When I arrived in Washington I was not followed. I made sure of that. I was not tailed to Kevin Sheppard's house either. You had lost contact with me, and Jefferson did not know where I was." He paused. "Last night I broke into Sheppard's house, and found something I was not supposed to. It was not in your plans, Mr. Murphy. I should not have discovered that Sheppard was your accomplice.

"Anyway, I found the judge's secret collection, and I phoned only one person. My close friend Peter Bohlen. I used a public phone, so nobody could tap the call. And yet, the house burnt down. Only then I understood. It must have been Peter, who knew at every stage of my research where I was, what I had found. Peter again, who suggested the idea of the Goering book. And if it was Peter, it was his master's voice. Yours, Mr. Murphy. That's why I told Peter this morning that I was flying to Guanajuato, to get Oates's papers. I had no doubt that he would alert you immediately. I knew that you were the main character in the conspiracy."

Murphy listened, immobile.

"And even though you tried to talk me out of the whole project," Clint continued, "you knew that I would not back out at that point. On the contrary. I am sure that your people were behind all those attempts on my life. I did some thinking while I waited for you here in the darkness. When I started my research, the whole theory about Goering's treasure seemed too farfetched." He smiled faintly. "Even I could not really believe that thirty-five years ago, a mysterious killer had disposed of Skolnikoff, Brandl and Goering, and stolen the most fabulous treasure ever. But when people began threatening me, shooting at me or trying to run me over with their cars—I started to believe. If somebody wanted me killed, then I was on the right path after all. That also explains Bohlen's press conference immediately after we signed the contract. He wanted me to suspect that Jefferson—or someone else—had learned about my research as a result of all that publicity. That's why I believed all those people were trying to kill me."

"Go on," Murphy said.

"That was my mistake," Clint said. "But your first mistake was that you agreed to come to my aid. You, the famous public figure sticking your neck out to help me find the owner of the numbered Swiss deposit." He shrugged. "Well, I guess you had no choice. I could not find that the deposit belonged to Jefferson without help from someone as influential as you, and you had to provide it. But you ran a hell of a risk by exposing yourself. Now I remembered that you had been in the OSS, and you had served in Germany during the war. And you, personally, put me on the right track."

"Did I?" Murphy asked softly. "And how was that?"

He remained very still, waiting, listening. He wanted to find out exactly what Clint knew, what precautions he had taken, what danger he represented, before using the ugly bluish object that lay in his lap.

"Just think, Mr. Murphy. Why was Oates assassinated? His daughter said that he had had an idea while he was reading an American magazine. What kind of idea? Let me tell you. He saw the picture of somebody whose name he did not know till then, the man behind Otto Brandl's murder. He suddenly recognized the stranger who had approached him in Stadelheim jail, talked him into murdering Otto and whisked him out of Germany with a carful of gold and money. And the simple mind of the former first sergeant reached the conclusion that he could blackmail you into arranging his return to the United States."

Murphy's right hand moved imperceptibly. Then stopped.

"At the beginning," Clint continued, "I thought he had seen a picture of Jefferson. That was a mistake. Jefferson was a well-known politician, his picture appeared very often in

258

the papers, and Oates certainly knew all about him. He never tried to get in touch with him.

"But you, Mr. Murphy. You had been keeping your picture out of the papers for years. The secluded, secretive millionaire. The former master spy. This morning I called Consuelo, and asked her what magazines her father used to read. She mentioned *Time*, *Newsweek* and *Life*. Oates was murdered, as you might recall, in July, six years ago. Well, I checked the magazines of that period and I found what I wanted."

"Please continue," Murphy said.

"*Newsweek* of June twenty-fourth. Business section. Rare photograph of William F. Murphy, oil and press tycoon."

Murphy did not say a word, yet Clint noticed that the hand gripping the Magnum was trembling slightly.

"You killed him, didn't you? You had no choice. The only other man who knew your identity was Kevin Sheppard. Sheppard was not dangerous, of course, being involved the way he was. Your security was the treasures he possessed. If he talked, he would have to reveal that he had them. But Oates had to be removed, and by nobody else but yourself." Clint mopped the beads of sweat that had appeared on his brow. "I guess that after you got Oates's letter you flew your own plane to the landing strip at Silao. How far is that from here? Fifteen miles? You came, you shot him, and were back at your ranch in New Mexico by noon. Exactly as you intended to do tonight. I heard your plane coming, Mr. Murphy. I guess you cabled ahead to have a rented car waiting for you at Silao."

There was a long silence. Murphy sighed deeply and said, almost conversationally: "Well, I am afraid that you don't leave me any choice, Mr. Craig.

"You can't walk out of here and start spreading those stories, can you?" Murphy went on in the same detached tone. "It might hurt my reputation. You are too clever; Peter made a mistake in choosing you. We should have picked somebody less inquisitive. I shall have to kill you."

"Are you sure?" Clint said quickly, raising his eyebrows. "Are you sure I did not take some precautions before I put out the lights and opened the windows so that you could easily enter? I am not alone here, Mr. Murphy."

Murphy slowly got up, shaking his head. His voice was heavy with contempt. "There is nobody here but you and me, Craig. I checked the garage as well. No cars."

Clint nodded. "That's right. Both cars were taken away this afternoon, as soon as I arrived. And I ordered everybody out of the house. I did not want you to run into anyone before you met me." He took a step backward. "I had a lot of trouble persuading Consuelo not to show up before we had our talk." He pulled the study door wide open and called: "You can come in now, Consuelo."

Something rustled faintly in the darkness, and the girl walked in. She was wearing the same white dress that she had worn on the night Clint had come to see her.

She seemed stretched tight, almost in a trance. Her skin was pale, and her opaque eyes had a faraway look. She walked slowly, her movements strangely mechanical, the small revolver in her hand incongruous. Then she looked at Murphy, and her eyes lit in recognition. She started to tremble and her lips moved. At first no sound came, but finally she managed to say: "It's him. It's him." She repeated the words over and over again. Clint had a feeling of unreality.

As if in a dream, the girl raised her hand and leveled the gun at Murphy. The weapon was shaking in her grip. Instinctively, Clint dived toward her and snatched the gun from her hand. A high-pitched scream, like an animal wail, burst from the girl's chest. "Give me that," she moaned, her breath coming in quick, shallow rasps. "Give me that, he is mine, give it to me . . ." She tried to grab the gun and, failing, broke into sobs. Clint grasped her shoulders, but his eyes did not leave Murphy's face. "No, Consuelo," he said. "Not now." The girl writhed in his arms, her eyes burning with a strange fire. Then, abruptly, her body went limp and she fainted, collapsing on the tiled floor.

Murphy took a step backward and the hand holding the Magnum imperceptibly moved upward.

"Don't use that gun," Clint said. "Consuelo is not a danger to you now, but Esteban is behind you. He will kill you if you don't drop that gun."

Murphy shot a quick glance over his shoulder. A blurred figure was visible behind the gently swaying curtain, and the barrel of a shotgun formed a small, steady bulge in the wavering fabric.

Murphy looked at Clint.

"Now drop the gun," Clint snapped. It suddenly fell from Murphy's hand.

Clint kicked the Magnum away and slumped in the armchair where he had waited in the darkness for Murphy to arrive. His hands were trembling. He reached in his pocket for a cigarillo, but the flat tin box was empty. His voice was very low. "It's the end of the road for you. No way out. Do you understand that?"

Murphy did not answer, yet there was a hint of resignation in the sagging shoulders and in the slack hands that fell to hang limply at his sides. Clint continued. "These people here are determined to kill you. And even if they don't, even if you manage to escape, there is no place for you to go. No place in the whole world. You'll be hunted down as a despicable common criminal. That's the end of the Murphy empire, of anything you ever built. I can have you arrested in twenty-four hours on charges of multiple murder, robbery and high treason."

Murphy did not answer. "What do you want?" he finally asked, his voice barely a whisper.

"I want you to answer some questions," Clint said.

"Why should I answer any of your questions?" Murphy asked bluntly. "You said that I had no way out." He paused, then added with finality: "You are right."

"Let's say that I can make it easier for you. You will be free to leave, without anybody shooting at you."

"But . . ." Murphy began and Clint looked directly at him, trying to convey a message. "There is no escape," he repeated. "But you can get in your plane. You can take off. There will be no murder charges. No disgrace." He added very slowly, "And nobody will know."

Murphy suddenly stiffened. He understood the hidden meaning of Clint's words, the veiled suggestion they contained. He looked at him, ashen-faced, then nodded almost imperceptibly. A strange bond of understanding had suddenly sprung up between them. "What do you want to know?" he asked wearily.

"Why did you want me to unearth Jefferson's secret?" Clint asked. "You got away with murder and with the biggest robbery of modern times. You had built your empire. Nobody suspected you. Why dig up the past? It was a double-edged sword. I can't see the logic behind it."

"Can't you?" Murphy smiled bitterly. "For years Jefferson had been trying to solve Otto's murder. As a senator, a couple of years ago, he asked to see the files of the OSS agents who had been in Munich at the same time as him. He also asked for their photographs. You see, he got the names and addresses of people who had been entrusted with portions of Otto's treasure after the war. He intended to show them the photographs of the OSS agents, hoping to pinpoint the man who had cleaned out those caches. But he never got those files. The CIA has the right to refuse that kind of information about its present or former agents. To a senator, but not to a President. I could bet that on the very day of his inauguration he would order the CIA to bring him those files and photographs, on the double. He couldn't afford to have the blackmail threat and the Swiss deposit hanging over his head in the White House."

"And you believe that he would have found you?" Clint frowned dubiously.

Murphy nodded. "In a matter of hours. There were not that many OSS agents at the time, you know. Three or four hundred guys—and only forty-five in Germany at the end of the war. And I was the only one who turned millionaire."

"But there were other ways to stop Jefferson," Clint exclaimed. "You could have hired a killer and had him murdered. That would have been even easier."

Murphy shook his head. "That's what I wanted, from the start. That was the only solution. I wanted to kill him, and I could get the man to do it. But . . ." He hesitated. "I . . . I was not alone in this operation. I had allies who wanted him out of the way for a different reason."

"Allies?" Clint looked at him sharply. "What kind of allies?"

Murphy hesitated. "I thought you had guessed that by yourself. OPEC of course. OPEC and its chairman, Ali Shazli. They wanted Jefferson out of the way."

So that was the missing link. That was why Jefferson had hinted that Clint was being used to destroy him. OPEC had plenty of reasons to want Jefferson out of the race.

"And they ruled out assassination?" Clint pressed on.

Murphy nodded. "They would not agree to murder. They forced me to abandon my plans. They were ready to go along only in a scheme to compromise Jefferson and smear his name. They wanted me to find some dirty secret from his past." He cleared his throat. "I went through his record with a fine-tooth comb. And I didn't find anything. So I had no choice left. The election was approaching, and I had to take the risk. I told them about the Brandl affair, and they jumped at it."

Clint cocked his head. "Did they know that you were also involved?"

262

"In Otto's killing?" Murphy shook his head impatiently. "Of course not."

"I still don't understand." Clint stirred restlessly. "Why did you need OPEC's help in the first place?"

"I needed men to carry out several assignments. I could not send my own men; it would be too risky. I needed people to stage all those attempts on your life. I needed people to break into this very room and plant here"—he pointed to Oates's chest—"the note with Jefferson's deposit number for you to find." Clint nodded. Things were becoming clearer now. The break-in at the hacienda, a week before he came, had been part of the frame-up. Murphy's envoys did not try to steal Oates's papers as Consuelo had thought. On the contrary, they came to plant another clue for Clint, to keep him on Jefferson's trail. How devious, he reflected. All those people moving ahead of him, sowing evidence for him to find, making sure that he would follow the right track, with the right timing, planning everything with meticulous precision so that the ugly exposé would explode before Election Day, ending Jefferson's chance to become President.

"And Dr. Hoffmann?" Clint suddenly remembered. "The old doctor in Nuremberg? Your people killed him, didn't they?"

Murphy nodded. "He could talk," he said. "He was the one who smuggled the cyanide capsule to Goering along with the news that his appeal for clemency had been rejected and he would hang at dawn. At the time Hoffmann thought that he was accomplishing a noble deed. He had kept quiet for years, but I did not want you to question him. He might have remembered that it was Kevin Sheppard and myself who sent him to Goering with the poison."

"And after your people killed Dr. Hoffmann, they almost killed Jill Jefferson," Clint said.

Murphy shrugged. "That was an accident. They had instructions only to scare you, but the girl got in the path of a bullet." His voice was detached, and a wintry smile hovered around his thin lips. "Accidents do happen," he said indifferently. "You also found Sheppard's cellar by accident."

"Kevin Sheppard," Clint repeated. He suddenly visualized the distinguished old gentleman sipping his rum punch on a powdery Caribbean beach, under the rustling leaves of the royal palms, and wondered if he had already been informed of his personal disaster. "By the way, how did Sheppard

263

smuggle all those art treasures into the country? It must have been quite an operation."

"Not at all," Murphy said. "After the war the OSS shipped hundreds of crates of captured German documents, equipment and advanced weapons for further research in America. I had no trouble at all dispatching Sheppard's crates and my own with the OSS material. Customs was not allowed to open them, you know."

Clint nodded. "I gather it was Sheppard who promised Goering that he would not hang if he disclosed the location of his caches."

"Yes," Murphy confirmed calmly.

"But he did not kill anybody."

"Oh, no," Murphy exclaimed, and Clint could swear that there was a perverse pride in his voice. "I was the brains of the operation. I found Otto's papers in his Paris office, at rue Adolphe-Yvon, after the liberation. I killed Skolnikoff at Ronda, and substituted a German tramp for Oates when I burned his jeep. I also had to do some preliminary work on Otto, in Stadelheim, until he spoke. He was tough; he did not talk easily. When Jefferson arrested Oates, I was ten yards behind him. I couldn't kill him on the spot, though—it might have made people suspicious. So I had to wait for him to get out before . . ." He stopped abruptly. "Any other questions?"

"No," Clint said, getting up from his chair.

Consuelo stirred on the floor. Her eyes were still closed, but a soft moan escaped her lips and she ran her tongue over her mouth.

"I think you should go now," Clint said hurriedly. He looked over Murphy's shoulder. Dawn was breaking and Esteban's immobile figure, holding the shotgun, appeared clearly now against the gray sky. Outside, early morning birds were chirping.

"Go back through the window," Clint ordered and turned to the majordomo. "Move back, Esteban," he said in Spanish. "Let him go—it's all right." Esteban soundlessly stepped aside.

Murphy quickly looked around him. His eyes locked on the Magnum lying in the far corner.

"It won't save you, Murphy," Clint said harshly. "I told you, there is no other way."

Murphy walked slowly to the window. Clint followed him with his eyes. Murphy suddenly turned back. "You don't know my wife," he said scornfully. "She doesn't care about money. She will certainly donate all of it to some refugee fund."

For the first time that night Clint smiled cheerfully. "Isn't that what they call poetic justice?" he said suavely.

Murphy shot a murderous glance at him, and was gone. They heard his running steps around the house. An engine coughed a couple of times, caught, and its throb quickly subsided on the downhill road.

Clint and Esteban walked slowly to the front veranda. In the morning light, the hills of Guanajuato looked singularly close and well-defined, as if an artist's brush had accentuated their contours against the translucent skies. As the morning breeze dispersed the clouds around the huge statue of the *Cristo Rey* on top of Cubilete hill, the giant monument loomed majestically into their sight.

They heard quick steps on the tiles. Consuelo ran toward them, swaying. Her hair was disheveled. "Where is he? Clint, where is he? I want him. You promised . . ."

Clint caught her by the shoulders. "I let him go, Consuelo."

"No, no, it's not true, you couldn't do that . . ." Stunned, she turned to the majordomo. "Esteban, say this is not true, he couldn't let him go. He is mine. I want him! He killed my father. Esteban! *El mató mi padre!*" She threw her head back and spat at Clint's face.

Esteban did not move, his eyes looking at the wretched girl with infinite tenderness. Clint wiped his face with his sleeve and said softly: "It's better that way, Consuelo. If you had killed him, the police would have learned the truth about your father as well."

But she was not listening. "You let him go," she screamed again.

Clint's eyes suddenly shifted to the right, and he said: "Look!"

A silvery speck appeared above the Silao valley, slowly gaining altitude. Clint's eyes were riveted on the rising airplane. The first rays of the emerging sun touched the smooth surface of the plane wings, transforming it into a gleaming firefly. Up and up it went, in widening circles, then suddenly changed its direction and sailed straight toward Cubilete hill. Consuelo's screams died in her throat as she followed the flight of Murphy's plane sparkling against the enormous black statue of Jesus, between the open arms outstretched in peaceful blessing.

The dazzling silver dot glimmered once again. Then, suddenly, a huge ball of red and black flames exploded at the base of the monument. For a second the blaze engulfed the huge statue, and a muffled thunder rolled over the valley of Guanajuato. As the flames subsided, the *Cristo Rey* emerged again, tall and unharmed amid the wisps of smoke still hovering around its pedestal.

Esteban was down on his knees, crossing himself. "He died as he lived," he murmured in Spanish, "in blasphemy."

Chapter Fifteen:

November 5—November 7:

PHANTOM

The big ballroom of the Hotel Richemond in Geneva looked like the setting of a riot. Hundreds of people were fiercely struggling in a desperate effort to get close to the small platform in the back, where a table, a battery of microphones and three chairs were bathed in the glare of several hastily installed spotlights. Many of the people pushing their way through the crowd carried cameras. Others brandished microphones, mobile spotlights and television cameras. More than three hundred reporters crammed the ballroom, and the crowd swayed to and fro like a giant tidal wave, threatening to break against the small podium and submerge it completely.

Outside the hall, in the narrow lobby, a throng of less fortunate journalists were elbowing their way to the ballroom doors, waving their press cards. The nervous employees of a Geneva public relations firm, positioned by the doors, were virtually overwhelmed, unable to cope with the reporters' repeated assaults. Even the detachment of police, hastily alerted to restore order, was at a loss. Since the announcement of the sensational news about the presence of James Jefferson, candidate for the presidency of the United States, and his forthcoming press conference, throngs of reporters had been swarming to the Richemond.

The press conference, originally scheduled for 2 P.M., had been postponed twice to allow the European electronic media to dispatch their reporters to Geneva; the major American TV networks had rushed their Paris and London-based teams to the Swiss city. Satellite communication with the United States had been established, and the networks had announced that the press conference would be transmitted, live, as soon as it started. Since Jefferson's strange disappearance seventy-two hours ago, the most fantastic rumors about his whereabouts and his intentions had swept the media. The interest in his sudden appearance in Geneva had doubled when persistent reports had linked his secret voyage with the presence of a mysterous Russian delegation in Switzerland.

The crowd stirred as a small door in the back of the hall opened, and a tight group of bodyguards escorted three people to the platform. Jefferson's leonine head was easily recognizable, but the two younger men at his sides became the subject of whispered inquiries. The bespectacled man in the center stood up, blinking in the dazzling lights, and reached for the microphone. Silence settled in the big ballroom, interrupted only by the angry shouts of the reporters who remained outside.

"Ladies and gentlemen of the press, good afternoon," the man said briskly. "I am Ralph Dowden, manager of Mr. Jefferson's campaign in the United States. I am pleased to introduce Senator Jefferson and Mr. Rodion Korchagin, member of the Politburo of the Communist party of the Soviet Union." As the public gasped in amazement, Korchagin pulled Dowden's sleeve and hastily whispered something in his ear. Dowden nodded, and quickly added: "Many of you know Mr. Korchagin, of course, in his capacity as editor in chief of *Pravda*."

Jefferson could not suppress a smile. Korchagin was doggedly fighting to stress his newspaperman's status, in order to minimize American criticism of the Soviet government for its unprecedented step. He did not blame him. Korchagin was walking a tightrope. After a nerve-racking sequence of consultations with Moscow, agreement had been reached for the publication of a joint statement, but under special conditions, which the candidate's campaign manager was stating at that very moment. "I shall provide a joint statement agreed to by Mr. Korchagin and Mr. Jefferson. Afterwards, Mr. Jefferson will make a statement of his own. Then they will both leave, and I shall answer your questions." The Soviets had been adamant that neither Jefferson nor Korchagin should be present while Dowden commented on their communiqué.

Ralph buried his shortsighted eyes in a typewritten sheet: "Senator James Jefferson and Mr. Rodion Korchagin, member of the Politburo of the Soviet Communist party and editor in chief of *Pravda*, met in Geneva on the initiative of Senator Jefferson. They discussed the oil situation, which has become the object of a growing concern in both the United States and the Soviet Union. They agreed to call on their respective governments to convene, in the near future, a summit meeting between the leaders of both countries, with the aim of working out a common approach to the oil crisis and defining practical solutions, for the benefit of all the nations of the world."

While the reporters scribbled furiously, Jefferson reached for the microphone. "During my campaign for the presidency I have repeatedly stressed that we should put an end to the brutal blackmail used against us by the OPEC states. I was accused in return of being a warmonger. However, while studying the issue of oil consumption in the world, I found out that in two years' time the Soviet Union will also start importing oil to satisfy the needs of the popular democracies that are her allies. I did not believe that the Soviet Union would yield to blackmail. I thought she might be tempted to use other means. That new reality could create an explosive situation and trigger a new world war. Therefore, I reached the conclusion that the two major powers, motivated by common interests—to secure their need for oil—should reach an agreement on oil production, quotas and prices, and . . ."—he paused briefly and raised his eyes—"*persuade* the OPEC states to accept it." A ripple of laughter ran through the hall.

"I contacted the Soviet government and asked to meet its qualified representative, to discuss that possibility with him. My friend Mr. Korchagin was appointed to the task and we met in Geneva. I suggested to him that our countries should convene a new Yalta conference, like the one that took place at the end of World War Two. That conference would work out the arrangements we are going to submit to OPEC. The idea was accepted, to my full satisfaction. I am sure it will be carried out by any American President, should he be Mr. Wheeler or me."

He paused, then continued. "In order to meet with Mr. Korchagin, I had to cancel the final stage of my campaign and come to Geneva in the utmost secrecy. My supporters and my closest associates were left in the dark. In America, my sudden disappearance caused the wildest speculation. I want to apologize to the American people for my unusual behavior. I sincerely believe that it was justified. I believe that by our joint initiative, today, Mr. Korchagin and I will put an end to the OPEC blackmail, in the interest of all peace-loving nations."

Jefferson stared for another second at his audience, folded the sheet of paper and put it in his breast pocket. Then he

269

reached over the head of Ralph Dowden and warmly shook Korchagin's hand. Applause broke out in one corner of the hall. Blinding flashes exploded over the room, and TV and radio commentators whispered urgently into their microphones. Reporters jumped to their feet, waving and shouting: "Mr. Jefferson! Mr. Korchagin!" Both men, however, left the platform and quickly walked out of the ballroom.

Ralph Dowden was left alone on the platform. "I am ready to answer your questions," he declared to the press.

Crouching near the left of the podium, Stanley Carmichael of *The London Times* quickly jotted the lead for his first page article: "By a cunning maneuver of the eleventh hour, James Jefferson secured his election, tomorrow, as President of the United States." He threw a look at what he had written, then suddenly realizing the meaning of the last part of his lead, he crossed out the word "cunning" and substituted "brilliant."

Chuck Belford was waiting for him at the door of his suite. "You'd better stay with me, boys," he said to the bodyguards, and moved closer to Jefferson. "Somebody is waiting for you inside," he whispered in his ear.

"Who?" Jefferson frowned.

Chuck's eyes twinkled. "You'd better see for youself. I took the liberty of inviting the gentleman in."

A man was standing by the window, his back to the door, looking at the lake. His posture singularly reminded Jefferson of his own agony as he stood at that very place night before last, waiting for Jill and Clint to come in. The man was tall, and his hair was jet-black. He was wearing an impeccable pin-striped suit, and the collar that enclosed his neck was dazzlingly white. The soft click of the closing door made him turn, and Jefferson found himself staring into the black eyes of Sheikh Ali Shazli.

The OPEC chairman bowed with a faint smile, and said without preliminaries: "There is an old Arab proverb, Mr. Jefferson." He said something in guttural Arabic and quickly translated into English: "Kiss the hand that you cannot cut. That's why I am here."

Jefferson had some difficulty in overcoming his initial shock. Trying to conceal his embarrassment, he mumbled: "Why don't you sit down?"

"No, thank you," Shazli said. "I should be on my way. I

270

only wanted to congratulate you as the next President of the United States."

Jefferson sat on the edge of the dining table, crossing his arms. "Don't you think that these congratulations are a little premature?"

"Not at all," Shazli said in the same soft voice. "After your agreement with the Russians you'll win by a landslide. Nothing can stop you now."

Jefferson studied him quizzically. "How do you know about my agreement with the Russians? Were you at the press conference?"

The lean, swarthy face wrinkled in a knowing smile. "No, I was not at the press conference, but I knew about the agreement. As a matter of fact, I have followed the negotiation with great interest since your arrival at the villa in Cointrin." Noticing the amazed expression on Jefferson's face, he added pleasantly: "I have my own sources, you know."

Jefferson remained still for a second, then slowly raised his eyes. "If what you are saying is true, then . . . you could have leaked the story about my presence here and caused the immediate breakdown of the talks."

Shazli paused a second to light a black Sobranie cigarette, exhaled the thick, acrid smoke and nodded. "Yes," he said, "maybe you are right. I had not thought of that."

Oh yes, Jefferson wanted to lash back at him, *you certainly thought of that, Sheikh Shazli. And that's why you are here, to let me know that I owe you something. Something I should not forget to repay you when I reach the White House. How quick, how cunning, Mr. Chairman!*

But aloud he said: "I admire your resourcefulness, Mr. Shazli."

"And I admire your tenacity," Shazli said quickly. "You will make a good President."

Jefferson could no longer play the OPEC chairman's game. "But you did all you could to stop me!" he said, his voice hoarse with sudden anger.

"Not *all*," Shazli candidly pointed out. "I was not happy with your candidacy, I admit. But my attitude changed in the last twenty-four hours."

"Is that so?" Jefferson said. "And what made you change your mind."

The Arab smiled again. "You will be surprised. I changed my mind because of your agreement with Korchagin."

Jefferson was taken aback. "What do you mean?"

"It's very simple," Shazli explained. "You are a man who means what he says, Mr. Jefferson. When you threatened to take the oil by force, I was worried. I did not want an American task force to land on the shores of the Arab gulf. It could bring about the total collapse of all that we had built for years. But now, after your agreement with the Russians, you'll impose on us quotas and prices, which we shall accept, as we shall have no other choice. No military intervention will be necessary. And I prefer by far to cut our oil prices than to have my country occupied by a foreign power." He laughed softly. "And if the worst comes and I lose my position at OPEC, I can always go back to my job as oil minister of Saudi Arabia. Didn't you tell Mr. Korchagin that we shall be in your sphere of influence?"

Jefferson couldn't help but smile back. "You are a clever man, Sheikh Shazli. But I am afraid that your friend, Mr. Murphy, will be very disappointed."

"Bill Murphy?" An expression of profound grief settled on Shazli's face. "I gather that you haven't heard yet. Bill Murphy was killed last night in an unfortunate accident. His plane crashed on a hill in Mexico. A malfunctioning of his altimeter, I guess."

Jefferson's eyes widened in surprise. "Murphy? Killed? Nobody has told me."

Shazli shrugged. "I assume that the body has not been formally identified as yet."

"But you've got your own sources," Jefferson said.

"As a matter of fact, no," Shazli replied, looking at him intently. "I received a strange phone call, from a man named . . ."—he frowned, as if trying to remember—"Craig, Clint Craig. He was nearby when it happened."

"Do you know him?"

"Never heard of him," Shazli said, putting out his cigarette in an ashtray. "It was very strange. He asked to speak to me, and told me: 'Your friend Bill Murphy is dead.' I was so shocked, I couldn't utter a word. And then he said: 'Do you hear me? Agent Jones is dead.'" Shazli stopped and the astounded Jefferson could swear that there was a message for him in the liquid black eyes, as Shazli's urbane voice whispered: "Agent Jones. I wonder what he meant by that. Good day, Mr. Jefferson."

The pack of reporters was there already, mounting the traditional all-night watch on the candidate's doorstep. The big television floodlights focused their blinding glare on the heavy gates and the pleasant lawn that stretched beyond, gently sloping toward the house. The TV crews had finished assembling and checking their equipment. Now they grudgingly awaited the authorization to move to the house for the first public appearance of the candidate as soon as the outcome of the vote was known. Jefferson had refused to have any reporters inside the house earlier, and Rita Malden, his attractive press secretary, had regretfully canceled her plan to transform the huge foyer into a pressroom. Outside the locked gate, the reporters were moving about restlessly in the cool Washington night, throwing weary glances at the swelling crowd of dedicated Jefferson supporters brandishing portraits and slogans.

He made his way through the crowd that pressed against the gate of the Jefferson residence, and showed his credentials to the uniformed guard. "Mr. Craig?" The guard consulted his pad. "The senator is expecting you, sir. This way, please."

He slowly walked up the driveway and into the house, repeatedly presenting his ID at the request of the Secret Service agents posted along the way. There was a new alertness about them, a grim concern in their faces as they checked his papers and frisked him for concealed weapons. No official results of the vote had arrived, and yet they already behaved as if it were no longer a candidate they were protecting, but the next President of the United States.

Ralph Dowden was waiting for him at the library door. He warmly shook his hand, and his shortsighted eyes blinked happily under the crown of blond hair. "It's almost final," he announced. "We are only eleven electoral votes short, and in a half-hour I'll make a first statement to the press." Clint patted his shoulder and walked in.

The big library looked strangely peaceful and serene. The only illumination came from two standing lamps in the far corners of the room. Their thick shades, made of a coarse tan fabric, softened the light and bestowed a relaxed atmosphere on the large room with its floor-to-ceiling bookcases.

The first person he saw was Jill. She was standing by the French window, her silhouette clearly outlined against the curtains. She was wearing a dark blue gown, and her blond hair made a golden pool on her shoulders. She quickly moved to him, and her soft lips brushed his cheek. He held for a second the searching look in her eyes, and smiled uneasily.

"How are you, Jill?" he asked. His voice sounded tense, distant.

"Clint." Jefferson got up from his armchair, his hand outstretched. He was in his shirtsleeves, his collar open, a wide grin painted on his face. "Where have you been? We have been looking for you all over the country." He suddenly remembered something and half-turned to his right, where a third person was gracefully curled on a deep-cushioned sofa, a glass in her hand. "I am sorry," Jefferson said. "I should have made the introduction. Mr. Clint Craig, Miss . . ."

"I know Miss Ross," Clint said, taking the delicate hand of the beautiful woman, who smiled at him knowingly. "We met a couple of times, some years ago."

Jefferson looked slightly embarrassed. From Clint's lack of surprise, he understood that Clint knew more than he would admit. To overcome his uneasiness, he quickly repeated his question. "Well, where have you been? Ralph even tried to locate you in Mexico this morning."

Clint accepted the glass of cognac that Jill brought him with a curt nod. "I had to see my daughter," he said. "I had not seen her for a couple of months, and I missed her." He took a sip from his drink. "Later, I waited for a person-to-person call to Geneva."

"Geneva?" Jefferson looked at him quizzically.

Clint quickly glanced around the room to make sure that Ralph Dowden was not there. "Does Miss Ross . . ." he began.

"Rosalynn knows everything," Jefferson said quickly.

"Well, I had to take care of your treasure," Clint continued, and as everybody stirred, he quickly explained: "There is no longer a deposit in your name in the Banque Suisse Centrale, Jim."

"What?" Jefferson's voice was a mixture of puzzlement, and hope, and immense relief.

"Deposit number SF seven-five-six-three-two-four does not exist anymore," Clint said. "And by now"—he looked at his watch—"the copy of the receipt attached to the deposit must already have been destroyed."

Jefferson grabbed him by the shoulders, almost crushing him. "You are serious, Clint? How did you do it?"

A note of diffidence crept into Clint's voice. "As a matter of fact, it was much easier than I had expected. I called Mr. Chavet, the vice-director of the B.S.C. The man seemed fairly frightened anyway, and quite disposed to cooperate."

274

"Chavet was the man who showed the deposit to Clint," Jill told her father.

"Yes. He knew who you were, of course, and I made him an offer he could not refuse." Clint smiled. "The offer consisted of a threat and a bribe. I threatened to make public his part-time job for the CIA. You know how touchy Swiss bankers are about that kind of thing. It could have ruined his reputation forever."

"And the bribe?" Jill asked.

"Well, the bribe was one million dollars of Nazi gold. It must be worth at least ten times as much today."

"You mean that the man can just pack the crate and walk away?" Jefferson asked incredulously.

Clint shrugged. "I guess he will have to make some minor changes"—he stressed the last word—"in the bank records. I don't think he will have any difficulty doing that. A vice-director has a lot of clout in a Swiss bank and . . . they keep very few records of secret deposits."

Jefferson let out a deep breath. "I can't believe it," he murmured. "I have been carrying that burden for thirty-five years and all of a sudden . . ." His voice was thick with emotion. "It seems like a miracle. Too good to be true. Too easy."

"Let's wait and see, then," Clint said.

Jefferson put a hand on his shoulder. There was tremendous gratitude in his eyes. "I can't tell you how . . ." he started, and stopped abruptly. He walked to the window, pulled the curtain and looked into the night.

Jill held on to Clint's arm. He felt that she was trembling. "And the others?" she asked. "The surviving witnesses?"

Clint moved away, approaching Jefferson. "What witnesses?" he murmured, as if talking to himself. "Justice Sheppard will never talk. There is no evidence against him. Everything has been destroyed."

"All those art treasures . . ." Jill began, and the image of Sheppard's mansion briefly flashed in Clint's mind. The exquisite paintings on the ground floor, the statues, the golden collection, the sleek ancient figurines. And downstairs in the locked cellar, the fabulous treasure cavern with its priceless objets d'art. A figure emerged from his memory—the sad, white-haired curator of the *Musées de France* on that mellow Paris afternoon, as he was reading aloud the list of the lost paintings: Sisley, Renoir, Corot, Mirò, Paul Klee . . . They were all lost forever now. But the charming French gentleman would go on hoping till his dying day that they were still

275

waiting to be discovered, in the depths of some abandoned salt mine in Germany. He will never know, Clint thought, for nobody would ever talk.

"The art treasures are lost, and Justice Sheppard will carry his secret to the grave," Clint said aloud, returning to the present. "And Bohlen, my good friend and publisher"—his voice was bitter—". . . I don't know. I still don't know to what extent Bohlen was a member of the conspiracy. I'd rather say that he merely carried out Murphy's instructions."

Jefferson had slowly turned back, and was listening intently as Clint went on. "Even if he was in league with Murphy, he will never admit it. He will stay on his job, and never stand trial. For what? He can always pretend that he didn't know a thing, he just commissioned what seemed to be a hell of a book. Period."

"A book," echoed the musical voice of Rosalynn Ross. "What about your book, Mr. Craig?"

Jefferson nodded, and Clint read the same question in his eyes. "Don't you understand?" he asked softly. "There is going to be no book. What did they call it? The 'Phantom Operation.' That's what it all was—a phantom, an illusion. A fata morgana." He looked at the startled faces around him. "It never happened. As far as history is concerned, Otto Brandl hanged himself, Goering swallowed a concealed capsule of poison, Michel Skolnikoff was murdered by persons unknown. And the treasure was never found."

There was a discreet tap on the door, and Ralph Dowden peered in. "J.J., Dick just called from Chicago. The count in Illinois is almost over, and he says that we've got their twenty-six votes. We stand at two hundred and eighty-four, which makes a tentative majority." He was surprised at the lack of reaction. "Do you want me to say something to the press?"

"Wait." Jefferson strode across the room, and conferred with Ralph in a low voice.

Jill touched Clint's arm. "Let's go out to the garden," she said. He nodded, and followed her. She threw a tan coat over her gown, opened the French window and walked to the terrace and down the steps. Dawn was imminent, and the sky had a gray, blurred color. The air was chilly and humid, and some wavering patches of morning mist hung near the low bushes. The place was quiet; the massive bulk of the house isolated them from the crowd and the commotion at the gate.

She took his arm.

His heart was thumping in his chest. He vividly remembered her hostility that night at Jefferson's suite in Geneva, when he searched in vain for a sign of tenderness, of understanding. "It's all over, Jill," he said again, and his voice quivered.

She turned to face him and he noticed the unusual paleness of her face. "I . . ." she began, bit her lip, tried again to say something but failed. Then, on a sudden impulse, she reached for him and tightly wrapped her arms around his neck. Her cold lips were soft and sweet.

He took her by the shoulders, trying to remember the words he had rehearsed on his way here tonight, when the doubts about her true feelings were painfully gnawing at him. "There is no use pretending anymore," he said in an uncertain voice.

She kissed him again, her silken hair brushing against his cheek. "I never pretended," she softly said, raising her eyes to him. "Not for a single moment." Her voice was muffled, and he suddenly realized that she was as troubled as he was. "I love you, Clint."

He did not answer, just stood there in the cold dawn, holding her close to him. For a second he remembered her in her hospital bed in Nuremberg, when he had first said the same words to her. Could it really be? That in the midst of all that game of double-dealing, something true and pure had happened? He stole a quick glance at her. Her lips were trembling. "Remember Abélard and Héloise?" she suddenly asked in a small voice.

"How could I forget?" Jill's image rose in his memory, her eyes riveted on the old house at the Quai aux Fleurs in Paris, her young, intense voice telling him the enchanting story of an impossible love.

"I thought . . ." she stammered, searching for the right words, "I thought that Héloise could have spared both of them all their troubles if she had only agreed to marry Abélard." She stopped, and quickly averted her eyes.

He cupped her face in his hands. "Are you trying to tell me something, Jill?"

She nodded slightly. "Yes, Clint, I certainly am."

He remained silent for a long moment, trying in vain to suppress the wave of emotion that enveloped him. And then she was in his arm again, and he was covering her face with kisses.

"Remember"—he tried to joke and failed miserably—"remember that you asked for it."

His last words were drowned in a loud roar coming from the other side of the house. The crowd massed in front of the Jefferson residence was cheering the new President-elect of the United States.

November 8:

MAYBE

The tricky autumn weather had brusquely changed again, and the city of Nuremberg awoke that morning to a thick layer of virgin snow. Inspector Helmut Brandt arrived in his office at 8 A.M. sharp. He thoroughly brushed the snow off his Swedish-made coat before he hung it in the closet. He unlocked the file-cabinet, took a middle-sized file and briskly climbed the stairs to the second floor.

Before entering the commissioner's office, he rearranged the knot in his tie and removed a tiny speck of dust from his lapel. In the outer office, the commissioner's secretary bent over the phone, whispering huskily in the mouthpiece. Brandt coughed discreetly. The girl looked up, flashed him an engaging smile and beckoned toward the inner office.

Brandt knocked on the door, paused, then walked in. Commissioner Stoff was engaged in a low-voiced discussion with the two men sitting by his side. They fell silent abruptly as he entered, and Brandt was quick to assume that they had been talking about him. The way they were sitting, all three of them lined behind the large desk, brought to his memory a photograph of a revolutionary tribunal in East Germany.

"Good morning, Inspector Brandt," the commissioner said. He was a wiry little man of fifty-five, almost bald, with watchful gray eyes, a beaked nose, a small tight mouth and a stubborn chin. He was sitting very erect in his chair, his hands spread flat on his desk. "I hope you are satisfied with your trip to Geneva."

"Very satisfied, yes, Mr. Commissioner," Brandt said. "I handed in my report yesterday morning."

"I read your report." The commissioner nodded. "And so have these gentlemen." Brandt raised his eyebrows in mild puzzlement as Stoff went on: "I'd like you to meet Mr. Kluger from the Foreign Ministry"—the white-haired fat man on his right smiled and limply shook Brandt's hand—"and Mr. Firth, from the *Bundesnachrichtendienst*." The Intelligence Service official, tall and ruggedly handsome, had the stiff posture and the calm confidence of a former officer. He was dressed in a conservative dark suit, a light-blue shirt and a striped tie. While he grasped Brandt's hand in a firm handshake, his cold blue eyes intensely studied the inspector's face.

"Have a seat, Inspector," Commissioner Stoff said. Helmut Brandt took a chair and sat in the middle of the small office, placidly watching the three people behind the desk.

"I see that you have brought the file," Commissioner Stoff continued, glancing at the pink cardboard file on which the titles "Dr. Hoffmann" and "Jill Jefferson (Hobarth)" had been successively crossed out, to leave a one-word inscription: "PHANTOM." "Could you tell us what documents you have in that file?"

It was a kind of tribunal after all, Brandt reflected, or at least a sort of commission, which had to proceed according to a specific set of rules. He opened the file. "We have two sets of documents," he explained. "The first set concerns our investigation in Nuremberg." He started leafing through the documents, quickly reading the titles of the various papers. "Police report on the death of Dr. Hoffmann; police report on the shooting at Sommerweg Street, where Miss Jefferson, alias Miss Hobarth, was wounded; minutes of the interrogation of Miss Jefferson, 29 October; minutes of the interrogation of Mr. Clint Craig, 25 October; transcript of a phone conversation between Mr. Craig and a Mr. Peter Bohlen in New York, 26 October; transcript of phone conversation between Mr. Craig, calling from New York, and Miss Jill Jefferson, in the Nuremberg Municipal Hospital, 31 October; transcript of a phone conversation between Miss Jill Jefferson and presidental candidate James Jefferson, 31 October." He raised his eyes.

"Where are the recordings of the phone conversations?" Firth asked.

"We destroyed them, according to Commissioner Stoff's instructions," Brandt explained. Firth nodded.

"Please proceed," the commissioner said.

"The second part of the file," Brandt explained, "was prepared with the cooperation of the Geneva police, following the offical request by the criminal police and the judiciary authorities of the State of Bavaria, addressed to the corresponding authorities in the canton of Geneva." Brandt started reading: "Report of Detective Juliot, *Brigade criminelle*, Geneva police, on the activities of Mr. Clint Craig in Geneva: arrival on 1 November, visit to the Banque Suisse Centrale, descent to the vault in company of Mr. Chavet, vice-director of the bank. Mr. Craig returned then to Hotel Richemond, where he met Miss Jefferson." He turned the pages. "Report by Detectives Brosco and Fratelli, *Brigade volante*, on the visit of Mr. James Jefferson to Geneva on 2 November, and his meeting with Mr. Korchagin at Cointrin, and with Mr. Craig and Miss Jefferson at the Hotel Richemond; report by Detective Brosco on the meeting between Mr. Jefferson and Mr. Ali Shazli, Chairman of OPEC, in the Hotel Richemond on 5 November."

He picked up the last document in the file. "We were allowed to tap only one phone, the private phone of Mr. Chavet, vice-director of the Banque Suisse Centrale. We have here the transcript of an incoming person-to-person call put by Mr. Craig, from New York, on 6 November." He looked sternly at the three people facing him. "In that conversation Mr. Craig and Mr. Chavet agreed that deposit number SF seven-five-six-three-two-four, in the name of Mr. James Jefferson, should be removed from the bank vault, and any record of its existence would be destroyed." He closed the file.

"The recording?" Firth asked again.

"Destroyed, immediately after the transcript was made." Brandt unwaveringly held the gaze of the secret agent. "The Swiss police did not keep any copy of the recording."

Commissioner Stoff stretched out his hand and Brandt handed the file to him. The commissioner systematically worked his way through the file, intently examining every document. Each paper was in turn perused by Kluger and Firth, who had moved nearer to Stoff. Brandt waited patiently. Finally, Stoff closed the file and straightened in his chair. His face was grim and preoccupied as he looked at Brandt. He did not speak.

The uneasy silence was broken by the Foreign Ministry official, Herr Kluger. He was very pale, almost livid, and stirred restlessly on his chair. "You were right, Commissioner Stoff," he said gravely. "This file is a time bomb. I also read Inspector Brandt's report, as soon as I arrived last night. Early this morning I had a long conversation with the foreign

281

minister, who consulted the chancellor. They feel that any leak of the contents of this file could set off an international scandal of unprecedented magnitude. Therefore, the investigation should be discontinued, the case closed and the file destroyed."

The commissioner looked searchingly at Firth. "I certainly do agree that the investigation should be closed," Firth said. "On the other hand, I fail to understand the excess of zeal as far as the destruction of the file is concerned. It looks more like panic to me. Why destroy the file? Why not keep it?"

"The chancellor's instructions are quite explicit on this issue," Kluger said icily.

Firth shrugged. "In that case, any further discussion will be a waste of time," he said, glancing at Brandt again.

Commissioner Stoff got up. "Inspector Brandt," he said formally. "I believe that you understand the situation. The 'Phantom' case involves friendly foreign powers and world leaders. Our government believes that any further probing into this affair may be harmful to our national interest. Therefore, according to a decision taken at the highest level, the 'Phantom' case is henceforth closed. You will leave the file with us, as we shall destroy it. I must remind you that according to the Official Secrets Act, you are not allowed to discuss this affair with anybody. You may go now." He quickly added: "And allow me to congratulate you for a very thorough job." He managed a wry smile.

Helmut Brandt got up and shook hands with the three officials, Firth holding his hand a fraction of a second longer.

He left the office, smiled politely at Stoff's secretary, who was still chattering on the phone, and walked out.

Everything had happened exactly as he had expected. Kluger and Stoff had done their job. The "Phantom" case was closed, or so they thought.

But there was something they did not know.

They did not know that the previous afternoon he had gotten an urgent phone call from Firth, whom he had never seen before, that he had met Firth in a small *Weinstube* in the old city, that after their conversation he had returned to his office in Police Headquarters. There he had personally photocopied all the documents in the "Phantom" file and deposited the photocopies in his private safe at the Dresdner Bank. The Federal Intelligence Service, Firth had told him, considered the affair to be of the utmost importance. The evidence

282

should be kept in a safe place, as it might serve the interest of the nation one day.

He walked into his office on the ground floor. The "Phantom" case was over. No one would ever touch it again.

No one but Helmut Brandt. One day. Maybe.

AUTHOR'S NOTE

The preceding story is a work of fiction. Nevertheless, its historical and political background is based on fact. The plundering of Europe's treasures by Hermann Goering and the *Einsatzstab* Rosenberg is well known by historians, and has been described in several books dealing with the second World War and the Nuremberg trials, as well as in the various biographies of Goering. Still, no major book on that subject has been written yet. Various sources can provide the reader with fragmentary descriptions of that unique phenomenon. In *Le front d'art* (Paris, 1961), Rose Valland deals with the brutal activities of the *Einsatzstab* Rosenberg in France; some of her findings have been contested since. Matila Simon has also tackled the subject in *Battle of the Louvre* (New York: Hawthorn, 1971). A detailed survey of the robbery of Europe's art treasures has been published in the *ZEIT Magazine* of December 1, 1978. It mentions the fact that many of the art treasures have not been found yet. The most outstanding among them is the famous amber room, stolen from the Tsarskoye Selo Palace near Leningrad in 1941.

Otto Brandl and Michel Skolnikoff are real-life characters, and many Frenchmen still remember their shady activities in Paris. The best account of their tumultuous lives and strange deaths has been published by the French historian Jacques Delarue in his book *Trafics et Crimes sous l'occupation* (Paris: Fayard, 1968). Delarue maintains that a great part of Otto Brandl's treasure has never been recovered. The fate of the treasure remains a mystery to this day. Another mystery surrounds the suicide of Hermann Goering.

The more recent events in the book are also largely based on fact. The State Department secret study about American retaliation against the oil-producing Arab states (Chapters 4 and 5) was published in Jack Anderson's syndicated column on August 13, 1979. The CIA report indicating that the Soviet bloc would start importing oil in 1982, in ever increasing quantities (Chapter 11), was leaked to the American news media on July 29, 1979. The warning that the Soviet Union might use force in the Middle East to assure its oil supply (Chapter 11) was issued by the OPEC chairman, Mani Said Utaiba, in a meeting with the prime minister of Japan on October 17, 1979, and was reported by the news agencies.

Finally, horror fans will appreciate the ghoulish flavor of the Guanajuato mummies in an album published by Harry N. Abrams (New York, 1978). It includes, besides the chilling photographs by Archie Lieberman, a reprint of the classic Ray Bradbury story "The Next in Line." The album is entitled *The Mummies of Guanajuato*.

M.B.

"The Reef"
Teague Bay, St. Croix
U.S. Virgin Islands

**SWEEPING FROM JERUSALEM
TO BEIRUT, ROME AND PARIS,
A FAST-PACED, TAUTLY WRITTEN
NOVEL OF INTERNATIONAL TERROR**

DOUBLE CROSS

BY

MICHAEL BARAK

**AN ORIGINAL HARDCOVER NOVEL
FROM NAL BOOKS
OCTOBER 1981 RELEASE**

Chapter 1

Monday, January 22, 3:35 P.M. An off-white Chevrolet station wagon turned the corner into the rue Verdun in West Beirut, closely followed by a desert-yellow Range-Rover. The two cars slowed down as they approached a modern apartment house, its brown walls still soaked with the midday rain. From a second-floor window across the narrow street, a middle-aged European woman intently watched the approaching vehicles. She nervously brushed away some brown wisps that had escaped the tight bun crowning her birdlike head and were fluttering before her eyes. The sun that suddenly appeared between the clouds over St. George's Bay made her squint. But as the Chevrolet drew nearer, she spotted the youthful figure of a handsome, black-haired civilian, huddled amidst four uniformed bodyguards clutching Kalachnikov assault rifles. She noticed two more guerrillas on the front seat of the Range-Rover, also heavily armed and wearing red-spotted kaffiyehs—the traditional Fatah headdresses. She shuddered. The phone receiver in her left hand became moist with her own sweat and her arm slightly trembled as she raised it to her mouth. "Yes," she softly said into the mouthpiece.

In an apartment farther down the street a curly-haired dark man drew a deep breath as he heard the single syllable and hung up at once. From his window the approaching cars were perfectly visible, although he could not make out the faces inside. His eyes glued to the Chevrolet, he slowly reached for the remote-control radio device on the small commode to his left. The red-coated switch felt smooth and cold between his fingers. He waited one more second, watching the Chevrolet's approach.

The Chevrolet sailed smoothly past a blue Volkswagen Golf, parked by the curb. Now. The dark man pulled the

289

switch. At that very second the Volkswagen exploded, metamorphosing into a huge ball of fire. The Chevrolet, engulfed by the blaze, blew up in turn. Chunks of metal, splinters of glass, parts of human bodies were projected violently upward as a roaring column of fire and smoke spurted from the devastated vehicles. Tiny bits of iron buzzed by the windows like stray bullets and sprayed the nearby walls with tremendous impact; the twisted chassis of the station wagon, heaved off the ground by the explosion, crashed heavily to the pavement, where the flames immediately turned it into a gigantic torch. An old Syrian street vendor, eyes wild, toothless mouth mumbling incoherently, stared with horror at the dismembered bodies of the Chevrolet's passengers, strewn about the smoldering debris. A sleek, gold-buckled Bally shoe, torn off the foot of a dead civilian, rested incongruously in the middle of the havoc, absurdly clean and undamaged.

The strident wail of police cars and ambulances broke out in the distance, and a frightened crowd warily started to assemble around the corpses. In the apartment across the street, the European woman wiped the cold sweat off her brow with a shaking hand, then slowly dialed a number on her old-fashioned telephone. The acrid smell of burning tires wafted through the window as the Mediterranean breeze gently blew away the dense cloud of black smoke hovering over rue Verdun.

Nine miles away, the telephone rang in a public booth at the Beirut International Airport. A small gray-haired man, wearing a moth-eaten moustache and wire-rimmed spectacles, calmly picked up the receiver. "The package was delivered," the woman said in English, trying to sound casual. Without answering, the little man replaced the receiver cradle and left the phone booth. He unhurriedly worked his way through the noisy crowd in the big departure hall, joined the line before the twin immigration desks, and patiently waited for his turn. When he finally stood before the stout Lebanese officer clad in an olive-green uniform, he neatly laid on the counter his plane ticket, boarding pass, and Austrian passport. The Lebanese examined the boarding pass. *"Vol 263 de la Turkish Airlines pour Istanbul,"* he stated pompously. He leafed through the worn Austrian passport and compared the photograph with the man's face; the square chin, the rather piteous moustache, the straight nose, the round glasses, the clear blue-gray eyes that held his with a placid, candid gaze. The large forehead was topped by a heavy mass of gray hair,

290

combed backward. The Austrian was sixty-four years old, according to his passport, and, even though short, had broad shoulders and solid arms which must have been quite strong years ago. His thick gray overcoat was inexpensive; so was his ready-to-wear woolen suit. The outmoded blue tie was gauchely knotted. "You were here for pleasure, Mister . . ."—the officer glanced at the passport again—"Mr. Kinski?"

"Business," the short man replied in a deep voice with a clipped accent. "Electrical appliances. I am with the Siemens–Österreich export department."

The officer nodded absently and stamped the passport. "Bon voyage," he muttered and looked over the Austrian's head to the next in line.

In the Turkish Airlines Boeing 727 the little man walked straight to his aisle seat in the last row of the nonsmoking section. He deftly folded his overcoat and put it on the upper rack, sat down, and buckled his seat belt. During the short flight to Istanbul he sat still, his arms folded on his chest, his eyes dulled with a faraway look. He politely declined the refreshments served by a plump Turkish hostess. His neighbor, a bourbon-reeking Texan, tried to engage a conversation but gave up when his repeated attempts were rewarded by laconic, noncommittal answers. The man obviously wanted to be left alone, and the Texan switched his attention to a fading, black-eyed beauty on his right, who stupidly laughed at his jokes and readily accepted the drink he offered.

In Istanbul the old man collected his medium-sized suitcase and calmly walked through customs. The immigration desks were heavily manned by grim, suspicious police officers, but they did not bother with the harmless-looking Austrian. An impassive look, a quick stamp on the passport—and the old man was past the immigration desk. When the crowd of taxi drivers assaulted him in the arrival hall, he seemed to hesitate for a moment. Finally he chose a tall young man, sporting a fierce moustache, who was dressed in a black turtleneck pullover and a short sheepskin coat. The Turk took his luggage and walked out of the terminal. It had rained heavily in the afternoon, and the bright fluorescent lights of the building projected red and yellow patterns on the trembling surface of a nearby puddle. The Turkish driver threw a brief look behind him, then walked with long, easy strides to his old Ford, parked across the road. Another man sat smoking a cigarette in the front seat, but the little Austrian did not seem surprised. He gave the stranger a perfunctory nod, got in the cab, and sat upright in the back seat. The driver started the engine and smoothly maneuvered his battered vehicle into the stream of outgoing cars. Just for a second his eyes met those of the Austrian in the rearview mirror and conveyed to him a mute, anxious question. The small man nodded reassuringly.

The cab did not go all the way to Istanbul, whose fairyland skyline glittered on the horizon. Barely five minutes after setting out from the airport, the driver left the main road, plunged into a maze of narrow, poorly illuminated streets, and stopped by a tawdry apartment house in the suburb of Bakirkoy. The old man followed the driver into the building without sparing a look for the man who remained in the cab. They took the aged elevator to the fifth floor. The tall Turk fished a key from his pocket and unlocked the door on their right. They walked into a small apartment, furnished with cheap carpets and chintz-covered sofas. All the lights were on; a dark girl in a white sweater and brown slacks was sitting in an armchair facing the entrance. "Hello," the Austrian said as he closed the door behind him, and the girl nodded.

The driver turned back to face him and quickly asked in English, "Well?" The girl had half-risen from her chair, her eyes equally concerned, her small hands clutching her heavy bag.

The Austrian smiled tightly and raised a sturdy finger to his mouth. "Not now," he said, flashing a quick glance around as he crossed the living room and disappeared into the bathroom at the end of the small corridor. He closed the door behind him, removed his jacket, tie, and shirt, and busied himself with the plastic bottles and cream pots that stood on a rack over the sink. Fifteen minutes later he came out of the bathroom, slowly buttoning his shirt. Gone were the moustache and the glasses. The mane of gray hair had turned pure white and was neatly combed to one side, still soaked with water. The short man walked into the adjacent bedroom and opened the closet. He took out a dark-red tie, a sleeveless V-neck pullover made of gray wool, and a herringbone tweed jacket. He changed his black shoes for a pair of crepe-soled brown moccasins that added a full inch to his height, then plucked a tan raincoat from the rack. He stopped briefly before the mirror as he put on a narrow-brimmed hat made of brown felt. In the living room the girl and the cab driver were talking in low voices but fell silent abruptly as he entered. They did not seem surprised in the least by the outward change in his appearance. "Let's go," he said to the cab driver. "We don't have much time." As he passed by the girl, he paused and rather clumsily patted her shoulder. "Don't worry," he said, his voice just a shade softer. "They will be all right, all of them." She managed a wan smile. The tall driver killed his foul-smelling cigarette in a glass ashtray on the living room table and followed the old man to the door. The girl was in the bedroom already, gathering the clothes left by the visitor.

Half an hour after his arrival in Istanbul, the old man was back at the airport. As the car stopped, the man beside the driver turned around and handed him a blue plastic pouch. "Your papers," he said.

The white-haired man quickly scanned the contents of the pouch: a flight ticket, a paid hotel bill from the Istanbul Hilton, some Turkish bank notes and small change, and a Belgian passport whose entry stamp certified that its owner had arrived in Istanbul from Brussels eight days ago. He nodded to himself and got out of the cab, dragging his suitcase after him. On a sudden impulse he turned back and stuck his head through the cab window. "Thank you," he said. "Everything worked out fine. You'll read about it in the papers tomorrow." It had started to rain again, and the heavy drops blossomed into big brown stains on the shoulders of his raincoat as he hurried, stooping, into the departure hall.

He boarded the biweekly evening flight of El Al to Tel Aviv that landed at the Ben–Gurion International Airport shortly after eleven P.M. In Israel the skies were clear, but an ice-cold wind was sweeping the runways, blowing the skirts of the ground hostesses who stood beside the airplane shivering in the cold and trying to hold on to their coquettish little hats.

The white-haired passenger was discreetly whisked into an inconspicuous commercial van that took him to the security wing of the main terminal building. In a small room, guarded by two plainclothesmen, half a dozen people were waiting. They were all senior officers of the Mossad, the Israeli secret service. The old man blinked uneasily at the sight of the familiar faces; otherwise he appeared unperturbed as they enthusiastically shook his hand. "Congratulations, Jeremiah," murmured a tall, balding man in Hebrew. "It was on the evening news already. The prime minister called twice. He wanted to talk to you personally."

"What about our people, David?" the white-haired man asked with a note of anxiety in his deep voice.

The bald man reassured him with a quick smile. "Everything is being taken care of. Most of them are out already, the rest will be by tomorrow. The clean-out team will get there on Wednesday, as planned." He paused, then added warmly, "I can imagine how you feel, Jeremiah. You got him at last. After all these years."

The old man shifted awkwardly, suddenly looking ill at ease. "Let's go," he said finally. "Where is Danny?" His driver, a supple, ruddy-faced young man, came forward from the far end of the room. "Let's go to the office first, Danny," Jeremiah said. "I want to drop by the Situation Room."

His assistants stared at him in wonder as he turned to go. "I told you this guy is inhuman," a towering, black-haired man with vaguely Oriental features murmured behind the old man's back as he approached two of his colleagues. "He just got Salameh himself, and—nothing! He walks by as if he couldn't care less. In his place I would have thrown the biggest champagne party since we brought back Marcelle and the boys from Egypt. How long did he work on getting Salameh? Six years?"

"Seven years and four months," the man called David whispered in return. They looked at Jeremiah Peled, the head of the Israeli secret service, as he purposefully strode away. Nothing in his behavior betrayed any satisfaction in the killing of Ali Hassan Salameh, the Red Prince, the most cunning and deadly figure of international terrorism. After seven years and four months Peled had finally avenged the massacre of the Israeli athletic team at the 1972 Munich Olympics.

ABOUT THE AUTHOR

Michael Barak is a pseudonym for a well known Israeli author. He was born in Bulgaria where he survived the fascist tyranny. Raised in Israel, he studied in Paris and has traveled the world, visiting Europe and especially the United States many times. In the Six Day War, he served as press secretary to General Moshe Dayan. As a paratrooper in the Israeli army, he crossed the Suez Canal into Egypt during the Yom Kippur War. He is the author of the suspense novel *The Enigma,* available in a Signet edition.

Bestsellers from SIGNET

- ☐ **THE INTRUDER by Brooke Leimas.** (#E9524—$2.50)*
- ☐ **THE SUMMER VISITORS by Brooke Leimas.**
  (#J9247—$1.95)*
- ☐ **THE DOUBLE-CROSS CIRCUIT by Michael Dorland.**
  (#J9065—$1.95)
- ☐ **THE ENIGMA by Michael Barak.** (#J8920—$1.95)*
- ☐ **THE NIGHT LETTER by Paul Spike.** (#E8947—$2.50)
- ☐ **ASTERISK DESTINY by Campbell Black.** (#E9246—$2.25)*
- ☐ **BRAINFIRE by Campbell Black.** (#E9481—$2.50)*
- ☐ **BLOOD RITES by Barry Nazarian.** (#E9203—$2.25)*
- ☐ **LABYRINTH by Eric MacKenzie-Lamb.** (#E9062—$2.25)*
- ☐ **UNHOLY CHILD by Catherine Breslin.** (#E9477—$3.50)
- ☐ **COLD HANDS by Joseph Pintauro.** (#E9482—$2.50)*
- ☐ **TULSA GOLD by Elroy Schwartz.** (#E9566—$2.75)*
- ☐ **THE UNICORN AFFAIR by James Fritzhand with Frank Glicksman.** (#E9605—$2.50)*
- ☐ **EDDIE MACON'S RUN by James McLendon.** (#E9518—$2.95)

* Price slightly higher in Canada
